I0672023

In the Shadows

of the

MOSQUITO CONSTELLATION

ALSO BY THE AUTHOR:

CHILDREN'S BOOKS:

A Pair of Docks

A Quill Ladder

NOVELLAS:

The River (Synchronic Anthology)

Resistance (Tales from Pennsylvania Anthology)

In the Shadows
of the
MOSQUITO
CONSTELLATION

JENNIFER ELLIS

MOONBIRD
PRESS

Cover Design: Design for Writers
Editing: David Gatewood
Proofreading: Warren Layberry
Interior Design: Shelley Ackerman

ISBN-13: (print) 978-0-9921538-2-3
ISBN-13: (ebook) 978-0-9921538-3-0

Moonbird Press

For my mother

CAST OF CHARACTERS

FARM MEMBERS

FAMILY

The Johnstons

NATALIE – Established the farm with the help of Richard and Daniel
RICHARD – Natalie's husband and former mayor of Vancouver
ANDREW – Natalie and Richard's youngest son
JUSTIN – Natalie and Richard's oldest son; studying to be a doctor

Richard's Family

DANIEL – Richard's twin brother and the farm vet
TERRENCE AND OLIVIA – Richard and Daniel's parents
KRISTEN – Richard and Daniel's younger sister
LEON – Kristen's husband
CHRISTOPHER – Kristen and Leon's oldest son

Natalie's Family

MIKE – Natalie's older brother and the farm doctor
JOANNE – Mike's wife
RACHEL – Mike and Joanne's oldest daughter
SARAH – Mike and Joanne's youngest daughter
SCOTT – Natalie and Mike's younger brother

Friends

ANNEKE – Natalie's best friend and the farm cook
ALAN – Anneke's husband
KATIE AND STEVEN – Anneke and Alan's children
PATRICIA – Natalie's friend
PAUL – Daniel's friend and former minister in Tanner's Ridge
CYRUS – Paul's partner
SIOBHAN AND SOLOMON – Organic farmers in charge of the farm gardens
GRACIE – Siobhan and Solomon's daughter

Refugees
BOB AND RAMONA – Married couple; arrived on raft on Syringa
JANE – Came with Bob and Ramona
KARL – Arrived after Bob and Ramona
COLLEEN AND BRENT – Married couple; former neighbors

PEOPLE FROM "OUT THERE"

RIDGE PEOPLE

CRAIG – Raider shot the night of the fire
RAFE – Leader of the ridge people
JOE – Craig's father
OTHERS – Elena, Carson, Marta, Hans, Ranjeet and Virginia

TRAVELERS

LIZ – Tarot reader who shows up one night

NEIGHBORS

ILENE AND FRED – Trappers; organize gathering in Jerry
NEIL AND LAUREN – Live on farm halfway to Tanner's Ridge
HANNAH – Neil and Lauren's oldest daughter

JERRY

CASEY – Minister in Jerry
EARL – Doctor establishing the field hospital

VANCOUVER

ALFIE – Richard's former campaign manager
CLAIRE – Alfie's wife
PETER – Casino owner
SILAS – Richard's employee

CHAPTER 1

THE WHEEL OF FORTUNE

———⚬⚬⚬———

NATALIE

For one to rise, the other must fall.

An inferno seethes in the night sky, engulfing the forest to the west of the farm in its forked claws. Smoke fills the air with sooty denseness. Natalie stands in the bucket-line at the edge of the cornfield in her pajamas and an old gray sweater. She takes the bucket from the person closest to her, sloshes water on the flames at the edge of the field, and hands the bucket back. It's still early, well before dawn. She'd been in bed, huddled against one of the house cats, listening to the thunder and praying as lightning fractured the sky and bit into the tinder-dry bull pine forest around the farm. Then came the crack, the shouts, and the call, followed by an outpouring of farm members from their rooms and cabins.

Natalie scans the mountains and the edges of the farm for movement, for the flicker of a torch among the trees. A forest fire would offer the perfect opportunity for a raid. Richard, her husband, is supposed to be on lookout, but he isn't watching. He's busy giving orders, being Richard. Natalie sees nothing, but doesn't feel comforted; beyond the fire, hidden within the smoke, an army of predators could be out there waiting unseen. Natalie refocuses on her work. They have to save the barn and the fields.

She hears a wild cacophony of bleats, whinnies, and protests as Daniel, Richard's brother, leads the animals to a holding pen. The rooster chokes out a guttural simulacrum of his morning cry. The dogs circle the farm animals, their training winning out over a fear so great the whites of their eyes can be seen across the field. Dark clouds linger to the north of the farm, and the rumbling thunder warns of the possibility of more lightning. Thunder, but no rain. There is never enough rain.

Every August, fires rage across the land unchecked, restoring dense forests to grassy fields. As soon as the weather turns warm, the farm members await the plumes of smoke that will hang in the valleys and turn the sky grainy.

They prepared with buckets and drills, or so they thought. But it's not like she expected. Flames tower above them, blistering their eyes, turning night to day. Their stench and ferocity tweak every instinct in Natalie to run. Earlier, a ball of fire shot through the sheep stable in the western pasture before anyone had time to react. Patches of the cornfield burn, and the air hangs with the scent of singed wool, popcorn, and burned flesh. The sound of fire surrounds her like the roar of a thousand jet engines.

Frantic hands clutch for the buckets passed down the row. Why didn't they realize they would need more buckets? Soup tureens, bowls, and emptied feed bins have been added to the containers being handed off.

Natalie panics every time her hands are empty, when she must stand and wait, useless. They fill the containers fuller and fuller, but there is not enough.

Anneke passes an overfull bowl, her glasses reflecting the firelight, and her face grimmer than Natalie has seen in their many years of friendship.

Icy water soaks Natalie's arms and legs. Blood pounds in her fingers from the strain of curling around handles and rims. The farm members work with an industry that can only be a product of pure fear. It's etched in everyone's eyes.

Except Richard's.

His face is almost a mask of euphoric pleasure, pupils dilated. He's always thrived on danger. He strides among them, shouting orders, breaking up arguments, redirecting, and ensuring they stick with the drill. His shoulders are thrust back and his chest puffed out.

He looks like the rooster.

Natalie feels a twist of scorn for herself. She should be glad of Richard, at least tonight. She is. She just wishes he were doing this differently.

One of the farm members runs across the courtyard toward Richard, shouting, "We need to move some people over to the outer cabins. Sparks are jumping from the pines." Alan, she thinks, from the shock of white hair and the slightness of his form, as the smoke fractures her vision and bites at her eyes.

She leaves her bucket line to join them.

"I don't think so. Not yet," Richard yells over the din of the fire. "Let's just stick with the plan for now. We need all hands on deck here."

Alan turns away, his expression unreadable. *Argue*, Natalie thinks. *Tell Richard he's wrong. Why does it always have to be me?* But Alan nods and leaves and Richard almost preens.

"Alan could be right. We might need more people at the cabins," she says.

Richard's blue eyes glint. "Not yet. We've got this under control."

"We don't have *anything* under control."

"Nice, Nat. Real helpful." Richard walks away.

Natalie wants to grab him by the hair on the back of his head.

Yells echo from the central courtyard as Daniel leads the last of the horses to safety. Richard's white stallion rears, eyes glazed with fright, nostrils flared, teeth bared in a spectral snarl. A shower of sparks falls into the cornfield. They descend in slow motion, brightening the air like fireworks. The field team runs in all directions. Natalie sprints back to her post.

"Can you please help? We could really use another set of hands here," Natalie says the next time Richard passes.

Richard curls his upper lip. "What do you think I'm doing?"

You look like you're walking around, Natalie wants to yell, but she doesn't. She forces her voice to be calm. "Everyone's getting tired. Please, just come and help us."

"Yup. Got it. I'll be there when I get there." Richard strides off to the barn.

Natalie's eyes rake the field for her sons. Her boys are the only children old enough to be included on the fire teams. Justin, with his white-blond hair glowing in the firelight, helps Daniel with the livestock. Andrew runs the well pump. The other children huddle in the farmhouse, safe, unless the fire gets out of control.

Years ago, they'd pushed up berms of dirt to serve as a fire line around the barn, the farmhouse, the cabins, the orchards, the gardens, and the fields— around everything that keeps them alive. But in the intervening years, the exhaustion from growing enough food to survive led to complacency, and each year grasses and weeds took greater root on the berms, leaving them looking like frothy, flower-dotted hillocks. Now farm members work desperately with shovels and pitchforks turning over the dirt and weeds. The others race about with buckets and damp blankets, stamping out small blazes in the fields and watching for flames on the buildings and in the orchard. They've held the fire to the forest and fields west of the farm. So far.

They hurl bucket after bucket of water on sparks and patches of flame, knowing they can't afford to waste so much. In the late summer, the aquifer feeding the well wanes to a cranky trickle. If they drain the well, it will mean time-consuming trips to the river and less water for the tomatoes and squash. Natalie runs a mental inventory of the food needed to get thirty-eight people through the winter. But in the smoke and heat, she can't do the math. Starvation scenarios swim in her mind, and she tries to stop the quaking in her thighs.

Daniel appears in front of her, his black cowboy hat and broad frame silhouetted against the fire, Justin standing close behind. "We're done with the animals. Where should we go next?"

She continues to lob water at the flames. "The cabins. Go help with the outer cabins. Take some men with you."

Daniel's eyes are bloodshot and teary from the smoke, but there's a grim determination in his gaze and the set of his jaw.

She brushes his hand with hers and draws a fragment of courage from the blunt tips of his fingers. Daniel turns and hurries away with his half walk, half jog. She lets Justin follow even though she wants to pull her son back and push him to the safety of the farmhouse.

Abruptly, the wind shifts east and picks up, sending the flames directly toward the farm. The fire in the trees blazes to dizzying heights, and showers of embers cascade into the fields. The heat spikes. Natalie's wedding ring sears her finger like a brand. She and the others on her crew race to put out the new blazes.

Screams and yells erupt from the north as darting tongues of flame encase the roof of one of the cabins.

Natalie barely has time to look. She and Anneke beat the burning corn with blankets, while others splash water on it.

The flames take only minutes to balloon into the sky a full story above the cabin. Farm members stand and stare with their buckets and shovels in hand.

Richard sprints in that direction, his body hurtling across the farm with remarkable speed. He snatches a shovel from someone. "Come on, folks, don't just stand there! Dig a fire line around the cabin!" he bellows.

Natalie detects a shade of uncertainty in his voice, which is the most terrifying thing of all.

Daniel and Justin grab shovels from some of the other farm members. The rest of the berm crew snaps back into action and starts to dig.

For a few minutes, it looks like it might work. The farm members work doggedly, and the trench around the cabin is almost complete. The fire has moved north of most of the main fields, leaving the field crew to deal with fewer outbreaks. But fatigue has set in, and the barn crew lounge at their posts, hypnotized by the flames, the adrenaline-high that drove their earlier efforts now yielding to a numb drowsiness.

Natalie feels the wash of exhaustion in her own muscles. They mustn't stop. Not yet. She'll just give them a few minutes to rest. She allows herself to breathe and shuts her eyes against the burn of the smoke, feeling the lurch of sleep shake her body. Her eyes snap open. Everyone's movements have slowed as they watch the fire move away from the farm, through the trees toward the river. They look like they could sink to the ground in heaps. She hears, faintly, one of the men in the cornfield say, "We did it."

Two women hug, and men slap each other on the back. Relief starts to creep into Natalie's veins and arteries.

A blur of movement in the western pasture catches her eye. Natalie turns. Shadows scurry between the clumps of smoldering oats, and an arrow sails past her and hits the barn wall with a loud *thwack*. A row of ragged men stand on the edge of the farm in the eerie orange light, bows drawn. Alarm rips through Natalie's heart. More arrows follow. Farm members scream and scatter. Richard throws down his shovel and runs to the barn, to the armory.

The farm had let down its guard. The dogs, confused by the smoke and flames, failed to smell the armed attackers.

The men closest to the barn follow Richard. The cabin and barn crews race to take cover behind the hay bales nearby. Farm members in the cornfield drop to their knees among the stalks. Richard and the other men take up positions in the hayloft, and the crack of rifle fire starts to emerge from the second-story windows of the barn.

The pace of the oncoming arrows slackens as the raiders hunker down behind the berms. Daniel runs from the hay bales to the barn, but he seems to only inch along, and Natalie can't watch. She too races to the barn, bursting from the cornfield and dashing through the courtyard, arrows slicing the air around her. She sees Justin behind the hay bale, while Andrew has made it to the barn.

Daniel grabs her arm, his nails digging into her skin. "That was stupid," he says. Dark rings underscore his gray eyes, and there is an urgency to his glare.

"I ran fast," she says. "Hard to hit a moving target. You said so yourself."

"Not if there are enough shooters."

Daniel turns to mount the barn stairs. Natalie grabs his sleeve.

"The children! Nobody's guarding the farmhouse!"

Gray eyes meet hers. "You think they're going to go around that side?"

"The cows are all over there."

Daniel wheels around. Solomon and Karl have arrived at the barn door. Solomon snatches up a rifle and runs for the side door, a ferocious look on his bearded face and his black dreadlocks trailing out behind him. Solomon's daughter, Gracie, is the youngest child on the farm, and it's clear he's already heading in the direction of the farmhouse.

Karl hesitates by the gun rack when he sees Natalie standing there. With the old knife wound scoring his cheek more bleakly delineated with soot, she barely recognizes him, but she clutches his arm.

"We have to go to the farmhouse."

Karl looks from her to Daniel, who nods firmly, and the three of them follow Solomon out the side door into the dawn-streaked sky. Daniel whistles, and Mitch and Daisy, his two most trusted dogs, race from their post by the farm animals to join their master.

The farmhouse sits shrouded in early morning shadow, the fire casting a glow on the west wall. As they near the house, Mitch and Daisy growl into the darkness. In between gunshots and screams, Natalie hears the low yips and whines of the dogs left to guard the cows in the east pasture.

Daniel curses under his breath, motions Natalie and Solomon inside, and rounds the corner to the east of the house. Karl follows.

Natalie steps inside. Rachel, Natalie's sixteen-year-old niece, has been left to tend the children and is peering through the kitchen window; the children are clustered together in a pile of blankets in the living room, dressed in patched and unmatched pajamas, their faces dirty and scared. Two of the older boys are dressed and standing by the window, scowling and agitated.

Natalie automatically does a headcount. Eleven.

Rachel holds Gracie, Solomon's daughter. Gracie gives a cry of recognition and practically jumps into her father's arms, burying her face in his shoulder.

"We heard gunshots." Rachel's words jump over each other.

"Raiders," Natalie says, struck by the fact that the children are growing up in a world where her remark requires no further explanation. She tries not to think about her sons in a shootout by the barn or Daniel approaching armed men outside. "You have to get down to the cellar. Bring your blankets." She grabs two candles from the table.

Two of the younger girls start to wail as other children stumble around, grabbing blankets, muddled and unfocused from lack of sleep.

Gunfire erupts just outside the kitchen.

Natalie thrusts the candles at Rachel, scoops up two children, and races through the door to the basement. "Get moving! Now!" Bare feet smack against the wooden stairs behind them. Solomon brings up the rear.

In the flickering candlelight, they troop past the neatly lined jars of vegetables, pickles, jams, jellies, honeys, and fruits, past the bins of sand where the carrots and garlic are stored, and past the shallow tubs where the potatoes, squash, onions, and apples are checked weekly for rot. One of the shelves holding the jars conceals a small room built for the expected raids.

Natalie wishes Andrew and Justin were also on their way down to the room. But at sixteen and eighteen, her boys would scoff at being escorted to the cellar.

Solomon pushes aside the shelves in front of the door. The frigid air and smell of rot and mold surrounds them. The children stand around the door, holding their blankets, jostling Natalie with their small bodies, refusing to go any further inside.

Natalie clenches her teeth. She has to get back outside.

She gives two children a small push into the room. "You need to get inside. Just sit tight, and don't leave the cellar."

The children don't move, but continue to watch her with stunned, hopeful expressions, as if they think it might be just a drill.

Solomon sits on one of the benches in the small room with Gracie on his lap and pulls two of the other children to the bench next to him, his long arm encircling them. He begins singing in his gentle baritone. After a few seconds, Rachel joins in with a watery voice. One by one the children sit, and a few of the girls chime in with their sweet, reedy voices, their teary, filthy faces huddled together in the candlelight.

Natalie swallows her own tears, backs out of the room, slides the door shut, and pushes the shelves back into place before returning to the darkened kitchen and pressing her face against the window. The sound of gunfire comes from the barn, but it's silent to the east.

Sepia orange clouds and smoke hang above the eastern pasture, and the cows huddle together in a creamy mass. Mitch and Daisy stand watch on either side of the herd, their steadfastness reassuring. Natalie can't see Daniel and Karl, so she pulls her gun out and creeps out of the door and around the corner of the house. The gunfire from the barn is louder outside, and she fights the urge to run and check on Andrew and Justin.

She heads across the field toward the cows. Surely Daniel would have gone that way. A white and black heap crouches on the ground—the slight body of one of the border collie pups, her fur matted and streaked with blood, her breath coming in labored wheezes, still staring dutifully at the herd she'd been set to guard.

A human body lies on the ground just beyond the dog.

Natalie creeps over to it, her heart hammering. It's a raider. A boy, perhaps nineteen, thin, filthy, and dressed in threadbare dress pants and a Budweiser sweatshirt. Blood streams from wounds in his shoulder and foot. It's fresh, not yet coagulated. An older man lies just beyond the boy's supine form.

Natalie jumps when the boy moves and moans. She kneels and feels for a pulse. It's erratic. The boy is shaking, close to shock. She hears a faint "please" from his lips; she rips off the kerchief holding back her hair and presses it against his shoulder.

"I'll come back," she says. "Try to hang on."

She knows he'll bleed out soon. She leans over to check the older man. Blood drains from a bullet wound on his neck, and his face is already white and gaping with death. No pulse. His body convulses once and then goes limp.

After years of raids, the deaths still torment her. They can't keep living this way.

Natalie loops her curls in a knot at the back of her head and stands still to listen for any sign of Daniel and Karl. Away from the fire, the chill of the morning air sends shivers down her bare arms. The gunfire at the barn is more intermittent now, and she thinks she hears voices to her right, in the wooded area edging the eastern pasture.

She makes her way across the field, gun drawn. As she enters the trees, she's grabbed from behind and pulled into the bushes, a hand over her mouth. Tensing, she struggles against the arms around her until she recognizes the tear in the right sleeve of Daniel's shirt and the drift of hair across his hands. She drops to her knees next to Karl.

Two raiders stand in the clearing some distance away.

"They should be here by now. Where the fuck are they?" growls the larger, darker one. A gnarl of ebony tattoos snake up out of his shirt and encircle his neck. His face and hair are a mix of black stubble and scabs, as if he's scraped his head and cheeks with a dull, rusty razor. The butt of a pistol sticks out of his pants.

"I don't know; those last shots sounded pretty close. Maybe they got caught," says the smaller, mousier one. His scruffy blond beard and spiky hair twitch, and he seems almost electrified with fear.

"Fuck." The tattooed man spits a stream of green saliva into the dirt through a gap in his teeth. Pot, the pain reliever of the new world. "I'm going to check on the cows. I don't think we tied 'em tight enough. You get your ass back and check on Ray and Craig. If they're hit, you know the drill. Just leave 'em to die. You got five minutes to get back to me, so hustle. You know what happens to your little Lisa if you don't." He stalks off into the woods.

The smaller man turns and starts heading toward Daniel and Natalie. Despite his unkempt hair, he looks like a regular person, like he might have been a construction worker or an electrician or a teacher, before the peak. His features haven't dropped into the slack-jawed expression of not giving a crap. Yet.

Daniel leaps out of the bushes, snatches the scruff of the man's coat, and thrusts Natalie's pistol into the man's temple.

Natalie stares. She's never seen Daniel move with such speed and grace. For as long as she's known him, his movements have been more measured, have *had to be* more measured.

"Where are you camped?" Daniel murmurs into the man's ear. "I know the places you're not. So don't lie."

The man looks over his shoulder for a rescuer.

Daniel shakes him. "Where?" he repeats.

The man's face scrunches into tears. "Across the river, on the ridge. Please, we're just trying to survive. I have a wife and children up there. Please help us."

"Stealing and shooting aren't the way to ask for help."

"Please, you don't understand. You gotta let me go. I only have five minutes."

Daniel hesitates, but then pulls the man's head closer. "You go up and tell your leaders not to come around here looking for food or animals." Daniel's lips are pressed against the man's ear. "And don't even consider staying up on the ridge over winter. You'll freeze your asses off, and we're not going to be your supply cupboard. Your friends are dead. Now get the hell out of here, or I'll shoot you." Daniel gives him a shove and the man stumbles before taking off into the woods.

Karl and Natalie rise to their feet, and the three of them slip back into the field in silence.

"What's the plan, Dan?" Karl squints. "Are we gonna follow them and get the cows back?" He stares into the trees.

"We're not following them," Daniel says, a note of impatience in his voice. He hands Natalie her gun, and takes his rifle. "Who knows how many armed men they have in the woods? There are only three of us. We let them go."

"We should go back, get Richard, and take them down." Karl takes a few steps toward the woods.

Daniel fixes Karl with a stern stare. "No. *We*"—he pointedly emphasizes the word—"just shot a kid and killed a man. That's enough for tonight. We need that guy to deliver the message that they should move on." He continues across the field without looking back.

Natalie trots to keep pace with Daniel's lengthy stride. He's moving too fast, his breath coming out of him in short heaves, his hand pressed against his heart. His half-assed gimpy heart, as he calls it. Her own heart rate accelerates. She cannot lose Daniel.

Karl mutters to himself as he follows.

It's darker than before, and as they reach the field, the clouds open, bathing them in a torrential downpour. That's how it happens now. No rain for months, and then a season's worth in fifteen minutes. Natalie wants to fall to her knees in thanks, but she has to get back to the kid, and to Andrew and Justin, and make sure Daniel is okay. She lifts her lips to the onslaught of water and prays it's a long, hard storm.

A few feet from the edge of the forest, Daniel turns to Karl. "You stand watch here to make sure that the raiders don't come back."

Karl looks mutinous, but takes a seat on an overturned water bin, rain cascading around him, still grumbling about fucking taking them.

Natalie leads Daniel to the two bodies, and Daniel bends down to scoop up the boy.

"Are you sure you should carry him? I'll get someone else," she says.

"I'm fine." She knows he hates to be asked. Maybe he *is* fine.

Daniel carries the barely conscious boy to the farmhouse while she trails behind, fretting. Anneke greets them at the door with her gun in hand, her face and glasses smudged with soot. Several of the other women, with pinched and nervous faces, loom in the darkness.

"We're here to protect the children. The fire's moved past the cornfield and Richard has the raiders on the run. Are there raiders in the east too?" Anneke directs her words at Natalie.

Natalie nods. "I think they're gone though."

Daniel pushes past Anneke with the boy.

Anneke steps aside, her eyebrows scrunched together, her gaze suddenly focused on the youth. "Who's that?"

"A raider boy. Gunshot wounds to the shoulder and foot. I need to get back to the barn," Natalie says. Daniel continues on through the kitchen toward the infirmary.

Anneke places her hand on the doorframe as if to steady herself. "He needs medical attention." Her voice sounds strained, almost unnerved.

"I'll send Mike as soon as I can," Natalie calls over her shoulder as she steps back outside. Rain pounds against her head and body, washing the soot from her arms in streams. The gunfire has ceased. Mushroom swells of smoke and steam fill the forest. The cabin has collapsed into a heap of smoldering ashes, smoke rising in sinewy curls, as a few small flames glow in the tops of the trees that line the river. The trees near the farm had been so dry they burned like a forest of paper sticks, leaving almost no fuel to maintain the fire. They'll have to patrol for sleeper fires for a week or two. But it's over.

Soot-streaked farm members mill around the wounded lying on the barn floor. Mike, Natalie's brother and the farm doctor, sits white-faced with a blood-soaked shoulder giving directions to Justin, who tries to stop the bleeding from Alan's hip. She scans the barn for other casualties but sees none.

Richard emerges from the stairwell when she enters the barn. He has the unruly, pumped look he always gets when he's been shooting. The other men are close behind, rifles still in hand, and Andrew is with them.

"We got them!" Richard crows. "They just took off with their tails between their legs! Bit off a little more than they could chew coming here." Richard chuckles and raises his rifle jubilantly.

Several men and women cheer and give Richard congratulatory smacks on the back. Natalie wants to give him a good hard push. For his hubris, for his endless well of optimism, for his delusion that he is sufficiently important in the universe that all will be fine.

The math comes more easily to her now. They lost twenty sheep, four cows, a dog, the oat field, a cabin, and an eighth of the cornfield. They used gallons of precious water, Mike and Alan are wounded, and there's an armed encampment on the ridge. She has to add Daniel's heart to her list of worries, and Richard continues to run the farm.

CHAPTER 2

THE QUEEN OF WANDS

NATALIE AND ANDREW

The Queen of Wands is the fire in the room and always pursues what she wants.

Natalie hustles across the courtyard to the creamery, the exhaustion from the night before heavy inside her skull. She's wasted time checking on Mike and the raider boy and assigning some of the men to bury the dead and check for ground fires; but Richard cannot find her neglecting her own chores, or he will flash her that knowing smile and use her lapse to his advantage. She has no time to weep for the trees west of the farm—now a smoldering grove of black sticks, like cropped hair under a microscope. She has no time to weep for anything. The tears gather and pool in the hollows behind her eyes, always threatening to spill over and choke her.

Yet the day is undeniably beautiful. Wasps dive in and out of the fruited fields, making the air around her itch with industry. A brilliant sun bathes the gardens and orchards in crisp light. The angled brilliance of a British Columbia fall—her sixth on Blue Moon Farm.

Other farm members go about their tasks, lids heavy and movements sluggish. The fall harvest, planned out to the last detail, doesn't allow for days off. Although it's still putridly hot by midmorning, nightfall brings cool shards of air, gasped in relief after the heat of day. But winter breathes down their backs, hastening their steps and focusing their efforts.

Sweat forms in uncomfortable prickles in Natalie's armpits. She hates long sleeves in the heat, but the intensity of the sun leaves no choice. Sometimes it feels like the sun is burning a hole through her center. She imagines the world's icebergs have dwindled into a single mass the size of a sailboat, bobbing alone on seething oceans that have erased cities, while the world's remaining population wanders homeless and unfed. The farm has become like the berg, an island in the mountains. But perhaps the poles remain encased in ice, and beyond the borders of the farm new cities flourish. They have no way of knowing.

The smell of hay, earth, and fur, tinged with the sweet stench of urine, wafts out the barn door. Now it's threaded with a faint odor of smoke. With a dairy, canning kitchen, windmill, storage for hay, and coops and stalls for the farm animals, the barn is practical enough. The massive beams and sparkle of sunlight on dust always remind her of a church. It *is* their new church in a way.

Natalie descends into the cool darkness of the barn root cellar, candle aloft, swallowing mouthfuls of sweet cold air. The cream has been skimmed off the milk every day for a week and left to sour in the barn root cellar. She pours the soured cream into the butter churn and begins plunging with a practiced hand, turning the paddle a quarter turn with each downward motion, while mentally running through her list of chores.

The September job chart has to be posted. There will be the usual accusations of favoritism. The number of tasks required to keep them alive is mind-numbing, and each farm member has his or her set ways and preferences. She's tired of pissing people off, of holding the weight of all the job assignments in the knot between her shoulder blades. She wants to be back at her desk reading case law and writing legal briefs. But she's convinced they'll all die if she stops taking control, if she leaves things to Richard.

The sliver of light on the worktable expands briefly to cast a dim rectangle as the trap door above her is opened. Her heart lurches when she sees scuffed steel-toed boots and the black outline of a cowboy hat. Daniel bows his head to duck his six-foot frame through the hatch and small stairwell. Natalie glances up but keeps working.

He stands at the worktable, facing away from her, moving the handle of the cheese press up and down in methodical strokes. "Did I choke, Nat? I couldn't kill the guy. I believed him. Part of me *wanted* him to have those cows." He turns to face her. The skin under his eyes is puffy from lack of sleep.

"It's okay," Natalie says, breathless from churning the thickening cream.

"Richard laughed at me. Called me a big tit. He says I just gave them an invitation to come back. He's right. But I can't keep killing people. I hate it."

"Ignore Richard. You know how he is. We have to start exploring other options." Natalie scoops the butter out of the churn, places it in a bowl, and starts working it with a paddle.

Daniel sits heavily on the lone bench in the cellar, takes off his hat, and runs his hand through his hair. There's a slight indentation where his hat had rested. Natalie imagines her lips pressed against the mark, letting them drift down his face to his mouth. But she cannot. She will not.

"Like what? A refugee camp? Why can't people just leave us alone?" As he speaks, Natalie lowers her eyebrows fractionally. Daniel's face softens. "I'm sorry. I know that's stupid. I'm just tired. Don't listen to me. I just want it to end."

Natalie pours off the additional buttermilk to be taken to the kitchen for biscuits and bread, and risks sitting next to Daniel on the bench. She allows herself to feel the warmth of his thigh against hers, inhaling his particular mix of sweat, leather, and hay. The top few buttons of Daniel's shirt are open, and she can see his pulse beating in his neck and the hint of hair in the hollow of his chest. His pectoral muscle curves away from his sternum, vanishing under the folds of his shirt.

"Is everything okay? I noticed last night you seemed to be struggling a bit." She doesn't want to add: *with your heart.*

He emits a snort of air through his nose. "I'm fine. Fine as I'll ever be."

She leans her head into his shoulder without touching him so her hair grazes his arm. They sit still for a moment, the only connection between them the edges of their legs and the weight of her hair, and she's sure he feels it, too. That he'd be okay if she placed her hand on his thigh. But then he puts his hat back on and stands up. She rises too. The cloth on her lap flutters to the floor. He mutters something about getting back to work and climbs the stairs back into the light. Natalie returns to her butter, pouring cold water and salt into it and working it until every last bubble is pressed out.

After washing her hands, she heads back to the farmhouse to check on the patients. Heat rises from the compacted dirt in undulating waves. Grasshoppers, energized by the mid-morning heat, storm through the air around her, their claws hooking into her hair and clothes. She steps through the mirage of heat over and over, but more waves always appear beyond her.

SHE KNEW ON THE NIGHT of her wedding to Richard that she was making a mistake. It had been Daniel whom she had first noticed, that night at the party more than twenty years ago. It had been Daniel she had first approached, tentatively, weaving through party-goers with slick fingers clasped around her beer to stand a little closer so he could approach her. But then Richard had popped into the scene, dominating the conversation with his charisma and wit, and Daniel had faded into the background, smiling and nodding at everything his twin had said. It was Richard who had asked her out, who had pursued her with a flamboyant confidence that had won her over.

And then on her wedding night, encased in yards of French tulle, and surrounded by nine bridesmaids—*nine*: what had she been thinking—she knew with sickening certainty that she had feelings for Daniel. But what could she do? Call off an event that cost more than many Canadian families earned in a year, paid for by Richard, high on the confidence of becoming a partner in a wildly successful telecommunications startup? She couldn't do that. She couldn't do that to Richard. So she said the words, swished across the floor in her twelve-thousand-dollar creation while flashes lit the room, and tried not to look at Daniel. She would tell Richard in a year or two. She would move far away and live alone with a cat and her books.

But then she got pregnant with Justin after a night of foolish drinking with friends, and her life became focused on her precious babies. She made the best of it and appreciated Richard for his good qualities. She would leave Richard when the kids grew older, extract herself from their circle of friends and colleagues and their expectations, and retreat to a small condo and spend the rest of her life in solitude. But then the world as they'd known it had ended. And she and Richard were trapped together on this farm, locked in a pitched battle of survival. And every year the fractures in her relationship with Richard blossomed, and her love for Daniel grew with a furtive and cursed insurgence. And she could not escape either of them.

It was hard to believe sometimes, the bilge of excess from which they'd come. "I think we need to move, Richard," Natalie had said in their airy country kitchen in Kitsilano eight years earlier, just after Richard had been elected mayor of Vancouver for a second term. She tossed beets and pea pods from the garden into a salad, a half-empty glass of wine next to her. Andrew and Justin were engaged in a wild game of hide-and-seek outside, their whoops and altercations echoing through the open window.

Natalie had spent the afternoon at a Vancouver Food Strategy Association meeting, where the talk had been animated and worrisome. The Association's food strategy plan looked great, with localized agriculture, backyard gardens, and reclamation of golf courses. They might have enough food, but Natalie had a nagging fear that, in Vancouver, with gangs, elaborate water and transportation infrastructure, and just *so many* people, food might not be their only concern.

And peak oil—she'd never even heard of it. But with each book and article, she felt a tightening sense of dread. Everything about their lives, and the lives of most people around them, had been built around oil. What would happen if it was all gone?

Richard caressed her buttock and grabbed a handful of the pea pods. "What is it this time, Nat? SARS? Terrorists? Flu pandemic? Mad cow disease? Earthquake? What's the crisis *du jour*? Can't be cancer because you said *we* instead of *I*." He chuckled, downing his glass of wine and pouring another. He always had to make fun of what he perceived to be her fears.

But the emotion she was experiencing wasn't quite fear. The notion of being trapped in the city when the pumps went dry terrified her. The city, with its clawing, mindless masses of people with no idea where their food came from. But it wasn't only fear that drove her to flee.

Perhaps she just wanted an escape from the city. The competition over kitchens, vacations, children's achievements and dinner parties. The ridiculousness of their conversations. *Of course you must come to Barbados with us. I don't know* how *people raise children without a swimming pool. We've decided that we really must buy a ski chalet.* The treadmill of their lives, with fundraisers, grocery shopping, activities, and trips.

Perhaps it was Richard she was trying to escape. Richard and his political life. Smiling tightly at functions. Gulping wine as she engaged in the hard-pumping handshakes and the affected seriousness of policy talk. Playing her part, polished and well-spoken, but never outspoken, except when she screwed up, which was often in the early days, when her opinions were too extreme, or she took offense to some chauvinistic remark, and Richard chastised her for it. Making life easy for Richard, so he could do important work in the community and the boardroom. The charitable part of her argued that she was doing it for the boys, that she cared about Richard, that this was what marriage was like. Besides, she wasn't sure if she could make it on her own. She mostly did pro bono legal work for environmental groups when she could fit it in around the family schedule. She hadn't had a career job in years. Richard was proud of her work and trotted it out frequently at political events, but he never failed to remind her that he made most of the money.

Maybe peak oil was the escape hatch from her life: an elaborate reset button.

Most of her friends and family laughed. There's lots of oil, the oil companies are just controlling the prices, there are alternative energy sources, things won't go off the rails if we run out of oil, they would say. Richard laughed the loudest. Peakers are a bunch of whack jobs, a cult, Chicken Littles, he said.

But Richard had always wanted acreage. A remote farming retreat had a wild back-to-the-land appeal to him. So when Natalie proposed it, he agreed. He spent several weeks strutting about the house flexing his muscles and pretending to chop wood, shoot chipmunks, and take down deer with his bare hands.

He balked at selling their house in Vancouver, though. Instead, he managed to wrangle a portion of his inheritance from his parents. That summer they purchased one hundred and sixty-seven acres of ranch land northwest of Tanner's Ridge in the interior. The Syringa River ran through the property, which was bordered on three sides by Crown land, miles from the nearest town.

They had the land, but no money to build. "We'll just finance it as we go," Richard suggested. "If it's all going to go belly up, it's not going to matter if we're overextended anyway." Natalie fretted about this until Daniel showed up one day with a check.

"It's my RRSP savings," he said when she looked at him with a raised eyebrow. "I've always wanted a farm. It'll get us started."

Daniel the hermit, as Richard called him. "Maybe the farm is just the place for him to hole up further from society and avoid ever doing anything with his life," Richard said later with a guffaw and a glass of chardonnay.

When Natalie announced that she planned to take the boys and live in a trailer while she had the farmhouse and barn built, Richard's reaction bordered on incredulous. He couldn't go, or *wouldn't*. He had constituents and businesses. He wandered around the house for weeks, flummoxed by the fact that she thought she could function without him. Then he stopped mentioning it, assuming that she wouldn't go. When Natalie loaded her new Jeep Cherokee and left with the boys, Richard stood on the front step waving, his face wreathed in bewilderment, as if he couldn't quite understand why she had packed suitcases to go to the grocery store.

The next year was a blur of construction, learning to till fields and dig in gardens on a limited budget. Daniel started driving out on weekends to help, and eventually weekends became weeks as he moved his veterinary practice and found he liked digging and building. The choices were impossible. What would they need? Richard sent emails with lists of local pool vendors and preferred brands of four-wheel-drive tractors. Natalie and Daniel overruled him, and Richard sulked. Daniel acquired dogs and livestock by offering veterinary services in exchange for new animals. But there were so many unknowns. Should they buy solar panels, or plan to operate with no electricity? Should they buy thousands of mason jars, rings, and lids? Drugs? Seeds? Hand tools? Or was peak oil just a myth—a question that ran gratingly through Natalie's head—making their efforts and money wasted and useless? Making them fools?

But then Natalie would study Daniel. Gray-eyed, enigmatic Daniel, leaning against the flatbed truck with his hat cocked and brow furrowed while he tried to puzzle though the pile of sketches for the gardens, sheds and pastures. She would study him, and she would question her own motivations and morals.

❊

ANDREW PAUSES FROM HIS SHOVELING to wipe his brow and have a drink of water. His cousin Christopher leans on his own shovel. Removing the shit from the outhouse composting bins is not a vied-for job on the farm, and sweat slides down Andrew's exposed chest. Despite his mother's frequent reassurance that humanure, once left to sit for two years, is a safe and necessary addition to the garden, Andrew shudders whenever the steaming mixture grazes his skin.

The job does, however, enable him to spend a few hours watching the luscious Siobhan in the garden, not to mention deliver the manure to her. He spent several hours the previous day anticipating her expressions of glee as he brings her the full wheelbarrows. In his imagined scenarios, both he and Siobhan wore significantly fewer clothes. But at this point, any interaction with an attractive member of the opposite sex is a good one. Pickings on the farm being slim and all.

Andrew's father is supposed to be helping them, but Richard set the boys to work and then excused himself from the task, muttering something about a well pump. Andrew just rolled his eyes, but hopes that his mother doesn't happen across the field and discover that Richard is absent. Another argument in front of Siobhan is the last thing he needs.

Andrew shed his shirt earlier to show off his tanned muscular form. But his pecs and stomach are getting tired from trying to keep them flexed in case Siobhan is watching, and Christopher keeps giving him sidelong smirks. Siobhan's joy was sufficiently gratifying when he trundled up with the first wheelbarrow. But her later responses have simply been gestures of where to dump the manure—a dismal contrast to his hoped-for outcome.

Andrew wonders if one can die from lack of action, or any prospects of future action. The only female on the farm over the age of twelve and under the age of twenty who isn't related to him is Katie Wood, Anneke and Alan's daughter, a squat and blemished gnome-like creature. Siobhan is his only hope. But she's married to Solomon and seems oblivious to his interest.

His cousin Rachel rounds the corner of the barn with some of the younger girls, their baskets laden with herbs and the wildflowers used to scent the soap. Great. The girls get wildflowers, and he gets shit.

When Rachel spots him, which takes a while because she's half-blind, her face breaks into a satisfied smile. She approaches slowly, with feline grace. Andrew imagines a tail switching behind her.

"What's up, cousin? The shit pile got you all hot and bothered, or are you stalking the gardener again?" The other girls titter.

Andrew turns on his most charming smile. "Can't blame a guy for trying. At least I have prospects. There's not one available guy on the farm older than ten who's not related to you."

Rachel throws her dark hair over her shoulder. Andrew cannot help but notice how hot his cousin has become, with her dusky blue eyes and milk-white skin. Her haughty demeanor is almost sultry. Fuck. Now he's fantasizing about his cousin. Things are really getting desperate.

"Until now," Rachel says. "Now we have Craig, the injured raider, don't we, girls? Who happens to be very cute. And as for *your* prospects, Siobhan wouldn't notice you if she tripped over you naked in her garden." The other girls giggle.

"All right, girls, you laugh, but we'll see who hooks up first."

Rachel purses her lips into an upturned pout. "Well, that's hardly any interest of mine."

"Oh no?" Andrew says. "That's why you pout and thrust your tits at Solomon."

Rachel leans in really close. Andrew feels the warmth of her breath faintly on his neck, the softness of her breasts against his arm and the silky brush of her hair on his chest. She whispers in his ear. "That, cuz, is just practice."

She tosses her hair over her shoulder as she leaves, her minions in tow. Andrew admires the curve of her ass. Cousin, he reminds himself. Off limits.

⚬⚬⚬

NATALIE ESCAPES THE BRILLIANCE OF the courtyard for the dim corridors of the farmhouse. The sounds of rhythmic chopping, muted talk, and snapping wood float down the hall from behind the oak door of the kitchen. It's canning season, and the kitchen is an inferno.

She enters the infirmary. Her brother Mike sits in a chair by the beds while Joanne, his wife, chides him for leaving his own treatment for last. Mike's ashen face is stark against the coal darkness of his hair and beard. Justin tends the boy, who lies on the bed shivering despite the heat. The boy's ragged sweatshirt is cut and pulled open at the shoulder, and streaks of filth and blood coat his clothes and body.

Joanne rises when Natalie enters. "I'm off to the schoolhouse," Joanne says. Streaks of soot still mark her face, but her eyes, while puffy with fatigue, shine with the resoluteness that Natalie has become accustomed to in her sister-in-law. No matter what the calamity or hardship, Joanne carries on. Natalie wonders if the woman is borne by the happiness of her relationship with Mike or just by some bloody-minded inner strength. Either way, she'd like to leverage some of whatever Joanne has.

"Cancel school for the day," Natalie says. "You just lost your cabin."

Joanne shrugs. "Can't. Colleen's already on about the farm caste system again."

Natalie feels the vice grip of her own tensed muscles. Some farm members manage to find something unfair with every aspect of farm life. Natalie often feels like a contortionist in her efforts to please Colleen, yet Colleen becomes more supercilious and domineering toward her every year. Richard finds Colleen's complaints hysterical and maintains that Colleen just hates Natalie because Natalie is beautiful. Natalie catches a glimpse of her frizzy hair and beleaguered face in the infirmary mirror and decides that Richard's theory is half-baked.

Joanne brushes Mike's cheek with a kiss. Their fierce intimacy hangs in the air even at the darkest of moments, and Natalie suppresses a pang of envy.

"How's the kid?" Natalie asks after Joanne leaves. She watches Justin start washing up, admiring the smooth efficient movements of her eldest son.

"He's stable," Mike says. "He took two bullets to the shoulder, one to the foot. We removed the bullets, but we had a pretty hard time controlling the bleeding. Anneke was a big help. We should train her as a backup medic—the woman's got nerves of steel."

Natalie feels a rumble of incongruence somewhere in her brain. Anneke never helps in the infirmary, yet there's no denying she'd probably be good at it. "There's lots of things we should train Anneke for. But go ahead, if she's interested."

Mike motions Natalie into the corridor, where he leans against the wall and speaks softly. "I just thought I should let you know we're running out of antibiotics, and the ones we have left are past their expiry, which means they're getting less potent." He pauses. "I need to know: are we using the remaining ones on the kid—Craig—or saving them for one of us? Alan and I are going to need them, as I'm sure those arrows were dirty. The bullets were probably cleaner, but the one shredded Craig's foot, so there's still a pretty good chance of infection."

Natalie presses her fingertips against the throb of her temples. There's always something. "How low are we?"

"With courses for Alan and me, we have enough to treat five or six more major injuries or illnesses. At the rate that we get injured and sick around here, that won't last a year."

Mike trembles slightly. Natalie pushes him into his tiny office that adjoins the infirmary. He sinks onto the couch, the bright pink flowered material thin with age and stained with blood from injuries sustained over the past five years.

Mike leans his head heavily on his good arm. "Craig could suck up a lot of our remaining stores if he gets an infection. I don't want to be heartless, but is that where we want to put our resources?"

Natalie closes her eyes. She wants to go to bed and not get up. "Okay, leave it with me. Farm Council will have to decide."

"All right. I need an answer sooner rather than later, so I know what to do."

"We could collect natural antibiotics, like Goldenseal or Oregon Grape," Natalie says.

Mike shrugs. "If you want. They might work for sinusitis and ear infections. But I doubt they're going to be much help against sepsis."

Mike forms the tips of his forefingers into a bridge and stares at it. "We also need to start thinking about more advanced medical services, Nat. I need to know if there's anything out there, any hospitals, any place I can refer people to when they get something I can't handle. I was okay with sewing people up for a few years, and I'm okay to continue doing so. But let's face it, we're all getting older. We're going to start getting diseases that I can't treat. If there are any medical services available, beyond my needle and thread, ethically I should know about them. My poor daughter needs corrective lenses so badly it's not funny. And," Mike flicks his head in the direction of the infirmary, "your son needs to go to a real medical school. I can teach him a lot of things, but it's not the same."

"I'm not sending him off the farm. What if there's nothing out there?"

Mike stares at his hands again. When had the curves beneath his cheekbones become so sunken, so indented? "Then there's nothing out there. But I think we're getting to the point where we have to know. Anyway, I gotta get back to the patient." He stands abruptly and leaves her alone in the office.

Natalie watches the play of shadows from the elderberry bushes on the wall. Mike's right, of course. He always is. But it all seems like too much to deal with. Richard's relentless optimism and confidence used to buoy her; now they just make her tendency toward darkness seem all the more maladaptive. Richard drops hints all the time that he thinks she's depressed, that she's just like her mother. Maybe she is.

Years ago, she never knew who she was going to get when she called home: the exuberant manic, or the needy depressive. Natalie could barely remember her father; he had been killed in a farm machinery accident when she was seven. Her mother's episodes started a year or two later. They would descend the stairs to find that the furniture had been rearranged overnight, every corner swept, surfaces gleaming, and her mother wearing a fresh apron and the smile of the Joker. And then the pendulum would swing, and dinner would be pancakes made out of old cake mix served by a woman who seemed to be sinking into the kitchen floor.

Either woman could be dangerous. One drove too fast, gave away money, and flew into tempers. The other left the gas on and played with matches. They devised signals—she, Mike and their younger brother, Scott—to exchange in the hall outside the kitchen. Thumb to the lips meant all was okay. One finger up against the nose, to represent an exclamation point, meant she was manic and anything could happen. Two fingers up and curved signaled the arrival of the black dog of depression and to stay out of the way.

Mike's escape was medical school. Scott's was the bottle. Was Richard hers?

Their mother tried—tried very hard—to keep things together. And she loved them. But there were probably impacts associated with living under a regime of chronic uncertainty.

Natalie stands and shakes it off. She will cling to hope. She just wishes that hope did not always have to look like Daniel.

Natalie leaves the farmhouse through the side door, past the fleet of old SUVs and trucks that fill the old carport. The remaining fuel in the vehicles was siphoned off for use in the tractor years ago, and their bodies have been stripped for parts. She walks back through the ripples of heat. She is on canning duty for the rest of the day, until the acids of the tomatoes and apples make her fingers burn, and the heat of the woodstoves bakes her face.

Andrew feels the ache of mental and muscle fatigue as he heads to the former closet in the farmhouse that he and Justin share. Justin, he knows, will sleep in the infirmary.

Most of the farm members have retired early, but Andrew stayed up to play cards with Karl, who is on night watch. Karl was a professional poker player before the peak, or so he said; but based on his like of the weed, Andrew wonders if Karl wasn't just a big dope smoker. Karl was the last refugee they took in before Andrew's dad and his Uncle Leon said that was enough, that they must close the farm to new people, and convinced Farm Council to vote with them. Andrew plays cards with Karl because he figures if anyone knows what it's like out there, it would be Karl. But whatever Karl knows, he keeps to himself, other than to reiterate, "It was bad out there, man."

Andrew creeps past Anneke and Alan's room. The light of the waxing moon floods the hallway, but the glow of candlelight flickers under their closed door.

"It was him in the raiding party, over to the far left. He wasn't shooting. He came late, after I was hit, and hung back a bit. I'm sure of it. I saw his face. Were you still in touch with him?" Alan's voice has a tone of mild rebuke and resignation, like this is a conversation he's had before.

Andrew freezes. In all their years on the farm, he's never heard Alan raise his voice to Anneke. The last thing Andrew needs is for the floor to creak and Anneke to fling open the door. The woman scares him. She can cast a gimlet eye that can cow even Richard.

Anneke's laugh sounds forced. "You're imagining things, Alan. It was dark and smoky. You had an arrow sticking out of you, and you're myopic. It was probably just someone who looks like him. I haven't spoken to Joe in years."

Nobody speaks for a few seconds.

"Maybe you're right," replies Alan slowly. "Let's just go to bed. I'm beat." The candle glow disappears, and the creak of two figures settling into the bed slips under the door.

Andrew finds his heart beating curiously hard as he shuffles silently to his room.

CHAPTER 3

THE KING OF CUPS

RICHARD AND ANDREW

The King of Cups understands people and knows how to influence them.

Richard watches Natalie sleep. He knows better than to wake her. Sometimes he deliberately lets her oversleep, just to put her in her place a bit. She's easier to manage when she's a little off her game, and it's a fair return for putting up with her chronic sleep problems.

Her hair lies in unkempt folds over the pillow, a wheaty mix of honey and gray. She's not as attractive when she sleeps, her features too slack. Natalie's allure was, and still is, always in waking, in the utter animation that possesses her face and eyes when she speaks. Richard watches the eyes of other men crawl all over her. It almost gives him a hard-on, possessing this woman whom other men want. Not that any of them could handle her. He would never have chosen her if she hadn't been so damn beautiful and pragmatic—relative to other women of course. Even now that he's seen her at her most base and unattractive, she's still impressive. A more compliant wife would probably have been far more useful, but divorce was always a death knell for politicians, and he could end up with a woman far more irritating. Especially since, Richard reflects, he's easily irritated. And despite her claims of being a small town hick, she is a defter political animal than she thinks. He needs her. For now.

She tossed and turned half the night, pulling him from his slumber again and again, rising and standing at the window, watching for intruders, demanding that he rise and look or listen. But it was ghostly quiet all night. The silent forms of the farm's night watch shifted about like wraiths, the shrouds of their breath hanging in the cold fall air.

NINE YEARS AGO, WHEN OIL prices started to climb, Natalie would stand by the window at night, haranguing him with her forecasts of doom and declarations that they would all die. Richard would scoff that it was temporary, a blip, and that Natalie was worrying too much, as always. He suggested antidepressants, but she refused, preferring to haunt him until he did something. *Do something yourself, and stop keeping me awake*, he wanted to yell. And so she demanded that he buy a farm in buttfuck nowhere, which he did, and then she fucked off to it with the boys, followed, inexplicably, by Daniel, his social misfit twin.

But shortages *did* start to occur across North America and Europe. Gas stations hung out "no gas" signs. They were limited at first, just a couple here and there. The governments of the world and media talked about distribution problems, refining capacity issues, and the Saudis withholding oil. When the shortages became more widespread, the developing countries, and importers with little global power, saw their pumps go dry within months. In Japan, transportation ground to a halt. The news showed commuters waiting day after day for electric trains powered by oil-fired power stations. Trains that never came. Richard had a good guffaw over the suited Japanese, ever dedicated and hopeful, arriving each morning with their briefcases. Most of them showed up every day for over a week before giving up. In the oil-producing countries and regions with pull, mostly North America, Europe, China and India, queues began to form at the gas stations that still had gasoline. They were calm enough for the first few days—people patiently enduring a temporary blip in their comfortable lives—but as news of what was happening in the rest of the world spread, hoarding quickly became a problem, and people jostled against each other to fill cars, jerry cans, and lawn mowers. And once the riots began around the world, most governments nationalized their gas stations, developed gasoline-rationing systems, and churned buses onto the road. This allowed most people to continue their daily commute for a few more months.

For Richard, it was electrifying. The sheer complexity and opportunities for leadership made him feel like he was high on coke and sporting an erection all day. He gave speeches touting that the government was in control, that everything would be fine. He built a team of respected politicians and civil servants to lead Vancouver out of the dark days. They would have Victory gardens and electric cars, and become world leaders. He turned over the first shovel of dirt at the new solar panel plant. People begged him to speak at dinners and rallies. Business leaders relied on him, and the newspapers lapped up his words, printing them over and over again until he could plaster his walls with the clippings. It was the best time of his life.

Richard may have been on the fast track to political fame and fortune, but the global economy was not similarly blessed. Retail started to tank as a result of the gasoline rations and the lack of shoppers. Weekend trips to Wal-Mart and other box stores didn't happen, and retail prices spiked everywhere as transportation costs quadrupled. People started to hang on to their cash and wear old clothes. To make matters worse, horrific storms pummeled the East Coast of Canada and the United States and other parts of the world, causing untold economic damage. Some climate tipping point related to greenhouse gas concentrations in the atmosphere, the experts said. Whatever it was, it led to some totally whacky weather. Richard dumped the Kitsilano house at a loss while there was still a market, squirreling himself away in a little condo with faux marble countertops. The eight hundred square feet boxed him in and drove him nuts, but he felt like a martyr as well as a hero. The automobile industry went down the tubes, followed quickly by the travel industry and purveyors of luxury goods, such as dog clothes, purses, and home décor. Richard's favorite suit store, aptly named Richard's, went belly-up in six months. Some people just didn't know how to manage through a crisis.

Richard expected calls from companies all over BC begging him to be their CEO and dig them out of their troubles, but when they called, it was to demand his help as mayor of Vancouver, to forgive their property taxes or otherwise prop them up somehow. For free. Stupid requests that wouldn't see them through the downturn in the way his strategic leadership could. With tight-lipped anger he helped them, and they stayed afloat for a while. The offers of CEO-level compensation never came. After limping along for a year, Target announced bankruptcy, the stock market crashed, and the true unraveling began.

When Vancouver became too lawless and food became too scarce, Richard made a run for it, to the safety of the farm where he now sits, wasting his time, his political career languishing while he gets older by the second.

RICHARD PULLS ON HIS WORK clothes and glances out the window to the clear September morning, the watery rays of sunshine breaking over the surrounding mountains. The trees east of the farm decorate the valley and foothills in a frenzy of red, yellow, and orange, giving way to the inky green of the conifers dotted with yellow tamaracks at higher elevations. To the west, the blackened trunks and limbs of the trees look desolate and sinister, like an army of toothpicks ready to obey the orders of some otherworldly command.

The farm, which never really sleeps, given the constant need to stand guard, is changing shifts. The night watchers creep back to their cabins, making way for the more lively sounds of day. Richard sneaks down to the den and sits at his desk, organizing his ideas and writing out his expectations, until the clatter of the woodstove and the banter of children echo down the hall. He clears his thoughts for a few minutes, then braces himself and heads for the kitchen. The twelve farm children line the benches of the long harvest table, eating porridge. The older girls—Rachel, Sarah and Katie—cluster together deep in discussion at one end. Rachel glances up when he enters and looks him up and down, her eyes lingering on his groin with alarming candor. *That girl's going to be trouble.* He's glad he has boys. The three youngest boys trade chestnuts, squirrels' tails, crystals, and old baseball cards. Andrew and Christopher throw jibes into the mix. Justin usually eats in Mike's office, poring over medical books.

The counters and floors overflow with baskets of green and red tomatoes and peppers. The sour smell of the morning bread competes with the acrid undertone of unwashed bodies, as the kitchen canning crew chops tomatoes, their backs a huddle of natty sweaters, whacked out buns, dreadlocks, and old sweatshirts. Natalie is among them, her hair a torrent of uncombed curls. At least Natalie isn't subscribing to this new bun code. Richard hears an anxious undertone to their chatter. *The hopeless hens.* They work themselves into a frenzy of clucks and ruffled feathers every time something goes wrong. Their prattle threatens Richard's hard-won centeredness. He feels the slivers of a headache coming on.

He pours himself a cup of steaming tea and turns with a smile to face the day.

"What have you been doing?" Natalie says. She doesn't bother to hide the accusation in her voice. Natalie was the last to leave the canning kitchen the previous night and then spent hours reviewing the supply books before bed. Her knife still flashes into a tomato even as she glares in his direction. She works hard, no question—but he has no idea why she expects him to follow suit. He's explained to her again and again the need to work smart and take breaks, to lead, rather than spend all of one's time in the trenches. The hens watch with interest, knives poised above plum tomatoes. If he and Natalie were alone, he'd give her some pushback. But in a group it's easier to look pleasantly receptive, let Natalie's temper ramp up, and wait for someone to feel sorry for him. Fortunately, Natalie usually plays right along.

"You were supposed to help Anneke with the bread this morning," Natalie continues, her voice bordering on a hiss now. Richard dons a benign expression, trying to pass her some of his positive energy.

"I'm sure Richard is on his way there now," Olivia says.

Richard plasters a smile on his face. "Absolutely." Saved by his mother. Natalie's face contorts into a bug-eyed gape, and he sees her lips twist—her tell that she's trying not to cry. He should stop playing his little games with Natalie; she gets too wound up, and then he pays for it later. His games are fine for most people; they don't even notice, or they like the attention. But Natalie can't take a joke. He turns and pushes through the door into the pantry— a claustrophobic, off-white closet of a room, the shape of an apartment galley kitchen, with a heavy swinging door behind which Anneke hides, planning meals, mixing dough, and prepping food.

Anneke greets Richard with a wide smile, frightening in its intensity, her hands deep in bread dough, wiry blond hair pulled back with a hairband. As a general rule, Anneke and Richard hate each other, dating back to the days when Richard was a buttoned-down patchouli disdainer and Anneke was the Birkenstock-wearing president of the Civil Justice League. Anneke usually refuses to even make eye contact with Richard. To be received by Anneke with a smile is shocking, and Richard almost staggers off his center before pulling back together. She must want something.

He pulls his lips across his teeth in a sort of awkward grimace and stands waiting to be told what to do. It's best not to show too much initiative in the pantry. Anneke always tells him he's doing it wrong anyway, and the less useful he is, the more likely he won't be reassigned to bread duty in the future.

"You're making rolls for lunch. The recipe's there." Anneke gestures to the counter. Richard begins the laborious task of hand-grinding the wheat, letting his mind wander to more pleasant thoughts—of his days as mayor of Vancouver and the coterie of people that surrounded him, people that were excited about ideas and actions to make the city a better place. He had been so close to making the jump to provincial politics, where he could have made a real difference, not to mention a lot more money. He longs for the dim elegance of his favorite restaurant in Kitsilano: Luna, with its endless wine cellar, impeccable service, lively vibrato of customers, and comforting smell of garlic and fresh bread. It was packed to the rafters every Friday, and yet they would find a table for Richard at a moment's notice, a table where he could be part of the scene, where he could interact with his constituents, where it would be evident that he had made it.

"So," Anneke says. Richard jumps. She seldom addresses him, preferring to work next to him in seething silence. "What are you planning to do about the raiders?"

Richard swivels his head, wondering if Beelzebub himself has decided to have a conversation with him, but all he sees is Anneke's squat form, with large pores and a scattering of blond hair fringing her upper lip. He suppresses a shiver.

Richard shrugs. "Dunno. Go up and drive them out, I suppose."

"Do you really think that's the best idea?"

"Well, they shot at us, and if they stay up on the ridge, they'll be a constant threat." He punctuates this with a chuckle, his usual approach to emphasizing the reasonableness of his plan and the stupidity of her question. In actual fact, Richard respects Anneke for her sharpness and clarity. Sometimes he almost feels she's more similar to him than anyone else on the farm. But the lines of mutual dislike are too well established to allow Anneke any hint of this. Best to stick with the script.

Anneke punches the bread dough against the side of the bowl. It flattens with a *blurp* and emits a faint smell of sour wild yeast. She says nothing more, but Richard feels the bulk of her frame standing too close to him. She sniffs occasionally with a sharp, aggressive intake of air. Richard proceeds to make the rolls, and tries to pull back to his meditative calm. He just needs to get through this farm life thing for a few more years, wait for things to settle down a bit, so he can get back to real life.

***

ANDREW HEADS TO THE BARN to hitch the quarter horse team to the wood wagon. He chopped wood with several of the men in the burned-out forest all morning, and his shoulders and hands ache. He jumps when the shed door opens and his father pokes his head out.

"Andrew. Just who I was looking for. Can you help me for a few minutes?" Richard disappears back into the shed.

Andrew follows reluctantly. The other men are waiting in the woods.

The shed smells of dust, smoke, and grease. Sunlight filters in through two dirty windows, casting patches of light on the workbench strewn with tools and parts. His father stoops over the vice in the gloom, trying to fit two pieces of a pump together.

"I really have to get back. What do you want? Can't you find someone else?"

"Andrew! Always so impatient, just like your mother. I just need you to hold this pin steady for me so I can pound it in with the sledgehammer."

"With my hand?"

Richard chuckles. "Oh come on, Andrew. I won't hit you. Just help me out here."

Andrew takes the pin with a scowl. It occurs to him that his dad has not proposed that he himself hold the pin, while Andrew swings the sledgehammer.

After a few swings, which thankfully land on the pin, Richard says, "I was thinking. It's time we get you off the farm."

"What do you mean?"

"I think you need to start experiencing life a bit more."

The hammer slams against the pin and slips off, barely missing Andrew's hand. "Shouldn't you focus on what you're doing?" Andrew says, cringing.

Richard stops and wipes his brow with his sleeve. "Don't want to send you out into the world unprepared." Richard flashes a knowing eye roll and a swath of white teeth.

"Am I going out into the world any time soon? 'Cause last time I checked there weren't any Greyhounds driving past."

"No need to be smart, Andrew. What I'm asking is, if you want to join the scout party to check out the raiders, I'll pave it over with your mother. She tends to worry about things."

"I don't need to get off the farm. I just need a girlfriend."

Richard picks up the sledgehammer again and nods to Andrew to resume his post. "Don't rush into the girlfriend thing. Enjoy your free and easy days while you can. Girls can be trouble, and most women are crazy. These days it's easy for a woman to get pregnant, and then you're trapped." Richard hammers on the pump and yells to compensate for the noise. Andrew winces with each strike and sentence. "Just make sure you use your head, not your thingamajig, to make decisions. I think it's time to get you out in the world a bit."

Richard puts down the sledgehammer and examines the pump.

"Is that it then?" Andrew says, starting to back away.

"And remember you can always ask me if you need any advice."

"Right, Dad. Thanks." Andrew makes a hasty exit.

Andrew breathes heavily in the lukewarm pools of sunlight outside the shed. Grasshoppers leap around the outskirts of the shed, basking in the last vestiges of warmth. Andrew wonders how many of them are fornicating; how easy it would be to be a grasshopper. Leave the farm? The prospect fills him with an excitement and fear that he can feel from his teeth down to his groin.

⌐∞∞∞⌐

RICHARD PLUGS THE ELECTRIC WELL pump into the ammeter. The door of the shed flies open, and Natalie marches in with a fierce look in her eyes. Chicken blood stains her work overalls, and chaff clings to her hair and shirt. The sun has started to drop into the hills, and a gust of chill air follows her into the shed. Richard knows that he was on the schedule to help with the threshing and winnowing, but it looked like everyone else had it under control, and he really wanted to get the new pump working.

"What are you doing?" Natalie asks. There is a measured quality to her voice that doesn't match her eyes. He hates this habit of hers. She's not really interested in what he's doing. She's setting him up to criticize him for not doing what he's supposed to be doing.

"I reworked the old electric well pump so we can hook it up to the wind turbine."

"Do you think that's the best use of your time?" Natalie begins.

"Yup." He adds an edge to his reply, a warning. He doesn't need the lecture or her micromanagement.

"Well, the current pump works fine, and we really don't have to spend a lot of time pumping." Natalie's voice trails off.

"Oh, come on, Nat, I don't question how you spend *your* time. Why do you always have to do this to me?" Richard picks up the wrench to tighten the last few screws on the pump.

"Because I'm always working, and I'm not in here trying to play hero."

Richard smacks his wrench against the pump. Natalie jumps.

"Oh, is that what you think?" he says. It's a restrained yell. Hardly even a yell. But Natalie visibly shrinks away from him. As if he would ever hit her. Her reaction infuriates him. Why can't she ever appreciate his inventions? But he pulls back. "Nice, Nat. You really want to go there?" This question always shuts her down. He doesn't know what number that nutty mother of hers pulled on her, but any suggestion that they'll be reviewing her failings instead of his makes her pull back immediately.

She pulls her lips into a hideous facsimile of a smile, but her eyes still flash with fury. "Forget I said anything. It's great that you're working on the pump. I was wondering if we could schedule a Farm Council tonight to talk about the raiders and the antibiotic situation."

"All right, but does it have to be tonight?" Richard asks.

She shakes her head—with what, disappointment? Disgust? He doesn't understand why her reactions toward him are so negative sometimes. "Well, why not? It's pretty important," she says.

"Because the deer are clustering in the orchards, and it's going to be a full moon with a clear sky, so it'll be a good hunting night. We can do Farm Council tomorrow night." He doesn't even know if this is true. It's just his policy to always object first to most things, especially with Natalie. He labels it a political strategy in his mind—never give in on the first ask—but sometimes he half-wonders if it's just habit. Still, it's important that she doesn't think she can always get her way.

"We need to deal with the raiders sooner rather than later," she says.

But there is doubt in her voice, and this reassures him.

He turns back to the well pump. "Relax, Nat. That level of stress is not healthy. Just wait until you see my new water machine. It will blow your mind." He smiles to show that all is forgiven, that he can get past this. She doesn't smile back.

"Fine, tomorrow night then. I'll let everyone know," Natalie says. "And can you talk to Leon? He's smoking up again and didn't show up to help thresh."

"Yup," Richard says without looking up. Wordlessly, Natalie leaves the shed. Richard reaches for his center. Natalie's ongoing irritation with him is a small and unimportant thing. He is the bigger person. He will not let it bother him. He will move on to more important things to change the world and never do a day of manual labor again, especially not threshing.

Sometimes he wonders if he would be happier without Natalie. But his feelings for her are too complicated. He wouldn't call it love exactly, more like a jumble of dependency and respect. She is, generally speaking, a political asset, except when she lets her emotions spiral out of control. Her sensibilities are usually in line with his, or maybe it's just that she's sensible, unlike many women, without being a complete stick in the mud. Besides, she seems so unable to cope without him, and realistically most other women give him the heebies. And despite her proclivity to moroseness, there's a fire in Natalie that he still finds captivating—or perhaps it's her perfect ass. He doesn't know. Whatever the reason, he's still inclined to stick their marriage out, despite her mood swings.

He often wonders if something happened to Natalie when she was younger. Like if she was raped, or if her parents hit her. Something that would explain her moods and fears. He expects she would have told him though. Maybe she's just going through something. Some hormonal thing perhaps. Richard shudders. He would not want to be a woman.

⸺◦∞◦⸺

ANDREW PICKS HIS WAY DOWN the rock-studded gravel embankment to the river for his evening swim that doubles as a bath. The evenings are biting, and the river temperature will soon drop, leaving them to fester in their own filth for much of the winter. The river is lower than it has ever been, and the banks are drying and crumbling, forcing him to scrabble down to the water holding on to roots and bushes sticking out of the bank. There had once been a rope, but it was removed in case it might attract the attention of anyone using the river for transport.

Andrew hurries down to the water. Siobhan, Solomon and Gracie went down early, and he hopes for a glimpse of Siobhan in her underwear before the rest of the crowd arrives.

To his surprise, Gracie sits playing in the mud on the riverbank alone. Andrew edges closer, silently hugging the bank. Has something happened to Siobhan and Solomon? They wouldn't leave their child unattended on a riverbank. The image of him rescuing Siobhan from a raider sends a quiver of excitement down his back. Her lips close to his, breasts pressed against his chest as he carries her to safety, the feel of her body sliding down his to the ground. Andrew searches for a stick.

A low moan startles him, and Andrew shrinks into the bushes. Siobhan and Solomon stand entwined farther down the riverbank, their partially clothed bodies pale in the waning daylight. Siobhan's gaze is fixed on Gracie, and she hasn't noticed Andrew. Solomon's hand cups Siobhan's rounded breast, his forefinger playing with her nipple, while his lips skate up her arched neck. His other hand curls inside her panties, exposing a hint of dark hair. The double-bunking required in most of the cabins doesn't leave a lot of room for marital privacy.

Andrew huddles in the shadows as unwelcome, but paralyzingly pleasurable, tingles arise in his groin. He reels back into the bushes wanting to whip out his cock—his tentative new name for the organ that seems increasingly to control his behavior—and jerk off into the trees. But he can't. The other kids will be coming over the bank any second. He decides to sneak back the way he came, wait to hear voices, and then emerge from his trail as if he has just arrived. He takes several steps and trips over a tree root, yelping as he falls. Andrew scrambles to his feet as he hears the crackle of dry leaves behind him. He whirls around. Solomon jogs toward him with his eyebrows raised. Andrew notices the vivid green detailing of the tree tattoo that snakes around Solomon's cut torso. Siobhan now holds Gracie in her arms.

"You gave us a bit of a scare there, Andrew. Are you okay?" The question of what he was doing hangs in the air.

Andrew flushes, stealing a look at his shorts to make sure nothing is sticking up, or out. "Tripped on a root coming down the bank," he says airily.

"Looks like you hurt yourself."

Andrew stares down at his knee. A stream of blood trails down his calf. "It's nothing. I'm fine. Just heading for a swim." He hopes his voice sounds nonchalant, but fears it sounds more croaky than breezy. Solomon nods with an arched eyebrow and returns to Siobhan.

"Oh, look who has a boo-boo." Rachel's voice carries over the bank. A rain of gravel precedes her as she descends, the younger children following. "Getting desperate, cuz?" Rachel murmurs as she passes.

"Smart ass," Andrew says, and then plunges into the cold water.

He needs to find a real girl, soon.

CHAPTER 4

THE KING OF SWORDS

—⟨∞⟩—

DANIEL AND ANDREW

The King of Swords is incorruptible and just, but he keeps his emotions in check.

Daniel hurries through the east pasture, trailing Mitch's white flag tail. The midmorning September air, tinged by the wafts of ripening apples, plums, and pears, bathes his face in thin warmth. He proceeds with caution. Bears patrol the orchard in the fall looking for any opportunity to feast on the fruit. The dogs and pickers keep them in check, but Daniel doesn't wish to come face to face with one without a gun, and he hates carrying a gun.

One of the bulls has taken a liking to a particular cow and is showing no intention of mating with any other members of the herd. The bull's preferred cow has already been removed from the pasture and taken down to the barn, but the bull keeps rushing the wooden gate to get to her. Daniel grudgingly respects the bull for his loyalty. Karl and Scott have gone ahead to try to head the bull off, and Daniel checks his pace, Mike's warnings echoing in his ears. Don't run too fast or too long. Don't exert yourself too much. If you have a massive coronary, I can't save you. They're the same warnings he's heard since he was a child, except now there's no ambulances or teams of doctors waiting to bring his heart back to life. And his heart is getting worse. He can feel it. He's been told it probably would with age. The shortness of breath, or "exertional dyspnea" as Mike likes to call it, comes more frequently now. It should be just called "pain in the ass," Daniel thinks. He curses and slows down.

Mitch stops to stick his nose into a pile of pitted bear excrement and then darts a guilty glance at Daniel, who shakes his head at the dog. Mitch looks away and sets off ahead at a trot, as if to suggest he wasn't really interested anyway.

When Daniel arrives, Karl's face is red and sweaty as he pushes at the bull's rump to turn him around so he notices the other cows. The dogs circle, trying to force the bull away from the gate. Scott holds two young cows ready to be mated, to attract the bull's interest. But the bull remains focused on escape.

Daniel pushes his hat back on his head. If the cows aren't settled, they won't freshen, and there'll be no milk in the spring, not to mention young cows for food. Daniel has already put the older bull on the slaughter schedule because, based on the miscarriage rate in the herd last year, he's probably a trichomoniasis carrier. He carefully selected the new bull as the healthiest of the male calves that summer, but the damn bull clearly isn't interested in his new job. They could go to artificial insemination, but he didn't think to buy an artificial vagina and he has no idea who's going to jerk the bull off. Daniel wishes he hadn't been quite so liberal with the scalpel on the young bulls. There is the other bull, of course, but Daniel had wanted to trade the bulls back and forth between the two herds to reduce inbreeding.

Karl bounces off the bull a third time. Daniel climbs into the pasture and adds his weight to Karl's, trying to steer the bull into the waiting cows without pissing him off. Even with the extra two hundred pounds, the bull isn't budging. Daniel has a sudden vision of dolling the cows up with lipstick and wigs and wonders if he's starting to crack up.

He takes the bull's halter and makes a mental note to start piercing the bulls' noses. He talks to the bull and then tries to pull him in the direction of the cows, but the bull digs in its front hooves and gazes at Daniel through heavily fringed brown eyes. Bastard.

Natalie and Andrew have joined the onlookers now. Daniel rakes his hand through his sandy hair and puts his hat back on.

"Okay, show's over, let's take a break. I need to reassess our strategy here. You two," he says, motioning to Karl and Scott, "take the bull down to the lower pasture so he doesn't wreck this fence."

"Poor old Rockster, being taken off the field." Karl walks around and rubs the bull on the head with his knuckle. The bull, which Karl insists on calling Rocky, snorts and jerks his head, almost pulling Daniel off his feet.

"Karl, you nitwit. How many times do I have to tell you never to approach a bull from the front?" Daniel feels a wave of exasperation.

"Oh god, Dan. I forgot. Sorry, man!"

Scott whistles, and he and Karl trot off down the field, leading the bull between them, the dogs following behind. Daniel glares after them. City folk turned ranch hands. After five years, their hands are calloused, but their farming instincts still suck.

"And you," Daniel says, turning to Andrew, "make yourself useful. I need to know how many cows are in heat."

"Sure thing, Dan," Andrew says with a salute, imitating Karl's habit of shortening Daniel's name. Daniel's lips tighten, but he knows it's Andrew's way of showing affection.

"So?" Daniel turns to Natalie, as they walk down the field. Natalie automatically slows her pace to match his. She must be here to talk about Farm Council. Daniel dreads Farm Council. All the stupid posturing and pettiness. He toys with skipping it every time.

"I need to know how we're doing with our stock of veterinary antibiotics," she says. Her hair is untamed today, and her eyes subdued. Not sleeping again probably. But she holds herself together, her compact form moving down the rutted orchard with the grace of a dancer. For all her steely determination, her edges and eyes remain soft and delicate, as if she were meant to be a wood nymph dancing in the trees with flowers in her hair, not a farmer in filthy overalls and gum boots. There's a wildness about her in the play of intensity around her eyes, the way she watches him and everyone, always assessing, the way her lips sometimes seem to arch upward in some lush secret. He wonders if she brings that wildness and intensity to bed. His mind leaps forward with the inevitable imagining of it: her perfect almond skin and halo of curls, her nakedness and that knowing smile. He clamps down on the fantasy immediately, ushering it out of his mind with a determined and practiced force.

The intensity and frequency of these imaginings concern him. It's like his mind and body, in some sort of act of joint defiance, are trying to convince him that the Natalie that he loves to stand next to, talk to, and smell, is an available woman. A woman he could someday touch, hold, and fuck. A woman who is not his brother's wife.

Daniel readjusts his hat and pulls back his hair, which feels slick with oil and dirt. "We're almost out. We've been managing without them, but it's not a big deal to put down a sick animal to prevent something from spreading. Why?"

Natalie hesitates.

"You're thinking we could use them on humans," he says.

"Yes." She pauses. "I'm also thinking that we could restock at some of the local veterinarians. All the pharmacies will have been cleaned out, but maybe people don't know about using animal drugs on humans, or haven't thought about who might have had supplies."

"They're all going to be past their dates. And the dosages are going to be different. I suppose we could work that out, but there could be compounds or impurities in them not suited for humans. It's risky."

"I know," says Natalie. "But if someone's dying already, better the chance of a reaction to the drugs than have them die of a routine infection. If we know they're less potent, we could increase the dosages."

"Who's going out there in search of them? That's going to be a dangerous trip with a very questionable outcome."

Natalie stops walking and turns to him. "I was hoping you would."

"Me?" Daniel feels a rippling wave of doubt. Danger could linger behind every goddamn thing out there—every tree, every hillock, every godforsaken house— every inch of the new world a relief map of risk. He would most likely end up dead in a ditch. He rocks back on his boots, fingers hooked in belt loops, searching for some way to express this to Natalie without seeming like a total loser.

Natalie's words emerge in a flood. "You're the best horseman, and the farms where you treated livestock would have had supplies." Daniel remains silent, rocking. "Richard and most of the other men are going to be wrapped up with the raiders." She pauses, then adds, "I'd go with you."

"You, with me?" Daniel repeats. This at once makes the trip seem both more doable and undoable. He wouldn't be alone. But he would be alone with her.

"I know the area as well as you, and I think it's time to see what's out there— if there are any signs of trade, if we're on our own, or if there are other people around us. We're low on so many things: salt, medications, clothing."

"I don't know."

Natalie's lips tighten. "I'm not incapable, even if Richard thinks I am."

Daniel feels a twinge of anger that she would think him like Richard. But then again, Richard seems to have an ability to keep her tied in knots of uncertainty. Of course, Richard seems to have the same knack with him, too. "I don't see you as incapable. But it's not totally out of line for me to be worried about your safety, or mine. I'll think about it. But I'll be honest with you, the idea scares me." He pauses and stares into her upturned eyes, freezing a bit when he realizes how close together they're standing. "I have to go deal with the bull. I'll see you tonight."

His tone is gruffer than he intended, and he expects her to be angry, like she often is with Richard. But instead she reaches her hand up and presses it against his cheek. Dirt weaves its way through the small crevices in the skin of her fingers, like a fine etching. The warmth of her hand sends a surge of current down his legs, and he jerks his head back fractionally. She snatches her hand away, turns, and heads in the direction of the farmhouse, picking up her pace, leaving him to continue to work his way down the field toward the barn, alone. He turns his hand over and examines his own fingertips, the faint bluish-purple that permanently marks his fingernails. He still feels the outlines of her fingers on his cheek.

DANIEL FINDS RICHARD BY THE well, attempting to install what looks like a new pump, his tongue thrust out and to the side as he concentrates. His hair bristles in all directions, stubble shadows his cheeks, and the muscles of his broad shoulders strain at the tattered flannel shirt he wears. He looks more like a backwoods lumberjack than the Armani-suit-wearing politician he once was.

"You're here to talk about Farm Council," Richard says without looking up.

"I assume you're going to propose leading a scout party to check out the raiders?"

"Yup," Richard grunts as he tightens a bolt.

"Okay. I'm thinking of going in search of antibiotics and other supplies."

Richard loosens a screw with a wrench and shakes his head. "I don't think it's a good idea. You can't go alone. What if something happens to you? And we'll need all hands on deck if we have to go up there and rout the raiders out."

Richard always did have a way of reminding Daniel of his limitations.

"Natalie says she'll go with me," Daniel says, feeling unusually exposed. He says it with a deliberate casualness, as if his face bears the traces of the betrayal his mind and body keep trying to spring on him. He's decided he wants Natalie to go with him. He'll just keep it in neutral, enjoy her company, and avoid all thoughts of feeling her skin against his in the tent. In fact, he had better avoid thinking of the tent altogether.

Richard's face contorts into a smirk. "Really? You want to take Mom, too?"

"Don't be such a dick, Richard."

"I'm just kidding." The sky-blue eyes that gleam up at Daniel shine with the fraternity of a shared joke. Richard always thinks he's funny, and he is; but Daniel has grown weary of life always being a punchline. Richard heads to the second room of the shed and gestures for his brother to join him. "Take a look at this!"

Daniel follows Richard and blinks in surprise in the darkness. Richard has rigged up one of the unused water cisterns on an old wagon bed with a seesaw handle and a hose.

"Whaddya think? It's our new fire truck. Just in case we have another fire." Although Richard has clearly been shirking his chores again, Daniel has to admit that there is some serious creative genius in Richard's inventions.

Daniel's reply is interrupted by the arrival of Natalie, a basket of seeds on her hip. Richard turns his attention immediately to her.

"Daniel tells me you plan to go with him to search for antibiotics." Richard's voice is neutral, almost joking, but its underlying chords seem taut and steely.

Natalie shifts her gaze to Daniel, her eyes slightly narrowed, as if to determine what Daniel has already said. Daniel widens his eyes fractionally as if to declare his innocence, although he's not sure to which one of them.

"I want to see if there are any signs of rebuilding," Natalie says.

"I haven't picked up anything on the shortwave," Richard says.

"I know, but who knows what's happening locally?"

Richard studies Natalie and then, as if he's found what he's looking for, returns to work on the pump, his features suddenly sunny. "All right. I'm going to take Andrew with me to deal with the people on the ridge." Daniel braces. He knows Natalie won't react well to this announcement.

Natalie straightens her spine and squares her shoulders. "What? Richard, we're not trading horses here. You can't take Andrew just because I want to go on the antibiotic run. It's way too dangerous."

"I'm not trading horses. The two issues are unrelated. Andrew's sixteen. It's time he started getting off the farm and exploring."

"Exploring?" Natalie says. "Is that your new euphemism for shooting people?" Daniel stares at the ground. He never knows what to do when they fight. Richard can be irritating as shit, but Natalie won't ever just brush him off. Daniel doesn't quite understand why she gets so upset, why every fight seems to shatter her completely. Richard is always alluding to Natalie's mental health issues and instability. Daniel can't quite reconcile that with his own image of Natalie. Besides, Richard thinks most people are cuckoo.

Richard slams the pump the rest of the way into the casement. The clang of metal reverberates around the yard. Natalie flinches. Richard's voice is calm, almost friendly. "Right. So, next time a raiding party arrives, I'll go out and greet them with complimentary bottles of wine. Is that what you want?"

Natalie stares at Richard, silent, her face tight in anger.

"Andrew will be fine, Nat. He'll be with me. I'll look after him," Richard says. His tone borders on reassuring. But Natalie is, as always, acutely sensitive to the faint, possibly unintentional, undertones of condescension that can shade Richard's voice.

"This isn't your 'protected' shit again, is it?"

"It's not shit. Do I call your stuff shit? You need to have a little faith."

Natalie turns to Daniel. "Richard thinks he's 'protected by God' and that nothing bad can happen to him." Daniel looks back at Richard. God? This is a new one even for Richard. What would be his angle on this one?

Richard lifts his shoulders and smiles almost sheepishly. His ability to morph his features into the image of cherubic innocence is startling, no matter how many times Daniel has seen it. "That's not exactly what I said. I said the Universe, not God. And I do believe there's a plan for all of us."

"Fine, whatever," Natalie says. Daniel knows Richard likes to describe Natalie as being mad as a hornet all the time, but if he had to describe her expression, it would be more one of resolute disappointment and despair.

Richard rolls his eyes and shakes his head. "Nat, you're overreacting. But if you really don't want me to take Andrew, I won't. Let's not fight." He grabs at her and tries to draw her into his arms. The seed basket thwacks against her thigh and gets pushed out from between them. Richard's smile at Daniel over Natalie's shoulder is both childlike and conspiratorial, as if they're sharing an exciting joke. Natalie angles her head and shoulders away from Richard, who pats her head and releases her with chuckle.

"I just want you to *agree* with me, instead of doing it *for* me," she says before turning and walking away, wiping her nose with her dirty sleeve.

"I said I wouldn't take him, if it's important to you," Richard calls to her back.

"That's the point, Richard. I want it to be important to *you*," she says.

Richard gives Daniel a look of hapless exasperation. "You really want to take *that* with you to look for antibiotics?"

⁂

ANDREW HAS RETREATED TO THE hayloft to analyze what's going wrong in his campaign to win Siobhan, who seems inexplicably attached to her husband. He also hopes for a snooze. His arms buzz from chopping wood, and he chafes more and more every day at the drudgery of farm life. He remembers a trip to Disneyland they took when he was eight, a lifetime ago, the roller coasters and greasy food and warm air by the tiki pool. Disneyland was heaven to him then. Would be now too probably, if it still existed.

He constructed his hayloft hideout slowly and carefully, gradually edging the stack of hay a few feet from the wall, not enough that anyone would notice, creating a small enclosure he could crawl into. He doesn't sneak off often. But after two days of shit and chopping duty he feels entitled. He just wants a day at Disneyland. Preferably during the National Cheerleading Championships or something.

Andrew concocts a much more satisfying fantasy about Siobhan's delight at receiving the compost. A fantasy that involves touching Siobhan's ass and her naked body moving against his until he lies shuddering in the hay feeling a bit stupid. Siobhan thinks of him as a kid, and this new driving need to spend time alone with his hand down his pants is as discomfiting as it is enjoyable. He needs to get off the farm and find a girlfriend, if there are any girls left. Maybe there aren't. He falls into a doze and dreams of refugee camps teeming with skeletal boys and men holding empty food bowls, with bleeding gums, withered cocks, and dark circles under their eyes.

He awakens to voices in the barn below him. His father and Uncle Daniel.

"So I have your vote then on the scout party?" his father says.

"Yeah, I guess. I'm tired of this," Daniel says.

"Chin up, little camper. We'll get through this."

"Why would you say that?"

"I don't know. I just think it'll be over soon."

"What will? The raids? Peak oil? The farm?" Daniel's sarcasm almost makes Andrew laugh. Part of him likes to see his father pinned. But his father never seems cowed by anything. Richard gives a little chortle. "Always such a negative Nestor. I just think things will start to get back to normal soon. You'll see."

Andrew rolls over as silently as he can and peers over the edge of the loft. The only things visible are his uncle's black hat and hands as he cleans some tack. Daniel doesn't reply to this last comment.

"I was thinking," Andrew's father continues. "Natalie listens to you. Could you talk to her about letting Andrew go help deal with the raiders and go on some other missions? That woman is as stubborn as an ox." Twangs of apprehension press at the edges of Andrew's gut. His father is working really hard to get him off the farm.

"No way. I'm not touching that one."

"All right, fine. I just thought I'd check. You know how she is. She gets so emotional about everything. The boy needs to get out there for his own good. If he spends too long holed up on this goddamn farm, he'll end up as barmy as the rest of the folks here."

"And it doesn't hurt that he's the best sniper on the farm." Daniel's voice is sly. Pride snakes slowly down Andrew's back. He didn't know his uncle thought that.

"Well, that doesn't hurt. But that's not the reason I'm pushing for it. You gotta get out there if you want to get anywhere in this world." Andrew wonders if this is a rub, an allusion to his uncle's habit of not leaving the farm, which his father seems to find hilarious. "So how many cows do we have again?" Andrew hears the tap of his father's cowboy boots on the cement floor. He seems to be walking in circles though, not leaving.

"Twenty-five, why?"

"Have you given any thought to my suggestion to increase the herd by making better use of the southern pasture?" The shifting squeak of leather drifts up from the barn below.

"We already talked about this. I don't know why we'd want to increase the herd. We have enough for food and milk, and I can't manage too many more animals. Will you get off that saddle? It's not a toy."

"Just making suggestions, Daniel. Always looking to make things better around here. You should set up a suggestion box. Oh, and you might want to watch out for Mom." The squeaking increases. Andrew strains to see through one of the cracks in the loft floor. His dad must be bouncing around in one of the saddles.

"Why's that?"

"She heard through the farm gossip mill that Jane and Patricia have the hots for you, so she's out to set you up with one of them." Andrew's father lets out almost a giggle. "Jane's a bit of a fish face, but Patricia's not so bad. A big-boned girl of course, but not too bad."

"Tell Mom I'm not interested. And please get off the fucking saddle."

"Just practicing my moves. I should have been a cowboy. You should at least take one of them out on a date. Christ. Do you want to die a virgin?" Andrew shifts his gaze back to his Uncle Daniel. Could someone live to be Daniel's age as a virgin?

"Only you would think I'm a virgin."

"All right. Well, I'm just saying, you gotta dip your stick sometime, and there isn't a lot of choice around here. People will start wondering if you have a thing for the animals." He chuckles. "Okay, got to get back to work, or the commandant will write me up. You might want to give this place a clean. It stinks like a barn in here." Andrew hears the tap of his father's boots as he retreats. Daniel stands motionless, his black hat angled in the direction of his brother's departure.

"You're such a fucker sometimes, Richard," he says, too softly for his brother to hear.

Then he puts down the tack he was cleaning and walks to the office, the rubber soles of his riding boots thudding gently on the barn floor.

Commandant is how his father refers to his mom when talking to Daniel, or to other men on the farm. Andrew's dad likes to name people: Commandant for Natalie, Pumpkin on Stilts for Colleen, Jesus for Solomon, Rumpelstiltskin for Brent, Beelzebub for Anneke, and the Quarreltons for Bob and Ramona, who are always arguing. He does this only in front of his immediate family of course. He's very careful never to get caught by anyone else.

Pussy is his father's favorite term when talking about Daniel to Natalie. He always says it with glee, as if impressed with his own daring, like a schoolboy using a bad word. Years ago, when Richard declared Daniel to be a pussy for his inability to ask women out on dates and his reluctance to travel, Andrew thought his father was likening Uncle Daniel to a small cat. His father still trots out the pussy label—whenever Daniel struggles to speak out at Farm Council, or shies away from disciplining the men who work in the barn—but now Andrew knows what it means. He wonders if Daniel knows that his own brother calls him a pussy.

THE SUN SETTLES INTO THE mountains, its final rays of warmth and light streaming almost horizontally through the boughs of the fruit-laden trees in the orchard. In a few minutes, the wisps of sunlight will vanish, and the afternoon will slip into the darkness of a fall evening. A Farm Council evening.

Daniel sits in the barn office. He missed dinner, and his stomach echoes with emptiness.

His old golden retriever, Oscar, ripped open his leg and belly in a fight with a bear on a hunting party a few weeks ago. Oscar took the ordeal bravely, limping around on his bandaged limb for the first week. When the leg puffed up to twice its usual size, Daniel amputated it, but now the wound on his belly is infected and Oscar lies on his side on a bed in the office, staring at Daniel with pleading eyes. He pants on and off, as if he's exerting himself just to stay alive. Daniel has tried airing the wound, dressing it with goldenseal, and changing the compresses hourly. But it's no use. He sits at his desk with his head in his hands, a bottle of amoxicillin in front of him. They need it for the people. They need it for the food animals. He can't use it for a dog. Not an old dog, and especially not a three-legged dog. It's against Farm Council policy.

Natalie pokes her head in the door. "Farm Council is starting soon," she says. Daniel swats his damp eyes with his sleeve, but she crosses the threshold of the office and sees him, sees the amoxicillin, sees Oscar. Oscar gives a small thump of his feathery golden tail. Daniel brought Oscar to the farm with him six years ago; he was the first farm dog. He had been Daniel's first real dog. Mitch, his new dog, his more functional farm dog, keeps wagging and thrusting his head into Daniel's lap, dismayed by Daniel's tears.

Natalie sinks to the ground, wraps her arms around Oscar and kisses the dog between the eyes.

"I think you should give him the drugs," Natalie says. "It's Oscar."

Hope winnows its way into Daniel's brain, but he crushes it quickly before it takes over and he does something stupid. "I can't. Oscar doesn't have that many years left. He can't do any more work. It's against Farm Council policy. Food animals only, and only if the infection is threatening the whole herd or flock." He woodenly repeats the farm rules, the rules that Richard and Leon forced into place last year. Not that Daniel disagreed with them.

Natalie doesn't loosen her hold on Oscar's neck. Her honey-brown curls fall over Oscar's back, and she rests her cheek on his occipital bone. "We won't tell anyone."

Despite the circumstances, this suggestion of collusion sends a frisson of something down his spine, as if her willingness to align herself with him on this one thing means that her loyalties lie far more with him than he expected. "We can't, Nat. He'd need at least a week of pills. We'd be caught for sure. Leon has seen Oscar. He'd report me. And it's not that the policy is wrong." He says this, but he really wants to stand up and say fuck policy and shove the pills down Oscar's throat.

"You're not thinking of putting him down, are you?"

Daniel looks away. It's enough that his dog looks pathetic; he doesn't need to see her already somber eyes take on another sadness.

"Yup." He hates this part of his job. No matter how often he's done it, even when he had no bond with the animal, every time he has to play God, it rips him apart. On hunting parties, the other men just think he's a bad shot, but the reality is he has dealt out death so often with the farm animals that he just can't bear to be the one to take down another living thing. The men have their guffaw and clap him on the shoulder and say he couldn't hit the side of the barn if he was standing inside it, and he lets them think that.

Oscar lets out a low whine and resumes his death pant. Daniel has no choice.

He gathers up the syringe, needle, and barbiturates, slings his stethoscope around his neck, and prepares to carry Oscar to the woods where they bury their dead. There will be a grave already pre-dug. Farm Council policy. Whenever someone is buried, as the raiders were yesterday, the grave-digging party has orders to dig a few new holes, so they're always ready. His tears tumble from his face onto the dog.

"No," Natalie says. "I can't let you do this."

"I have to. He's suffering."

Natalie pulls at the folds of his sleeve. "We can try tetracycline. Mike put it aside. We can't risk using it on humans anymore because it's too far past its expiry. But maybe we could take the risk with Oscar." Daniel allows a small glint of hope to nudge at his heart. He used all the cycline drugs he had stockpiled for the animals first because they were believed to become toxic with age. But this is uncertain, and studies hadn't confirmed precisely when they became toxic. He'd forgotten that Mike had some left.

"Are you sure? What if we need to use them on a person?"

"We can't. Remember? We agreed not to. Farm Council policy," Natalie says with a half-smirk. "That damn policy has gotta be good for something. I'll go get them." She runs off before he can say anything else, and Daniel sinks to the office floor and presses his face against Oscar's velvety ear.

"We're going to try to make you better, buddy," he whispers.

CHAPTER 5

THE FIVE OF WANDS

⸺⠿⸺

ANDREW AND NATALIE

A time of difficult ethical choices when head fights heart and both are in conflict with conscience.

Bodies crowd the kitchen, a jostling mass of faded fabrics and tanned skin. The odor of stale perspiration hangs in the air as too many unclean people fit shoulder to shoulder in a room intended for a smaller crowd. The adults sit at the table, while the older kids jockey for position on the hearth. Andrew's female cousins cluster on one end. Andrew avoids them and plunks himself down between Justin and Christopher, forcing the other boys to move apart to make room.

"Thanks for saving me a space, bro," Andrew says.

Justin rolls his eyes. "No problem."

The fire, the first of the fall, leaps at Andrew's back. He surveys the room with keen interest. With two major issues to debate, this evening promises to be exciting. And Farm Council always gives him an uninterrupted opportunity to stare at Siobhan.

He's enjoying an unobstructed view of Siobhan's breasts when he sees his mother weaving through the crowd in his direction, her tiny form slipping in and out of the other bodies. "Watch out," Justin says. "She's been waiting for you."

A faint stain of red marks his mother's cheekbones and her forehead is bunched together. Andrew wonders what he's done this time. She points at the doorway and he follows. In the living room, she turns to him. "Your father tells me you might go on the ridge mission. Did you *ask* to go, or did he *suggest* that you go?" She stands with her muscles taut, always ready for a fight. Even though he's a foot taller, he's not sure he could beat her in hand-to-hand combat.

"Dad suggested that I go."

"Do you *want* to go?"

"I don't know. I think so." Andrew feels his father is expecting him to prove himself now, to become more a part of the group of men on the farm.

And there might be girls out there, somewhere.

His mother blows a huff of air out of her nose. Since his parents rarely agree on anything, Andrew usually humors his mother. It's safer. And although she can be a bit of a freakshow about things, she's always been the more real and reliable one. His father has always been kind of random—sometimes checked out and distracted when he talks to them, with no clue what they like to eat or who their friends are, while at other times playing the theatrical role of their father, providing them with elaborate speeches on the important things in life, and taking them on expensive trips to Disneyland or ski resorts. At least that was what he was like before. Now on the farm, he and Andrew seem to have formed some strange man-to-man bond related to hunting and shooting raiders that Andrew doesn't quite get.

"Andrew, the ridge mission is going to be very dangerous. You could end up getting shot, or worse. Your father can't be depended on to take care of you. You know that. He'll be involved in the conflict, and you could be left unprotected."

"I'm not helpless. I'm the best shot on the farm."

His mother makes the huffy noise out her nose again. "Sniping is not the same as combat. I understand you want to go, but you're only sixteen."

"Mom, I'll hang back when the action starts, if there is any action."

"If your father's involved, there's almost always action," she says. Andrew can tell she's thinking about it. That she feels guilty for always keeping him here on the farm. "I don't think you should go. In a year, maybe. Promise me. We better get back in there. They're starting." Andrew barely has time to nod before she turns and leaves the room.

Andrew squeezes back in between Justin and Christopher. His mother takes her seat at the head of the table, between Richard and Daniel. Although every-one can sit where they want, they sit in the same spots meeting after meeting, as if they unconsciously, or consciously, align themselves with the sides that some-times emerge in the discussion. His mother's two brothers, Mike and Scott, and her two best friends, Anneke and Patricia, always sit with their backs to the window, and to the right of the threesome at the head of the table. On the left, with their backs to the fireplace, is his father's family, including Andrew's grand-parents, Terrence and Olivia, his father's sister, Kristen, and her husband, Leon.

Even the refugee farm members stick to the same positions. Those who usu-ally agree with his mother sit on the right. Those who usually agree with his father sit on the left. The swing votes sit at the foot of the table, except for his Uncle Daniel, who generally sides with Natalie, but occasionally votes with Richard.

Not that all Farm Council issues are contentious. Often his mother and father are in alignment, aside from minor bickering around the margins of how something is going to be implemented. But when it comes to raiders and refugees, there are almost always arguments.

NATALIE TAKES HER SPOT AT the table and tries to pull out of her tailspin of worry over Andrew and now Oscar. She should be grateful that her sons are almost men, that she doesn't have to face the strange new world with a pair of toddlers. But it was simpler when they were little—when she had an excuse to watch over them every second of the day and spent her nights with a small head tucked under her chin. It was simpler still when she carried them inside of her, and they announced their vigor and presence with kicks and rhythmic thumping with two feet that made it seem like she was growing small rabbits, not humans.

Maybe she should let Andrew go. She knows Richard will do his best for the most part to look after him. She knows she's too protective. She was probably too harsh with Richard earlier. She doesn't understand why he has the capacity to enrage her. Perhaps he's right. She *is* unreasonable. She has to start being more reasonable with Richard. He's her husband, for God's sake. She affects a genial smile in his direction and reminds herself of all the reasons Richard is great. Her lips feel strained against her teeth.

Natalie feels the body heat on either side of her and sniffs the vague musk of sweat. It's Daniel, for Richard rarely perspires, and Natalie finds the faint scent comforting. They gave Oscar a first dose, and Daniel wanted to stay with his dog. But she told him she needed him at Farm Council. Now Richard stands slightly in front of her, his broad back blocking her view of the table. She tries to catch Daniel's eye, but he seems lost in his own thoughts.

Natalie finds it painful to watch Richard chair Farm Council, to become a different Richard, *official* Richard. His words become rounded and resonant. He self-deprecates and pokes fun at others. When things go his way, he adds in lots of loud guffaws and backslaps. When things don't go his way, he becomes white-lipped and sarcastic, like he can't believe it. He plays fast and loose with the rules, sometimes failing to call for official votes and motions. Richard calls it synergistic facilitation. Natalie calls it sloppy, as decisions are sometimes called into question and farm members don't understand what they agreed to. But she cannot deny that most of the other farm members seem completely entranced by the Richard show. She used to think she could be a politician too. But after years of watching the eyeballs of both men and women automatically swivel to Richard instead of her when important things are being discussed, or when she disagrees with him, she no longer thinks this.

"Tonight we're meeting regarding two critical issues: the antibiotic shortage and the ridge encampment. Any additions to the agenda?" Richard says.

Colleen raises her hand, the permanent frown ridges that indent her face swept up in temporary importance. Natalie tenses. She works her ass off to placate Colleen, but still the woman seems try to undermine her at every turn, just out of spite. Richard says she's a stupid bossy cow and that Natalie should ignore her, but she can't. "I would like to talk about the unreasonable work schedule."

"What do you mean?" Richard says.

"Well," Colleen says, in an excessively patient and sweet voice, as if addressing a collection of nitwits. Natalie feels, irrationally she knows, like it is directed only at her. "Some of us feel that we are expected to do too much. We need to cut back on our work schedule." She draws her broad round shoulders up and thrusts out her heavy chest.

Richard's smile contains the edges of a sneer. "Colleen, my question in response would be, do you want to survive the winter or not? You've been here for two years now. Fall is our busiest season, and it's not like any of the tasks we do are for *funsies*." Richard draws quotation marks in the air with his hand. "What would you suggest dropping?"

Colleen smiles and gives her annoying little headshake. "I'm sure if things were run better around here that we could find time for days off and sick days." Natalie's fury obliterates any words she might have offered in response. She glares at Richard, willing him to defend her.

"All right, so you think you can do a better job?" Richard says.

"I can't believe we're actually talking about this," Anneke says in a loud voice.

"Anneke, we don't have to get like that. Everyone can have a say," Richard says. "After all, I'd like to be able to get off the chain gang sometimes myself." He chuckles. Natalie wants to twist the skin on his leg in her fingers and then run back to the barn office and sit alone in the dark. What is it about Richard that makes her unable to be reasonable for fifteen minutes? "Perhaps, Colleen, you could review the job schedule with Natalie and try to find those days off. And Anneke, you and Colleen can review the menu plans to see where we can find some savings. What do you think, Colleen?" His tone is almost sing-songy. It's his talking to women or stupid men voice. His synergistic facilitation voice.

Colleen nods and puffs up her body in a pleased fashion. Natalie records the action item, seething with rage. Richard has once again pushed the problem off onto her. Anneke casts Richard a look of utter loathing.

⸙

ANDREW WATCHES HIS FATHER AT the front of the room—the way his shoulders are drawn back to make himself look taller and broader, the slight flair in his arm movements, everything about him brighter and more electric, squeezing every last bit of influence out of his natural charisma. "Okay, let's all give ourselves a pat on the back for solving that first problem. Let's move on. I assume you all read the post about antibiotics on the bulletin board. Mike, do you want to add anything?"

Mike rises with difficulty, his arm bandaged and in a sling. "I want to stress that we use antibiotics all the time, mostly because we get wounded, but we also use them for pneumonia and upper respiratory tract infections. We've gotten so low that we're going to need to start restricting them to the worst infections, which means people may start dying. The raider boy, Craig, has an infected foot. I have to give him some of the remaining antibiotics or amputate. We need to have a decision on that tonight." Mike sinks back into his chair. A swell of muttering overtakes the room as farm members turn away from the head of the table and lean in to whisper to seatmates. Richard stands and waits until the room quiets.

Jane raises her hand. "The post says you're going to start using animal medicine on us." Jane wears her thin brown hair slicked back in a minuscule bun, accentuating her beady eyes and sallow complexion.

"I wouldn't exactly say that." Mike rubs his forefinger against the space between his brows. "The intent is to have a stock of veterinary antibiotics that we can use if need be. Hopefully we won't need them."

"Well, I, for one, don't think it's safe." Jane crosses her arms under her breasts with a side-to-side sway of her head, as if she's an overturned pendulum clock.

Mike strokes his beard. "It isn't a perfect solution, although the medications are exactly the same. We should be able to determine the right doses. There could be ingredients that are human allergens or toxins, but I doubt it. At this point, we don't have much choice."

"I think we're missing the point here," says Bob, one of the recent refugees, his sonorous voice echoing. "We haven't even procured the veterinary medications yet. They're to be the goal of some cockamamie chase across the countryside. There may not even be any to be found, and if there are, they're probably in someone else's possession and that person is not going to just hand them over. So to me, the only real question is, what are we going to do with the existing supply of human antibiotics?" He pauses, then adds, "Are we going to use them on the boy, or save them for us? I think we should save them."

"Very good. Thanks, Bob," Richard says.

Natalie waves her hand and shakes her head, flicking a dirty look at Richard. "No. Wait. That's *not* the only question. We also have to discuss whether we're going to attempt to find the veterinary antibiotics."

"Oh, that," Bob says with a wave toward the head of the table. "That's already been decided by you people, and frankly if you want to risk your necks on some harebrained operation, I suppose we could rubber-stamp it."

"Bob, that is not the case. All decisions come to Farm Council," Richard starts.

"Why would we use our antibiotics on this kid?" Jane interrupts. "We don't know him, and he was part of a raiding party."

"We didn't know you either, until two years ago," Anneke says. "I think we should use the real drugs on him."

Colleen sniffs. "If amputation is an option, why don't we just do that?"

Natalie stares at Colleen, her eyes so wide that her sclera seem like broad white frames for her irises. Her bulgy-eyed look, as Richard calls it. "Because it's a difficult operation that he could die from," she says. "And then he'll be footless with no prosthetic. Amputation should be our last resort."

Andrew's Uncle Leon pushes to his feet. His sunken cheeks and hawk nose cast an angled shadow on the wall, and his brown eyes glow almost black, except for the spooky patch of murky blue in his left eye. "I say we use the cow drugs on him. Then we'll know if they're safe for us." Nods of assent ripple down the fireplace side of the table.

Paul raises his hand and waits until Andrew's father nods in his direction. The bald spots on his head glow in the firelight and he looks around the table with his earnest plain face. "It would be unchristian to experiment on a prisoner. Isn't there some sort of prisoner-of-war convention, the Geneva Convention, that forbids that? I believe we're obligated to save his life using the proper antibiotics." Andrew finds Paul excessively sincere, and he brings God into the discussion too much, but Andrew generally respects his opinions. Paul's partner, Cyrus, nods his head in agreement and takes Paul's hand.

"Pardon me, but some of us aren't Christians," Jane says. "When one of us is sick and dying, and we have no antibiotics, I'm sure we'll be glad the boy's alive and well waiting on the ridge to shoot us. The raiders aren't going to follow any Geneva Convention. They'll just murder us in our beds."

Uncle Leon sings, "God is dead, beer isn't available, and people are crazy," in a dissonant undertone.

Richard looks about to speak, but Natalie stands and pushes him to the side. Richard throws his hands in the air theatrically, as if she pushed with excessive force. "Mike and Daniel are confident that the veterinary antibiotics will be fine," Natalie says. "We wouldn't recommend it if we thought it was too dangerous. Craig was part of a raiding party, but he may not have had a lot of choices. I think we could try some of the veterinary antibiotics on him. I know it doesn't seem like the humanitarian thing to do, but maybe it's the best compromise. And we need to take a more positive outlook on the antibiotic run."

Bob's wife, Ramona, fixes Natalie with an intent gaze. "With all due respect, you don't really know what it's like out there. You haven't left the farm since this all began."

Daniel cuts in. "Look, we know the risks. But it's worth a try. Nobody's left the farm in two years, except for hunting parties. Sure, we don't know what it's like out there. But maybe things have changed. Even if we don't get the antibiotics, at least we'll know what's going on."

Richard holds his hand in the air. "It looks like we have agreement. We'll try the veterinary antibiotics on the boy, and Daniel will lead the antibiotic run. Any objections?"

Anneke snaps to her feet. "I object! It should go to a vote. Perhaps we should try to remember that we're human beings." Her voice is sharp as always, but there's a hint of unusual immoderation in her tone and movements.

"Fine," Richard says. "All in favor of trying the veterinary antibiotics on the boy and letting Daniel go on an antibiotic run?" Hands rise all around the table. A clear majority. Anneke's lips pull into a tight gather.

"I'll take that as assent then," Richard says. "Perhaps Daniel, you can tell us your plans for your little trip and who's going with you."

Daniel stands and removes his hat. "The plan is to leave in a few days, once I know the new bull is working out. The trip will probably take a week and a bit on horseback. Since the horses aren't used to really long distance travel and neither are we, I figure we'll cover thirty kilometers a day." Daniel pulls his hand through his hair. "There were a few large farms along the Syringa that may have stocked veterinary supplies. Tanner's Ridge is a hundred and forty kilometers away. We'll skirt the town. The vet's office there was on the south side. Then we'll head east before cutting back. It's going to be a dangerous trip, and you'll have to spend an entire day on a horse if you want to come."

"I'm going," Natalie says in a low voice.

The corner of Richard's mouth arches into a slight upturn. "Atta girl," he says. "Daniel, just make sure you bring my wife back. And don't let her do too much shopping. Any other ladies joining?" Richard smiles, but a thread of ice weaves through his tone. A few people chuckle. Natalie stares away, her face flushed.

No one else speaks up, so Richard continues. "Now on to the big issue. I'm going to lead a scout party to the ridge tomorrow morning to assess the raiders' numbers and see how well armed they are. We'll be back by tomorrow night. Then we'll have a better idea how many men we need."

"Or women," Anneke says.

"You are always welcome to join, Anneke. Just remember there won't be any pee breaks," Richard says. Laughter ripples down the table. Anneke shakes her head.

"Have we even considered a nonviolent solution to the ridge encampment?" Paul says. "I can hardly believe that going up there and shooting at them is the only answer. What about a diplomatic approach—like asking them to leave, or considering inviting them to join the farm?"

"Well, Paul, we haven't found diplomacy super-successful in the past," Richard says. "They shot at us and stole four of our cows. So they've hardly established a track record of being open to negotiation. And in case you don't recall, we have a no-refugee policy."

"Yes, but policies can be changed by Farm Council vote, unless I'm mistaken. Has anyone even talked to the boy?" Paul says.

"He's not very talkative," Mike says. "Probably wonders what we plan to do to him."

Leon thrusts his hand in the air. "I agree with Richard. We need to stick with our zero-tolerance policy of not tolerating violence against us." Justin shudders with suppressed laughter next to Andrew. Uncle Leon always comes drunk to Farm Council.

"Since when did we have a zero-tolerance policy? We haven't voted on a policy, have we?" Paul says. Natalie shakes her head.

"Well, we have a zero-tolerance practice," says Leon. "That's the same as a policy."

"And I don't think we should start opening up policy tonight," Richard says. "We established the no-refugee policy two years ago, and if you want it reopened, it needs to be on the agenda in advance."

Paul ignores Leon and Richard and turns to Natalie. "If we wanted to consider it, could we feed extra people?"

"It depends how many of them there are," Natalie says. "Extra hands means extra workers, so we could produce more food next year. It would mean double-bunking till spring and tight supplies for this year. If they have some supplies too, it might be doable. The one man Daniel talked to did ask for our help. We have to start thinking about community building instead of isolating ourselves. But it's risky. I didn't like the look of that other guy."

"Nat's right," Daniel says. "We have to start considering our future position and building some allies, not enemies."

"Well, aren't we all a bunch of Mary Poppinses this evening? Why don't we all go dance around with our umbrellas?" Richard says. "And if there's lots of them and they have no supplies, and we bring them down here and find out they're not the kind of people we want to have on the farm? Then what?"

"Oh, pardon me for not wanting one of the life lessons I teach my children to be 'Shoot first and ask questions later.'" The flames of the fire glow in the lenses of Anneke's glasses.

Andrew surprises himself by standing. His knees shake a bit, but his voice sounds level at least. "What about the fact that we need more people on the farm? That there are some of us who need girlfriends or boyfriends? Or at least some hope in that department."

Andrew's father gives him an incredulous look and then emits a big belly laugh. "Andrew, we're not talking about having a dance party. Has everyone forgotten that we really have no idea who's up there?"

Andrew sinks to his seat, his face hot. *It isn't just about girls*, he wants to shout, but he's not actually sure. It was stupid of him to say anything.

"In case you haven't noticed," Anneke says, "your son has a point. We're aging and we're not reproducing. Our children are going to need partners. Just saying."

Andrew's father's eyeballs look like they might explode out of his head. But he contains himself and gives Anneke a wide smile. "Then I would suggest that we go out and select the people we want to have come live with us, and not just snap up the first set of folks that come knocking, or rather *shooting*, at our door."

Voices spiral into the air as everyone starts to speak out of turn. His father rolls his eyes and picks up the gavel that he uses occasionally to keep order. The front door swings open, and the two sentries walk in, leading an older woman in a black woolen overcoat. Beneath the coat, Andrew can see tattered maroon sweatpants and white Velcro sneakers. The woman's matted white hair sticks out in all directions and her cheekbones are leathery and sunken, but her vibrant blue eyes sweep the room in sharp darts before she dons a broad guileless smile. Out of the corner of his eye, Andrew catches the slight movement of Anneke rising an inch off her chair before sitting down again.

Silence falls over the room. "She just walked down the driveway. Says she's looking for shelter," says Andrew's Uncle Scott.

"I see. And does she have a name?" says Richard.

"I'm Liz, and I'm just a lone traveler," the woman says. "Could I ask you for food and a bed? I'm willing to work."

Richard squints. "A woman traveling alone? From where?"

The woman doesn't flinch. "There's a farm to the west, five days' walk from here," she says.

"Where are your bags?" Richard says.

"I travel light. I would be ever so grateful for even just a few days' stay."

Andrew's mother, father and Uncle Daniel exchange looks. Travelers are uncommon, and his parents have to be wondering if she's connected to the raiders. But he can't imagine them turning out an old lady.

Anneke extracts herself from the bench seat at the table and goes to stand next to the woman. "I'll take her and feed her so you can finish the meeting," she says.

Natalie gives a nod to Anneke, who takes the woman by the arm into the pantry. Scott follows, his gun still drawn.

Richard moves down the line of men sitting by the fireplace and speaks quietly to several of them. They jump up and go out the door, collecting their rifles on the way. Richard turns back to the now subdued room. "Okay folks, we can't proceed any further tonight. We need to scout the perimeter of the farm. We're going to take Liz, or whoever she is, into custody for tonight. The rest of you should go to bed. We can't decide anything until we know who's up on the ridge. I'm going to take a scout party up to the ridge at five tomorrow. Natalie and Daniel will interrogate Liz and Craig. Then we'll make some decisions." Richard's voice is firm, and everyone moves off to his or her room or cabin.

CHAPTER 6

THE MOON

———⟨∞⟩———

NATALIE AND ANDREW

In the moonlight, things are not always as they appear.
Let dreams and visions guide you.

The men return to report that all appears clear. Natalie, working alone in the den by candlelight, nods and dismisses them. She tries to be relieved but still feels watched as she gazes out the window into the gloomy night. Richard retreated to bed half an hour ago with instructions to wake him if the men find anything.

Natalie works for another fifteen minutes. Colleen will imply that Natalie does a shitty job with the farm schedule. Natalie considers just handing the job over to Colleen and seeing what Richard does. On her way to bed, Natalie glances at the small den where Liz has been put for the night. Colleen's husband, Brent, stands guard outside the infirmary and den. A brief conference with Anneke, who fed Liz dinner, revealed little. Just that the woman claims she travels from farm to farm alone, but Anneke suspects from the bruises on her arms that she might have been in an abusive relationship or gotten forced out of somwehere. Natalie will have to interview the woman tomorrow.

In the bedroom, Natalie pulls the curtain aside and glances out into the moonlit yard. Daniel and Jane stand first watch. Jane prattles in Daniel's direction, while he stares out at the fields. Natalie watches Daniel—the way the moon plays across his face and paints his sheepskin coat in ghostly hues. She studies his lips as he rocks back on the heels of his boots.

Twenty-one years ago, Richard and Daniel looked somewhat alike to her, for even though they're only fraternal twins, they dressed more or less the same, had similar mannerisms and were always together. Now she can draw each of them in her mind, down to the smallest detail. Richard's full head of almost black hair, youthful features, and eyes as blue as cornflowers. Daniel's more serious gray eyes that flash suddenly green in the right light, craggier face, and finer dun-colored hair. Richard's broad shoulders and brute strength. Daniel's more stately posture and grace. Richard pops like a Vegas stage show, affecting wild surprise, excitement, anger, and disdain in an instant, while Daniel is like a muted winter sunset, his emotions carefully hidden: the shadow twin.

But Richard's lips have always irked Natalie. The way they twist into a smile, mocking her, or pull into a rosebud of disdain at everyone or everything. Daniel's lips possess a suppleness of expression and a generous and sensuous solidity. He thrusts his lower lip forward when he concentrates, when he's determined, and, she imagines, when he makes love.

And yet, if Daniel is not wearing his hat, other people still mistake them for each other, as if there is still some solid core of sameness, of twin-ness, that Natalie can no longer see.

Leon smirked when she announced she was going with Daniel to look for antibiotics. Smirked and looked at Terrence and waggled his eyebrows as if to suggest *see I told you she was a good-for-nothing whore*. Men have a fraternity that way, a way of looking out for each other's interests, defending the brotherhood, defending Richard. Natalie has little doubt that most of the farm-women would throw her under the bus, or the wagon as it were, at even the slightest suggestion that she's having a dalliance with Daniel, which she is not. Even if she were to do it by the books, and leave Richard long before approaching Daniel, she doubts it would ever be accepted. It would be too scandalous, too disloyal to beloved Richard, and women who leave their husbands almost always shoulder the blame. Richard would play the victim exquisitely. She can see it now, the puzzled and stoic expression. Even *she* would feel sorry for him.

Natalie pulls the curtain closed with more vigor than it requires. The rod clatters in its bracket and Richard looks up with a perplexed expression.

"Oh, you're still awake," Natalie says. "Sorry."

"I was just thinking," Richard says, stretching his arms up into the air and placing them behind his head, "that I should become a minister like Paul."

"What?"

"Well, I miss my groupies, you know, that I used to have as mayor. Ministering seems like a pretty good gig. I could travel around, tending my flock, taking care of the poor. We could get off this farm and see the country."

"Oh yeah, well you're so good with the disenfranchised." Natalie's words are dry, but she tries to make them gentle. Why does Richard persist in imagining himself in these pursuits, trying to find some place for himself, some place that always seems to come with admirers?

To her relief, Richard laughs. "You're probably right. Maybe that isn't the job for me. I could give great sermons though."

"I'm sure you could, Richard. Do you really think Brent should be posted alone watching Craig and Liz? He's a bit unreliable."

"Nat, relax. I had a talk with him. He's going to try harder." Richard pats the bed beside him. "Why don't you get into bed. Maybe we could…you know."

Right, relax. I just need to relax more, Natalie thinks grimly as she casts back in her mind for when they started calling sex "you know." She undresses and blows out the candle as she climbs into bed. She tries to picture herself surrendering to sex, the way she did their first time, when he made jokes about her libido.

"That was mean what you said to Andrew about the dance party. He's right, you know," she says. She injects as much kindness into her voice as she can muster. "The kids on this farm need to have the chance to find future partners. As it stands, with the current farm population, they won't have that."

"Hmm, you're right. I shouldn't have said that," Richard says. "Don't get bent out of shape about it. Andrew's time will come." Richard's hand snakes up her leg to her inner thigh, pulling it against his groin, and he starts bucking against her backside with his hips. Natalie tries to convince herself that she must respond. Richard has a right to marital relations. But her imagination fails her.

"Not tonight, Richard, please. There are too many things on my mind."

Silence, and then the hand and groin are withdrawn. He rolls over and settles into his pillow. She lays motionless until she hears light snores. Richard prefers sex with the lights off and his eyes firmly shut, and there are parts of both of their bodies that he will never name.

SHE AWAKES AT MIDNIGHT AND stands in the streaming moonlight by her window, studying the long shadows in the yard. Jane and Daniel have moved out of sight. Suppressing a stab of concern, or perhaps jealousy, she grabs a sweater and descends the stairs.

Silence hangs over the dining hall. Only small embers remain of the fire, pulsing with red heat. The scuff of her slippers on the wood echoes in her ears.

Brent is slumped in the hall by the infirmary door, his breathing deep and regular. The den door lies ajar and the room is empty. Natalie curses and considers sounding the alarm, but a light flickers beneath the infirmary door, and Brent's gun still lies beside him. Natalie collects Brent's gun and creeps into Mike's office next to the infirmary.

Justin sleeps on a cot. She gently lays her hand on his arm, her finger pressed to her lips. He blinks into consciousness, unsurprised to see his mother standing over his bed with a gun. A sign of the times. She motions to the connecting door to the infirmary, the gun held in front of her. Justin pauses only for a second to remove a knife from beneath some files in Mike's drawer before coming to stand behind Natalie at the door. She feels the brush of his long blond hair on her shoulder. She turns the knob quietly and edges the door open a crack.

Liz sits bolt upright by the bed, her eyes closed. A small candle sputters beside her. Craig appears to be asleep, his face still ashen. Cards lie on the bed beside him.

"What are you doing?" Natalie says, crossing the threshold into the infirmary.

The woman's hooded blue eyes flutter open. "Sorry. I was just saying a little prayer for this young man here."

"Why are you in here? Do you know this boy? Are those…tarot cards?"

"I heard him moaning and came to check on him. Then I did a reading for him."

The woman seems so benign and kindly that Natalie has a hard time staying angry. But nobody can receive special treatment these days. "Liz, you can't just wander around and go into people's rooms. You need to stay in your room." Natalie's eyes drop to the tarot cards, which seem somehow both absurd and alluring—as if a deck of cards could give her answers or hope. She shakes off the ridiculousness of the notion.

Justin moves to the other side of the bed to check Craig's vitals.

"Oh, dear. Sorry. I didn't know. It sounded like he was in pain." Liz collects her cards and rises. She steps around the end of the bed toward the door, but catches her knee on the crank on the end of the bed. The deck slips from her hands and scatters on the floor. She drops to a crouch and begins picking up the oversized, deep blue cards, muttering apologies.

Natalie bends to help the woman. She runs her fingers over the smooth backs of the cards and gathers them into a stack. The urge to turn one over, to see what it says, is overwhelming. She flips a card, revealing a man and woman holding cups and gazing into each other's eyes.

"Ah, the Two of Cups. True Love," Liz says.

"Yeah, we tend to brim over with that around here," Justin says, his mouth twisted with the irony that he so often affects.

The infirmary door opens to reveal Daniel, with a sheepish-looking Brent behind him. "Is everything okay? I saw a light," Daniel says.

"We're okay," Natalie says, more tersely than she intends. She softens her voice. "But thank you for checking on us. We're just escorting Liz back to bed."

Daniel surveys the room. "She better stay put this time. I'll be outside if you need me."

"Thanks." Natalie gives him a slight wave.

Natalie hands the gun back to Brent, who resumes his post, avoiding her eyes. She motions for Liz to follow her back to the den. Once inside the room, Natalie turns to the woman. "Tomorrow we're going to have a talk about who you are and what you're doing here. Until then, you need to stay in your room."

Liz nods. "Of course." The woman places the stack of cards facedown beside the couch, flips over the top card, and looks at Natalie. The card shows a large heart pierced by three swords. "The betrayal card," Liz says. She cocks her head at Natalie and then nods. "Ah, I understand now."

Natalie pictures a sword lacerating Richard's heart and feels a surge of anger and guilt. What could the woman possibly think she understands? "We don't put a lot of faith in cards around here," she says.

Liz shrugs. "Love always matters. In bad times even more so." She lies down on the couch and closes her eyes.

Natalie considers responding but, finding nothing convincing to say, retreats to her bed. She falls into strange dreams about ironing Richard's shirts. As she irons, Richard stands behind her, caressing her, insistently and intrusively thrusting his groin against her buttocks. The children play on the floor nearby. Richard dangles a yellow viper over her shoulder. The viper watches as the iron moves over the cloth. She pleads with Richard to get rid of the viper, to get rid of all of the vipers, that they will harm the children. But he laughs as she begs.

Natalie awakes, trembling, and finds the bed beside her empty. She jumps out of bed and flings the curtains wide. The scout party rides into the dusky morning air, guns slung over backs. Andrew, astride his chestnut stallion, is among them.

Natalie dresses with shaking hands and runs downstairs. Only the early kitchen shift, Ramona and Sandra, move about silently by candlelight, clearing the men's bowls and preparing for the next set of arrivals. Natalie brushes past them to the pantry, to Anneke.

"How did Andrew end up in the scout party?"

Anneke gives Natalie a strange look. Natalie knows her hair must be on end and her eyes wild. "Richard said he could go."

"Richard knew I was opposed."

"Richard seemed quite keen to have him go." Anneke's voice is neutral. She pours wheat into the grain mill and starts to turn the wheel.

"Bastard," says Natalie. "Why does Richard always do this?"

Anneke shrugs. "There's nothing you can do about it now, unless you ride out and drag him back."

"Maybe I should," says Natalie.

Anneke looks up from the mill. "They have a ten-minute head start. By the time you tack up, it'll be thirty, if Daniel even lets you take a horse out alone, which he won't. And you don't even know which way they went. Get your mind off of it. Andrew's sixteen. They'll be back tonight."

"Fine," says Natalie, recoiling at the hint of harshness of Anneke's words and trying not to imagine all the ways Andrew could be killed. "Where's Liz?"

"Sleeping. It's five-thirty, remember? I'll get her up. She can help me in here."

Natalie snaps her head around to look at Anneke. Anneke doesn't look up from her grinding.

"Since when do you want anyone in your pantry?"

"I could use the help, okay?"

A cold tug of suspicion washes over Natalie, accompanied, in equal measure, by a prick of jealousy. Anneke dislikes almost everyone. But she always has preferred unusual characters and hard-luck cases. Before the peak, Anneke's house was an endless parade of odd, socially challenged ducks with leftist political leanings, no fashion sense, halitosis, bad teeth, and the tendency to stand too close when talking. It's a never-ending congregation of kooks, Richard once declared after wincing through one of her dinner parties, where he was called Roy and Raymond by men in beanies and generally dismissed as an inconsequential pretty boy.

Natalie decides to let it go. It's probably just one of Anneke's quirks. "I'm off to the greenhouse, then. Can you tell Mike to come and get me when Craig wakes up?"

ANDREW REFLECTS ON HIS SMOOTH exit. It helped that his mother wasn't yet awake. The other men welcomed him readily. He pushes aside a slight twinge of guilt.

They cross the Syringa using an old wooden bridge a few miles south of the farm and wend their way through the forest into the foothills of the Selkirks, under a canopy of Douglas fir and ponderosa pine. The limited undergrowth makes for easy going for the horses. Steam emerges from the horses' nostrils, and Andrew pulls his coat closed at the neck. The midday sun will burn away the chill.

Winter was something that Andrew never thought much about before the peak. It just came. Even Christmas had required little action on his part. Now winter occupies many of their waking thoughts. Even Andrew's. Winter and war. The war talk on the farm has come and gone over the years. There's always someone willing to suggest that the raids are minor skirmishes leading to the inevitable: someone forming an army. When his father talks about it, he seems almost excited. His father has always envisioned himself as a general, devising strategies and giving orders, but he's never been on grave-digging duty.

Andrew has buried enough bloodied bodies to know that war is not something he's prepared for. Bodies of raiders with lice still crawling over their scalps, rotting teeth, and loose empty folds of skin because they had once perched in front of their TVs eating Ding Dongs and Big Macs. War usually ends with you dying and alone, not even sure what you were fighting for.

He views days like today as practice. Opportunities to develop the skills that he needs. He savors the adventure of it, even if the notion of being "out there" gives him a kind of sick feeling.

Every so often, his father looks back and gives him a big smile. Andrew knows that his father prides himself on his youngest son's marksmanship, and thumbs his nose, ever so slightly, at Justin's pacifism. "Taught him myself," his dad says whenever Andrew takes down a buck or a grouse. "That's my boy. He could hit a moving target at eight hundred meters." Andrew wonders if his father has the slightest inkling that, in shootouts, Andrew often fires up and over the raiders' heads.

⊸≋⊶

NATALIE STANDS STARING AT THE pile of knapweed she's yanked from the garden, the dream of Richard and the viper still heavy on her shoulders. The dawn pokes its furtive rays over the hillside. Natalie's fingers are stiff from the cold and the wiry stems of the knapweed.

The dreams started not long after she met Richard. They were always of some betrayal, some unforgivable act that Richard committed. Cheating, abandonment, loss of one of their sons, and always, in the dream, Richard seemed unapologetic. The dreams were so emotional that she would wake crying. In the early years, just waking and seeing Richard, and knowing that he hadn't betrayed her made her feel better. A few years later, the dreams upset her so much that she'd needed to wake Richard to be comforted. Eventually they became so frequent, and his comforting so halfhearted, that she stopped waking him. A few times, in a half sleep, she pushed him or punched him, sobbing. And after getting over his anger at being struck, Richard would laugh.

She could never understand the reason for the dreams, for Richard never gave her reason to believe he would betray her so dramatically. She felt guilty for even allowing her subconscious to advance the notion. What kind of wife *was* she? Perhaps her brain had a way of accumulating her perceived little daily betrayals into an anger so deep that her brain manufactured more dramatic acts of treason. But surely most of those little betrayals were all in her head. Richard was certain they were, and she felt it likely that he was right. She was just too sensitive.

Then, about ten years ago, she started having an altogether different kind of dream, a recurring dream that was always the same. She was doing something unremarkable—working, spending time with family, at a dinner, on a picnic. There were no words exchanged. Nobody was even paying attention to her, but there was always a hand held firmly in hers. A hand that gave her more comfort than she had ever thought possible. Daniel's hand.

Impossible.

Natalie looks up to see Siobhan with her notebook in hand, her dreadlocks coiled into a giant bun on her head. "I'm sketching this year's layout today. Do you want to help?" Crops have to be rotated each year so that heavy feeders that take nutrients from the soil alternate with light feeders, and insects and crop-specific diseases don't take hold. Siobhan doesn't comment on Natalie's early arrival, or the size of the weed pile.

Natalie brought Siobhan and Solomon to the farm as workers before the peak. For years they had been members of World Wide Opportunities on Organic Farms—they called themselves WWOOFers—working on farms all across the province, learning how to grow in every possible condition. If it weren't for Siobhan and Solomon, with their knowledge and unassailable optimism, they'd probably all have died of scurvy years ago.

"Thanks for the offer, but today I just want to cut and dig," Natalie says.

Siobhan looks up from her notebook and flashes Natalie her dimples. "Okay. We're pulling the frost-susceptible veggies 'cause it's been so cold at night. Why don't you start with the beans and spinach and then pull about half the carrots? Solomon's clearing the new garden area by hand. We're out of newspaper, so we're just going to turn over the sod and put down compost."

Natalie feels a rush of gratitude for Siobhan, one of her few unflinching allies. She scoops up two of the garden tubs and heads to the beans. She settles in to work, and tries not to worry about Andrew.

Paul and Cyrus work their way down the rows of tomatoes and peppers, removing the cloches that keep the plants warm at night. Paul and Cyrus were acquaintances of Daniel's in Tanner's Ridge before the peak. Daniel met them at the Tanner's Ridge Stargazing Club and struck up a sort of offbeat friendship. Paul and Cyrus showed up on the farm with their two sons, Hayden and Nick, after life got lawless in Tanner's Ridge. Richard initially got a big charge out of the "gay gardeners," as he calls them, and made all sorts of allusions about Daniel's friendship with them. In the early days, Richard loved to imitate Cyrus's more dramatic gestures and could often be found at Cyrus's side wearing a wild smile, only to return to Natalie to squeal, *"They're just so gay."* The two men have seemed a bit cold to Richard of late though, and Natalie wonders if Richard went too far.

Natalie concentrates on the lush purple bean pods dangling from the plants. Fall requires all hands on deck, all day, every day. Her body vibrates with exhaustion, but the retreat into work, into the rhythm of doing what is required, is a relief.

⁓

THE SCOUT PARTY ARRIVES AT the ridge just after lunch. Andrew's father smears his face with the charcoal and mud he brought, pulls his camouflage cap low over his forehead, and creeps up the hill. He returns fifteen minutes later to report that the ridge dwellers have no dogs to sound an alarm and that he's found a spot from which two people can watch. He suggests they take turns of ten minutes each, with him as the lookout.

When his turn comes, Andrew covers his own face with what's left of the mud, takes the proffered camo toque from Karl, and creeps up the hill to join his dad. The camp is nestled on a grassy plateau. A cluster of teepee-like structures, constructed of a mishmash of canvas, tarps, and animal skins, form a circle around the camp. A wooden wagon with bicycle tires holds bins and containers of supplies. Two of the stolen cows graze in a pen, and four horses are picketed nearby. The carcasses of a deer and the third cow hang on sticks a small distance from the camp. A mass of flies swarms over the dead animals like a seething cloud. Either they aren't afraid of attracting bears, or hope to. They're not above eating bear on the farm, but the greasy sweetish chunks of it make Andrew gag as they slide down his throat.

Several fires burn in the center of the camp, and the smoke rises in lazy curls and hovers in the windless afternoon. Skewers of fish and meat are suspended in rows over the smokiest of the fires. Andrew's father pokes him in the side and points dramatically at something toward the eastern edge of the camp. Andrew strains to see, but can only make out a pile of branches that's been placed against a frame, probably hiding the pit toilets. He glances back at his dad, who gives him a big thumbs-up. Over toilets? Sometimes he has no idea what his father is trying to tell him.

Andrew does a headcount. Four armed men stand sentry on the outskirts of the circle, while four others scuttle about piling firewood and shaving sticks for spears. Two small children sit huddled together by one of the fires. Andrew turns his attention to the women, who move about the camp engaged in tasks such as washing, cooking, and laying out herbs to be dried. Many of the women look young, and he feels a small lurch of hope until he sees the bumps that occupy many of their stomachs. He scrutinizes them one by one. There are eight of them, but only three that don't seem to be carrying a baby. They don't talk to one another, and the sentries don't help when one of the pregnant women falls to her knees, moaning in pain. Instead, one of the other women guides her over to a bench by one of the fires, where a pot hangs from a spit made out of sticks.

An outcrop of rocks to the west and the mountain to the north offer the camp some protection against the wind, but the teepee material ripples in the slight breeze. Andrew shudders. Six months of winter in one of those structures would freeze a person down to the bone. It's adequate from a defensive perspective if they placed lookouts in the rocks on the mountainside, although he wonders why they haven't done so today. In fact, the overall number of men seems small considering the extent of the attack they were able to launch against the farm. Andrew buried four dead raiders after the fire, and he was sure he counted more than twelve shooters that night.

CHAPTER 7

THE SEVEN OF SWORDS

—❧—

DANIEL AND ANDREW

Beware a loss due to cunning and trickery.

Daniel and Natalie sit beside Craig's bed. Craig keeps his eyes averted. A scar runs from the corner of his right eye down to his mouth, like the tracks of a tear. Dark stubble dots his head. Farm protocol. Newcomers' heads must be shaved to prevent lice outbreaks. Craig's gaunt arms rest on top of the blankets, fragile and wasted like those of an old woman. The breakfast plate on the bedside table has been licked clean.

Daniel feels faintly nauseated. How many people live like this? How long will it be before they're *all* knocking on the farm gate? Daniel removes his hat, places it on his lap, and studies its rim.

Natalie leads, as he expected she would. "Hi Craig. I'm Natalie, and this is Daniel. We need to ask you some questions about where you're from, and what happened to you after the peak."

The clump of boots and the scrape of benches travel down the hall from the kitchen. Lunchtime for most of the farm members.

"If you help us, we'll consider how we can help you," Natalie adds.

Craig looks back to the window. "Not much to tell. Same story as everyone else," he says. Daniel recoils when the boy opens his mouth. His gums have recessed, revealing pockets of decay and blood at the base of his teeth. Pre-scurvy. "Grew up in Kimberley. Just me and my mom and my sister. When things started to go bad, we held on for a while, but Mom lost her job at the school and money got tight. Couldn't afford the gas to go work somewhere else. The bank threatened to take the house. But everyone else was in fore-closure too, so what could they do? Then the trucks stopped bringing food. Grocery store was empty. We got pretty hungry. We tried to grow stuff, but people started going house to house, stealing anything they could find. That's when things got really bad." Craig stops. "Are you going to let me go?" he says.

"We'll definitely consider it, if you tell us as much as possible," Natalie says.

"How do I know you won't just shoot me?"

"We wouldn't waste our time and supplies trying to save you if we were going to shoot you," Natalie says. Craig licks his cracked and blistered lips and looks away for several seconds.

"Will you help me?"

"I can't promise that. But the more you tell us, the more we are likely to consider it."

Craig studies them and then continues talking. "We had no idea what we were going to do. Then my dad showed up on our doorstep out of the blue, saying that he'd come for me and that we were going to head to Creston on foot. He figured that since it was an agricultural place, they'd be more organized in terms of growing. My mom said that she and my sister—she's not his daughter; we're both adopted—were going too. But everyone else must've had the same idea. All these people on the road just walking, half-starving, killing each other for food, only to discover nobody had any. Most of them just died by the side of the road. The stink was so bad. My dad had a shotgun but no ammo, but we pretended we did and people steered clear."

Daniel's mind drifts to darkness, imagining scores of people marching along the roads with no place to go. Roads of bones. His brain conjures mem-ories of black-and-white pictures of people in concentration camps and world wars, and he wonders if that's what the whole world looks like now, beyond the edges of the farm.

Craig continues. "At night, the animals came. You'd never have known there were so many animals living around us. Bears, coons, coyotes, dogs, cougars, rats—they were all there, just walking beside us, just in the shadows, waiting for one of us to fall. Every so often, you'd walk past someone you thought was dead, and they'd grab your leg, beg you for help. As if you could help them." Craig pauses and flicks at the IV tube looped around the bedrails.

"We ran out of food early on. We got so hungry we hunted for bugs and worms. We even considered eating the bodies by the side of the road. Carved a piece off one guy. Figured we could fry him up, but we couldn't do it. Tried to kill animals with rocks. But they were too fast. So we ate maggots. Picked them from people's bodies. Cooked them on a stick…"

Craig trails off. Daniel stares at his hat. He wept over a dog last night. But elsewhere, dogs may well be dinner.

"We met up with my dad's buddies in Cranbrook—another family and a couple of Indian guys. They had crossbows. Things got better after that because we had meat. It was getting later in the summer, so we could find berries and old orchard trees. And we went off the road, so we were safer. Thought we'd keep walking till we found a safe place. Maybe it hadn't all gone to shit everywhere."

"And did you find a safe place?"

"There is no safe place. We made it to Creston, but it was just the same as Cranbrook. All the grain storage units looted, everything gone. We stayed on the outskirts of town first 'cause we could see the watch fires burning in town. We went door to door, breaking in, looking for food. Most of the houses were empty or the people were dead inside. But the cupboards were bare. Then my dad saw a house with the lights on. We could barely see them. The guy had put black paper all over the windows. So we broke in. It was one guy with a whole bunch of food stored up, dried stuff, army rations, years and years' worth of stuff. We tied him up and started eating. He begged us not to eat all his food. Finally he said if we left him some food, he'd take us to other people who had food. People like him who had prepared."

Daniel interrupts. "How'd he know where other people were?" Not the smoothest of interjections, but at least he now feels like he's not letting Natalie do all the work.

Craig picks at a spot on the sheet. "They had a network. Doomers, he called them. They were very secretive about their bug-out locations, but he knew where a few of them lived. So we spent a couple more weeks there and then packed up the food he had left, along with his supplies like tents and candles, and headed out. He came with us. What else was he going to do? Most of his buddies were holed up alone like him. They were easy to take down. We didn't kill anyone—that was my dad's rule, and we always made it clear we were sorry for what we were doing. We'd stay awhile at each place, and then when we were done with most of the food, we'd offer to take the person with us to the next place.

"And they went?" Natalie says.

"Some of them did. They didn't want to die, and they were scared shitless to head out anywhere alone. Others looked like they'd sooner kill us than come with us. When spring rolled around, we had run out of places to go, but we'd collected enough seeds and gardening tools from the Doomers to consider starting out on our own. So we found an abandoned farm and set up shop. Some of the Doomers stayed with us, figuring there was strength in numbers. We made it through a couple of years half-starving, with raiders looting us just like we'd looted others."

"How did you end up here?" Natalie says.

Craig hesitates before answering and his tone shifts. "Too many people were getting killed. So my dad decided we had to relocate and set up camp somewhere more remote." He watches them now as he speaks, whereas he had previously recounted much of his story with his eyes downcast. This part is definitely a lie, Daniel decides. *But why?*

"How long are you planning to stay?" Daniel says.

"I dunno. That wasn't decided."

"Do you have your own supplies?" Daniel watches the boy for any change in expression, but he has made his face almost blank.

"We have some."

"Enough to get through the winter?" Daniel says.

"Looks like there's enough game around here."

"Can you tell us about them? How many of them are there?" Natalie says.

Craig doesn't respond for a few seconds. "There were sixteen men and ten women when we arrived a few days ago. I expect you shot a few, though. A lot of the women are pregnant. If you let me go, I'll convince them to move on," Craig says, twisting the IV tube in his fingers.

"Do you know the woman who came in to see you last night? Liz?" Natalie says.

"Nope. Never seen her before." Craig folds his fingers together on his chest as if he's about to say a prayer, then pulls them apart quickly and places them at his sides.

"Who were those guys you were with on the night of the fire?"

"Rafe and Carson. Rafe's the one with the tattoos."

"And is he your leader?"

Craig's lower lip tightens for a second. "I suppose you could say that."

Mike appears from his office and checks Craig's pulse. "Sorry guys, I think that's enough for now. He's sicker than he looks, and he needs to eat."

Daniel nods a thank-you to the boy and rises quickly. Natalie darts him a questioning look but follows him out the door. She catches his arm in the hall. "Do you think we should have tried for more?" she says.

Daniel shakes his head. "I think we need to think more carefully about what we're going to ask." He pulls her into the den, out of earshot, and tries to ignore the surge in his heart when his hand touches hers and they're alone in a room together. She looks up at him expectantly, leaning in so he can keep his voice low. The closeness of her reverberates off of him in waves, like sonar. It would be so easy to wrap his arms around her and pull her in to him just for a second. But he doesn't. He won't. She would be horrified, and Richard is his brother. She is Richard's wife. Daniel blinks his eyes and repeats this mantra to himself quickly. "Let's wait until the scout party gets back, then see what we can piece together. There's some weird power structure going on here. That guy in the woods, Carson, he seemed more afraid of his buddy than he was of me. And I think there's something sketchy about why they ended up here."

Natalie flicks her eyes from place to place in thought, purses her lips, and then nods. "I can buy the weird power structure. He's a kid though, and has been through a lot of trauma, so let's not glom onto any little tic in his story. I think they could have just been trying to relocate, but let's see what Liz has to say." She looks up at him intently, checking, as always, to see if her words have caused upset, and her fingers graze the tips of his. "Okay?"

He feels the skin above his eyebrows crease a little. "Of course." He can't imagine why it wouldn't be okay, why she's so conscientious about checking.

THEY FIND LIZ IN THE dining room, shelling scarlet runner beans under Anneke's supervision. The woman's scalp is shaved and cloaked in a red kerchief. Natalie sits down next to her, and Daniel settles in across the table. Anneke debones chickens by the sink.

Natalie surveys the woman. "Let's talk about who you are and how you got here."

The woman's lips form a tight, tired little smile. "I lived in Nelson before the peak. I was a part-time psychic. When the peak hit, I stayed for a while, till it got too dangerous. Since then, I've been wandering from place to place, exchanging my services for food."

"People give you food in exchange for fortune-telling?" Daniel finds this proposition utterly flabbergasting.

"People are more eager for my services now than they ever were."

"Why didn't you see the peak coming, then?" Daniel says.

"It doesn't work like that. I can feel people's energies and read their cards. But I can only answer the questions they're asking—so if nobody asks the question, I don't see that aspect of the future."

"Are you associated with the ridge people, or Craig?" Natalie says, giving Daniel a slight look, as if to tell him to stop asking questions about Liz's psychic abilities. Liz shakes her head, the flaps of the kerchief swishing back and forth.

"I swear I'm just a lonely traveler. I've come from the Wellburn farm several days' ride away. People may feed a psychic for a few days, but not many want one on staff."

"And the bruises on your arms?"

Her blue eyes harden. "A little disagreement over payment."

"Are there many farms like ours, where people are alive?" Natalie says.

The woman pulls her sunken jowls into a grim smile. "More than you might think. But raiders, starvation, and sickness have taken care of most people. You don't want to head into any of the cities. Not if you want to see your next birthday."

"Well, we were planning on heading to Tanner's Ridge," Natalie says. "So we'd like to know as much as possible about it."

Liz's gaze falls to Daniel's fingertips on the table; she catches his hand in hers with surprising speed and flips it over. Daniel suppresses the urge to snatch his hand back. Something about the woman's blue eyes spooks him.

"You haven't done much living in your life, have you?" She peers at him as if expecting confirmation. "You're not as fragile as you think. Don't lend anyone that which marks you," she says.

"What? What do you mean?" Daniel says. Psychic stuff has always made him nervous, like someone is off sticking pins in a voodoo doll of him or something.

Liz shrugs as if he should be able to answer his own questions. "Like I said, I get feelings." She releases his hand and returns to shelling. "As for Tanner's Ridge, I haven't been in, but I've heard you should bring as much gold as possible."

"All right, thanks," Natalie says. "We may have more questions for you tomorrow. You're going to have to stay under Anneke's supervision during the day and under guard at night. We have a no-refugee policy in effect right now, so you can stay for a few days, but then you'll have to move on, unless you want to apply to Farm Council to change the policy. And if you want to even be considered for refugee status, we demand that you tell us the complete truth because if you're found to be lying about *anything*"—Natalie pauses to emphasize the word—"you'll be out. So just keep that in mind."

Daniel watches Natalie as she speaks. He is so used to watching the Richard and Natalie Punch and Judy show that he's always surprised to find Natalie so efficient and comfortable to work with. How utterly competent she seems to be when she's away from Richard.

DANIEL AND ALAN SPEND THE afternoon harvesting corn. It's a small crop, used mostly for fodder, that's even smaller this year due to the late, wet spring and the loss of several sections of the cornfield in the fire. They do a count as they thrust the cobs into bins, and when they're nearing completion, Alan consults Natalie's meticulous records. Less than half of last year's take. They wanted to leave half the stover in the field to improve the soil fertility, but they'll have to use it for fodder. Daniel stews about the corn, and about his certainty that Craig is lying. Why did he lie? The boy wasn't asking to be taken in. He was as much as saying they would clear out, that he *wants* to clear out. Bits of pollen and sweat trickle down Daniel's back.

Mitch's frantic barks shatter the afternoon peace. He's wandered away from Daniel, and his barks seem to be coming from near the barn. The sounds of the other dogs are curiously absent. Where are the other damn dogs? They should be on patrol. Daniel runs from the cornfield and arrives at the barn at the same time as Natalie. Other farm members are close behind with tools and axes in hand.

Three armed men—one with a gun, and two with bows and arrows—stand by the chicken coop holding Sarah, Mike and Joanne's youngest daughter, captive with a gun to the temple. The guy with the tattoos from the night of the fire is one of them.

Rafe.

The men border on grotesque, with shaved heads, skeletal eye sockets, and red scabs on their faces and arms. They're all covered in tattoos, thin black lines that snake out of their clothes and adorn their faces in jarring locations. Prison tats, Daniel realizes with a mild jolt. Rafe's tattoos are more elaborate and decorative, and he definitely appears to be in charge, but perhaps just because he's the one holding the gun. A purple welt marks Sarah's face and her shirt is torn. Mitch crouches low in front of them, his upper lip curled back.

Joanne runs from the farmhouse making whimpering noises. Mike overtakes her and skids to a stop a few feet from the trio. The men wave their weapons.

"Stay right there," Rafe says.

The other farm members jostle behind Daniel and Natalie. Their worried murmurs pulsate through Daniel's ears amid what sound like muffled barks from the dogs. He feels a building sense of panic in the absence of Richard. Where are the dogs, and what should he do?

"Don't come any closer, and we won't hurt her," the man says. The other man opens the chicken coop and starts thrusting chickens into a cloth sack. "Bring us some peaches and other fruit, and we'll let her go. Nobody'll get hurt."

Mike bolts for the farmhouse, his eyes like black pools of tar.

After a nod from Natalie, Solomon follows. One of the intruders turns to face away from them, to make sure they aren't assaulted from behind. The sack flaps and jerks with berserk chickens. Sarah and Joanne sob hysterically. Natalie looks at Daniel like she expects him to do something. He *should* do something, but what? Rush the men? The men look weak enough, but they're armed. Rushing them would get him and Sarah shot. Daniel tries to control the bloody shaking of his hands.

Mike and Solomon return with a bin of peaches and apples.

"Put it on the ground there, and get back," says Rafe. Mike and Solomon do as instructed, and the man with the chickens dumps the bin into another sack.

"We're going to back away. When we get to the edge of the woods, we'll let her go."

"Just give me my daughter, and we'll let you go," Mike says.

"Not a chance. Not until we make it safely away," Rafe says.

"No!" Sarah shrieks, holding her arms out to her father while Joanne moans no, no, no, over and over.

Mike's voice is ragged. "Take me instead. I'm unarmed and injured. Please."

"Or me!" Natalie steps forward. Guilt threatens to paralyze Daniel. *He should be volunteering, not Natalie.* But he always thinks too long, which means he's always late with his hand.

"We'll stick with the girl. No shooting at our backs, no jumping us. Don't even move. Heroes get killed, and it won't be pretty for this little girl if you don't let us go." Rafe wraps a strand of Sarah's blond hair around his finger. "Cooperate and we'll get our relationship off to the right start."

The three men start to back away.

"No, no!" Sarah screams. "Daddy!"

Joanne's cries are as guttural as those of a woman in labor.

Natalie grabs Daniel and pulls him and Mike into a huddle around Joanne. "What do we do?" she whispers.

"We have to let them go," Daniel says. "It's too risky to do anything else. If they don't let her go, we go after them immediately." Mike's eyes barely leave his daughter. Natalie nods. The men cross the fields. Joanne weeps and shakes.

The men vanish from sight at the edge of the woods. Everyone strains to see. The bile rises in Daniel's throat as he counts to thirty. At thirty, he's going after them.

At twenty-seven, Daniel starts to tense his legs, but Sarah races out of the woods and across the fields. Her thin legs shake and she stumbles a few times. Mike and Joanne sprint toward her. Mike snatches Sarah up like a toddler and jogs with her in his arms back to the farmhouse. Joanne and Rachel follow, as the dogs pour in a barking stream around the corner of the farmhouse and skid to a stop in front of Daniel.

"Get everyone armed," Natalie says to Daniel as she heads after Mike and Joanne.

Daniel organizes the distribution of guns after shaking a couple of the lead dogs by the scruff of the neck and marching them back to their posts. The dogs go with lowered ears and stricken looks. Jeffry, the yellow lab, trembles with fear. Daniel jogs from post to post, trying to keep his pace in check and figure out what distracted the dogs, but he sees nothing out of order.

The farm members cluster in groups, talking and looking over shoulders when he returns. Some of the women hustle the children to the farmhouse. Natalie sets Paul and Bob to guard the front and back of the farmhouse, and Solomon and Cyrus to patrol the perimeter of the farm on horseback. She no longer trusts the dogs. Then she orders everyone back to work.

"I'm sorry," Daniel says to her.

"For what?"

"For the dogs."

Natalie's about to reply when Justin joins them, his white blond hair pulled back and his fine features solemn.

"The dogs were in the pantry," Justin says. "It looks like they were being fed. Together." Justin elevates his pale eyebrows.

"Where the *hell* was Anneke?" Daniel says.

Justin turns his palms over. "I have no idea. I was guarding Craig, so I couldn't leave. They were going crazy in there. By the time I marched Craig with his IV down to the window to see what was happening, it was too late."

Daniel stares in stunned disbelief. Anneke knows not to do this. The dogs are to be fed in shifts. She *knows* this. Has always followed this rule. His first thought is that she's made a mistake. His second is that Anneke rarely makes mistakes. But the dizziness and cloudy vision of overexertion start to overtake him, and he's forced to go sit in the barn office for a few minutes and collect himself.

DUSK DRIFTS INTO THE UNDERBRUSH as the last light of day vanishes over the trees. Andrew's father rides at the front of the scout party. When they reach the foothills of Selkirks, well away from the ridge, he stops. The other men gather around him expectantly, their horses pulling and nudging with swishing tails. Andrew, the least experienced on a horse, arrives last.

His father surveys the group until they quiet down. His eyes and teeth gleam white amid the charcoal and mud, which is smeared and caked. Lichen dangles from his hair, and in the growing twilight he looks like some sort of swamp man. "Good work today. I don't think we have anything to worry about. A couple of men with guns and they'll turn and run like lily-livered jellyfish." He winks. The other men respond with whoops.

Andrew decides not to point out that jellyfish don't run and writhes with the idea of sending so many pregnant women off to probable death in the winter.

His dad seems pleased with his announcement and lifts his silver flask in salute before taking a pull, then slips it back in the folds of his riding jacket before anyone else can ask for some. Always the germaphobe.

"What do you say, a bottle of plum wine on who has the fastest horse back to the farm, and can keep his ass in the saddle?" The other men cheer, and heels are dug into flanks as the party charges into the night, pointlessly of course, Andrew thinks, because his dad is the best rider and has by far the fastest horse.

Andrew tries to keep up in the semi-darkness. His father slows occasionally, weaving through the trees on the side of the path to check on him and shout encouragement. Andrew's ass is numb from the saddle. Brent hogs the path in front of him, the wide butt of the other man's brown palomino appearing in front of Andrew every time he attempts to work his way ahead. Brent, Colleen's husband—or Rumpelstiltskin, in Dad-speak, due to his short stature and somewhat misshapen appearance—always enjoys putting Andrew in his place, giving him play punches to the head that hurt just a little too much, or farting in Andrew's face. Andrew grinds his heels into Sherlock's flank and goes wide to cut through the trees. But Sherlock, spooked from the race and the dark, cuts too far left. Andrew sees the low-hanging tree branch and tries to rein Sherlock in and duck—but it's too late. He feels the bludgeoning smack of the branch against his forehead, and then everything goes black.

⁂

DANIEL AND NATALIE STAND IN the sweaty warmth of the kitchen, eating stew. Natalie clutches a glass of elderberry wine and stares fixedly out the kitchen window. She only quit working in the garden after Daniel shooed her in for dinner with admonishments not to be out in the dark alone with raiders around.

They agreed to confront Anneke together after dinner. He's on early watch, so it'll be a late night, and Daniel's bones already feel weighted and uncooperative. The fatigue associated with his heart condition dogs him more and more these days. The talk at the table is hushed. The farm members are afraid now, and talk of what to do to the raiders has turned nasty. Liz has been returned to armed guard in the den.

"They might not come home tonight, you know. They took provisions for overnight in case anything went wrong or they needed more time," says Daniel, in a tone that he hopes is reassuring, not condescending or dismissive.

"I know. I can still hope, though. I know I'll have to let go someday, but I just don't like Andrew out there." Daniel nods. He knows well Natalie's fierce attachment to her children. She downs the last of her wine. "I guess we should go talk to Anneke now."

Daniel follows Natalie into the pantry. She probably expects him to do the talking. They're his dogs, his orders regarding feeding. Anneke turns to face them when she hears the door, her solid legs braced squarely on the floor in beat-up Birkenstocks. She holds a wooden spoon aloft.

"Yes?" Anneke says.

In the narrow pantry, the side of Natalie's arm presses against Daniel's. He moves aside to give her more space, and she gives him an almost anguished look before turning to address Anneke. "We just wanted to check in on what happened with the dogs. We heard that they were fed all at the same time."

The edges of Anneke's lips flip into a smile, but her eyes narrow fractionally and she shrugs. "That cinnamon bear was harassing them again. I didn't want him to hurt them. He's becoming a total nuisance. He needs to be shot."

"But we agreed not to feed all the dogs at the same time," says Daniel. He tries to make his voice diplomatic and reasonable like Natalie's, but it comes across edgy and annoyed.

Anneke eyes widen slightly, and she pulls her lips sideways into a long inexpressive line. The skin of her forehead creases into defiant furrows. "The bear was acting really aggressive. I brought them in to protect them. I'm sorry if you don't agree with my choice. You can feed them yourself from now on if you wish."

Daniel feels the anger billow in his mind and he almost wants to shake the woman. "Well that's terrific. Maybe you should go explain to Sarah how you had the dogs' best interest at heart. Where were you during the incident?"

"Oh, is this the inquisition now? I was down in the cellar doing inventory with Liz. We didn't hear a thing."

The clatter of horses and loud voices in the courtyard echoes in through the window. Natalie pushes past Daniel out into the kitchen. He follows in time to see the kitchen door swing outward, revealing Karl standing to the side. Boots clomp on the porch, and then Richard enters, carrying the front of a makeshift stretcher, holding Andrew covered in vomit, mud, and blood.

CHAPTER 8

THE TWO OF SWORDS

—∞∞∞—

ANDREW AND RICHARD

A decision in a balance; a conflict between two equal powers.

Andrew stares at the white plaster ceiling of the infirmary. His head throbs despite the Tylenol, and the porridge in his stomach lurches about. After clutching his hand for much of the night and morning, his mother departed for the garden with promises to be back in a few hours.

Andrew tries not to let his gaze linger on any one object in the room, as his eyes seem to twist and blur, sending his gut reeling. He settles for closing his eyes and trying not to focus on the spots dancing on his eyelids.

In the adjacent office, Mike provides instructions to Justin regarding head injuries and the neurological exams Andrew should be subjected to for the remainder of the day.

Craig huddles in the next bed, his head turned to the window. Earlier, he and Craig had made eye contact a couple of times when they ended up rolling to face each other accidentally. After that, they settled for an alternating schedule of only turning toward each other's beds when they were sure the other person was facing away. Anneke had passed through with Craig's dinner and stopped to murmur some words to the boy in an uncharacteristically kind tone.

"Did you see a girl on the ridge?" Craig says. "Dark hair, sixteen?" Andrew jumps at the sound of Craig's voice, sending pain spiraling down his neck. He rotates his body without turning his head. He's struck immediately by the immensity of Craig's eye sockets and the degree to which Craig appears like a skeleton sheathed in a thin layer of skin.

"There were a lot of girls up there," Andrew says.

Craig shifts impatiently. "Attractive. Very attractive."

"I think I saw her. She your girlfriend?"

"None of your business. Is she okay?"

"She looked okay."

Craig nods and starts to roll away.

"How far along is she?" Andrew says, wanting to continue the conversation somehow, and grasping at anything to say.

Craig's face tightens in disdain. "A long way."

"Are you the…" Andrew doesn't quite know the appropriate way to ask about paternity, but he wonders if perhaps someone should not make the suggestion that Craig should be present for the birth of his baby. "…father?" Andrew tacks a weak smile on the end of his question.

Craig stares at Andrew as if he's so far out of touch that he no longer qualifies as human. "Um, no… Slaves don't get to father babies around our camp. We leave that all to Rafe."

Andrew feels another queasy turn in his stomach and wonders if he would even survive out there on his own. "What? Who's Rafe? What do you mean you're a slave?"

"Rafe and his men are a former prison gang from the Idaho State Correctional Center. Seems once the shit hit the fan, there was nobody left to keep the prisoners behind bars. Rafe was a serial killer and rapist. Well, I guess technically he still is, but we don't classify it that way anymore. The rest of us… We're the slaves. We do the work, and the women get to service Rafe and his men." The eyes in the hollow sockets burn at Andrew now, making him feel inconsequential and completely sheltered by his life on the farm.

"How…"

"They took most of us hostage on our farm. Then they picked up a few more women along the way, just for fun." Craig stops talking and turns over to face out the window.

Andrew stares at the stepping stones of vertebrae down Craig's back. The discussion seems somehow to be over. Andrew has no idea what he would ask at this point anyway.

RICHARD LETS THE STEAMING WATER encase his aching muscles. Only being able to shower once a week is absurd. He doesn't give a shit about being dirty, but his back needs the hot water. He should have special dispensation to shower more because of his injuries. But Natalie won't hear of it and tells him it's his own fault for the fall from the horse that screwed up his back. And her rule about not being able to draw well water for bathing is ridiculous; there's plenty of water in the well. Maybe he could rig up some more hosing on the barn roof to heat more water, and find some container to use as a third cistern to collect rainwater. A wood-fired hot tub that wouldn't have to be refilled each time would be great, but the thought of sitting in water that other farm members have occupied gives him the creeps.

He glances at the fat pendulum mantel clock perched on the top of the shower stall, counting down the time until the water has to be turned off, its wood warped and peeling as a result of its constant exposure to the steam of the shower. He strikes a bodybuilding pose and lets his eyes trace the lines of his body. His arms and legs are still cut, tanned, and strong. The tiny hints of a gut play around his sides. He should go on a diet before he resumes his political career. But overall, he's maintained an impressive physique over the years, the kind that cows other men and draws the hopeful silly eyes of women. It is a body that effortlessly maintains its muscle mass and propels him across the fields faster and farther than the other men. It is a body that has served him well. He imagines what it would be like to live in the unreliable vessel of skin that Daniel occupies, always worried about pushing too hard, about dropping dead. That would be an insufferable trial. And it has made Daniel too much of a chicken. About everything.

Richard saunters across the courtyard in his towel. He winks at a couple of the farm ladies as he passes, and takes his time dressing. Best to enjoy the one break that he has. When he's finished, he goes to find Natalie.

He makes his way through the kitchen as quietly as possible. Anneke and

Natalie talk, and as Sun Tzu says in *The Art of War*, it's always useful to know as much as you can about the enemy. Richard has amended this wisdom to include his allies as well. And although Natalie and Anneke rarely discuss anything of serious interest—just their kids, their endless worries, the many failures of husbands, and the sorry state of feminism—Richard likes to gather random details that he wouldn't be expected to know, and then drop them casually into conversation later. It puts people on their heels. It's always good to have the upper hand. So he lurks by the door.

AMID THE SOUND OF KNIFE blades hitting cutting boards, Natalie's voice emerges low. Richard strains to hear. "Would you leave your husband, now, the way things are, having to live on the farm? Or would it just be impossible?" Richard braces himself against the doorframe. He hadn't even considered this. Has Natalie really come this far? Or is she just speaking hypothetically? Or is she speaking about Anneke and Alan?

"Well, I've never been particularly good at leaving my husband," says Anneke. "So probably not. I guess the good news is you wouldn't have to shuttle the kids between two households. The bad news is everyone would watch and judge you as your life collapses in on itself, and it wouldn't be pretty."

"What do you mean?"

Anneke's tone is cool, certain. "It would be one of the best dramas going around here. A divorced woman is still a fallen woman, as far as I can tell, and will be so until the end of time. Don't think we're that far above chattel even to some of the so-called liberated men on this farm. They may *believe* they think women are equal, but when it comes to their emotions and threats to their manhood, they retreat to the cave pretty damn fast and take no prisoners on the way. And some of the men are just waiting for an excuse to blast us back to the Dark Ages in terms of women's rights. I hear them talk. Don't kid yourself."

Richard resists the urge to barge into the pantry playing a mock violin. Typical woman, thinking she's so hard done by.

"Do you really think so?" Richard can't tell from Natalie's tone whether she's humoring her friend or actually believes what Anneke is saying.

"Yup. Unless the man is proven to be an abusive cheating lout. And even then there'll be 'he said, she said' and a lot of the men will side with the man. Your best hope is that your husband dumps you…or dies. Otherwise, I would make the best of it."

Richard almost chuckles at the starkness of Anneke's words. He can't believe women think like that.

"Well at least Alan is lovely. Even if your relationship isn't perfect. He must be fairly easy to live with, isn't he?" Richard can hear the timidity in Natalie's voice. Natalie doesn't like to judge, or make assumptions about others. But he wonders if what she's saying is that he, Richard, *isn't* easy to live with. He feels a billowing of disgust at all the sacrifices he's made for her; sacrifices she clearly doesn't appreciate. *She* is hardly easy to live with.

A knife clatters against the counter sharply. "Alan *is* lovely," Anneke says with her customary curtness. Richard has to hand it to Anneke. The woman doesn't air dirty laundry. Richard is about to make his entrance when Anneke speaks again more quietly. "I've heard Leon talking. They're bitter about this whole peak oil thing. And when men feel like they've lost power, they turn around and try to control the one thing they can, and that's us. They'll start slow, ease it over our heads. Like the 'no women in hunting parties' policy that Leon and Richard proposed last month."

"Yeah, but we voted that down," Natalie says.

"I know, but do any women go hunting now?"

"Well, I'm not sure if they did before," Natalie says. "But I take your point."

"It's the first step."

Richard grinds his teeth together and lifts his hand to slam it against the doorframe. He only supported Leon's dumb proposal because he needed Leon's vote on the new cabin-building policy because he had to get some of the new refugees out of the farmhouse so he could have a little privacy and space again. Not a single woman ever volunteered for a hunting party anyway. Trust Anneke to warp the whole thing. He doesn't get why women always have to be so god-damn crazy.

Richard hears some of the other women on the porch, returning from gathering more tomatoes for canning. He tiptoes hastily back across the kitchen and then returns, this time letting his feet fall heavily on the wood floor. He pushes open the pantry door.

"Ladies," he says. "Having a little chitty chat without me? I'm hurt."

Natalie stops, her knife poised in the air above some rainbow chard, a flush of guilt creeping up her neck. Anneke glares at him through smudged and crooked glasses.

Natalie places the knife on the counter and pushes past him to the kitchen while he just stands there, smiling. He knows a lecture about Andrew is coming—best to play dumb as long as possible and try to ensure that the confrontation occurs in front of others. The other women mill around the counter, preparing the hot water bath for the tomatoes. Natalie gives him her stricken look, and stalks off to the den. He follows reluctantly. He doesn't get what he does to inspire that look all the time. Then again, he shouldn't assume her numerous issues have anything to do with him.

Liz's black coat sits on the couch. Richard tweaks open a pocket with two fingers and glances inside. He's just about to reach inside when Natalie's face looms in front of him. She swats at his hand but doesn't make contact.

"What are you doing?" she says.

"Hey," he says, snatching his hand away.

"You can't go through someone's pockets!"

"We don't know who the hell she is! She could be one of *them* and she could be packing a gun. I have every right to look in her pockets."

"Scott already patted her down for weapons."

"I'm just going to give it a little look. I won't take anything." Richard lifts the coat off the couch and begins rifling through the pockets. Natalie heaves a sigh and shakes her head at him.

"Why did you take Andrew with you yesterday? I thought we agreed that he should stay behind," Natalie says.

"He showed up and he wanted to go. I thought we agreed that he could."

"No. We didn't." Natalie's voice is flat.

Richard shrugs. "Sorry. I guess that was a misunderstanding, then." He tries to recall the precise nature of their previous discussion and wishes she didn't think she has an encyclopedic memory for every conversation they ever had.

"And then not only do you take him, you make him participate in a dangerous race through the woods for no reason other than your fun and games, and now he's got a concussion and could have been killed. What were you thinking?"

Richard tries to control his anger. Why is he always being berated? Andrew wanted to go. She has to start letting go of those boys. She's so fucking mental sometimes. "I don't know. I guess I wasn't thinking."

"Well, you need to start thinking. This isn't a game, Richard."

"Sure thing," Richard says, and walks out.

EVERYONE ASSEMBLES FOR FARM COUNCIL after dinner. Richard's attempts to grill Craig that afternoon were futile. The boy shrank away from Richard and kept his mouth clenched shut. It doesn't matter, as far as Richard is concerned. The ridge people need to be run off, Craig included, so anything Craig tells them is kind of useless. The kid seemed off anyway, and the whackadoon woman who thinks she's a psychic is even worse.

Richard feels centered and charitable toward Natalie again. She may be high-strung and a pain in the ass sometimes, but she's a good mother and far more practical and attractive than most of the other women on the farm. He admires the perfection of her cheekbones and her reserve as she sits huddled beside him. She still looks like one of those women they used to cast as the wife in Harrison Ford movies. Beautiful and classy, but not too showy or sexy. Exactly the kind of wife he wanted.

He stands and addresses the group. "There are eleven men, eight women, and two children living on the ridge. They're armed, but they aren't well stocked. They look pretty rough, and they've attacked us twice. So it's pretty safe to label them as hostile. I know what *I* think should be done, but I want to hear your thoughts."

Alan proposes taking them in, which Anneke promptly supports, but Alan looks rebellious and like he might only be doing it because his wife is making him. Richard manages not to sneer or roll his eyes. Leaders must appear receptive to the opinions of others. That was drilled into him a long time ago. The rest of the farm members look uncomfortably at the table, even the ones who usually fall on the bleeding-heart side of issues. Bob, forever the academic, contends in ponderous tones that the farm doesn't have enough supplies to support a doubling of population, and that these are clearly not the type of people wanted on the farm. Siobhan proposes providing them with supplies to get them through the winter.

Jane sniffs. Insipid Jane, Richard calls her. "An armed encampment right by the farm? In the dead of winter?" Richard wonders if he's ever seen Jane smile in a manner that isn't spiteful. But at this point, Jane is saying exactly what he wants her to, so Richard gives her his most dazzling of smiles. He's sure she'd love to have the opportunity to sleep with him.

"We go up there and shoot the men and run the women and children off. That's what we do," Leon says.

"Killing the men is just a slow death sentence for the women and children," Paul says.

"Not to mention completely inhumane," Anneke adds.

Richard just nods and listens. It's always best to let them exhaust their stupid ideas and then convince them of the right path.

After twenty minutes, Richard stands again. "Let's review the facts. At current population levels, it would be very risky to take them in over the winter. We might all die. They've already shot at us with the intent to kill, injuring two people, killing a dog, and stealing four cows. Then they came back and took Sarah hostage to steal more supplies. When their food runs out this winter, which it will"—Richard pauses, looking around the table—"we all know they're going to come here. Do we want to watch over our shoulder at every moment of every day?"

"Let's not forget, they could have killed someone on their last raid, but they didn't," Natalie adds.

Richard snorts. "That's just because they don't want us to come up and blast them into next year. The way I see it, we have three options. Option one, we go up and force them to move on, and take out a few of their key men while we do it. Anyone who surrenders will be given the chance to leave, and we'll patrol widely to make sure that they've gone. Taking out their men will reduce the chances that they'll attack us in the future."

"And reduce the chances that they'll survive the winter," Anneke says loudly.

"Option two, we take supplies up and negotiate an agreement. If they agree not to attack us in the winter and move on in the spring, we'll provide them with more supplies and seeds then to help set up their own farm."

"And run the risk that they murder us in our beds on Christmas Eve," Jane says. Richard affects a grave look of agreement. He doesn't know why he always has the temptation to laugh in these circumstances, why he finds most of the farm members and their tics so ridiculous.

"And finally, option three, we offer those who are willing to work and follow the rules a spot on the farm. That would mean providing an exception to the no-refugee policy on a one-time basis. We are not reopening the policy at this point." Richard pauses theatrically. He pretends he's an actor in a movie when he addresses Farm Council, like Al Pacino or Marlon Brando in *The Godfather*, except without the accents and weird voices. He does kind of wonder at the irony of his pretense, though. The issues he's dealing with are real and serious, and they were merely stars reading a script. "Given the sensitivity and importance of this issue, we need to have a silent ballot. All of us need to feel free to vote with our conscience without fear of moral judgment."

While Natalie and Anneke rip up squares of paper, Richard retrieves the old shoebox from the den. When everyone finishes casting their ballots, Richard and Daniel tally the votes. A smile curves on Richard's lips as he places the pieces of paper in neat piles. He pats the winning pile. He loves being right. As he stands to speak, he keeps his voice measured to avoid sounding too smug. "Option one carries the day."

"I VOTED FOR OPTION TWO. I really think we need to start building a community." Natalie says flatly, staring out the bedroom window.

"Of course you did," Richard says, caressing her shoulder as he passes on his way to the bed. "I wouldn't expect any different. But are those really the people you want to start building a community with? They look a bit squirrelly and dangerous. You wouldn't like it one bit if some of those guys were sleeping in the bunkhouse right now." She doesn't answer, and he knows he's right.

He rubs the palms of his hands together. "You've got to give it to democracy, though. When it comes down to it, even though people spout bleeding-heart liberalism at the table, in the privacy of the voting booth they vote with cold hard self-preservation. I love it." He considers that maybe he and Natalie should have sex. Wins always give him a hard-on. When she climbs into the bed he gives her leg a little rub.

She shakes her head at him. "I'm not sure why you'd be excited about turning us into cold-blooded killers."

Richard pulls his hand away. She always has to be such a bitch. Natalie blows out the candle, and the darkness hangs like a scythe between them. He drifts off to sleep while Natalie tosses and turns. He knows that he's right, and he knows that no matter what moral high horse she pretends she's riding, she's relieved that option one—the right option—was selected.

⬦

ANDREW COUNTS THE NUMBER OF times the watch lights pass the infirmary window. On any given night, if you're moving at a reasonable pace, you can do the inner circuit—farmhouse, Daniel's cabin, shed, barn, bunkhouse, greenhouses—at least twenty-seven times in a four-hour watch period. Watchers aren't required to skirt the outer cabins or the schoolhouse, but they can if they choose to. Diligent farm members usually do the outer circuit every few laps. Andrew can tell from the way the passing light moves more perpendicular to the infirmary window every fourth lap, in the direction of the schoolhouse, and then takes longer to return, that it's probably his Uncle Daniel or Uncle Mike on watch. Daniel and Mike do the outer circuit every fourth lap; his mother, Paul, and Cyrus do it every second; and Siobhan, Solomon, and Alan do it every third. The other farm members don't ever do the outer circuit.

He glances over at Craig. They weren't able to hear the Farm Council decision when it was made, but Andrew's Uncle Leon and Brent spent some time in the hallway afterward talking loudly about it, and it didn't take long to figure out the nature of the decision. Craig's face cinched together all tight, and he turned his back to Andrew for the rest of the evening.

Then Anneke came with their evening snack, a peach crumble that she made a ridiculous fuss over, given that he was still pretty much too nauseated to eat anyway. Now Andrew lies awake worried that, given the decision, Craig might decide to try to wrap an IV tube around Andrew's neck and escape in the night. He knows that Justin sleeps in Mike's office next door, and that there's probably a guard outside the infirmary, but it seems to be assumed that he, the head injury patient, is fine being left alone with a raider overnight. If it comes down to straight-up hand-to-hand combat, Andrew feels confident he can take Craig, who is little more than an ensemble of bones, sinew, and skin, thinner by at least forty pounds than him. But aren't people with concussions supposed to sleep more deeply? What if Craig slays him in his sleep? Not that Craig seems like the type. He seems like a possible friend. But he is a raider and a slave, after all, and that might make him too desperate to be trusted. So Andrew lies there counting the laps of the watchers to stay awake.

"You awake?" It's Craig's voice, in a whisper.

"Yup." He wonders if he should call for reinforcements.

"You know much about computers?"

"What?" The question flummoxes him.

"You know anything about hooking up computers?"

"No more than the average person who was ten the last time they touched one."

Craig lets out a huffy wheeze at Andrew's sarcasm. "Do you have old computer equipment, like an old laptop and modem and a radio transmitter?"

"Yeah, sure."

"Do you know where they are?"

"I could probably find them. What are you getting at?"

"We need your help. We need to get free of those bastards up there. We just need a little help. Look, we have Internet access. It's not like the old Internet, but it has its uses. I can get you hooked up, if you help us."

The Internet. The source of endless good things; at least the old Internet was. Andrew experiences an undeniable sliver of interest. "What do you want in return?"

"Guns."

"Guns?"

The lights of the watchers rounding the corner of the farmhouse cast just enough light for Andrew to make out Craig's eyes. They stare at him from sockets that are too deep and sunken for a young man. "Just a few. I swear we won't use them on you. Just give it some thought."

CHAPTER 9

THE NINE OF SWORDS

⎯⎯∞⎯⎯

NATALIE AND ANDREW

Worry is a trick of the mind that keeps you from your destiny.

It drizzles on the morning of Natalie and Daniel's departure. The fog cloaks the mountains and fields in furls of ivory; the aroma of wet earth filters through the morning air.

Justin stands in the barn with his horse when Natalie arrives to saddle up. Justin's saddlebags bulge, and he wears a battered blue jacket and toque. The look on his face implies that it's pointless to argue with him, and she won't. His equanimity has always made for solid, if not chatty, company, and it means that she won't have to be parted from both of her children. Her younger brother, Scott, is also joining them. Scott, her chronically irresponsible, manic depressive, substance-abusing brother. Not the easiest of companions, but they don't have a lot of choices, and under Daniel's supervision in the barn, Scott's work ethic and attitude seem to have been improving of late although he wears a mutinous expression this morning.

Daniel has outfitted the horses to be ridden with saddlebags and panniers. Two packhorses huddle by the barn door laden with camping gear and food, plus items to trade for information, antibiotics, or free passage. They all go about their travel preparations in silence, cinching saddles and double-checking supplies, and then Natalie goes and curls herself around Oscar, who sleeps under Daniel's desk in the office, and covers his silky head with kisses. The tetracycline has not done him in yet. There is hope.

Several farm members come to see them off. For better or for worse, they're a community, almost a family, Natalie thinks, until their collective guilt spins them apart. She had wanted to delay the trip until the raider issue was dealt with, but Daniel and Mike convinced her that they need antibiotics, particularly if the ridge conflict turns ugly.

She hugs Andrew goodbye and makes him promise again that he'll stay safe. Richard struts around, making a show of tightening saddles and checking the supplies that Natalie and Daniel meticulously packed. She tightens her shoulders. She doesn't want Richard near her. He gives her a knowing half smile, as if daring her to kiss him here in front of everyone. She contorts her face into some sort of beseeching expression. But she's not sure what she's asking him.

She pulls him aside. "Promise me you won't take Andrew with you to the ridge."

He smiles and winks at a couple of the men behind her. "I promise."

"And promise me you won't just go up and murder everyone on that ridge."

Richard scrunches up his face and scratches his head. "Nat, we're not going to do that. We might not kill *any*one. But we have no idea how it's going to go down."

"So what you're saying is, you *won't* promise me."

Richard raps his knuckles against his forehead in a joking sort of way, like she's paining him. "I *can't* promise you."

"I'm scared." She doesn't know why she continues to tell Richard this. He only has one stock answer.

"You'll be fine."

"You always say that. You have no idea if we'll be fine."

"What do you want me to say? Don't go?"

"I have to go."

"Then go." Richard blinks his eyes and shakes his head like he's vibrating, like she's driving him mad. The unexplainable but constant inadequacy of their communication is shattering. She knows they're both to blame, but she doesn't know how to fix it. She turns away from Richard, and her eyes meet Daniel's. What must he think of her and Richard's constant bickering?

They mount their horses and head across the fields into the mist. With every fall of the hooves in the mud, Natalie feels a tiny bit lighter.

They travel in silence—Daniel in the lead, followed by Justin and Natalie, with Scott bringing up the rear. Daisy trots ahead of Daniel while Mitch runs circles around the group. Natalie absorbs the splendor of the fall countryside, every so often letting her eyes fall on Daniel's and Justin's backs. Their shared awkwardness and inscrutability renders them unknowable to all but the most determined. Natalie wonders if Daniel would possess Justin's fleetness of foot if he didn't have a heart condition, or Justin's sweet vulnerability if he hadn't had Richard constantly mocking him when they were younger.

They make slow time. The horses are unused to being so burdened, but Natalie worries that Daniel's reluctance to push the horses is in deference to her limited experience riding long distances. He says nothing, but often looks back to check on her. By midday they're following a narrow path along the Syringa River, cutting across fields where the river loops lazily. An old highway runs on the other side of the river. Every so often they see abandoned vehicles with broken windows and missing tires, eerie reminders of the expansive life they lived five years ago. But they encounter no people.

Natalie's bones buzz with exhaustion by the time they stop for the evening. They picket the horses and set up camp in a sheltered clearing away from the river. They cook corncakes, carrots, and a small bit of chicken in a frying pan. They will have no more fresh meat on the trip, unless they find something to kill. Natalie sits on the ground, watching showers of sparks snap out of the wet wood. Daniel sits next to her on top of his saddlebag. He's so close that she could reach out her arm, curl it around his calf, and rest her head against his knee. As if sensing her thoughts, Daniel excuses himself to check on the horses and motions Justin to follow him.

Natalie watches her younger brother through the flames. She and Scott have never been close. Scott always seemed so self-destructive, moving from job to job, never seeming to fit in.

Scott pokes the fire with a stick. "I take it Richard told you about the bullets we found."

Natalie sits up, her lethargy dispelled. "No. He didn't say a word."

"Well, he probably didn't have a chance," Scott replies. She recoils at his tone. Is she such a horrid wife that everyone feels they have to defend Richard?

"What did you find?" Natalie tries to keep the anger and hurt out of her voice.

"We found a full box of bullets on the way back from the ridge, just on the edge of the eastern pasture. The same brand and type we use for big game hunting. They're premium bullets that Richard picked special 'cause they expand gradually inside the animal. So it was a bit strange. Not an impossible coincidence, but strange."

"Maybe you guys left them behind on one of your hunting trips?"

"Nah, we pack 'em in ammo cans. We never take a box."

"And how did Richard react?" Natalie says.

"Well…" Scott hesitates. "He didn't think it was a coincidence. He thinks someone's smuggling bullets off the farm."

Daniel and Justin slip back through the darkness. Daniel takes a seat on the other side of the fire, his luminous gray eyes on her. She can't tell if he knew about the bullets or not.

"I see. Does Richard have any theories who that might be?"

"Not that he shared. Said he'd ferret out the traitor."

"He should have brought it to Farm Council," Natalie snaps, and then winces at her words. Her anger is almost always seen as bitchiness. She wills Daniel to say something. He tosses a stick into the fire.

"I don't know. Wouldn't that just tip the traitor off?" Scott says, whittling the end of a stick to a sharp point.

"Well, he sure as hell should have told me about it before I left at least." Andrew and the farm suddenly seem far more vulnerable.

"He probably just didn't want to upset you," Scott says.

"I see." Is that what everything is about, not upsetting her? Don't tell the emotional woman. She might get upset. Is that how all the men around her function? She can't look Daniel in the eyes. She stands and stalks off into the enveloping night.

Natalie leans into the firm softness of Serendipity's warm neck and waits for the predictable arrival of someone to tell her to relax. That she's overreacting. It's Daniel who appears out of the gloom and comes to rest his arms against Serendipity's back.

"Nat, I know you're probably worried about the farm and Andrew." He pauses and she nods, trying not to feel pathetic. "I know you don't always trust

Richard, and God knows you shouldn't, but he's not dumb. The bullets will be under lock and key, and the farm is already on high alert. Richard even sent Karl and Brent up to watch the raiders' camp. Besides, you know Richard. I don't drink his Kool-Aid. He might have taken that box of bullets out there himself and forgotten about it. There might not even be a traitor."

Except that Anneke fed all the dogs at the same time, Natalie thinks, then buries the thought. "He should have told me," she says.

"I agree. But he didn't."

"Should we go back?"

"If there's going to be a conflict, finding antibiotics is just as important as running off raiders." Daniel hunches so he can look up into her downcast eyes, his face a pale hopeful moon with a kindly smile and craggy edges. The outlines of her heart swell and hurt at the same time. "I think we should carry on."

Mitch wedges his way between them and presses against her leg. "I'm just afraid that something will happen to Andrew while I'm gone—and I don't think I could live if anything happens to one of the boys. This new world…it's too dangerous for the fainthearted like me."

He hunches again, so that his face is only inches from hers, but this time his face is more serious. "I know. For the record, I don't think you're fainthearted. Does it help to know that half the time I'm scared shitless myself?" He shifts his eyes to his feet, and then back to her. "I wish I could tell you it's going to be okay, but if I did I'd be lying. But the boys are still alive and well, and if you spend all your time consumed with worry over them, you aren't living yourself. And in this new world, your window for living might be a lot shorter, so I suggest that you live—at least a little bit. " His lips are so close she can feel the faint puff of his breath on her chin. He seems to inch closer fractionally, and Natalie feels hope and shock thunder through her body in a massive swell. Then he pulls away and shakes his head at the sky. "Ha ha. Listen to me, spouting shit that I don't even do myself."

Natalie's heart slows in a grind of disappointment. She must stop wanting him, stop hoping that he'll kiss her.

"Well, you *should* do it yourself," Natalie says, not even sure what she's telling him he should do. His face is shadowy in the moonlight.

"I guess we should get back," he says. "They'll be wondering."

The sky has cleared, and she stares up into the vast swath of stars that canvases every inch of the ebony sky, a brilliant spill of glitter over a planet with no more light pollution. The stars have become their signposts and guides—and, for Natalie, a bellwether that the universe, at least, is still intact. She wonders how many satellites still circle the earth, faithfully beaming their signals to a world no longer able to listen. She would give anything for a signal or a signpost to tell her that loving Daniel isn't wrong. That it would be okay if they were together someday. But the stars glow back at her, unrelenting in their silence, telling her nothing. She hears the snap of the campfire in the distance.

"Which constellation are we following back to the fire? In case I get lost." She says this in jest; she knows the way back to the fire. But Daniel always likes to walk looking at the sky.

He cocks his head at her. "Let's go with Aquila. It's just on the southern horizon there right now. It pretty much looks like an arrow." Daniel starts walking in the direction of his outstretched arm. Natalie follows, trying to pick out the constellation from the jumble of stars.

"Aquila, the eagle, known for its acuity of vision, guards the arrow of Eros, Sagitta. Sagitta is right over there." Daniel pauses and directs his finger at another part of the sky.

"The arrow of Eros?" She allows a hint of suggestion to creep into her tone.

Surprise flits across his face, and then his eyes meet hers. "Yes, known to make even the gods lovestruck," he says. His tone is casual, but the momentary flash of something in his expression—in any other man she would think it desire—jolts her. She wants to pull him to her and breathe him in, but they have arrived at the campfire, and her brother and son both look up expectantly.

Daniel dons his usual neutral expression, and they take seats next to Justin and Scott. Natalie clasps her hands on her lap so she doesn't reach out for Daniel without thinking. Daniel starts talking about Cygnus, one of the other avian constellations, which is farther overhead. Natalie allows herself to stop listening and just watch his lips.

—⦵⦵⦵—

ANDREW CRAWLS INTO THE HAYLOFT, his head still throbbing from his fall. His father spent the day pacing about in the shed with Terrence, his go-to man for any sort of military strategy, even though Terrence's qualifications extend only as far as watching every war show the History Channel ever produced. Hand-drawn maps of the ridge and potential approach positions hang from the walls of the shed, and Richard wears a puffed-out, twitchy look. With his mother and Justin gone, and his father distracted, Andrew has been able to collect what he needs without interference.

Andrew plugs the laptop, wireless modem, and radio transmitter into the extension cord he's run from the main floor of the barn; then, with shaking fingers, he flicks them all on. Stealing some of the small amount of power that the windmill produces is strictly forbidden in the Farm Code, and Andrew hopes he's concealed the cord well enough against the back wall of the barn. Even as a first offense, it would be punishable by many weeks of shit jobs. The old Macintosh hums to life. Andrew unfolds the list of directions that Craig scribbled out and inserts the tiny memory stick that Craig gave him. He clicks on the radio app, as the directions specify. Then he opens the terminal window and types, his fingers searching awkwardly for each letter:

ping mercury.network.org

He checks it twice and then hits return. He barely breathes as the modem lights blink. Lines appear on the screen:

PING mercury.network.org (73.240.210.190) 56(84) bytes of data.

64 bytes from mercury.network.org (73.240.210.190): icmp_seq=1 ttl=52 time=87 ms

It works then. He had scarcely believed it would. Andrew types in ssh craig@mercury.network.org and then the password that Craig provided. Three lines of text appear. Three emails. The first email, from hans@mercury.network.org, is highlighted. Andrew hits return and then R, and types Craig ok and Will have plan soon. Then he hits Control-X, and the word Sending appears on the bottom of the screen.

Craig told him that it might take a while to receive a reply. That Hans can only check email occasionally, when Rafe isn't watching. Andrew already feels the creep of his betrayal down his neck and back. It rests heavily in his gut, but in his head it engages in a pitched battle with his dad's plan to run off the raiders—a group that includes children and pregnant girls, as well as Craig, Andrew's sort-of new friend. This is only a test to see if the new Internet works the way Craig promised. He has agreed to nothing yet. He could turn Craig in at any time.

A reply flashes across the screen. Andrew hits return and the words make his stomach quiver:

We'll be waiting.

Andrew unplugs everything hurriedly. Richard acted strangely at dinner, roving around the room, gazing ponderously at each farm member in turn. It was almost farcical, and yet most farm members just ate or chatted, seemingly unaware that they were being examined. Their obliviousness was almost as unnerving as Richard's behavior. Richard constantly talks about how dumb most people are. Andrew rolls his eyes at this—discreetly of course; he'd never let Richard see. But tonight his father seemed to be right. Perhaps he, Andrew, is also stupid. Perhaps he only thinks Richard has no idea what he's up to.

He stows the laptop and modem under the hay, returns the radio and extension cord to the barn office, and then sneaks back to the farmhouse in the shadowy night.

MEET AT MIDNIGHT IN THE *cellar*, Craig told him. Andrew's not sure whom he's going to find there. If other farm members are present, going to the meeting will mark him as being part of the betrayal. Of course, he could just later claim he was collecting information on the traitors, but attending the meeting seems like it will push him past that terrifying precipice of commitment.

Andrew hovers in the kitchen for several minutes, rubbing his sweaty palms against his pants, racking his brain for a reason to be in the cellar at midnight. Food is rationed, and being caught in the cellar near the food stores would be almost as bad as meeting with raiders. Maybe he could say he heard a noise? That might work. His night-owl tendencies are already known.

Maybe Craig pegged him as their helper based on some analysis of propensity for computer addiction. But the Internet could help improve their life on the farm. And it's the right thing to do; they can't just kill women and children.

Andrew wonders if this is some weird rebellion thing, if he's bored. Since he can't drink or party, he's going to betray the farm. Maybe it's the girls up there, and the potential that one of them could become his girlfriend. Maybe it's the head injury.

He opens the door and tiptoes down the stairs. It's pitch black, and someone grabs his arm. He hears steel scrape against a flint. A single spark leaps, and in the glow, Andrew can make out Anneke's glasses and haunted blue eyes. In the far corner of the cellar, Liz, Rachel, and Craig crouch together. He had sort of expected to see Liz as soon as Craig had said "us," but he's a little surprised by Anneke and Rachel. In the true spirit of farm desperation, Rachel and Craig already hold hands. Rachel goes to give him one of her cocky smiles, but her lips start to quiver partway, and she pulls them back into a tight-lipped grimace.

"Thanks for coming, everyone," Anneke says, as if she's addressing a much larger crowd. Andrew settles on the floor next to the others. The cement instantly chills his skin. "If you're here, we're presuming you've agreed to loan these people some guns so they can free themselves of their captors." She gestures at Liz and Craig.

Andrew raises his hand. Anneke turns in his direction with squinted eyes, but plasters a smile on her face. She nods.

"I'm just a little confused. Why don't we just tell my father the situation and maybe he'll help?" Andrew says.

"Your father?" Anneke says. "Even if he did agree to try to set the slaves free, which I'm not sure he would, he would never give them guns. He'd go up and do it himself in some big song-and-dance theatrical strike. He wouldn't know who was who. It'd get messy and more people would get killed. It's better to attack from within. There's too much bureaucracy with Farm Council. You know how they get. They can't tell their asses from their elbows."

"What if they turn around and come and down and attack us with our own guns?"

"Well, there are only sixteen of them, and seven of them are pregnant women." Anneke pauses. "And I know them." She glances quickly at Craig and Liz.

"You *know* them?"

"Liz is an old friend of mine. And there's another man, Joe, that I know. I told them about our farm—that's why they're here. You can trust them completely; your mother and Joe were…good friends." Andrew stares at Anneke. In the dim light of the cellar, she seems even more inscrutable than usual.

"Then why not tell my father that?"

"Like I said, it has to be done from within. We need you to get the guns. You have access to all sorts of places we don't, and I don't know what's what in that armory. And horses."

"Horses? You've got to be kidding me."

"Take the second-stringers. They're in the upper pasture all the time. Nobody'll even know they're gone. And we all have to promise not to reveal who was involved in this."

"I don't know," Andrew says. He hugs his feet in closer to his chest.

"Come on man, help us out," Craig says. "You're our last hope. We'll leave if you don't want us to stay, but help us get these bastards off our backs."

NATALIE WINCES AS DANIEL HELPS her into the saddle with gentle but firm hands. His fingers find just the right crevices in her body to move her into place easily, yet still feel somehow like a caress. Her whole lower body trembles from riding so far yesterday. It's raining again this morning. The drizzle shrouds the fall air, and the pungent stew of damp soil, leaves, and horsehair envelops her.

They make good time and, by midmorning, arrive at the outskirts of one of the farms from which Daniel once purchased livestock. Before the peak, the farm was a small operation with fifty head of cattle and a brilliant red silo. The silo, still a brilliant red, juts up out of the dirty yellows of the poplars and birch surrounding the farm as they approach—an ominously cheery beacon for passersby. It's quiet. There are no cows in the east pasture, only the thrum of the rain on the tin roofs of some of the outbuildings.

Natalie and Daniel and the dogs approach the farmhouse with a white flag, while Justin and Scott remain back, guns ready. The ceramic dwarves, gnomes, and cartoon characters that had festooned the yard now lie in shards, the still-beaming pieces of their faces staring up at Natalie and Daniel. No smoke rises from the chimney.

The well sits in the middle of the farmyard. A makeshift pump has been fashioned from a steel pipe and an old axe handle. Swirls of green grass grow around the casing for the now-useless electrical pump. A spider web, its perfection outlined by shimmering beads of rain, is suspended between the pump handle and shaft. Daniel cranks the handle. After what seems like an eternity, a small trickle of water dribbles out in a dusty wheeze.

"I don't think anyone's here," he says.

They raise the flag high and drop it quickly, their signal to Justin and Scott to approach.

Natalie swallows at the strands of fear that wind down her throat. "These people were farmers. I can't believe they couldn't make it."

Daniel shrugs. "It was an older couple, in their fifties, with two boys. They mainly did cattle. And hay. Maybe they didn't know how to grow enough food, or preserve it."

Scott and Justin join them. They tie the horses to a fence and wander about tentatively, as if under surveillance. The drizzle has stopped, and the mosquitoes descend relentlessly. The tractor sits the middle of a field—out of gas, probably, and impossible to move. Weeds twine around each other in a small garden plot. Natalie can almost feel ghosts drifting around her, whispering their despair, their utter shock.

While Daniel and Justin head to the barn, Natalie and Scott enter the farmhouse—where they find a skeleton on the kitchen floor. The bones lie randomly on top of each other, like the skeleton has been kicked aside, or the limbs carved off one by one. The cupboards stand open and empty. Raiders, probably, moving on and through. A thick layer of dust coats every surface. Pots cover the top of the woodstove. Whatever had been in them has long since been eaten by someone, or something. A hand-drawn calendar on the yellow kitchen wall marks off the month, date, and year in tidy script. The last date marked is January, three years prior.

A thud sends a wave of fear down Natalie's spine, but she relaxes slightly when a cat walks into the room, purring loudly and weaving in and out of their legs, sleek and plump and black as midnight. Natalie smiles slightly. "How did you survive all this, kitty? You must be a good mouser. I'm surprised they didn't skin and roast you."

Natalie walks through the kitchen and into the gloomy living room and on past the fireplace hearth littered with wood debris and ashes. She presses her forehead against the cool pane of the back window.

Three graves lie in the yard behind the house, carefully marked with stick crosses. The couple had two boys, just like hers. Natalie doesn't even want to know which one of the four had to bury the other three.

Natalie is standing in the front walkway when Daniel returns from the barn. The cat sits beside her, watching with unflinching eyes. Scott and Justin have gone to the outbuildings to search for supplies. As Daniel draws nearer, the cat—sensing the imminent arrival of the dogs—disappears into an opening under the porch.

"Do you think it was raiders?" Natalie says, her voice almost a whisper. She lets her body lean into his so they're only a few inches apart.

Daniel points across the field. "The well's dry. Looks like they were starting to dig a new one and couldn't stop the cave-ins. They used an electric pump to get the water up from the creek for the cows and the fields. I'm not sure what they would have done when the electricity cut out. There's a huge pile of cattle bones, so someone must have slaughtered them, rather than let them all just die. My guess is that they turned the cows down to the creek, but couldn't keep up the hay production. So come winter they slaughtered the cows one by one and ate them. Maybe malnutrition. But lots of things could have gone wrong."

"What if we could have helped, given them seeds, helped them dig a new well? We've holed up for the last five years saving our own asses, while everyone around us dies."

"Nat, we don't know what happened here. It could be a seasonal creek. Without water, survival would be pretty tough. Could've been illness. Or raiders. Or maybe they just ran out of cows. We have no way of knowing whether we could have helped them or not."

Natalie stares at the graves. "We could have tried."

The cat, emboldened by the dogs' disinterest, butts against Natalie, purring. Natalie scoops it up, feeling the tiny thud of its heart.

There is nothing of use in the house or barn. If there were once antibiotics here, or any other supplies, they have been picked clean. The four of them leave in silence, their horses walking single-file across the mist-veiled fields. Natalie keeps glancing over her shoulder, unable to shake the feeling that they're being followed. The silo bobs in and out of sight like a clownish specter. But only the shadowy cat trails them across the fields. After a while, anxious that the cat has ventured too far from his home, Natalie picks the beast up and places him on her lap in the saddle. The cat, surprisingly, settles in for the ride.

They reach the next farm a half hour later. When they arrive, Natalie and Daniel go ahead with the white flag, as before; Justin and Scott stay behind. Nobody emerges to greet them or shoot them. Chicory and vetch wind around the bean and pea plants in the large garden, and the tomato plants lie on their sides, unstaked and browned in the sun. Puffy white seed heads sprout from the carrots and lettuce. The garden was clearly planted out this year, and then abandoned. The stable door creaks back and forth in the slight breeze, and sprays of darkened blood cover the dry earth beside the empty chicken coop. Chicken blood, Natalie hopes.

In the house, cupboards and drawers sit open, their contents turned out into a jumble on the floor. Furniture is overturned or smashed. Natalie and Daniel wade through a churn of clothes, DVDs, dishes, and books, their boots crunching on glass, while wind seeps through the shattered windows. The chaos and emptiness are too overwhelming.

Back outside, Justin and Scott stand beside a recently dug mass grave in one of the fields. Natalie and Daniel approach, and Daniel takes off his hat as if he's paying some sort of respects, then runs his hand through his hair, which stands at a rakish angle. His eyes glow a darker, more luminous green, seemingly deeper in their shock and despair. "I think we should go. There's nothing of use here," he says.

Natalie nods. She doesn't try to hide the tears that course down her face.

They return to their horses as the afternoon sun settles into the mountains, walking slowly and in silence, as if part of a funeral dirge. The cat mewls desperately at the prospect of being left behind, and Natalie lifts it up onto the saddle. They ride off into the dimming evening. Daniel falls in beside Natalie.

"What if we find nobody alive?" she says.

Daniel opens his mouth to answer, when Justin pulls up on the other side of her, and gestures in the direction of the river. "Smoke," he says.

CHAPTER 10
THE THREE OF CUPS

—⟶⟨⟩⟵—

NATALIE AND ANDREW

It is time to find solace and solutions in community.

As they draw nearer, the faint lilting sounds of a banjo drift over the trees with the smoke. The fire illuminates the silver hair of a man and woman seated on stumps. A small tent sits next to the fire, and two horses stand phantom-like in the trees. A pot hangs from a spit, and strings of fish dangle from a central stake over the flames. Five years ago, this couple would be someone's kindly grandparents on a camping trip. Natalie and Daniel approach with the white flag and guns drawn.

The man and woman stand, grasping crossbows that had been placed within arm's reach.

The woman speaks. "Are you friendlies?" Her face has the rounded, almost furry look of age.

"Yes… We're friendly," Natalie says.

The couple's crossbows remain trained on Natalie and Daniel. The woman speaks again. "Are you qualified? Do you have a passcode?"

Natalie feels a clutch of unease. "I'm sorry, we don't know what that is. But we are friendly. We should all put down our weapons."

"Not until you give us your full names and birthdates."

"We're the ones with the guns here," Daniel says.

"You're the one standing in a leg snare," the woman says. Natalie becomes dimly aware of the glint of metal around Daniel's foot, of the foolhardy nature of their approach, their false sense of safety because the pair is elderly. Richard would have scoped them out and ambushed. The woman, as if sensing Natalie's fear, calls out, "It's a precaution. Do as we ask, please. We don't want to hurt you."

Natalie glances at Daniel, who lifts his shoulders slightly as if to suggest they should, and then she and Daniel each provide their full names and birthdates in turn.

"Again," the woman orders. Natalie and Daniel repeat their names and birthdays. It seems surreal to hear Daniel saying Daniel Levi Johnston, like they're taking part in some strange wedding vow.

"All right, Natalie Jeanine Johnston, that's good enough." The woman lowers her crossbow, and the man lets go of the wire that's attached to the snare around Daniel's foot.

"Nine times out of ten, non-friendlies don't give you their real name, and then they can't remember the name they gave you. There's always a hesitation. That's how you know. I'm Ilene, and this is Fred. You may come and sit awhile at our fire. Watch, though. There are snares and traps all around us."

Fred's gray hair and bushy sideburns stick out in all directions. His smile reveals oddly spaced, yellowed teeth. His pants, hoisted high by wide suspenders, ripple with folds and indents, indicating they once fit a much larger man.

"My son and brother are back with our horses," Natalie says. "Is it okay if they join us?"

"Yes. Weapons on the ground though."

Natalie picks her way through the perimeter of snare wires and traps, and leads Scott and Justin back to the fire. Introductions are exchanged, and they all settle around the fire, perching on their packs, still too wary to get out their food and cooking supplies. Daniel pickets the horses and posts the dogs well outside the perimeter of the camp. The cat—Shadow, as Natalie has dubbed him—weaves in and out of legs, tail aloft. Natalie scoops him up every time he seems intent on heading out toward the circle of snares and traps.

"Now," says the woman. "Tell us where you're from."

Natalie decides to be circumspect. "We come from a farm about a day and a half ride up the river. You'll have to excuse us. We've been to a couple farms today. Everyone was dead or gone. We weren't totally prepared."

Ilene nods. "That's understandable. There are some people alive, living on small farms, and there are folks in Tanner's Ridge, but we don't go there. It's too unsafe."

"And who exactly are you?" Daniel says with his customary bluntness.

Natalie places her hand on Daniel's arm and smiles at Ilene and Fred. "Tell us about yourselves, and about this friendlies thing."

Ilene's return smile is broad and genuine, and there's almost a twinkle in her demeanor, like she possesses a deep heartfelt optimism of the sort that Natalie hasn't seen in many faces over the past five years. Natalie allows her hand to linger on Daniel's arm for just a few seconds.

"Fred and I were trappers before the peak. We always had kind of a subsistence lifestyle anyway on our trap-line. We never went into town for much. Just salt, flour, and diesel."

Fred adds, "And toothpaste and ciggies, of course."

Ilene continues. "Before things started to go bad, we stocked up on staples. We just had a feeling that if Wal-Mart couldn't make it, we were bound for trouble. Besides, there'd been all the talk of course."

Fred removes the fish from the spit and places them on two awaiting plates. The smell of the crisp flesh makes Natalie almost dizzy with hunger.

"So we hid out for a few years and just kept living the way we'd always lived," Ilene says. "Kept to ourselves. Planted a bigger potato crop. Took up fishing. Used candles instead of light bulbs. We never had any kids so we didn't have them to worry about."

"So, tell us who the friendlies are?" Daniel plasters a broad, toothy grin on his face. Natalie almost laughs at his strained effort at social nicety.

"Last year we started venturing out to see what was happening," Ilene says. "Almost got our heads blown off more than a couple of times. When we tried to go back to Tanner's Ridge, we found that the gangs had set up a perimeter guard. But then we met some folks who wanted to rebuild like us, so we coined the term "friendlies" and made a list. When you meet a friendly on the list, they can qualify you. Then you get a passcode so other friendlies know you're safe. We're trying to set up a network."

"How do you know unfriendlies haven't infiltrated your group?" Natalie says.

"We don't for sure. You just have to trust sometimes, but usually it's around the eyes. People who have a desperate way of living start to have a desperate way of looking."

"And are there lots of these…friendlies?" Daniel says.

"Not as many as we would like. We know about twenty people in this area, and some folks like yourselves who we've just met passing through. We don't know about Tanner's Ridge. We've heard gangs have taken over."

"Have you seen any signs of reorganizing, in terms of government or trade? Is anyone selling anything yet?" Natalie says.

Fred tosses a handful of chopped potatoes, turnips, and carrots into the frying pan and glances up. "There's no government, none that's reached here anyway, but we keep to the woods. Heard rumors of a provisional government in Vancouver. But that's all speculation. I'll be surprised if them lawyers and CEOs can pull their heads out of their asses down there in Lotus Land any time soon. I'm surprised the US hasn't invaded yet, to be honest. A man passed through in the early summer selling salt from Utah. He had a whole entourage of guards. Wouldn't take money, only gold."

Ilene interrupts. "We're planning a community gathering for Remembrance Day, after everyone has finished the fall harvest. Kind of a summit to start reorganizing. We need to reestablish trade and some sort of government, or we'll find ourselves having to accept the terms imposed on us by others. We're inviting all the friendlies we meet to gather at the old church hall in Jerry. You're welcome to join us."

Daniel looks at Natalie. "Wouldn't that be incredibly dangerous? Raiders could kill us all. And what if there's a freak storm?"

Fred nods. "We'd have sentries of course, and the storms are worse in the spring."

"But what if they infiltrate and attack from within?" Daniel persists.

Ilene takes a mouthful of fish. "Maybe if we figured out how we could give these people places to live and food to eat in exchange for labor, we could all sleep better."

Scott snorts from where he's unpacking one of the saddlebags. "If you think you can just offer some of these people a place on a farm, and they'll work and be happy, you're wrong. You don't know what it was like in Vancouver after the fall. The gangs rose up and took over so fast. It was like they were already there, waiting, frothing beneath the surface of our so-called society. They won't be farmers." He stalks off into the dark.

Natalie stares after him. Scott doesn't usually say much at all. She rises and looks at Ilene. "I'm sorry. You'll have to excuse my brother. His wife was killed by a mob in Vancouver. He's still struggling with it."

Daniel looks at her, but she shakes her head.

SHE FINDS SCOTT ON A rock, his head in his hands. Natalie sinks to the ground next to him.

"I can still see their faces. They were laughing. Laughing while they killed her. They told her she should have gone back to her own country. In Vancouver. It's my fault she's dead. She wanted to leave earlier, but I thought we should stay. I thought we could wait it out. It's all my fault."

"Scott," Natalie says. "It wasn't your fault. How could you have known?"

He raises his head and glares at her with wild eyes. "It was *absolutely* my fault. But the good news is I'm going to die soon anyway." He rises from the rock and paces away from her. Natalie looks at the revolver in Scott's waistband. He was not unacquainted with suicide attempts.

"What do you mean?"

Scott twists his mouth into a sharp smirk. "Didn't Mike tell you? I have karma cancer."

"What?"

"Mike figures I have cancer. Stomach cancer. Serves me right."

"Oh, no. Scott." She speaks the stilted words of the stunned.

The moon slips out from behind the clouds, illuminating the clearing and Scott's fierce expression. "It's okay. I want to die. I have nothing to live for. Mike's pretty broken up about it because he can't do anything for me. But I'm okay. This is what I deserve." His mouth twists into a dark smile. "I'm thinking I'm going to take up drinking again, though."

Natalie stares at him. He's been clean for seven years, but who is she to argue with the vices of a dying man? She wants a drink herself.

"Please don't think you deserve this, Scott. That's crazy. We'll find a hospital. We'll fix this."

Scott's eyes glitter in the moonlight. "You can't fix this, Nat. You know what? It actually makes me feel better. It's like penance. Don't tell anyone. I guess when I'm choking up blood you'll have to say something, but not before then."

"But we have to do something."

"There's nothing to do. I don't want to talk about it. I'm not even going to think about it. But those two are fools if they think they're going to solve the problems of this world with a gathering. It doesn't work that way anymore. I'm not sure it ever did. We just lived in some sort of fantasy interlude for the last half of the twenty-first century. It was nothing but a fucking façade, till the zombie apocalypse came and got us all. Do not go to that gathering unless you have a death wish. Now if you'll excuse me, I need a drink." Scott turns and marches back to the fire.

SCOTT'S MOOD STABILIZES A BIT after his first cup of moonshine. Fred and Ilene invite them to share their camp for the night, and after exchanging a few uncertain glances, Natalie and Daniel agree.

They eat, and then Fred's fingers dance skillfully across his banjo, the melody spiraling into the night air like the sparks of their fire. They tell jokes and exchange hunting and gardening tips. They pretend that things are sort of normal. They are friends on a campout. They will go home to their warm beds, nice homes, jobs, and whatever else they cherished before the peak.

Natalie absorbs the heat of the fire and the comfort of companionship. Letting her thigh press against Daniel's occasionally is both deliberate and unconscious. An act of treason perhaps, but a necessary one. Her brother is dying. Who knows, maybe *she* is dying. She should live, just a little bit. She's sure that she feels a small answering pressure from Daniel and the graze of his fingers when he passes the moonshine.

ANDREW CHECKS OVER THE LAST of the supplies he's stashed in the woods. Six guns—probably not enough—and a few dry biscuits and pemmican. The pemmican makes him gag, but it travels well. He put it in a tin; he hopes something doesn't eat it before Friday. He can't think of what else they'll need. Guns and horses—that's all they agreed to. But one of them is just the old .22 his dad gave him. Richard's kept the armory locked since the last attack. Andrew's managed to round up the three guns he knows Richard leaves lying around, plus the Glock his mom keeps under her bed and his Uncle Daniel's Winchester from the barn.

Andrew just hopes Anneke knows what she's doing, and he wonders for the seven millionth time if he shouldn't just march directly to his father and tell him what he's about to do. But that would land him in a world of trouble. Anneke's right: there's no way his dad would lend out guns.

Andrew returns to the farmhouse to find Richard in the midst of a dramatic dinner-table announcement that they will head to the ridge Thursday afternoon for a nighttime attack. Andrew reels with horror. Thursday is in three days. He and Craig weren't planning to leave until Friday.

Adding to Andrew's unease, Richard goes into detail about the direction from which they'll attack, who will be positioned where, and what they'll do if it doesn't go as planned. Richard generally springs his plans on his men just beforehand. Makes the troops less likely to balk, Richard always says, when advising Andrew on how to lead men. And Richard usually flies by the seat of his pants, going on gut after gauging the situation. For him to have the attack this planned out, and to announce it to everyone, reflects a fundamental shift in strategy, which makes Andrew nervous.

Craig and Liz's arrival in the kitchen for their meal is met by hushed giggles from the girls, like the arrival of a minor celebrity. Rachel sweeps around the room tossing her hair and sending dusky pouts at Craig. Craig sits stiffly eating, despite the fluttering of girls around him. He doesn't know yet that the attack day is Thursday. Andrew just hopes he's making the right choice, and that his mother would approve of his decision to try to help these people. Because Andrew is scared, pretty much shitless.

<hr />

THE LIGHT ON THE WALLS of the tent plays irritatingly around the corners of Natalie's eyes. The crows snarl and thrash outside. The cold hardness of the compacted earth seeps up through her sleeping bag, making her hip bone ache. Shadow nestles against her, the only spot of warmth. Justin sleeps peacefully, his blond hair falling in a curtain, long pale lashes curling up at a sharp unexpected angle. Natalie marvels at the perfection of his unlined face.

She huddles deeper into the warmth of the cat. Surely forty-two is old enough for her to go after what she wants? But Richard's potential reaction terrifies her. Would he let her go with grace and goodwill, or do his best to torture her? Probably the latter; even if he made a show of benevolence, he would find a way to get his digs in, undermining her position on the farm, making it clear he's better off without her, proving to her again and again that she made the wrong choice. And what of Daniel? For all her imaginings of him, she really has no idea what he would be like as a lover or a partner…or how he feels about her.

And now her brother is dying.

Natalie zips up her fleece and emerges from the tent, the demands of her bladder forcing an early start to the day. The sun dusts the mountaintops with pink and orange light. Mitch and Daisy glance up from their posts. Natalie had taken the first watch, and Ilene took the second. Fresh wood has been added to the fire, and a kettle hangs from the spit. Ilene sits on a rock a few yards away, her back to Natalie, mug in hand.

After emerging from the trees, Natalie pours herself some tea and sits next to Ilene.

"Good sleep?"

"Short, but I'm used to that now," Natalie says.

The older woman smiles and tips her face up toward the sky. "Sometimes, on mornings like this, I think the world is nicer now with fewer people. It's certainly quieter without the hum of highways and jets. But then we spend time with people like you, and I remember why we have to rebuild. Humans can't survive in small groups without interconnections. How will the children find people to marry? How will we reestablish trade? We need community. I hope you and your husband will help with that. I have a good feeling about you."

"My husband?" Natalie says. "You mean Daniel? He's my brother-in-law."

Ilene blinks in surprise. "Oh, goodness. Sorry. I just assumed."

"It's no big deal."

Ilene is silent for a few seconds, and Natalie steels herself against the inevitable feeling of judgment. It's foolish, she knows, this perpetual fear. The farm members pick and rip at the details of each other's lives, like crows over carrion. But outsiders might not be so quick to condemn.

Ilene rises and places a hand on Natalie's arm and flashes a kind smile, a smile devoid of the inner laughter Natalie imagines in the eyes of so many of the people who share her life. "We'd better start breakfast. Can I count on you and your husband, or brother-in-law, or both if you like, to come to the community gathering in Jerry?" Natalie is nearly felled by the woman's touch and goodwill. She has almost forgotten how people who have never met Richard look at her.

Natalie nods. "We'll do our best. But…"

"I know," Ilene says. "No promises. There are few promises in this new world."

THEY BREAK CAMP AN HOUR later. Ilene and Fred head west across the river while Natalie, Daniel, Justin, and Scott continue south. It has turned cold, and the sun has taken on a more watery quality. Shafts of sunlight splinter the crisp air. Natalie huddles in her jacket, glad of Shadow's sinewy heat.

They plan to search two largish farms that stocked animal antibiotics, before heading for the outskirts of Tanner's Ridge that evening. Natalie keeps glancing back, attempting to evaluate Scott's expression. He looks stormy, but composed.

They come upon the first farm shortly after lunch. It's out of the way, a fair distance from the river, less likely to be stumbled upon by raiders. It looks like it's been abandoned for several years: the fields are almost reclaimed by natural vegetation, and the house is full of cobwebs, dust, spiders, and vermin that scurry into corners when they enter.

They divide up. Natalie and Justin search the house, opening kitchen cupboards and medicine cabinets. Mouse feces litter the floor and counters and Natalie tries not to think of hantavirus as she rifles through drawers. They've become looters now. Each item must be evaluated for its value versus its weight. EpiPens, salt, Bic lighters, matches, ballpoint pens, toilet paper: yes. Coins, liquor, canned goods, heavy tools: no. Not on this trip.

Natalie has accumulated a small pile of working pens when Scott appears ghost-like behind her, cradling several brown bottles. Natalie's eyes automatically skim the labels: Combi-Pen and Di-Methox. Broad-spectrum antibiotics.

"I found them in the barn. Tucked up behind some boxes. Daniel thought there was nothing, but I checked through every box, even the empty-looking ones."

Natalie embraces Scott. He stands stiff for a few seconds, but then relaxes marginally. Seven bottles. Expired of course. But even so, each one feels like a small miracle.

They complete their search of the house. Natalie looks at some of the children's clothes, willing herself not to think of who wore them. They need new clothes on the farm, but she can't bring herself to gather them up. They would be too bulky anyway. She approaches Daniel, who checks through the farm machinery for spare parts, his head down.

"You let Scott find them?" she says.

Daniel glances up briefly and shrugs. "Everybody needs to be the hero sometimes."

"Thank you." She places the tips of her fingers on top of his on the hitch of a tractor. This is bold, and yet far less than what she wants to do. She wants to fold herself into his arms, feel the length of his body against hers, press her lips against the skin of his neck, and know that he loves her.

A hint of panic flits through his eyes, and he looks away, but not before his fingers lift fractionally to intertwine with hers.

⸙

RICHARD HOLDS A MEETING TO finalize the plan of attack on the ridge. They will ride out Thursday around noon. Paul and Bob, never straying too far from their former pacifist—or as Richard less politely calls it, pantywaist minister and university professor—ways, argue rancorously about being forced to go. Bob blunders about, muttering about conscription and workers' rights. But with Daniel and Scott gone, and Mike too valuable to risk, they're the only choices. Ramona, Bob's wife, declares she's going, to "make sure Bob doesn't get shot."

Andrew tries to memorize the sketched map Richard has prepared. The best sharpshooters, Terrence and Solomon, will snipe from the east, while the rest of the party sweeps in from the south. They'll take out some of the key men on the ridge, and force the rest of the raiders to clear out. Richard bustles with vigor as he wanders around the room giving pep talks and telling jokes.

Anneke stands with her arms crossed during most of the planning session. The lunch stew is scorched and the buns burned. Anneke places the blackest bun on Richard's plate. Richard scrapes the bun into the garbage and helps himself to another, then approaches Andrew, suggesting they could use another sniper. If Andrew wants to go, Richard will smooth things over with Natalie. He cocks his head in shock when Andrew declines. But he claps his son on the back with a laugh, saying it's okay to be scared, that he understands. There will be other missions, just as long as Andrew doesn't go "permanently chicken" on him.

Chicken, thinks Andrew. More like Benedict Arnold. About to get exiled, or killed.

CHAPTER 11

TEMPERANCE

—ⷮⷮⷮ—

DANIEL AND ANDREW

Rebuild by adding the old to the new.

They start to pass more houses after they turn onto the rural highway that leads to Tanner's Ridge, most of them darkened and silent, with broken windows and overgrown grass. They don't bother with these places. They look only for the large farm operations that would have treated their own animals. Daniel scans constantly for threats, his emotions a jangle of knots. They cut through abandoned fields, keeping the highway in sight, but staying well out of the line of view of other potential travelers.

Daniel is in the lead as they crest a small rise. A blackened curl of smoke twists out of the chimney of a white clapboard farmhouse nestled in the valley. Mitch drops to a crouch, a growl rumbling deep in his belly. Daisy stiffens and starts to bark.

A man steps out from behind a tree, his shotgun cocked. Bulgy blue eyes look down the barrel. The man's clothes hang off his lanky frame.

"Please don't shoot. We come in peace," Natalie says. "We're just traveling to Tanner's Ridge."

The man doesn't move. "I don't trust strangers anymore, coming in peace or otherwise." A small girl with blond hair peers at them from behind a large gray rock several yards behind the man. Daniel almost cringes. They can't let this go bad. He grasps for any potential way to keep this under control.

"We have bullets and other items to offer in trade," Daniel says, "if you're willing to put down your gun and talk."

Something infinitesimal shifts in the man's face; raw desperation replaces the hostility for a fraction of a second. He needs the bullets. "Call off your dogs, and throw your guns on the ground," he says.

"I'm going to get off my horse," Daniel says. "Then we all have to put down our guns at the same time." He swings his leg slowly over his horse to the ground.

The man starts backing toward the rock. "Don't come any closer, or I'll shoot." His shaking hands make the gun vibrate. Daniel braces for the crack of the shotgun, but he only hears the whoosh of his own blood pumping in his ears.

Daniel places his gun on the ground in front of him. "Please talk to us. I've put down my weapon. Natalie and Justin will put theirs down next, and then you and Scott—that's him over there"—Daniel points—"need to put yours down at the same time."

The man stares at Daniel, his face grim with distrust. Natalie and Justin dismount, creep forward, and place their guns next to Daniel's. Natalie inclines her head slightly as if to ask Daniel if he knows what he's doing, if he's got this. He doesn't, of course. He's out on a limb with his pants down. But he can't let the little girl get shot.

"Let's help each other." Daniel removes a small tin of bullets from his pocket, relieved to see that his own hands aren't trembling. "I'm willing to bet your gun's not loaded."

"Don't assume that. What kind of bullets do you have?"

"Slugs for a 12-gauge."

"What are you looking for in trade?" the man says.

Daniel looks at Natalie. "You got any milk or cheese?"

The man shakes his head. Daniel racks his brain for what else they would accept in trade. "We'll take fresh vegetables or meat."

"We have no extra food."

"Then what do you have?"

The man smiles with bland tightness. "Same as most people. Nothing useful. TVs, an old laptop, cell phones, but I don't suppose you want any of that. I have some old jewelry. I hear they're taking that in Tanner's Ridge."

Two blond girls, twins, about six years old, appear from behind the rock and start to approach their father. He turns on them almost in a frenzy. "Stay there!" One of the little girls bolts obediently back to the rock; the other huddles on the ground in a ball, sniffling.

"It's okay," Natalie says. "Please. We won't hurt them. Can you give us information in trade? We'd like to hear anything you know about traders, strangers passing through these parts, or news from Tanner's Ridge. Are you part of the friendlies network? Ilene and Fred?"

The man's bushy brows draw together. "Those two kooks? They're going to end up shot with all their friendlies talk." But something in him has shifted. He glances around them. "We shouldn't be out in the open. We can go down and talk in the trees by my farm."

"We're taking our guns back then," Daniel says.

"Fair enough. But I'm bringing up the rear," says the man. "Consider it mutually assured destruction if anyone gets trigger-happy."

Natalie slips behind to walk with the man as they proceed down the hill. Daniel, Justin, and Scott lead the horses. Daniel hates the thought of a rifle at his back, but reminds himself it's probably not loaded. He strains to make out what Natalie and the man are saying, while searching the house and yard for any sort of ambush. The paint on the white clapboard house is peeling and an inferno of smoke rises from the chimney. The grass gathers in unmowed tufts, and freshly turned furrows of soil carve through the large garden, but piles of decaying plants sit on the side of the field waiting to be composted.

Daniel stops at the edge of the farm and turns around to face Natalie and the man. The two small girls run ahead and into the house. Natalie looks at Daniel. "Neil's wife is ill. I told him that Justin is training to be a doctor and you're a vet. I think we should try to help them." A nerve in Daniel's neck twitches. Treating humans scares the shit out of him. He's had to do it a few times, when there've been too many wounded and Mike and Justin have been busy. He's good with the needle and the scalpel, but not so good with the diagnoses. It's only a matter of time before someone dies because the vet made the wrong call. But Natalie, for some reason, has always seemed supremely confident in his abilities.

The man looks at Justin, who even at eighteen is unmarked by the shadows of facial hair and stands slight and elf-like. "Isn't he a little young?"

"I've studied for four years under a doctor," Justin says.

"I don't know," says Neil. "How do I know you know what you're doing?"

Justin seems unfazed by the man's skepticism. "I could take a look."

The man's mouth twists into a grim smirk that trembles around the edges. Daniel knows that look. It's the look of someone about to weep, someone out of options. He can't even conceive of the utter loneliness and desperation one would feel out here trying to make it alone. The man pulls himself together and nods.

Justin removes his small medical bag from the saddlebag. They follow Neil into the house, while Scott stays outside to guard the horses.

The kitchen is scorching. A girl of about sixteen chops tomatoes, her thick blond hair caught up in a knot, wet strands falling into her face. Her cheeks are slick and flushed. She draws her eyes open wide, but says nothing. A wood stove in the living room belts out heat while two pots perch on top at a full boil. Throat-parching woodsmoke and steam cloud the air. Neil sighs. "Hannah's trying to keep up with the canning, but she can't without help."

"We can help for a bit, while Justin checks in on your wife," says Natalie, removing her outer layers and rolling up her sleeves. A droplet of sweat slides down Daniel's back. Natalie nudges him further into the room and smiles at the girl. "I'm Natalie, and this is Daniel. Why don't you tell us what to do?" Justin and the twins follow Neil into a back room. Hannah clutches her knife and stares at them. Natalie smiles. "I can chop, and Daniel can watch the pot and restock the stove."

Hannah nods slowly. Natalie picks up a knife and starts chopping, directing Daniel with her eyes over to the stove. Steam hangs in a thick wall around the stove, and the heat almost makes Daniel stagger backward. He steadies himself against the brick hearth and stares at the pot. The water seethes and churns around the glass jars.

They work in silence. Hannah barely looks up from her cutting board. Her hands, abraded from the acids in the fruits, bleed at the knuckles. She's slender, bordering on underweight, but not starving, and there's a sensuous curve to her lips and cheeks. This girl would have known life before the peak, and now her life must seem akin to slavery.

Justin and Neil emerge from the bedroom and gesture to Natalie and Daniel to follow them to the porch. One of the twins scrambles up onto a chair on the other side of the stove to watch the pot, her face solemn, the tendrils of her hair straggly and damp.

Daniel sucks in the cool air outside with relief. The pallid sun hasn't penetrated the foggy clouds that bathe the mountaintops.

"The puncture wound on Lauren's foot is infected," Justin says. "It's bad. She needs antibiotics immediately, and we have to get her away from that heat to bring her fever down."

Neil's face sags with the weight of unshed tears. "Are you sure?"

"You saw the foot, those red streaks running up her leg. The fever. You don't need a doctor to tell you how bad it is." Justin raises his eyebrows at Natalie and Daniel.

Daniel doesn't clue in to what he's trying to communicate, but Natalie looks at her son and nods.

Justin turns back to Neil. "We have some antibiotics. I'll stay here, and treat her. The others can pick me up on their way back."

Daniel glances at Natalie. From the hollowness in her cheeks he can tell that her teeth are clamped tightly together. She won't like Justin's proposal to stay behind in the slightest.

"Why would you do all this for us? I can't pay you," Neil says.

"We're neighbors, and please don't get your hopes up. I'm going to go start the first dose, and then we need to move her to the barn or shut down that stove." Justin heads toward the horses.

Neil sinks to the ground and presses his face into his hands. Natalie follows Justin, leaving Daniel standing uselessly next to Neil. He can't make out Natalie's words, but he hears snatches of her voice and he knows she's upset.

Daniel studies the pale disk of the sun until it threatens to etch into his eyes. The winters have grown shorter, but more erratic, bringing wild snowstorms in the shoulder months. Sometimes Daniel thinks he can smell them coming, but today the air is still sweet with fall. He shivers. The sweat on his body has turned cold.

Daniel noticed Justin's double take when he looked at Hannah. Daniel knows the motivations, the needs, of an eighteen-year-old boy. Especially an eighteen-year-old boy living on a farm where there are no girls. Justin stalks into the house, his conversation with his mother clearly over. Daniel walks over to Natalie and Scott.

"I'll stay with him," Scott says. "And make day trips to other farms around here to see if they have any more antibiotics."

"Are you in any shape for that?" Natalie says.

"We'll be fine."

"How can you possibly say that?" Natalie says.

"We haven't encountered any hostiles," Daniel says. "We're only going to Tanner's Ridge. If we leave now, we'll be back in two days. I can leave Daisy with Scott and Justin." His mind reels at what he's saying. He's almost pushing for this, which is probably a bad idea, as it goes against rule number one with Natalie, which is to attempt to preserve the safety of her two boys at all costs. He cannot even imagine being responsible in any way for a plan that resulted in harm coming to Justin.

Natalie closes her eyes and tilts her head toward the sky. Daniel waits for her refusal. She will never agree to leave Justin.

"Okay," she says.

Daniel feels an odd quiver of shock. He can't believe she said yes. He is about to be alone with the woman who is the center of his fantasies and dreams. A woman he possibly loves; a woman who is his brother's wife. He curses his bad good luck and reins his emotions in tightly.

They move Lauren to the small barn on an old door, settling her on a bed of straw as Justin starts to apply cool compresses. Daniel tries to conceal his dismay at her flushed, quaking form. This is why he could never be a doctor. Justin goes about his care with practiced hands. Neil hovers about, watching. Daniel wonders if he should leave his nephew with advice or warnings with respect to safety, but most of the time the boy seems more competent at life than Daniel. Daniel settles for a nod and a curt "see you in a couple of days," and hopes to God the boy will be all right.

Scott unloads and tethers their horses and then goes about pitching the tent. Natalie stands in the yard, staring back at the barn. Daniel doesn't want to push her—perhaps she's changing her mind—so he stands and waits. After several minutes, Natalie heaves herself into the saddle and heads her horse west. Daniel follows, his heart a clamor of too many emotions.

❧

ANDREW LEADS THE HORSES THROUGH the trees. He has chosen three from the upper pasture—two older horses and one recovering from a torn ligament. Not exactly the most stellar of the bunch, but the least likely to be missed. Thank God the other men are distracted by their own preparations. His Uncle Daniel would notice right away, of course, but he's not there. Andrew feels horrible leaving the poor beasts by themselves for two nights, but he has the chance to slip off with them and it might not come again. He has to try and get saddles somehow tomorrow. He tethers the horses by their halters some distance apart, taking care to entwine the halters deep in low-lying bushes. If someone finds them, it might be plausible that they wandered off and got tangled in the bushes. He feeds and waters them and then makes his way to the schoolroom.

Three rows of students look up as he saunters to his seat. Joanne gives him her usual "whatever" look. In an independent learning environment, lateness is allowed as long as you finish your work. He opens his algebra notebook, a mishmash of recycled paper sewn together, and works the problems.

Math questions completed, Andrew stares out the window, trying not to let his edginess show. This whole math thing is a waste of his time. It's not like he'll ever go to university. He watches the glossy back of Rachel's head as she cranes forward from the front row, trying to make out the printing on the board. He just hopes Rachel comes through tomorrow morning. The whole plan borders on colossally stupid, but it might work. Jane, Colleen, and Mike are on early watch, and the two women will be useless without Mike. Andrew hopes. He's sent an email to Hans telling him to expect them on Thursday.

If they manage to sneak away tomorrow morning, they'll have time to get to the ridge before his father arrives with the rest of the ridge mission party, as long as Craig and Liz aren't missed too early.

⸞⸞⸞

DARKNESS SWEEPS THE LANDSCAPE BY the time Natalie and Daniel reach the outskirts of Tanner's Ridge. They make camp in the woods far out of town, keeping their fire small. The town, which once glowed with the lights of houses and streetlights, sits somber and dark, save for a few bonfires that form an uneven ring around the town.

The two of them sit by the fire, guns resting across their laps. Mitch sleeps close by, his breath coming in short puffs. They laid their bedding out in the single tent. Someone has to keep watch, so they're not going to be in the tent at the same time, but their side-by-side sleeping bags caused him to experience an unnerving cascade of images: skin and nakedness and whispered affections.

Daniel gropes for words, anything useful to say. But he's never been a conversationalist, and even the tritest commentary escapes him now. He swims in a welter of obscure discussion possibilities, while she studies him from the other side of the fire, probably expecting him to say something. She must think him a hapless lunatic, sitting across from her slack-jawed and stunned. He's so absorbed in his lack of conversation that he almost doesn't hear her when she speaks.

"Have you ever thought of where we'd all be if none of this happened?"

"Uh, no." He feels a vestige of panic at the direction of the conversation. Where is she going with this?

She cocks her head and the firelight casts a flush on her cheeks. "You don't imagine you might have wanted to get married? Have kids?"

Daniel searches for some reasonable answer. Some explanation for his interminable bachelorhood that doesn't involve confessing that, for the past twenty years, he has loved only one woman. She is probably just being kind. She's like that, always looking out for him, making sure he's included. Like a sister.

"Never met the right person," he says lightly. "And besides, I'm pretty good at being alone."

"What about me?" she says.

He stares at her in the gloom, struggling to process her words. "What?"

"What about me? Have you ever considered anything between us other than friendship?" she repeats.

A burn of embarrassment creeps up Daniel's neck. He casts his mind back for any inappropriate behavior on his part. "What? No."

"You don't feel anything for me?"

He feels like an elk in the crosshairs of her rifle, his pupils dilated, his feet frozen for a millisecond before bolting. How can he answer that? Why is she asking? Has she noticed the way he looks at her? Has Richard made some joke about him being a lovesick idiot? Is she trying to let him down gently? Guilt flutters in his stomach and collects in his throat. "No. I don't know." The rational safe part of him says this, while the rest of him howls defiantly in disagreement.

She nods and sits there for a few minutes staring at him, the firelight highlighting the curve of her lips and the shimmer of gold in her hair. He should say something more, but his heart is pounding mercilessly in his chest.

She smiles at him, and the faint wrinkles around her eyes that he has always wanted to kiss crease. "Go to bed. I'll take first watch."

Daniel moves into the tent wordlessly, his mind spinning. He crawls into his sleeping bag and stares at hers.

CHAPTER 12

THE SEVEN OF WANDS

~oeeo~

NATALIE AND ANDREW

Conquer your fear and stand up for what you believe in.

The dream is joyous, at least in the beginning. Natalie dances with abandon in the woods in dazzling blue shoes. When she returns home, mud cakes the bottom and sides of the shoes. She tries to hide them from Richard, but he reprimands her for trailing dirt through the house. Her fury and shame shake her awake.

"No. I don't know," Daniel had said last night. There was a possibility, then. A small thing to hang on to.

Daniel prepares porridge when Natalie emerges from the tent. They had switched over in silence in the early morning, carefully avoiding contact in the gloom of the tent, with no reference to their declarations from the night before. She notes the indefinable grace in his movements, in the set of his lips. Everything he does whispers to her of intimacy and truth and sex, and it wraps around her, pulling her in again and again. He skirts the outside of the camp as he makes breakfast, avoiding any potential intersection of their paths.

"I assume we're going to go around Tanner's Ridge," Natalie says.

He nods and looks relieved at the choice of topics. "We better. There're only two of us. There's nothing to be gained by going through. The veterinary office is way down South Road on the other side of town. I'm sure it's been stripped clean, but there are farms down the road."

She catches him watching her as they strike camp. She's used to the appraising looks of men, but Daniel's glances have always been different. Kinder, perhaps, hungry sometimes, but with a strange undercurrent of solidarity.

They skirt Tanner's Ridge. They pass travelers on foot or horseback, mostly in twos and threes, dressed in a jumble of old garb and travel cloaks made from blankets and plastic bags. Like Natalie and Daniel, they carry their weapons openly—deterrents for any would-be thieves or killers. The travelers avoid eye contact, and after a few attempts at smiles or nods, Natalie does the same. The protocols of the new world. These people are evidently not part of Ilene and Fred's network of friendlies, or perhaps they have their own network.

The houses seem to gape at them with their broken windows and blackened interiors. Most appear empty, but the windows of some have been boarded up, and smoke floats from the chimneys. Natalie cringes every time they pass one. Who might be watching them from inside?

They consider searching some of the deserted houses, but decide against it. It's too hard to tell if the houses are occupied, and even if they aren't, the neighbors might not be kindly disposed toward looters. The person going into the house alone would be in danger, and the person staying outside alone with the horses would be in danger. Without Scott and Justin, this mission is far more challenging—and, Natalie begins to realize, potentially fruitless.

At the end of a narrow country road south of town, Natalie spots the veterinary office. It's a squat cinderblock building surrounded by a thrash of wild grass that was once a lush lawn. The metal frame is all that's left of the front door, and a scatter of glass litters the white floor just inside. They decide to risk it; the building and surrounding area appear deserted. Daniel draws his gun and steps under the metal bar of the door, while Natalie takes up a post outside. A pileated woodpecker swoops down in a red and black streak and scolds Natalie from the roof of the office while Daniel crunches through the glass inside. Mitch, perturbed by Daniel's departure, chases around the outskirts of the building, thrusting his nose into each crack to sniff wildly. Does Mitch know something that they don't? Daniel returns and shakes his head.

"Everything's gone," he says. "I think we're wasting our time."

"There was a pet store in town. We could check there."

Daniel looks at Natalie and then turns to study the smoke that clusters thick over the center of town. He says nothing.

"We haven't met anyone who's threatened us. We've brought things to trade. Maybe we can trade, or at least buy free passage," Natalie says.

"Or we could be robbed and murdered," Daniel says.

"I think we have to try."

Daniel gets on his horse. Natalie follows. When they emerge back onto the main road from the lane, Daniel turns in the direction of town. They ride slowly. She has just demanded a fool's mission, and a possibly deadly one at that, and yet he is accompanying her without comment, without making her feel small and mistaken.

They pick their way down the potholed pavement flanked by silent houses. The heavy smell of smoke weights the air. Natalie isn't surprised when six men with drawn guns step out from a garage and block the road, but her heart begins to thud in dull, unforgiving heaves. The men wear mostly navy-collared shirts and jeans, old, but in good repair—almost like they've made an attempt at a uniform. Each man has a red strip of material tied around his arm.

The burly man in front speaks. His teeth flash white in his dark beard. "This is a tariff-controlled area."

"We are peaceful and come to trade," Natalie replies. Her rein hand shakes. Three men have moved to block the road behind them.

"You still have to pay the tariff to get into this part of Tanner's Ridge."

"How much is the tariff?"

"An ounce of gold per person. We also accept platinum, alcohol, tobacco, salt, munitions, fresh game, and slaves." His eyes snake down to her breasts and buttocks.

"And to get out?" Natalie says.

"Variable. Depends how long you stay and what you get up to." The white teeth draw into a tight smile.

"And if we just decide to turn around and leave now?"

"You still have to pay the tariff."

"I see." Natalie's thighs join her hands in quaking. She wonders if profiteering border guards and despots now litter the country. "We have jewelry. Will that work?"

"As long as you meet the required weight. Otherwise we'll take your guns and horses."

Natalie reaches carefully into her saddlebag and selects a handful of the jewelry that she collected from the farmwomen before departing. A shorter man steps forward to take it, lowering his gun. He wears jeweler's glasses and carries a briefcase. He sets the briefcase down, opens it, and withdraws a set of old-fashioned beam balance scales, a notepad, and a calculator. He weighs each item, checks the karats, punches some numbers into the calculator, and makes an inscription in his notebook. He nods to the first man, and the men blocking the road step aside.

The man smiles again. Natalie notices that his back teeth are all gold. "Thank you for your payment. Welcome to Tanner's Ridge. Enjoy your stay. No shooting, no stealing, no looting, no feeding the animals. We have the rule of law here, and we enforce it."

Natalie and Daniel proceed slowly past and head farther into town, and likely farther into danger. Natalie looks back at the men who have rearranged themselves around a table in the garage and resumed a card game. She wonders how many other men sit in garages around town extracting tolls.

"I'm sorry," she says to Daniel.

"No need to be," he says. "I agreed to this too. We have to play it out now."

Beyond the gatekeepers, smoke rises from chimneys, laundry hangs from lines, and rows of tomatoes and squash cover the fronts of yards. A few people walk up and down the streets or work in gardens. Most avoid eye contact, but a few look up, their faces wan and dirty. Everybody carries a weapon. Even the children have knives tucked into belts and pockets. The continuous clanging of metal on metal reverberates down the street. A blacksmith shop, Natalie guesses, not too far down the way. They can see the main street, with its board-ed-up windows and shattered glass fronts. Hand-painted signs hang from telephone poles, directing them to the Tanner's Ridge Trading Post.

"I assume that's where we're headed," Daniel says.

"Doesn't look like there's anywhere else," Natalie says. Daniel edges Shadowfax closer to Serendipity and looks like he's about to say something, but changes his mind.

"Let's get it done then," he says. The sun beats against the back of her neck. Midday. They need to be well away from town before dark.

They arrive at the main street. Several people walk purposefully down the road with baskets filled with produce and tidy paper-wrapped parcels. The hammering noise is fainter. *Tanner's Ridge Trading Post* is scrawled in big, blue, lopsided letters on a white stucco storefront. Music emerges from the tall brick building next to the Trading Post—a bar, or a brothel, Natalie realizes, when she sees women standing in lingerie in the window. Skeletal men and women in tattered clothes sit in a row on the curb with pots or blankets in front of them and signs begging for food. Small children lean against the adults, their skin lank and sagging, their bodies too compact and angled for their age.

Natalie dismounts and removes several pieces of pemmican and dried apple from her saddlebag. Her lunch. She thrusts it at the children. They snatch at it, but the adults are faster, pulling it out of Natalie's hands and shoving it into gaping mouths. A scuffle breaks out and two women claw at Natalie's pants and arms. Daniel leaps forward, waving the butt of his rifle as Natalie jumps back with a scream. The people fall back into their seats on the curb, their heads bowed.

A teen boy, not more than thirteen, watches from the sidewalk. "Don't you know you aren't supposed to feed the animals?"

"These aren't animals. They're people," Natalie says.

The boy shrugs. "They can't grow or hunt. Half of them can't even talk."

Natalie looks closer and sees the unfocused eyes and the slack in some of the faces. These would have been people in care before the peak, the infirm or mentally ill. A toddler with long lashes peers at Natalie from behind a woman rocking herself on a blanket.

"But you can't just leave them to starve," Natalie says.

"They get scraps here and there. Who's going to look after them?"

"Where do they sleep?"

The boy shrugs again. "Around. There're lots of empty buildings."

"But they have children," Natalie says.

"Look, I don't make the rules. They're lucky the Red haven't run 'em out of town. Are you going into the Trading Post? 'Cause if you are, I can watch your horses for a price. Can't leave 'em alone out front or they'll be gone in seconds."

"How do we know you won't take them?" Daniel says.

"I got a business to run. And besides, the Red don't tolerate horse thieves."

"But I thought you said they'd be gone in seconds."

"I said they'd be gone." The boy gestures across the street to an open square where a wooden platform stands with a solid wooden beam above it. A platform for hangings. "I didn't say the person would get away with it. But the horses would be impounded as evidence."

"How much to look after the horses?" Natalie says.

"Quarter ounce."

Natalie looks at Daniel. A flicker of uncertainty shifts across his face before he replaces it with an affected air of authority. "Half now, and half after we come back out and the horses and my dog are still here," Daniel says. He is not Richard in these situations, and that's sometimes good, and sometimes bad.

Natalie passes the boy a necklace, then unstraps the saddlebags containing the rest of the jewelry and bullets and hands them to Daniel.

The cool dimness of the Trading Post washes over Natalie. It's set up like a general store, with an open center floor and a counter running in a horseshoe around the room. Shelves of neatly arrayed merchandise extend from floor to ceiling. Most of the items are old. Looted, probably, taken from the homes of the dead, or the local dump. Pots and pans, old clothes, blankets, tinned goods. Wood stoves ripped out of walls, their chimneys leaning precariously, stand in a cluster in the center of the room. A produce section with fresh tomatoes, lettuce, and tree fruit stands at the far end of the shop, next to seeds, garden tools, and loaves of bread. Natalie's stomach claws at emptiness. They're low on food, and she wonders if they should buy some, but they're low on gold as well. A jumble of cosmetics and hair dyes occupies one shelf: shiny unopened boxes in the shades nobody ever wanted. An "Accepted Currencies" sign hangs over the till, advertising that in addition to gold they accept livestock, grain, and munitions.

"Can I help you?" The white-haired shopkeep wears the same navy shirt with red armband of the border patrol, and has an automatic handgun tucked into his belt. His expression is guarded but not unfriendly. A door to a back room is open and two men can be seen sorting stock.

Daniel steps up to the counter. He taps his boot on the floor, as if to emphasize his importance, and draws himself up to his full height. "We're looking for antibiotics."

The man snorts. "You and everyone else."

"For fish."

"You have pet fish?"

Daniel cocks his head. "Let's say I do. Do you have any fish antibiotics that you may have collected from the pet store in town?"

The man twists his mustache. "You a doctor?"

"No," Daniel says.

"We only sell antibiotics to doctors."

"Let's say I am a doctor then."

"Prove it and you're welcome to buy some."

"What's the price?"

"Two ounces a bottle."

Daniel emits a barky sort of laugh. "That's ridiculous. That's like eighteen hundred dollars for a bottle."

"Scarcity, my friend. Tell you what, you do a quick diagnosis and tell us the dosages for humans, and we'll give you a deal. An ounce per bottle. Maximum six bottles."

Daniel opens his mouth too wide in almost a snarl. Natalie cuts in. "Thanks. We need to talk for a minute." She draws Daniel back out onto the sidewalk. The horses thankfully stand patiently with the boy.

"This is highway robbery," Daniel says.

"Of course it's highway robbery. What did you expect? Can you tell him the doses for humans?"

"I don't know if it's by weight, or if humans tolerate less or more than animals."

"Well, you're going to have to give him some numbers and hope that they're right."

"And what if they're not? We could end up killing people."

"And the diagnosis?"

"Just do your best and let's get out of here."

Daniel's lip twitches and he narrows his eyes at her, but he says nothing.

The long-lashed toddler who stared at Natalie earlier has now wandered away from her mother on the curb and stands watching Natalie and Daniel with solemn eyes in a skull that seems hopelessly too large for her body. What are the ethics of stealing a child in these circumstances? What are the ethics of *not* stealing her?

They return inside. Six bottles of Fish Mox sit on the counter.

A wan and thin girl with a deformed and swollen neck stands beside the man. Natalie tries to control her own recoil, but feels some of the tension exit Daniel's body. The man gestures at the girl, and Daniel approaches and lifts his hand to her neck.

"May I?" he says. The girl inclines her head.

Daniel palpates her neck. "It's goiter," he says after a few seconds. "She needs to eat iodized salt, or take small doses of iodine."

"Are you certain?" the man says.

"Quite," Daniel replies.

"It's not cancer?"

Daniel hesitates for the briefest of seconds and then shakes his head.

"What if we don't have iodine?"

"Feed her the thyroid gland of a sheep or pig. It's in the neck."

The man nods as if satisfied and pushes the Fish Mox across the counter at them.

They pay the man, and Daniel writes the antibiotic dosages on a piece of paper. Natalie hugs the contours of their limited cache of jewelry remaining in the saddlebag. The price for exiting Tanner's Ridge better be the same as for entering.

Outside, Daniel pays the boy who watched the horses. Wanted posters reminiscent of the Wild West cover a bulletin board fastened to the white stucco. A poster in the bottom left catches Natalie's eye. It's a sketch of the tattooed raider from the ridge. *Wanted in the murder of 10 Tanner's Ridge residents*, reads the poster. And she had proposed taking him in.

Natalie's body slides into the spiral that precedes a faint: the narrowing of vision, the splotches in front of her eyes. She reaches for the wall to steady herself, and feels Daniel's arm curve around her ribcage to catch her.

"When's the last time you ate?" Daniel's voice comes at her from a distant tunnel. She always joked she'd be a shitty person to have around in a famine.

"I'll eat as soon as we get out of town."

He lets go of her and gently nudges her back into an upright position, and she tries not to ache at the loss of his touch.

They mount the horses. The early-afternoon sun sears at her eyes as they make their way down the main street. The faint sound of music filters out of the brothel.

They reach the border crossing without incident. The men emerge as before, but Natalie can't help but notice that they seem twitchier than they did earlier, and form a tighter circle around Natalie and Daniel.

The bearded man approaches. "Thank you for visiting Tanner's Ridge. We've been given to understand that this man is a doctor. So I'm afraid he'll be unable to leave."

"What?" Daniel says.

"Scarcity, my friend. We're in need of a medical practitioner here. The last doctor had an unfortunate accident. Your wife can stay too."

"What if we don't want to stay?"

The guns pointed at them jerk to attention and the bearded man shakes his head. "'Fraid that's not a choice."

Natalie opens her mouth to declare that Daniel is a vet, even if it means surrendering the antibiotics, when the blast of rifle fire shatters the air. One of the border guards drops to his knees. Armed men with green shirts have approached the circle of men from Natalie and Daniel's left and are firing at the guards. The border guards whirl and return fire.

Daniel grabs Serendipity's harness and kicks his heels into Shadowfax. The horses, spooked by the gunfire, hesitate. A bullet pierces Natalie's upper arm, and the pain that rips through her body is so intense that she nearly falls out of the saddle. The horses bolt, and she's jerked back and then careens to the side into Daniel, her leg pressed between the two horses. Blood streams down her arm. Daniel snatches at her, pulling her up and off Serendipity, but he can't quite hold her and she slips out of his arm and falls with a thud to the ground. The pain in her arm and the jolt of the landing are too much, and she feels the pavement rush toward her face as Daniel skids Shadowfax to a stop ahead of her.

NATALIE AWAKES IN A BED of straw in the stall of a stable, with Mitch's warm and furry body pressed tightly against her. Shadowfax and Serendipity stand in the stalls on either side of her. Her arm is bandaged, and pain still courses through her body with an intensity that makes her teeth chatter. Her head pounds with a shattering throb that reaches every indentation of her skull. Worse, though, is the feeling of fog that shrouds her brain.

"Daniel," she manages. Her voice sounds slurred.

A young woman in a green kerchief looks over the stall wall. "I'm afraid he's busy. He said he would be back soon."

"What? Where is he?"

The woman walks around the corner of the stall, a carving knife tucked into a leather thong attached to her belt. A low growl vibrates through Mitch's body. "I told you. He's busy. Operating."

"Operating? On what?"

"Not your concern. No more questions. Rest."

Natalie lets the murkiness in her brain rise up again and pull her in. She realizes, though, as she presses her fingers together, that her wedding ring is gone.

It was only a platinum band. She traded her diamond solitaire years ago, before the peak, for a pair of horses. She's taken the band off before, just to see how it feels to have a naked finger. The words engraved inside the ring had always rankled her. *Constant faith and abiding love.* She hadn't wanted the inscription, but Richard insisted. It had been hard to picture such enduring faith and love in her twenties. It had felt like she was setting herself up for failure, that the words pressed against her finger for years had been silently mocking her.

WHEN SHE WAKES AGAIN, MITCH lies by the stable door and Daniel kneels beside her holding a bowl. Her mind is clearer now, and she has the vague memory of Daniel yelling in the street, trying to rouse her, being carried somewhere by someone. Daniel thrusts a spoonful of oatmeal into her mouth.

Natalie swallows the oatmeal. More spoonfuls follow.

"Where are we?" she says.

"In a stable on the outskirts of town."

"What happened?"

"Eat first," Daniel commands.

Natalie starts to scramble to her feet. "We've got to get out of here." Splotches appear in front of her eyes and she reels with a wave of nausea.

Daniel pushes her back down into the straw and hands her a piece of stale bread. "We have to wait until after dark. The Red might still be looking for us."

"I'm sorry."

"What for?"

"You sound mad."

Daniel runs both hands through his hair, which stands in wild, almost electrified, tufts. "I'm not mad. You scared me. I pulled the bullet out of your arm. I think it'll be okay. Eat more. We'll leave in an hour." The skin beneath his eyes seems more deeply etched than before. Natalie realizes she has never ever scared Richard, and that it's a strange and almost gut-wrenching relief to scare someone. But she can't focus on that now.

Daniel goes around the corner and starts doing something with Shadowfax.

"Are you okay?" she asks. "What did they do to you?" She struggles to sit up.

Daniel appears around the corner of the stall, his jaw set and his eyes haunted. He stands looking at her for the longest time. Then he falls to his knees in the straw and wraps his arms around her, careful not to move her injured arm. The shock of his touch explodes through every nerve in her body. He is somehow tender and ferocious, one hand cupping the back of her head as lowers her back into the straw, his eyes locked on hers. Then he buries his face against her shoulder and she almost gasps with want.

"They made me operate," he says, his lips muffled against her clavicle. "On an old man with a tumor on his tongue. Their spiritual leader. I told them I was a vet. But they didn't care. Apparently doctors are in such short supply that they get abducted and people will settle for vets. I didn't know what the hell I was doing. I just hope to God I didn't kill him. At least they let me pull the bullet out of you first." He shifts, and she can feel the brush of his mouth against her hair, his breath on her neck. "As soon as I was done with him, they took off. They took your wedding ring, half the antibiotics, and the rest of our supplies. At least they left the goddamn horses, guns, and tent in 'payment' for my services, and they didn't find one of the stashes of antibiotics and oatmeal inside my riding jacket pocket. They insisted on giving you pain meds. I'm sorry. I think it was opium. I think they wanted you out of it while I operated, or maybe they just thought it was funny. I think they were all high as kites. I was so scared they'd kill you, or that you'd die from the drug while I was operating."

She inhales the grassy scent of his hair and allows her body to curve against his, each point of contact a heady mix of exhilaration and satisfaction. She has imagined lying in Daniel's arms so many times. Richard had led her to believe that Daniel's experience with women is limited, that he would be awkward and stiff and ridiculous in bed, but the confidence of his arms and posture suggest otherwise. They lie there, just breathing for a few seconds, every cell of her body finding a home with his.

Abruptly, he starts to disentangle himself. The shock and loss are visceral.

He takes her hand and helps her to her feet. "I'm sorry. I don't even know what I'm doing. It's the stress of everyone thinking I'm a goddamn doctor. It won't happen again. Please forget I just did that."

Natalie nods, not trusting herself to speak. He drops her hand, and they look at each other.

"Can you ride?" he says. "I don't know how long the drug effects last, but I'd be far more comfortable the farther we are from this hellhole. Those green-kerchiefed hippies claimed that we're out of the Red territory, but I don't even want to know whose territory we're in now. And we have to get back to warn everyone about the wanted poster."

He helps Natalie onto Serendipity. A sliver of moon hangs in the sky as they pick their way through yards and fields, going slowly so the horses make little noise. The haze of smoke dissipates as the houses grow fewer, and they allow the horses to gather speed as they try to put as many miles between themselves and Tanner's Ridge as possible.

Three hundred capsules of amoxicillin rattle in Natalie's saddlebag. A small bit of safety purchased with the symbols of love and wealth from the old world. Natalie tries not to run scenarios of death in her mind as they ride. Richard was right. The ridge people should be run off. Should have been run off right away, while she was trying to hawk visions of community and goodwill. She tries to erase the miracle of Daniel's arms around her. She is still Richard's wife.

Natalie is clinging to the saddle by the time Daniel calls a stop, her arm a stiff mass of shooting pain and her legs shaking. They pitch the tent and Daniel insists on taking watch. Natalie slips into the empty tent, with only one of the saddle blankets for cover, without argument.

WHEN NATALIE RISES IN THE half-light of morning, Daniel is pacing, the skin under his eyes puffy. "I'm sorry about yesterday," he says after making a few circles around the campfire. A tiny ember of hope kindles softly in her. He's still focusing on this.

"It's okay. You were upset. Nothing happened. It's fine."

"You won't say anything to Richard?"

"Why would I say anything?"

"Because I did something inappropriate."

"It wasn't inappropriate." She wants to shake him, to have him grab hold of the meaning of her statement, but he doesn't seem to.

"Okay. Well, it won't happen again," Daniel says, turning and looking back down the valley. "We need to go."

They break camp, hurriedly. Despite Daniel's determined words, something infinitesimal seems to have shifted between them. Their hands meet when they fold the tent and tarp. They stand slightly closer to each other than usual to load the saddlebags. He checks the dressing on her arm with great tenderness and care. Despite Natalie's constant yoke of worry and the burning pain in her arm, the world suddenly seems sharper and more full of color.

The massiveness of her feelings for him thrums through her soul, just as his embrace still aches on her skin.

She must stop this.

<hr />

ANDREW OPENS THE WINDOW A crack just after four a.m., his head thick with exhaustion. The only way to be sure to be awake for something without an alarm clock is to *stay* awake, but if his weird thoughts are any indication, he probably dozed off a couple of times. Andrew arrives at the window just in time to see Rachel enter the shed. He exhales in relief. He had been worried she would change her mind. A scream and a stream of squawks follows. The chickens that Andrew hid in the shed must have been plenty irritated. It was not unheard of for a couple of chickens to take refuge in the shed during the day and be missed in the nightly round-up. Six chickens was a bit excessive, but there needed to be enough for Rachel to have to spend time rounding them up. For their plan to work, they need Mike to accept Rachel's lie that she heard something in the shed and left the house to investigate.

Jane and Colleen—on watch together with Jeffry, the yellow lab, because the men have to rest up for tomorrow—hear the noise and make their way over to the shed cautiously. The two women stand outside the shed and confer, shifting from foot to foot for a few seconds, their guns twitching. Three lily-livers on watch together. At least they're predictable. Sure enough, Colleen goes inside and returns with Mike, who had been set to guard Craig's and Liz's doors. Andrew chokes with relief. Mike, the trusting sort, has left Craig's and Liz's doors unguarded, just as Andrew prayed he would.

Andrew takes the stairs two at a time, hoping he doesn't trip and plunge off a stair edge into the darkness. Craig and Liz emerge from their rooms at his knock, and they make their way noiselessly out of the house. They're also depending on Mike not to check on Craig and Liz when he returns. The best they can probably hope for is a three- to four-hour head start.

They race across the eastern pasture. The horses cluster together in the woods where Andrew left them. Once astride, the three of them ride off into the pre-dawn morning, Andrew's emotions a jangling mixture of fear and excitement.

Andrew's gut feels bubbly and unsettled. Liz and Craig plan to kill Rafe and his men with the guns rattling in Andrew's saddlebags. Andrew still reels from the notion that Liz is Craig's adopted mother. Anneke revealed this matter-of-factly at the meeting in the cellar, with an air of superiority, as if Andrew should have known or guessed. He wonders what the hell else they haven't told him. He just hopes nobody notices he's missing before he can circle around and come back. His compromise agreement was that he would collect all the guns when they were done and return them to the farm. Liz and Craig agreed to this. He just hopes they follow through on their end of the bargain. Realistically, once they get the guns, they could turn around and shoot him.

Liz believes she can convince Richard that the rest of the ridge camp should be taken in. Craig's sister, Elena, is one of the pregnant girls, and Liz is determined that Elena should have medical care when she gives birth. Andrew didn't want to be too discouraging about the likelihood of his dad taking them in. Craig said that even if the best they can do is get rid of Rafe's gang, it will be enough. And so here Andrew is, not only sanctioning, but aiding and abetting, murder. He feels, and not for the first time since agreeing to the plan, like he might throw up.

The horses plod along at a reasonably steady pace for second-stringers. Richard's old stallion, Augustus, seems happy to be on the trails again, and Andrew gives the horse a pat on the neck. Faint shafts of dawn break through the tree branches when they stop to water the horses. Liz flips through her tarot deck.

"Do you really believe in that stuff?" Andrew asks as he cinches up his saddle.

Liz smiles. "The cards help you to know who you are."

"We should get going," Andrew says. He hops back onto Augustus and gives the horse a firm heel to get him moving. He *does* want to know who he is. He wants an entire essay on it, as he's currently in the process of betraying his family for a pair of strangers, a two-bit Internet, and a potential girlfriend, who's probably pregnant. Or is he? Maybe he's just doing the right thing. He doesn't even know. Anneke assured him this was the right thing to do. He doubts there's a tarot card that could clearly spell out his motivations.

They continue their ascent. The trees around them begin to get sparse and scrubby; they're getting closer to the alpine meadows. Andrew looks over his shoulder at his odd companions. Liz's features verge on serene, like she's headed out on a picnic, her gray hair bobbing as she rides. Craig wears the mask of an undertaker. Andrew supposes that, like him, Craig is probably often on grave-digging duty.

An hour later, Andrew, Liz, and Craig leave the horses tethered to some trees well below the ridge. They circle around the ridge camp on foot into the rocks on the mountain above. Andrew feels naked without the horses. If they're forced to run, he has no idea what his endurance will be like. Or his speed.

They make their way down to the pit toilets and remain in the trees, watching.

The smoke from the campfires smudges the early-morning horizon. A few people wander about preparing breakfast and checking on livestock, but mostly they just sit and stare at the fires. The bleakness makes Andrew shudder. He thinks of the kitchen table at the farm with the familiar smells of Anneke's cooking, the clang of dishes, and the chatter of voices. At the farm, at least there's the vague hope that pleasure may once again trump survival, or at least rival it.

Rafe cleans his fingernails with a knife. The man on Rafe's left, Andrew guesses from Craig's descriptions, must be Donny, a short bald man with tattoos twining up from under his shirt. A blond hulk sits to Rafe's right, his hair a nest of long dreadlocks. According to Craig there are seven guys in the prison gang. All of the other men wear hoods and hats, and Andrew can't tell who is who.

Craig points to one of the girls who sits apart from the rest, huddled in a blanket, and mouths the word *Elena*. The bulge of her belly is evident.

When a dark-haired man heads to the pit toilets, Liz creeps in his direction and gestures to him, and Andrew realizes there is no turning back. The man ducks into the bushes beside them hurriedly and throws his arms around Craig.

Craig seems taken aback and almost takes a step backward. "I'm so glad you're alive, son," the man says. Craig's dad, Andrew guesses, the man Craig said he just met a few years ago. The man releases Craig and turns to Liz and Andrew. Andrew recoils a bit at the pale, clouded, unearthly blue of the man's eyes. Blindness? Cataracts? He walked across the field, so it must be cataracts. There is a brusque handsomeness to him with his icy eyes and Roman nose.

The man passes Craig a set of binoculars with a directed look at the cliff-side, and Craig scrambles off up the rocky slope to keep watch. The man inclines his head toward Liz and then looks to Andrew.

Andrew finds himself stuttering. "I'm Andrew. The helper. I emailed you, or someone. My parents, Natalie and Richard, own the farm." He feels lame that he chose to say his parents owned the farm. The man peers at him more closely, then extends his hand.

"I'm Joe. I know your parents."

Liz pushes between them. "We don't have time for chit-chat. Richard has some of the men on the farm completely inflamed, and they're coming here to murder half of us and drive the rest of us away. We need to get rid of Rafe and his men and then beg for refugee status immediately. Some of them are sympathetic to refugees, especially Natalie. They'll take us in if we play our cards right. You should see that farm. It's like flipping Shangri-La."

The sweat prickles on the back of Andrew's neck and palms.

"What's your plan?" Joe says.

"We brought guns. Six of them," Andrew says. Suddenly this sounds lame.

Joe squints past Andrew at Liz. "Guns? That's your plan? Rafe isn't going down without a fight. Some of us will get killed."

Craig's voice comes rushed and panicked down from the rocks. "They're here. The farm people. I saw them through the trees coming up the hill. They're only ten minutes out."

"They figured out we were gone." Andrew's stomach and intestines feel weak, like they might not be able to contain their churning contents. "Or," he hesitates as he considers Richard's behavior, "it's a trick. They always intended to come early. Richard thought you had an information source, and was hoping that you would be fed the wrong information."

"We have to go," says Liz, grabbing a gun. "Come on, Joe, at least we'll be armed so we can shoot back when Richard arrives."

"Whoa, whoa! That wasn't the plan!" Andrew squeals, grasping for the gun bag.

Joe snatches the gun bag from Andrew, giving him a firm push in the center of his chest, his spooky white eyes like a storm. Too late Andrew realizes he's put his own gun in the bag. "All right, we take Rafe and his men out and then beg for clemency, as much as I fecking hate begging for anything from Richard Johnston." Joe turns to Andrew. "Get on your horse and run interference with your dad. If he starts shooting at us, we'll shoot back." He whirls back to Liz and Craig. "Hans and Ranjeet are waiting for my signal. We need to do this with no hesitation. Approach from the east. Hold your fire till you're right on top of them, unless they see us, then get as close as you can before shooting."

"But I'm not even supposed to be here!" Andrew says in a hiss, but Joe, Liz, and Craig are gone. Andrew trembles in the trees until the first gunshots shatter the air at the encampment. His father's heels will have driven hard into the flanks of his horse the instant the sound pierced the air. He doesn't have much time. He has to head them off before there's a bloodbath—with the guns he gave the raiders. Andrew runs madly through the forest that skirts the ridge. Tree branches slap his face and arms.

He leaps on top of Augustus and hurtles through the trees down the hill. Someone wails on the ridge amid the jolting staccato of rifle fire. Andrew chokes back a sob, imagining the gore on the ridge above, a dead girl, a dead baby, dead children. Andrew has never had to bury a child before. Andrew and Augustus barrel out of the trees, almost smacking directly into his father's horse. Both horses rear and paw the ground as both father and son try to stay in the saddle. The rest of the farm members pull up their horses with stunned looks.

Richard's face compacts in furls of disgust. "You!" says Richard. "I would never have guessed it was you, Andrew. You've made a big mistake. What the *fuck* are you thinking? Get out of my way! You're in a world of trouble! But I'll deal with you later."

"No," says Andrew. His voice seems tiny and pathetic even to him, and his knees quiver against Augustus's rump, unnerving the horse and making him skitter from side to side.

"Are you kidding me?" Richard says.

"They've been taken hostage by a prison gang. They've been slaves. I gave them guns so they can deal with the gang. There are women and children up there. Seven pregnant women. We should help them. What are we going to think of ourselves in five years if we drive them away and they die? They have Internet access and one of the guys up there is a friend of yours, or at least you know him." Andrew's voice trails off, as he realizes he is uncertain of the nature of the relationship between his father and Joe.

"You *believed* them? You gave them guns? What is this? Some jackassed hero thing? You just made this ten times worse. Move!" Richard starts to push past. But Andrew wedges Augustus against Caligula and blocks the path. Richard's face is rigid with rage. Gunfire continues to echo on the ridge. Andrew's stomach froths with fear. What if his father never forgives him?

"I'm sorry, Dad," Andrew says. "Maybe I screwed up. But they know you're here now. They're armed. Don't go up there."

"Richard, he's right," Solomon says. "We can't just ride into a shootout."

"And wait until they come down to the farm with their newfound guns?" Richard spits the words back at Solomon, still glaring at Andrew. He draws his gun and fires six rounds into a nearby tree. Andrew's body leaps involuntarily with every blast. The horses jump and jostle and Andrew struggles to keep Augustus under control.

Richard reloads his gun with his back to them. At the back of his mind, Andrew registers that the gunfire on the ridge has become more intermittent.

Richard turns around. "No."

"No, what?" Andrew says.

"No, we're not turning back," Richard starts. But Bob and Ramona have already wheeled their horses around and started back down the rocky slope. "Where the hell do you think you're going?" Richard yells after them.

"To the farm," Bob says. "We're not going into an armed shootout. We were English professors, not military operands."

"Get your asses back up here, or you are no longer members of our farm!"

"We'll take our chances with Farm Council," Bob calls back.

The color evaporates from Richard's face, leaving his eyes like livid orbs in a sickly mass of putty. He makes a motion to slam his gun on the ground, but thinks better of it. A stream of cocksucking sonofabitch expletives pour from his mouth. Andrew is wondering if Richard is mad enough to ride over the ridge and start shooting alone, when Joe staggers down the hill holding his blood-soaked arm.

"We need help. Medical help. Please." He drops to his knees in a faint.

CHAPTER 13
THE SIX OF PENTACLES

———⊶∞⊷———

RICHARD AND ANDREW

It is time to help others who are not as fortunate.

"It could be a trap," Richard says automatically as Alan and Solomon dismount and begin examining Joe's arm.

Joseph Wharton. All the fury Richard feels toward Andrew collapses into a single nexus point. Charming, feckless, sneaky, fucked-up Joe. Natalie's ex-boyfriend. Richard had never expected to see him again. Natalie obviously told him about the farm. Trust the fucking bastard to bring a whole boatload of people with him. Richard's finger strums the trigger of his revolver.

"We can't just leave them," Paul says. Richard turns and stares at the look of concern on Paul's lined and bespectacled face. He wants to shove Paul's Christian charity up his ass.

"It's none of our business."

"I'll go check it out," Andrew says, turning Augustus.

"You will not!" Richard says. "Damn it all to hell!" When did his son become fucking Robin Hood? Richard shakes his gun at Andrew. "I'll go. You keep your ass parked. Leon, you're with me."

Richard picks his way up the hill with Leon behind him, cursing the day Joe was born. He dismounts and looks over the edge. Six men and two women lie bloody and unattended on the ground. A man performs CPR on a young woman. Two other men huddle around a small and crumpled child trying to apply pressure to wounds, while a woman wails beside them. A pregnant girl lies on her side in the grass with Craig and Liz, the traitors, hovering over her. Two other young girls and a woman with a crying child crouch by one of the teepees. He could just walk away, let these people die or kill each other. That would be the smart thing to do.

Richard heads back down the hill. "We'll help them," he says. He doesn't like the surprised and hopeful look on Paul's face. Now Paul will think Richard is ripe for conversion to Christianity and will start all his God talk again. That's the last thing Richard needs.

Liz yells at them when they crest the hill, their guns aloft, like she's in fucking charge, directing them not to touch the six men. Richard has no intention of going near them anyway. They look dirty, bloody, and dead. At least this is an easy way to take the ridge people prisoner with no bloodshed. Their fire has been scattered and patches of grass burn quietly, threatening to ignite the field. Richard directs Andrew to get water, as Liz grabs Richard's arm.

"Elena needs to see a doctor immediately. She's in labor."

Richard shrugs her off and heads for the child lying on the ground. He takes inventory as he goes: six women, two children, and four men, plus Craig and Liz. Fourteen people, but the woman receiving chest compressions doesn't look like she's going to make it. Liz dogs him like a gnat as he walks, wailing about Elena. Paul relieves the man giving chest compressions. Terrence and Leon start rounding up the uninjured.

The child has taken a bullet to the arm and leg. Blood pools on the grass beneath him and his face is the color of blue ice. His five-year-old body is too tiny and thin, and Richard almost crumples. They need to get the child to Mike if there's to be any hope of saving him. There's no way they can make Mike's "golden hour" though, not even at top speed. The men tending the child eye him suspiciously when he arrives with the first-aid kit in hand.

"I can help," Richard says in a little voice. Too little. He's embarrassed it came out of his mouth. This situation is unbalancing him, and he needs to pull back to center. He tries not to focus on the child, but rather to think like a doctor. The men don't move. The woman moaning and cradling the boy's head in her hands grates on Richard's nerves.

"Let me help," Richard says in a more assertive voice. Christ, he's not going to *beg* to save these people. The two men move aside this time, creating a small space for him. Richard elbows his way in to kneel beside the boy. He opens the first-aid kit and starts untying the filthy bandage that the men have placed on the kid's leg. One of the men makes a gurgling warning sound in his throat.

Richard holds up his hand.

"Do you want me to help, or not?" he says. "As soon as I remove this bandage, one of you needs to be ready to put pressure on it with the clean compress." Richard disinfects the wound and applies Celox to stop the bleeding. Then he applies a clean dressing and ties it tight. He does the same with the arm. Quickly, efficiently. He should have been a surgeon. He could have been famous and rich, and he wouldn't have to take shit from anyone.

Richard looks around the rest of the field. They need to get the boy to the farm immediately if they hope to save him. Terrence and Leon have rounded up everyone except the two men helping Richard. Liz still yells about something from the middle of the group, and the pregnant girl thrashes about and wails. Richard wishes they would both shut up. Andrew has put out the fire. Solomon and Alan have dragged Joe over the lip of the ridge and appear to be heading in Richard's direction. Blood soaks Joe's shirt. Paul stops giving chest compressions to the woman on the ground and shakes his head. Richard revises his estimate: thirteen people.

Solomon and Alan deposit Joe on the ground in front of Richard. Even pasty-faced, pale-eyed, and twenty years older, Joe remains a beautiful man. Richard presses his lips and teeth together. He's going to have to treat Joe's wound or let him die. He cuts the arm of Joe's shirt away to reveal a mash-up of skin, blood, and tendons, with glimpses of bone. Multiple knife wounds with a dull knife. Richard sparingly dumps Celox on the wounds, cleans them as best he can, applies gauze, and binds Joe's arm with a pressure bandage. If there are severed tendons, it can't be helped.

Joe's eyes drift open. "We need your help. We'll work hard if you take us in. Those men we've just killed are the ones who attacked you. I swear. We were hostages. We have skills. Hans has figured out how to connect to the Internet. We'll work our asses off." He almost gasps the words.

"Supplies are pretty tight on the farm. We have to look after our own first."

"You don't have to decide right now. Just get this boy and Elena some medical attention and then decide. *Please.*"

Richard grinds his teeth together. He knows that when Natalie sees Joe, Richard will have a hard time turning the ridge people out. Joe knows it too. Yet to not bring them to the farm now that Andrew and others know that Joe is among them would land Richard in a world of trouble with Natalie. And they have an Internet connection.

Elena's moans turn into howls.

Richard feels the rigidity of his own lips. "Fine, then. Turn in all your weapons. We'll transport the boy and the girl now. Pack your stuff up and make your way down to the farm. You can camp on the edge of the farm under guard until we make a decision."

ELENA'S SCREAMS AND GROANS ECHO up the farmhouse stairs. They've grown raspy and huskier in the last hour. Andrew wraps his pillow around his head. Giving birth without drugs is beginning to sound like a horror flick.

Andrew and Craig hauled Elena to the infirmary late yesterday afternoon after a harrowing ride down the hill, her skirt soaked with blood-tinged fluid. They took turns carrying her sidesaddle in front of them until their arms grew leaden and uncooperative. Each turn seemed to go on forever as she fought them and demanded to be put down so she could pant and moan in the bushes. And all the time, Liz's urgings came from behind them. They must go faster. They must save the girl and the baby.

Mike met them at the door of the infirmary, and helped hoist her onto the bed. Craig was escorted outside, and Mike shooed Andrew away from the infirmary in favor of Siobhan.

The shrieks continued as the other farm members arrived with the injured boy on a stretcher, followed by the walking wounded, quadrupling Mike's workload. Richard drew up the rear of the party, leading the two stolen farm cows. Then came Joe and the rest of the ridge members with their supplies. Once their camp was set, Richard gathered everyone and made a speech that the "newcomers better keep to themselves and work their asses off," and that "they are not to set foot in the farmhouse until further notice." Andrew was surprised Richard didn't hand out armbands or stars.

Andrew heard Richard storm out in the middle of the night, probably going to the barn office to sleep. Andrew wishes he could too, but he feels a strange loyalty to Elena after carrying her off the mountain. He pulls on his pants and heads to the infirmary. Elena lies naked from the waist down, her stomach like a bloated white whale trapped on the beach. Mike pops up from between Elena's legs, which are splayed in stirrups. His gloved hands are streaked with blood. Elena's face is twisted in agony, and her grunts and heaves remind Andrew horrifyingly of the feral pig he shot a few years before. Liz stands outside with her face pressed against the infirmary window.

"Andrew, the baby's coming. Get over here. I need your help."

Andrew almost gags from the stench, but joins Mike at the foot of the bed. He tries not to faint at the sight of the head cradled in Mike's hands, and avoids glancing at the opening from which it emerges.

"Grab those towels. The baby's almost out. I'm going to suction it and hand it to you. You dry it on that bed carefully. Support the head at all times. Do not drop it. Then put it on Elena's chest. Try to get the baby to suckle. Don't let the baby fall. You ready?"

"What about her?" Andrew flicks his thumb at Liz.

"Richard's banned her from the farmhouse. You ready?"

"I guess." Andrew picks up one of the towels, wishing he'd remained upstairs with a pillow wrapped around his head.

The removal and suctioning go more quickly than Andrew expects, and soon a howling blue bloodstained creature, a girl, is placed into his arms. The arms and feet thrust at him in fury, and he places it on the bed, doing his best to rub off the blood and white stuff. The blue begins to fade, and the baby becomes a deeper red. Andrew puts the baby on Elena's chest. She places her arms around it, but Andrew holds it still, afraid it will slip off. Mike massages Elena's stomach, still swollen like a giant dough ball despite the emergence of the baby. Something red and fleshy slips out, and Andrew hopes to God it is not the baby's deformed twin.

"Pull up her shirt," Mike orders. "Expose her breast so the baby can nurse. Help her to get the baby latched, she's bleeding too much."

"What?" says Andrew.

"Just do it. It helps to contract the uterus."

Andrew tries to wedge Elena's shirt up while she tries to maneuver the baby out of the way. The shirt is uncomfortably tight and it takes Andrew a few minutes to hitch it up. Her large breast flops out. Andrew tries not to recoil. This is not how he wanted to see any of this. Together they manipulate the baby into place, and to Andrew's surprise, the baby nuzzles the nipple a few times with her nose, then opens her mouth and latches on.

"Just keep the baby nursing," Mike says, continuing to press deeply into the doughy folds of Elena's stomach. The sense of panic fading, Andrew feels a vague relief as he watches the baby suckle. He rearranges the blankets to cover Elena and the baby and then turns to look out the window at Liz. She cracks a gap-toothed smile at him, and Andrew finds himself absurdly smiling back.

RICHARD WATCHES AS NATALIE AND Daniel ride alone across the fields to the farm in the mid-afternoon. The dogs dance and whirl around them, barking in joyous greeting. Stupid animals, so in love with Daniel. The mists drift silkily, almost lazily off the farm fields. Richard feels a momentary flash of concern over Justin's whereabouts, but Natalie and Daniel don't ride quickly enough to suggest an emergency, and Natalie doesn't look sufficiently suicidal for Justin to be dead, although he notes that her arm is bandaged and in a sling. The dogs skid to a stop when something leaps out of a basket attached to Natalie's saddle. A black streak tears across the field. A cat. Richard lets out a small puff of relief. Natalie wouldn't be transporting a cat if her son weren't okay.

Natalie and Daniel slow when they see the tents pitched in the south field. They stop their horses just outside the barn, and farm members crowd around them. Richard hangs back, waiting.

It doesn't take long for Natalie to spot Joe.

"Joe?" Natalie says. The incredulity in her voice is almost convincing, but Richard knows she must be faking.

"We were in the neighborhood. Thought we'd drop by for coffee," Joe replies, pausing, and then nods at Daniel. "Daniel."

"Joe," Daniel says, tipping his hat slightly to the man below him. He turns to Natalie. "I'll take the horses."

Natalie dismounts, and she and Joe hug. Richard assesses the distance between their bodies, the length of their embrace, the expression on Joe's face. Her wedding ring is missing, he realizes with a jolt. Traded or stolen probably. But he can't be sure, and this sends a flare of anger down his back. It's plain that the fucker Joe can still see well enough and that he still wants her. Of course, everybody wants Natalie. Richard used to get a charge out of this, having the woman that everyone wants, but now he's not so certain. He can't believe she told Joe about the farm.

Daniel leads the horses off. Natalie turns as he goes. Richard catches a flash of something new in the expression on her face, some strange desperation. He has no idea what that could be about. Some new anxiety or conflict with Daniel. Something he'll have to deal with.

Richard approaches Natalie, and the crowd parts for him. He makes a big show of hugging her and patting her buttocks; it's best to remind everyone that she's his. She flinches away with her eyes narrowed. He ignores her and smiles.

Richard addresses the crowd. "All right everybody, move along. Get back to work. We'll have Natalie update you on her trip at Farm Council tonight."

Richard turns to Natalie. "Where's Justin?"

"He's fine. He and Scott are helping a neighbor. The woman has a puncture wound and it got infected. They'll be along in a couple days."

"Are you sure that's safe?"

"No, but what can I do?"

"What happened to your arm?"

"Gunshot. I'm fine."

Richard takes her good arm and guides her to the farmhouse. Natalie pauses to hug Andrew and Mike on the way. Joe trails them like a dog, but hesitates on the front porch. Richard turns to tell him to buzz off, but then reconsiders. Joe might let down his guard in front of Natalie, and vice versa. Richard nods, and Joe follows them inside.

In the kitchen, Anneke gives Natalie a curious one-finger wave before bolting to the pantry. That woman is three shades of crazy. Richard and Natalie take seats at the table. Joe pulls out a chair too. Richard gives a theatrical neck twitch as if to suggest that he would rather stick his hands in a thresher than sit next to Joe. It's just a joke of course, but Natalie glares at him. Nothing is ever funny to Natalie.

Daniel slips into the room and sits at the other end of the table. Richard tells Natalie of the scene on the ridge, and provides Joe and Liz's story that Rafe and his men held them hostage. Not that Richard believes them, but he'll trot out the tale for now while he gauges reactions and figures out the truth. Natalie's face clamps tight in shock and anger when she hears of Andrew's presence and role. She'll blame Richard, no doubt. According to Joe, Rafe's men were all killed and Rafe was shot but escaped. They figure he's dead. Richard scans Joe's face for any sign of uneasiness as he says this, but Joe's attention is fixed on Natalie.

"I was pretty shocked to find that Joe was among the group. Thought you hadn't talked to him in years. But I guess you must have forgotten," Richard says. Joe doesn't blanch. Natalie jerks her head at Richard and creases her brows further together. Guilt? Or anger at his accusation?

Richard gestures at her arm. "Why don't you tell me how your little trip went? You obviously must have had some excitement."

Natalie stands. "Please don't talk to me like that. I need to go change." She marches out of the dining room and up the stairs.

Richard leaves Joe and Daniel at the table and follows her to the bedroom. She's such a drama queen. "Come on, Natalie, don't be silly. I didn't say anything to you."

"Really?" She turns her back to remove her shirt.

"Really." He tries a different tack. "Did Scott tell you about the bullets in the woods?"

"I can't believe you weren't watching Andrew more closely. How could you let him do this?"

"I didn't *let* him do anything. He's sixteen, not three. I don't watch him every second of the day. Can we please focus on the bullets?"

"Now I feel like I can't leave the farm ever."

"Don't, then. We need to figure out who put the bullets in the woods. Andrew has denied it despite repeated grilling, and I believe him. I don't think he even knew about them. Liz and Craig were always watched. And your boyfriend denies all knowledge of them. So we have to figure out who did it." Richard sits on the bed. He wonders for a second if Natalie left the bullets for Joe, but dismisses the notion. Natalie is a bleeding heart and too messy with her emotional entanglements with other men, but she wouldn't betray the farm or him like that. But if Natalie didn't leave the bullets, how would the person who *did* leave the bullets even know about Joe? Unless that Liz woman got to some-one with all her psychic crap and convinced them to help, just like she'd put some sort of spell over Andrew. Perhaps one of the meathead farm members just took the bullets out there and forgot about them. Or perhaps his wife is a traitor. He considers asking her, but settles for staring deliberately at her ring finger until she shoves her hand in her pocket.

"Please don't call him that."

"What?"

"My boyfriend. Joe was one of my best friends, not my boyfriend."

"Yeah? Well, friends with benefits then. Same thing in my books. I thought we agreed on the list of people we would tell about the farm, and as far as I recall Joe was not on it."

"I did not tell Joe about the farm."

Richard almost laughs at this, the bitter laugh that bubbles up when he knows someone is talking shit to him, but he forces his features into a bland expression. "I need to know whatever he knows about the bullets. And just for the record, I don't think they should be allowed to stay. I don't trust them. Half of them look like they have flipping scurvy, and that Liz woman is bat-shit crazy and a liar to boot."

Natalie's voice is clipped. "Fine. I'll talk to him. And what did you do about Andrew?"

"I was pretty mad, but he's got guts. To pull all that off." Richard cracks a small smile at his son's daring. Natalie doesn't smile back.

"And what are we doing for consequences?"

"Oh, don't worry, he's on shithouse duty for the winter." Richard tries to brush away his feelings of betrayal. If it comes to a competition between him and Joe over Natalie's affections, he'll win again, just like he did years ago. "The good news is they've got some sort of Internet connection. No sites or anything, just a way of communicating using the old phone lines. Hans, their computer programmer guy, is going to give me their contact lists tomorrow. Maybe we can finally start hooking up with the real world again."

"Okay. Just don't go overboard on it. You know how you get."

"God, Nat, do you think I'm like a total idiot?"

"No. You just get excited about things," Natalie says.

"Maybe we *should* be excited about this."

"Maybe, but please, exercise some control."

"That's me, no self-control," Richard mutters, as he follows her out of the bedroom.

THEY FIND JOE ON A bench on the porch, peeling apples. Natalie sinks onto the bench next to him—closer than Richard thinks is necessary or appropriate, but they were always that way, crawling in and out of each other's beds in university. Natalie has sworn repeatedly that Joe isn't her type. But why does she sit so close to him? She selects an apple and starts to peel. Natalie never just sits and does nothing. Richard makes as if to hang out on the porch, but Natalie glares at him pointedly until he leaves.

CHAPTER 14

THE HANGED MAN

---ΘΩΘ---

NATALIE AND ANDREW

To acquire one thing, you must sacrifice another.

"So..." Joe begins. "Strange times, Tallie."

Natalie feels an odd jolt at Joe's old nickname for her. "Indeed," Natalie says, studying him. Wrinkles have formed around the edges of his eyes, and gray dusts the stubble at his temples and chin. He looks haggard, but the irony and self-deprecation he's always armed himself with still undergird his voice. In university, Joe careened from woman to woman and job to job, his emotions hanging on the line at all times. Richard still loves to do an impression of Joe with his head down in the drink, moaning about some broken relationship or career fuck-up. Richard overstates it of course, but there's generally some small truth to Richard's imitations. Joe was always feckless and caddish, but he was charming and the life of the party and, before Richard, one of her dearest friends. They slept together on occasion when they were drunk and mistook their closeness for something more. But mostly they were just friends and roommates. But then Richard came along, and the two men spent weeks circling each other like deranged territorial cats, until Joe decided he needed to spend more time with his new girlfriend, and moved out. She and Joe tried to be friends after that, but they could never seem to find the same groove. Joe did not even attempt to hide his dislike for Richard, and Natalie thought Joe was being immature, and potentially jealous.

"Do you want to maybe walk me through the last few years and how you got here?"

Joe offers her his old familiar lopsided smile. "I became a chef of all things. I had a small restaurant in Nelson. Thought I had life by the tail. Then, of course, things started to go bad. Next thing I know, I get a letter telling me I have a son named Craig who had been adopted by a woman in Kimberley named Liz."

"What? You didn't know?"

Joe sighs. "Well, you know, I got around a bit in university." Natalie almost laughs at the degree of understatement in Joe's words.

"Anyway, all hell was breaking loose, so I went and got him, and brought Liz and Elena along too. Ranjeet and Hans are old buddies of mine. I didn't know if I should bring that many people here, so we tried to cope on our own. The six of us did okay for a few years as kind of 'nice outlaws,'" Joe lifts his lips in a half smile. "Then Rafe and his gang basically took us hostage. It got pretty shitty. We tried to get away but we couldn't, and I didn't want to abandon all the girls. I didn't know what to do, so I decided to head this direction. We tricked Rafe into heading this direction using Liz's tarot cards. He's such a fool he believes she's psychic. But then we got here, and I had no idea what to do. Rafe saw the farm as a gold mine, and I realized we had made a huge mistake. If it weren't for Andrew, we'd probably be dead by now, as I understand Richard was on his way to take us down."

"Well, we didn't know it was you, and I don't think he was planning to kill you. But what do you mean, you didn't know if you should bring that many people here? How did you know about the farm?"

Joe's brow furrows, and he cocks his head in that way of his that she still finds appealing. "You sent me a letter, five years ago, with the address. Saying if everything went down the tubes, I should come here. When I got it, I thought it was a joke. I was going to call you and tell you that if you wanted to be friends again, you didn't need to go out and buy a ranch. But I never quite got around to it."

Natalie blinks at him. There were letters that she, Richard, and Daniel sent to family and two friends apiece. She chose Anneke and Patricia. Daniel, in his usual solitary way, only made the case for Paul and Cyrus. Richard's friends never showed. Joe was not on the list. Richard went on some rampage about not having drunk screw-ups on the farm, and Natalie did not push.

"Was the letter typed, or handwritten?"

"Typed. Why?"

"Do you still have it?"

"No. I looked up the location at the time. That's why it took us a bit to find you. I didn't have the exact address." He leans down and cradles his forehead in his hands. "I'm really sorry about bringing so many people and Rafe here. I just… I didn't know what else to do. I was still trying to figure it out, when Craig got caught and then there was no way Liz or I were leaving. And then Liz insisted on coming down here."

Natalie sits stunned. Who sent that letter? She runs through the list of potential options. Patricia never paid much attention to him, Anneke hated him, and Daniel, Mike, and Scott barely knew him. Richard wouldn't.

"Joe, I need you to tell me who worked with Andrew, and who left you those bullets."

"I don't know anything about the bullets. And I don't know who was working with Andrew. I swear. I thought it was you. But maybe someone else just doesn't like the way Richard does things."

Joe throws a peeled apple at the bowl. It hits the side with a thud. He shifts his milky eyes to Natalie. Up close, his long lower lashes and freckles make him seem younger, more like the man she used to know. She feels a flash of longing for their free and easy days before the peak, before Richard.

"What happened when you were in Tanner's Ridge? I saw wanted posters of Rafe."

Joe elevates his eyebrows. "We didn't stay there long. Too many competing gangs. We were staying in a barn when the farmer came to kick us out, and Rafe freaked. The next thing we knew they were all dead, even the kids. He was an absolute psychopath. Please don't judge us based on him. Please, please let us stay."

She wants to reassure him, but she can't. She has no idea how this is going to end up, what Farm Council will decide. "Introduce me around, and we'll talk about this again tomorrow."

The rest of the day is a blur of updates and chores. Joe takes Natalie around to meet the other ridge folks. A dentist, a computer programmer, a teacher, a carpenter, and four emotionally damaged girls with no education—one with a new baby and three who are pregnant. Some potentially useful additions to the farm. More mouths to feed. Natalie manages to convince Richard that the newcomers should at least be permitted in the farmhouse for meals and that Joe should be allowed to help Anneke in the kitchen. *Probation*, Richard keeps reminding her and Joe, *they're on a two-week probation*. She wonders when the no-refugee policy will come up, if Richard is just waiting until he has access to this new Internet, but she doesn't say anything.

Everyone, including Richard and Joe, still thinks it was her that told Joe about the farm. And she doesn't know what to tell them.

She feels Richard's eyes on her everywhere she goes until she falls into bed exhausted. When he reaches for her, she closes her eyes and lets him press his body into hers.

NATALIE STUMBLES INTO THE KITCHEN the next morning chased by dreams of waiting for Daniel in the barn, in the dining room, in the greenhouses, only to have him replaced every time by a smug Richard. The morning sun illuminates the mountains west of the farm. They need it for the potatoes still in the ground. She runs through the names of the new people that Joe introduced her to the day before. Jane has already pulled Natalie aside and murmured that the farm needs new blood, no doubt spurred by the presence of the two single men. Natalie pushes the pantry door open.

Joe and Anneke face each other in an intense whispered conversation. Joe whirls and plasters a smile on his face. Anneke's blond hair, normally held back with a bandana, has been brushed into thin swirls that hang around her shoulders. Natalie had expected Anneke to refuse to share the pantry with Joe, but instead Anneke seemed almost eager about the new arrangement, and now stares almost stonily at Natalie. Natalie takes a step backward. Did Anneke send Joe the letter? What development in Anneke and Joe's friendship had she missed twenty years ago when she was preoccupied with Richard and university?

She opens her mouth to say something, but loses her nerve in the face of Anneke's glare. She'll have to confront Anneke later.

She's not even sure where her feet are taking her, but she finds herself in the barn. Daniel mucks out the horse stalls alone. There's an aloof and stiff quality to his movement. He, too, thinks she brought Joe here. She steps into the stall, grabs a pitchfork, and joins him.

"I think Anneke told Joe about the farm," she says. "I don't know what to do."

Daniel stops moving and leans on his pitchfork. "Anneke? Are you sure?"

"It wasn't me."

He nods as if this is sufficient explanation, and his body seems to loosen slightly. The tightness that had framed her ribcage dissipates. Having someone trust her this way is a strange and fragile thing.

"What makes you think it was Anneke?" he says.

"They were having some weird conversation, arguing, and she brushed her hair, and if it wasn't me, who else could it be?"

"Ahh, the old brushed hair clue. Always a tip-off." A hint of laughter plays around his lips. His checked navy shirt hangs slightly open and untucked over his faded Lee jeans. He's making fun of her. She's about to come back with some snappy response, but he's staring at her again with that intent look that he gave her just before he held her in the stable two days before. The stare shatters her composure, and she considers bolting. She's always stayed away from men that seem a bit dangerous, men that have clear ideas about sex and make her feel jittery or unnerved. She looks away and he returns to his mucking.

"What are you going to do about it?" he says.

"I don't know." Karl and Bob enter the barn with a wagon of hay, and Natalie takes a step back from Daniel and lowers her voice. "Should I tell Richard?"

"Probably."

"I think I need to talk to her first."

"That's probably a good idea."

The agreeable nature of their conversation almost confuses her. She is so used to arguing over every little thing. She hears Karl and Bob loading the hay into the rope elevator at the back of the barn, and she risks moving closer to Daniel. Another step and she could rest her head in the hollow at the base of his neck. His expression becomes intense again, his lower lip thrust out and his eyes on hers, questioning now. Her heart lurches with the danger of it. There is nothing to catch her. This will probably be her downfall.

She holds her position for a few seconds, willing herself not to look away, and then she slinks back to the garden to her designated chores, throbbing with guilt and furtive hope.

OVER THE NEXT TWO WEEKS, the newcomers work hard to fit in, but there are mutterings among some of the established farm members about the winter food supplies. They plant additional winter crops in cold frames and the woodstove-heated greenhouse, and Natalie sends the men on more hunting parties. Natalie spends several days down in the cellar doing inventory, while Anneke and Joe rework the meal plans. Richard occasionally appears in the cellar, ostensibly seeking out supplies or checking on the wine brewing in big oak caskets. He's watching her. She tries to work up the courage to talk to Anneke, but her friend is avoiding her, and Natalie lets it fall into the pile of unaddressed issues that seem to swamp her life. How is it that she's afraid of so many of the people she's surrounded herself with?

The question of whether the newcomers will be permitted to stay goes unaddressed. Richard was elated when she told him about Ilene and Fred's reports of a provisional government, and flits in and out of the den to sit in front of the computer screen with Hans whenever they have enough power, asking Hans questions about how the new Internet works, sending emails out to old colleagues. He insists on interviewing all the newcomers to find out what they know about the provisional government and life "out there," and emerges from his office each afternoon quivering with energy and jubilation. He seems to have forgotten about the questions regarding who might have helped the newcomers, or has decided he no longer cares about farm politics in the face of bigger opportunities.

Natalie doesn't know whether to put the status of the newcomers on the Farm Council agenda, or just let it be a rolling non-decision. What if Leon and Richard get it into their heads to turn the newcomers away in the dead of winter? The weather has turned cold and rainy, and she can't imagine running them off at this point. She debates whether they should make another trip to Tanner's Ridge to try to trade for more food, and if they can afford the time to send anyone to the community gathering in Jerry. But after her and Daniel's experience in Tanner's Ridge, it might be too dangerous; besides, drawing these questions to Richard's attention will alert him to the fact that they've not yet made a decision.

One chilly gray morning, Natalie and Siobhan are tending some of the cold frame vegetables when the dogs start to bark. A single horse carrying two figures gallops down the drive. Natalie tenses, praying it's not Rafe or other raiders. Several farm members start to cluster around the barn door, eyeing the locked armory. A slow certainty of recognition slips over Natalie. It's Claire and Alfie. Old friends of Richard's.

Natalie goes to greet them, but Richard overtakes her, crowing greetings and slapping Alfie on the back as the smaller man springs off his horse. Alfie and Richard have been friends since university, and have spawned many half-drunk schemes to get rich. Alfie managed Richard's re-election campaign when he was mayor of Vancouver, and there was enough suggestion of dirty dealings on the election trail for Natalie to beg Richard to fire him. Richard emerged squeaky clean, though, and simply rolled his eyes or got angry when Natalie questioned him about any wrongdoing. And so she felt guilt for thinking him guilty, while he blinked in innocence; and that guilt had a way of transforming itself into fury in her soul.

Natalie tries to muster some enthusiasm for Claire, who once spent most of her limited energies on housewares, spa treatments, and holidays. Natalie manages a weak smile and hug for both Alfie and Claire, while Richard makes some brief introductions and then ushers them inside, offering lunch and other refreshments.

Natalie ladles them bowls of steaming stew. Alfie's loud voice echoes around the room. "I'm telling you it's crazy out there, Richard. There's almost nothing left. Not many people, no jobs, no businesses. Nothing. The government's in disarray. I thought you were dead. Thank God you emailed when you did."

Alfie wolfs down spoonfuls of stew while he talks. Claire bends over her bowl, her fine pale hair falling like an afghan around her head, as she shovels the meat and potatoes into her mouth. Richard pours tumblers of brandy and ignores Natalie's pointed scowls.

"At first we had a terrible time finding a place to live. If you wanted to eat, you had to live in weird boarding houses like communes and nobody had much tolerance for Claire's migraines. It was like the hippie granola crunchers had taken over with their gardens and dreadlocks." Alfie gives Richard a wink. "But finally, I got hooked in through the new provisional leader, Ron Merlo. Of course when I heard you were here, Claire and I packed up and came right away. This is our chance, Richard. There's a leadership vacuum right now. I already have you set up. You just have to move to Vancouver." Natalie looks at Richard. Surely he has no intention of doing that. But his lips are pulled back in a smile and his pupils are dilated.

When Natalie returns to the pantry for more bread, Anneke looks through the crack in the pantry door. "Is that Alfie Hobbs?"

"Yes," Natalie replies. "He was Richard's campaign manager."

"I know who he was. He's basically a criminal." It's the first flash of the old Anneke she's seen in weeks. The Anneke who was her friend and ally.

"I know, but they never proved it," Natalie says.

"Do you mind if we go to our rooms and lie down?" Alfie says, as Natalie returns to the kitchen. "It was a long trip, and Claire isn't feeling well. You wouldn't happen to have any Advil or Percocet would you? I have a blinding headache. I assume you've probably stocked all that stuff."

Natalie opens her mouth to respond, but Richard sweeps her aside. "Of course. Whatever you need. I'll show you to your rooms."

Claire gives Natalie a feeble smile. "What time should we be down for dinner?"

"Six," says Natalie, gritting her teeth as she clears Alfie's and Claire's bowls from the table, wondering where Richard is going to take them.

Natalie is picking deer tongue lettuce when Richard comes to talk to her. He wears the sheepish look that Natalie knows means he's done something that will irritate her.

"Just so you know, I gave them our room."

"You *what?*" Natalie regards him blankly.

"Alfie was concerned about Claire's ability to sleep in the den because it's so close to the kitchen and so noisy. And some mornings she needs to sleep in because of her migraines. And with Alfie's bad back, the bed in the den would be pretty uncomfortable. There aren't any other rooms. We're stuffed tight. So I thought we could sleep in the den and give them our room. I packed up some of your clothes in a suitcase."

"You gave them our room?" Natalie repeats.

"I was just trying to make them feel at home. I'm sorry, Nat. I didn't know what to do."

Tell them to piss off, she thinks. "I'm not sleeping in the den," she says. "I don't sleep well either, remember? I'm going to see if Daniel will let me sleep on his couch."

Richard's gaze sharpens, just for a second, before lapsing into a neutral expression. "You could bunk with Andrew and Justin."

"They're teenage boys, and they have a room that was once a closet and a bunk bed."

"Fine," Richard says. She can't tell what he's thinking.

NATALIE IS SITTING ON THE couch in Daniel's tiny one-room cabin when he enters to wash up before dinner, Mitch on his heels. Daniel blinks in surprise, his eyes adjusting to the light.

"Richard gave Claire and Alfie our room. I was hoping I could sleep on your couch."

Daniel stares at her for several seconds, his eyes flicking to her suitcase. "And Richard was okay with that?"

Natalie shrugs. "He seemed fine with it."

Daniel catches her tone and turns defensive. "Well, I guess it's okay. I'm just used to my own space. But it's fine."

"You don't want me here then?" Hope is so perilous, so easily jettisoned.

Daniel pulls his hands through his hair. "No, I do. You can stay. Please stay. I want you to stay. It just came as a bit of a surprise. You should probably tell Richard that he can come and stay too. You can have the bed. I'll take the couch."

Richard staying with them is the last thing she wants, and the last thing she wants Daniel to want, but she nods. "Fine."

"I'll ask him," Daniel says. "I'm going to get changed." He points at her shirt, which is still caked with dirt from the greenhouse. "You probably want to change as well. And then we can go for dinner."

Natalie turns her back on Daniel and rifles through the suitcase Richard packed. It contains numerous items that are too fancy and constricting for farm work. Things she hasn't worn in years. She smothers her tears with anger. Is it too much to ask that Richard know what she wears?

"Hey, are you okay?" Daniel has removed his work shirt and donned a plaid shirt, the faint dusting of hair across his pectorals visible as he does up the final buttons.

"I'm fine. I just have nothing to wear." She holds up a silky blouse. "Richard apparently thinks I'm going to a cocktail party."

"Richard would like life to be a cocktail party. Do you want an old shirt of mine? Till you get your own stuff, of course."

She accepts a flannel shirt and he politely goes outside on the porch while she changes. Then they walk silently side by side through the starry night to the farmhouse. She wishes she could slip her hand into his, but after the incident in the stable, he seems determined to keep his distance, which is probably the right choice. She just wishes Daniel was more willing to make the wrong choices.

An empty bottle of farm-brewed brandy sits between Alfie and Richard on the dining room table. Alfie and Richard's guffaws dominate the room as they reminiscence about BC politics. Richard waves Daniel and Natalie over to the table, furrows his brow at Natalie's attire, and pours them each a glass of brandy before dispatching Solomon down to the cellar for another. Natalie cringes with every knee slap, every male bellow of laugher, every sardonic eyebrow waggle. She wants to shrink back to the quiet of Daniel's cabin and detach herself from Richard.

After dinner, Natalie packs a new bag and takes it to Daniel's, then returns to the office. She needs to figure out how the new Internet works. Hans has informed her that there are trading bulletin boards. Natalie seats herself at the desk and plugs the laptop in. Patricia walks in and sinks onto the den couch. Patricia, her bridesmaid, her college roommate, her friend forever, her backup when Anneke isn't available—except that Natalie's never been convinced that Patricia understands her in the slightest. Not that Anneke does either. Natalie aches to tell her, tell anyone, about Daniel.

"What's up, honey?" says Patricia.

"Oh, you know, the usual. Just stressed. Stressed about everything. And Richard is acting like a dickhead. I hate it when he gets like this."

Patricia smiles serenely, her usual response to any perception that Natalie is going off the rails. "Oh, Nat, you're so hard on him. He's so funny, and he loves you."

The words make Natalie feel like driving a nail between Richard's innocent and sparkly blue eyes. How could they be talking about the same person? Have her own perceptions of Richard become so warped that she no longer sees reality at all?

"Do you really think he loves me?"

"Of course. I watch the way he looks at you." Patricia pats Natalie's knee and nods soothingly.

"Yeah, but he acts like an ass all the time."

Patricia laughs. "Only *you* see that. You need to be nicer to your husband." Patricia's tone is gentle. Her comment is not meant to be a criticism. It's just a reflection of Patricia's worldview. But still, it cuts deep.

"What if I were to say I had feelings for Daniel?" Natalie says.

Patricia almost recoils and is silent for a few seconds. "Oh honey, is your heart going someplace it shouldn't?"

"Shouldn't?" Natalie says. The word makes her irrationally angry. Patricia widens her eyes in surprise at Natalie's tone.

"Well, that would be a completely impossible path." Anneke's deeper voice startles Natalie. She turns to see the other woman in the doorway. Laughter and bitterness skirt the edges of Anneke's expression of disbelief.

"Why?"

Anneke raises her eyebrow. "Because you're married to his brother! Everyone would take Richard's side. Besides, Daniel would never do that." Anneke counts the points off on her fingers while she speaks, and Patricia rubs the small of Natalie's back in circles.

Natalie nods. "I see. Is that how breakups go, then?"

Anneke rolls her eyes up and over to the side and then fixes Natalie with a piercing gaze. "When there's another man involved, yes."

"And everyone would take Richard's side because...?"

"Because that's what they do. And they see you mad at him all the time."

"What about the fact that he doesn't do his chores, or does a bad job of them?"

"Most people just hope that their own crappy work goes unnoticed."

"We just don't want you to get hurt, honey," Patricia chimes in.

Natalie forces a broad smile. "Richard and I are fine. Totally fine. There is no other man involved. Forget I said anything." Natalie rises and walks past Anneke, her head held high and to the right. She returns to the kitchen, where she sits across from Daniel, hoping for any form of reassurance. For anything at all. But Daniel has been drawn into the drinking game, and aside from a general acknowledgement, focuses more on Richard, Alfie, and the brandy than her.

RICHARD PASSES OUT ON THE couch after dinner, his buzzing snores reverberating around the dining room. Natalie and Daniel decide to leave him there for a bit. Natalie considers sleeping in the den, but her things are now all at Daniel's.

Natalie and Daniel slip out into the night between rain showers, the dark figure of Shadow creeping after them. The air seethes with an autumn resurgence of mosquitoes, and Natalie swats the air around her. She tries for something neutral to cover her unhappiness and hurt. "We need to drain the troughs and cover the rain barrels."

"That's what *I* am, you know," he says. "A mosquito."

"A what?"

"Pre-Inca civilizations used an insect zodiac. What we call Gemini in the modern zodiac was known as the Mosquito. When the mosquito constellation appeared in the sky, early farmers knew winter was coming. You're a grasshopper, I think."

Her heart still stings from Anneke's statements. "Couldn't they tell winter was coming because it started to get cold?" she says, trying to keep her voice even.

"It doesn't always get cold at the same time. The stars were like their calendar. Every thirty days a new constellation appeared in the sky."

"Can you show me?"

"It's in the southern hemisphere. I'll have to show you a drawing."

They walk the rest of the way to Daniel's cabin in silence. Inside they pull the shades and then stand in the dark.

"You're upset about something," he says, hunching in the way he does to look in her eyes.

"Why did you ignore me at dinner?"

Daniel sinks to the bed and places his hat on his knee. "I don't know, Nat. I didn't really. I was just drinking with Richard and Alfie. I'm not sure what you're talking about."

"I don't know. I just want you to notice that I exist."

Daniel offers a wan little smile. "I *do* know you exist."

Perhaps because of her anger, her hurt, and the harshness of Anneke's words, the truth shoots to the surface like a cork held too long underwater. "Okay. I love you. I just wanted you to know that." She thrusts the words at him, not unkindly, not harshly, but matter-of-factly, her voice thin and taut, daring him to deny them, daring him to deny her.

Daniel blinks once and then stares at her. Perhaps he hadn't known. Perhaps all those meaningful moments she thought they'd shared over the past twenty years had just been her imagination. She refuses to believe it.

"But what about Richard?" he breathes.

She breaks eye contact and walks to the window. This is not the hoped-for response, but her mouth shifts into a rueful smile, the relief of telling him, of starting this conversation, this relationship, exceeding any cares she might have regarding its precise trajectory.

"Sorry," he says. "I thought Richard and you were happy."

"How *could* you think that?" Has nobody, not even Daniel, seen her desperation?

"I don't know. It's easy to construct a lot of reality around other people's marriages. You fill in the blanks with whatever you believe to be true about relationships. I just assumed..."

"Richard and I haven't been happy for a long time. We may never have been happy. It's possible that I've *always* loved you." She exhales a faint sob. "I'm going to go out for a walk. I'll give you some space. Please, you don't need to love me back, but I just wanted you to know, so you don't think I'm behaving strangely, and, well, because I thought maybe you felt the same way... But it's okay if you don't. Just think about it."

She bends to pick up her coat, but pauses when she hears his footsteps behind her. When his hands grasp her shoulders she can feel the tremors in his body.

"I don't need to think about it. For the record, I do know that you exist. You're the only thing in that room that I was thinking about. The only thing I ever think about. Tonight and every night. And every night I remind myself that if I let myself go, everyone in that room will know how I feel about you. I just... I didn't know. I didn't *let* myself know."

Natalie feels his breath on her neck and lets his words blanket her like tiny bits of hope tumbling from the sky.

He takes her hand and pulls her over to his telescope, his gray eyes almost blue in entreaty. "Come here, I want to show you the Summer Triangle. It's made up of three stars from other constellations: Vega from Lyra; the Harp, Deneb, from Cygnus, the Swan; and Altair, from Aquila, the Eagle. It's a constellation that joins three separate constellations." Daniel orients his desk telescope east toward the Scarecrow Mountains and places his eye on the eyepiece. "Vega was the Northern Star a long time ago, and will be again in about ten thousand years, which means that the other stars will appear to rotate around it. I have the telescope trained on it now. You can also see it easily with the naked eye if you just follow my finger." The contours of his chest press against her back as she lets her eyes trace the line of his finger. She sees the Triangle, but mostly she feels Daniel's body.

Daniel lips graze her ear. "I know it sounds stupid, but you're like my Vega. You're the star around which everything else rotates for me. I do dumb things because I'm not great in social situations and because I can't show people how I feel about you. But never doubt that I always know you exist, and I know exactly where you are in the room."

Natalie bows her head and feels the brim of tears against her lashes.

The words almost shake out of him, he trembles so hard. "So, don't think I don't love you. I do. More than you can imagine. But he's my brother. We can't."

Can't. Always that word: can't.

"What if I leave Richard?" she says.

He moves away from her with effort and sinks to the bed, taking her hands in his. "It would be fine if we could just disappear together. But you would never leave the boys, and I don't know if I could face what people would say. My parents, Kristen, Richard, the farm members. Leon with his marriage sanctity and men's rights crap. It would be an absolute shit storm. And some people are already pissed off about the newcomers, and most people think you brought them here. If you left Richard, they might use it against you."

"Do you really think that nobody would accept us?"

"Not at Richard's expense. Not unless you left him and we got together years later."

"How many years?"

"I don't know. Three years…five…ten."

"That's an awfully long time."

"I know. I'm sorry. He's my brother, Nat. Even then it's going to be hell, and we might lose everyone that matters to us, including Richard."

Daniel's trepidation and uncertainty give her pause. But she knows he's right. Leaving Richard would court censure from all parts of the farm. Richard would play the hangdog with great aplomb and skill, and garner all the pity—even *she* would feel sorry for him—and she would be alone, laughed at and talked about, stripped of all influence on this farm that *she* built. Perhaps Anneke wasn't harsh in her reproach; Natalie knows all too well how the politics of divorce work. She wanted Daniel to be more certain, more reassuring. To erase Anneke's words and convince her that they could get through this. But maybe they can't.

"What do we do, then?"

"I don't know. Nothing," Daniel says.

"Is Richard worth that?"

"I don't know. It's not just Richard. It's everyone. It's us, too."

An impossible path, Anneke had said.

"So, we're just friends then?"

"No."

"So, what then?"

He flashes her a desperate look. "I don't know. Maybe over time things will change, and we can leave the farm. Maybe something will happen."

She stares at him for a few seconds, a tear trailing down her face. "Okay," she says.

He stands and leans toward her, his breath warm on her face, the folds of his shirt grazing hers, and lets his lips brush faintly against the curve of her jaw. "I want you, more than anything. I have for so long," he whispers in her ear. He catches the tear with his finger and traces it delicately along the hollow of her cheek, and then allows his mouth to fall on the same spot. Shivers of fear-laced desire spiral down her spine, and she lets out a low whimper. He steps back and presses his lips together, his breathing uneven.

They retreat to the couch to sit side by side in the dim light, poised to leap away at any second. Daniel shows her the drawing of the mosquito constellation and talks about the stars in the Summer Triangle, saying something about Aquila representing the secret hidden thing that lies at the back of our souls. Guilt hangs around Natalie, but the euphoria of touching Daniel, even just a tiny bit, outweighs it.

"We better go to bed," Daniel murmurs eventually. "I'm sure Richard will be coming to bed soon. I'll take the couch."

Richard. Why do they both fear and need him so? Natalie retires to Daniel's bed, which everywhere is marked with the smell of Daniel, every nerve of her body twigged.

SHE MUST HAVE EVENTUALLY FALLEN asleep. She wakes in the early morning to find that Richard has joined her in the night, the bedclothes twisted around him. He belches out stale brandy snores. Natalie dresses in the murky light, aware that Daniel watches her half-naked form through one half-open eye from the couch. The irony of the three of them sharing a room wraps around her. She thinks of the Summer Triangle. Three stars joining three separate constellations.

"Sometimes souls have been together for many centuries," a bespectacled old tarot card reader had said years ago at a seaside psychic fair in Vancouver. "Remember the triangle is the strongest shape in the world. But no good can come of these feelings of yours." What did that mean? She doesn't believe in interconnected souls. Or does she?

It would be easier to think of the three of them as being interconnected somehow, of her love for Daniel being inevitable, her fate written in the stars. Some days she does, but other days she thinks it was just written on her faithless heart. Still, try as she might to extinguish them, her feelings for Daniel glow on true and stark, like the stars that paint every inch of the canopy of their brave new world.

Daniel said she was his Vega, but she feels more like Altair, with a pool of secret things hidden at the back of her soul.

But what is in the pool? Lust. Anger. Pride. Hope. Love.

She doesn't know.

Clearly, even if their love is written in the stars, it's doomed. An impossible path, indeed.

CHAPTER 15

THE TEN OF SWORDS

⸺❧⸺

NATALIE AND ANDREW

*Your mental state and fear of ruin lead you to a conscious decision
that things will not work.*

The next several days take on an all-too-consistent arc. Richard and Alfie drink and exchange jokes in the evenings, tittering like frat boys. When he's not drinking with Alfie, Richard is keyed up and snappish, completing his chores with careless efficiency, and Alfie and Claire spend their time in their room, or walking about the property, as if they're visiting a spa. At least Richard has stopped watching Natalie now that he has Alfie to focus on, but he continues to act as if she and Joe are having a torrid affair—smiling maddeningly and wiggling his eyebrows at other people whenever she speaks to Joe, giving her bland disgusted looks when they're alone, and mercilessly mocking Joe whenever he's out of earshot.

Natalie assigns herself the early barn rotation, and she and Daniel milk, clean tack, feed the animals, and discuss how to double the chicken flock. The work and the conversations are necessary, but the smiles and the sweet thrill of togetherness, however restrained, are not.

Each day Natalie forces herself out of the barn to refocus on her work and her responsibilities. She and Daniel have not done anything really wrong, yet. It could all be erased and forgotten. That's what they should do. This message repeats in her brain on a constant cycle. Yet every morning she goes back, haunted by guilt, drawn by a longing she cannot seem to contain, to find him waiting for her; and they speak not of ending it, but of their hopes and desires, and their future.

Natalie returns to Daniel's cabin each night, where they sit on the couch in a state of frustrated paralysis, daring only to talk and exchange the barest of touches, convinced that Richard will show up at any moment. But he inevitably sidles in stinking of moonshine just as they've drifted into slumber, and every wasted evening that they could have spent in each other's arms slides into morning.

IT'S A GRIM DANIEL WHO greets Natalie in the barn office a few days before Thanksgiving when she shows up to help with the milking. "There's talk," he says in a low voice.

"What?"

"Leon's trying to get everyone riled up about the food supply and the newcomers. He's blaming you. I'm worried."

"What's Richard doing?"

"I don't know. He's offline. Seems totally distracted by Alfie and the Internet. I don't even know if he's paying attention to Leon."

"What are *you* doing?"

Daniel stiffens. "What do you want me to do?"

"I don't know. Defend me."

"I'm not your husband. That would seem weird."

"What about defending me as my friend?"

"There's not a lot of room for friendships between men and women in the man code."

"Oh, well, that's a great fucking code, then."

Daniel's eyes turn flinty at her tone. "And the woman code allows your friend to throw you under the bus to save her ass? That's a great fucking code too. You need to talk to Anneke. Get her to come forward. Or tell Richard yourself. Why are you protecting her?" Natalie recoils slightly at the bitter impatience in Daniel's voice.

"Richard won't believe me anyway. I have no proof. Not unless Anneke says it was her. Please don't talk to me that way. I hate it."

Daniel closes his eyes and bows his head, exhaling a big puff of air. "I'm sorry. I'm just worried. If Richard doesn't believe you, then get Andrew or Joe to say that it was Anneke. Leon's an asshole. You don't want him against you."

NATALIE APPROACHES THE PANTRY, THE cream-colored swinging door ominously still. She tries to envision what Anneke might be doing, shifting about the pantry in her systematic and focused way. A stock boils frantically on the woodstove. She watched Joe depart the kitchen for the now-depleted garden with a basket a few minutes before. The frenzy of canning has diminished as the fall harvest has proceeded. Now only the barn kitchen is required to keep up with the slower pace of putting up food for the winter. She hasn't spoken much to Anneke since their exchange in the den a few nights ago, but she must.

Natalie pushes open the pantry door. Anneke's face shifts from a welcoming smile to a more quizzical squint. A jumble of apples, cored and diced for a pie, lie on the countertop in front of her. Natalie forces herself to enter, and leans against the counter's aged green marble laminate. Anneke cocks her head at the fact that Natalie doesn't pick up a knife to work while she talks, but shrugs and returns to chopping.

"I didn't tell Joe about the farm," Natalie says.

Anneke meets her gaze squarely. "Bully for you."

Natalie keeps her voice even. "Which means I think you did, and that you helped the newcomers."

Anneke pushes her lips out in a speculative purse. "Does it matter? They're here now. They're helping. They needed our help, and you've said yourself we need more people on the farm. Maybe we should be questioning the morality of the plan to go up there to run off a bunch of innocent women and children."

Natalie considers this. "How did you know they were innocent?"

"Because Liz told me their story, and I believed her."

"Why didn't you bring it to Farm Council?"

"Because your ruddy Farm Council doesn't work that well sometimes. It all worked out. Can't we just drop it?"

"Well, some people aren't very happy about the new mouths to feed, and

I'm the one taking the blame because everyone knows Joe and I were friends. Even Joe thinks I did it because he got a letter—apparently from me. And, if you helped them by putting out the bullets and calling the dogs inside that day, you endangered everyone."

When Anneke turns this time, she still wears the resolute standoffish expression she has directed at Natalie for the last few weeks, but giant teardrops shimmer at the edges of her blue eyes. "Please, Natalie. I'm sorry. I know. But it all turned out okay. If Richard had gone up there and tried to run them out, it would have been a bloodbath, and who knows how many people would have gotten killed. It could have been worse. Just let everyone think someone left the bullets out by accident, and that the dogs were a mistake. Nobody thinks you helped the newcomers. You weren't even here, and nobody will go after you for telling Joe about the farm. Even if they did, Richard will protect you. He always does. And he'll forget about Joe. If people find out it was me, they'll turn me out, and probably Alan and the kids too. Alan and Leon already don't get along. Please don't tell anyone."

"But why, Neke? Why did you tell Joe about the farm? What don't I know?"

"Please don't ask that, Nat. Please. Just let them think it was you. Most people wouldn't dare question *you* for inviting an old friend here, at least not openly."

There's a hint of spite in Anneke's last sentence, and Natalie bites back the inclination to remind her friend that she's the one who built the farm while everyone else enjoyed city life and had a good laugh behind her back, and that she hasn't lorded it above anyone, ever. One vote for everyone for all major decisions. That was the basis for Farm Council, and they've stuck to it, no matter what the grumblers say. She supposes she may have more influence regarding some things, but she's not even sure of that. Most of the time the farm seems like it's spiraling far out of her control.

"Besides, if I'm out, Alan's coming too, and then you've lost two of your votes on Farm Council. You need me. Please."

"I'll have to think about it."

Natalie's head feels like it is spinning. She just wants her friend back. The friend she had before their lives all got too complicated by farm politics. The Anneke who came with her to peace rallies and left-wing coffee houses, who set Natalie up with earnest environmentalists, and seemed to adore Natalie's boyfriends as much as Natalie did. Well, until Natalie met Richard, anyway. She wants the Anneke who used to give her advice on whom to love and how to live, who would listen to her late-night laments about ever finding a man who would support her career and personhood.

But Anneke is right. Natalie relies on her vote.

Anneke has already turned back to her cutting board, carving the apples into ever-smaller fragments.

⸎

ANDREW STUFFS HIS HEAD UNDER the blankets. Rain pummels the roof, and Alan and Anneke are talking again. The tight living quarters are beginning to wear on him. Alan and Anneke seem to converse endlessly now, and although they keep their voices down, Andrew can hear their muffled conversations through their shared wall. If it's not Alan and Anneke, it's Elena's baby down in the den, or his dad and Alfie playing poker. Andrew feels like a stupid zombie going about his shithouse chores every day in a sleep-deprived fog. And now there's almost twice as much shit, and talk of digging another two outhouses.

Andrew has pretty much given up on his hopes for Elena. She's obsessed with her baby, and Natalie has already warned Andrew that girls who experienced what Elena and the others did with Rafe and his gang are terribly hurt inside and need to be given a lot of space to heal. Two of the other three girls from the ridge are pretty much just shadows going about their chores in silence. They leap at the slightest noise, and are always looking over their shoulders. The third, Virginia, traipses about in provocative clothing, and has already come on to a few of the farm men. Despite his mother's warnings, Elena seems to be doing better than the other three. From what he can gather from Craig, Rafe only dared to touch Elena once or twice because of Liz and her spooky predictions. But still, Andrew's mom is probably right. Yet there's only so much that can be accomplished with one's hand and imagination. Andrew needs to get off the farm somehow.

He decides to make his way down to the kitchen for a glass of water, hoping that Anneke and Alan will be quieter by the time he returns. The hall gleams ghostly in the moonlight. The dining room is quiet. Richard and Alfie must have cut off their nightly bender early. Andrew walks down the side of the hall, avoiding all the squeaky floorboards; he has no interest in waking the baby.

Eve, he reminds himself. If he has any hope of securing Elena's affection, he'd better start calling the baby by its name.

Andrew is positioning himself as Uncle Andrew in his mind when he hears noises coming from the small alcove living room. Breathing and shuffling noises. Andrew freezes. Is someone having sex in the living room? This is replaced by a wild and morbid curiosity.

Andrew hears a man laughing. He reverses direction as quickly as he can on tiptoes and slips into the shadows of the hallway that leads to the infirmary. He whips his head back just in time to see Alfie emerge from the living room. Alfie mounts the stairs to the master bedroom, his gait uncertain and tilting. A few seconds later, Virginia leaves the living room and slips out the front door into the night.

Andrew shuffles into the kitchen for his water, his heart pattering in his chest. Rumbles emanate from the living room. Andrew peers around the corner into the small room to see his father prostrate on the couch, his eyes closed and his mouth open in snore.

⸎

NATALIE CATCHES RICHARD OUTSIDE THE farmhouse two weeks into Claire and Alfie's stay.

"You and Alfie need to tone down the drinking. It's getting to be too much," she says.

Richard's face flicks quickly from rage to a controlled disdain. "Oh, come on, Nat. Can't I have any fun?"

"No, Richard, you can't. Not like this. You aren't at an all-inclusive in Mexico."

"Name one chore that I haven't done this week." He thrusts out his chin and his chest, and makes a small lunge-like move in her direction as if to punt her aside with his bulk. He wouldn't, but he's belligerent and hung over, his pores exuding the acrid stench of grain spirits.

"Claire and Alfie haven't lifted a finger since they got here. It's even worse that you and Alfie are drawing attention to yourselves by carrying on. And Mike says Alfie keeps dropping by the infirmary, even at night, looking for meds."

"Oh yeah? Well, has anyone said anything? Does anyone else think I'm not toeing the party line?"

"No..." This was technically true. Nobody had said anything. Farm members almost never said anything about Richard. She could never understand why.

Richard sticks out his jaw. "Then what's the problem? Is it just your problem? It's not like they're farm members. They haven't applied for refugee status. They're not staying, like your friends seem intent on doing."

"They can help out while they're here. Come on, Richard. *Everyone* works here. My 'friends,' if you want to call them that, are working their asses off, and Alfie and Claire are doing nothing."

"Fine, then. Put them to work."

"They're *your* friends. *You* need to talk to them."

"I'll see what I can do," Richard says.

"Please just do it. I don't know why you always give Alfie special treatment. He's pretty much a criminal as far as I can tell."

Richard's face gets tight. "Don't bring that up again."

"I won't. Just put him to work."

Richard's face morphs into a sunnier and more charming repose, one of his political expressions, his "ask" face. "Just so you know, I'm planning to head back to Vancouver with Alfie after Thanksgiving for a few weeks. They want to talk to me about a potential role in the provisional government. Claire wants to stay here. Just work her into the schedule. You're good at that."

Natalie stares at her husband's brilliant sky-blue eyes. She can't believe Richard's ego would allow him to fall for what might be another pack of Alfie's lies. If there's no leadership role, Richard might be hurt, or made to look foolish. But why does she care? It *is* his choice, and she *wants* him to leave her—doesn't she? And yet suddenly he seems vulnerable and she finds herself worried for him.

"You don't mean you'd actually move there?" she says.

Richard shrugs. "I don't know. I can't take this farm life much longer."

"I'm not moving." The words are automatic. Somewhere in her mind, she still sees their lives as connected. This could be her chance to let go, but she clings. To what? It pisses her off that Richard is always dissing farm life, as if there's some exciting life waiting for him elsewhere. Some life filled with parties and acolytes and single-malt scotch, where he'll be a political god. The life he used to lead. Bitterness reaches its acrid fingers around her concern. *We all want our old lives back, Richard.*

Richard is just dreamer enough to think that it's possible.

Richard smiles, as if her announcement has pleased him. "Don't worry. Nothing is set. I'm just going to check things out. I don't even know if I want the job. I won't be gone long. I promise."

"It's dangerous. You could be killed."

"I'll be fine. You and my milksop brother seemed to do okay out there on your own. It can't be that dangerous."

"You really have a way with words."

Richard cracks her a grin and a wink and saunters off into the rain. Natalie watches his retreating back. He was joking, but Richard's chronic insensitivity wears. Or perhaps his casual putdowns are more malicious than that. Perhaps she doesn't know up from down where Richard is concerned anymore. She wants to ask him about Leon, what Leon is saying about her, about the refugees, but she doesn't. She's scared of what he might say.

Natalie returns to the farmhouse and enters the dining room, her thoughts frayed. A crowd stands around the table, and as Natalie approaches, she sees that Liz is giving Claire a tarot card reading.

Delicate tendrils of blond hair curl around Claire's face. With her white skin and mournful green eyes, she is almost pretty, except for the permanently confused look on her face. Before the peak, Claire lived in a chronic state of illness: stomach problems, exhaustion, back pain, infertility, migraines. Claire had always wanted a baby, and spent many years depressed about her inability to get pregnant. Alfie paid little attention to his wife's wilting and posturing. Richard does a funny impression of Claire as a blood-sucking banshee, feeding on unsuspecting victims with her self-absorption. And now, even in utter disruption, Claire has managed to cling to her old ways. Natalie tries to suppress a surge of jealousy regarding Claire's ability to wallow in irresponsibility.

"I see here that your migraines and back problems will end very soon," Liz says.

Claire gives a slight wail. "Oh, good. They've become almost unbearable."

Natalie leans over to look at the cards, but Liz sweeps them into a pile.

"Oh, I was hoping for more. Is that it?" Claire says.

"Yes. That's it." A sharpness has crept into Liz's voice. She collects her cards and thrusts them into her pocket. Natalie continues through the dining room to the den to consult the work schedule. Siobhan and Solomon have declared that the potatoes must be harvested due to the wet weather, and Natalie has to reorganize some of the work crews.

Liz knocks on the door. Natalie looks up, and the older woman enters and sinks into the faded denim armchair beside the desk.

"I know you don't believe in what I do. But something bad is coming. Illness and death. I saw it in Claire's cards."

Natalie tries to push away her irritation. "Statistically, in this new world, bad things could happen to us at any time. Illness and death are always coming," Natalie says.

"I need to do a reading on you. To understand." Liz fans her tarot cards in front of Natalie. "Draw five cards," Liz says.

"No thanks. I don't have time," Natalie says.

"You must have more faith, my child."

"Not in cards."

"I will pick for you, then." Liz picks five cards and places them on the desk in the form of a triangle and lets her hands flow over the cards as if they emit energy. "The King of Cups, the King of Swords, the Wheel of Fortune, the Tower, and the Queen of Wands. All court cards and Major Arcana. Nothing pedestrian for you." Liz squints up at Natalie. "The Kings represent the two opposing forces in your life. The Wheel of Fortune and the Tower will resolve the conflict between the two Kings. And the Queen of Wands. Very Interesting."

Despite herself, Natalie's eyes fall on the black cat at the foot of the queen. Liz sees her glance and catches Natalie's gaze with sharp eyes.

"The cat represents the Queen's intuition, her shadow self, and her darker impulses."

"I have work to do."

The hooded eyes regard her. "You need to trust your gut and your heart."

A small bud of hope blooms in Natalie's chest. She quickly extinguishes it. It's an impossible path. "I'm afraid they're not very reliable."

Liz grasps Natalie's hand with her surprisingly warm one. Blue veins, rounded and bulbous with age, trace through the backs of her hands. "The time is coming when you must."

Natalie wants to snatch her hand away. What the woman is asking is an impossibility. She has always relied on her mind. She will not change.

The woman regards Natalie for a few seconds and then gathers up her cards and exits the room.

Natalie tries to refocus on potatoes. On duty.

NATALIE RISES THE NEXT MORNING to the crack of rain on Daniel's roof. The glorious September has given way to a frigid and rainy October. Most of the farm members have been diverted to potato harvesting today. The unseasonable rain is saturating the fields, making them a stew of mud and rotting plants. Harvesting in the rain is going to vastly increase the storage rot, but the alternative is to have the potatoes turn to mush in the ground. The rain and close quarters have invaded everyone's senses, and tempers and worries are at a high ebb around the breakfast table.

Natalie is scheduled to meet individually with farm members who wish to lodge complaints or who are to be switching jobs, something she does every three months. She wonders if she should cancel her meetings. But this would likely result in even more complaints. She'll just have to keep the meetings quick so she can get out to the fields.

Her interviews bring the common set of demands and suggestions. Most farm members are worn down from the summer of hard work, and are worried about the winter. Two of the cabins have started leaking, and their occupants demand that their repairs be higher on the list for the construction crew than building cabins for the newcomers. Several people complain about the reduced rations and the outhouse lines. New outhouses will have to be built before winter to accommodate the new people. But nobody suggests outright that the ridge people should be turned out. Except Leon, who points a crooked finger at Natalie and demands to know whether the old farm members will get preference when they run out of food midwinter. He laughs long and hard when she says no, and says he'll see what the others have to say about that. His words leave Natalie shaky and nauseated. Her influence is so tenuous. Claire staggers in, surprised that she's been added to the job chart, and flutters on about the limited skills she has to offer and that she'll be leaving soon anyway. Natalie wonders if Claire knows Alfie and Richard don't plan to take her to Vancouver with them. Claire settles on helping with the washing when she feels up to it and leaves with her brow scrunched in confusion.

The faces grow more and more strained as the morning passes and the reports on the potato crop start to roll in. Blight. Natalie's not surprised. It was only a matter of time, with no fresh seed potatoes. By midmorning, the rain dumps out of the sky in sheets, and Natalie pulls on her wool socks and boots to prepare to go help with the potatoes. Alan is her last appointment. She's surprised he signed up. He almost never has complaints or issues.

He shows up crushing his sodden felt hat between his hands, his red kerchief around his neck. Alan manages all the construction and repairs around the farm, and does an impressive job of putting things back together with nothing but string, old bolts, and scrap lumber. Richard likes to call him MacGyver. She hopes he isn't going to request a job change.

"I keep a careful inventory of our supplies," he starts.

"I'm sure you do," she says gently, wondering what seems to have him so torn up.

"The thing is, things have been going missing."

"Things?"

"Nails, some four by fours. A couple sheets of plywood. I keep track of everything because we can't afford to waste anything. And someone has been taking things."

"Do you know who?" Natalie sees Alan's knuckles whiten around the edges of his dark hat.

"I don't want to name names, but Leon's been hanging around after the shift is over, real chatty, making like he's helping clean up. But that's a new thing for him. It used to be he'd be the first one gone from the site. And the other night, I'm sure I saw him taking a bag of wheat from the barn. Just a small one, mind you, and it was dark, so I could have been mistaken, but I just thought I would let you know."

"Okay, thanks, Alan. I'll follow up on that. Can you do me a favor and keep an eye on him around the lumber supplies for the next few weeks? Don't say anything, just watch him."

Alan nods and scurries out of the office, pulling his cap tightly over his head.

Joe catches her on the porch on her way to the potato field. The rain runs in streams off his brows and nose. He took three of the men out on a hunting party the night before.

"Nat, we got nothing. Not a deer, not a gopher, not even a tick."

"It's okay, Joe. That happens."

Joe tries to shake off the worst of the rain that soaks him. "We've come up empty the last two trips. With all of us depending on game for food these days, it's possible we've thrown off the buck to doe ratio, or just plain over-harvested. Maybe we shouldn't stay. I'll move on with the men I brought with me. Just please keep the girls. They need some stability."

The cold, rainy air seeps under Natalie's undergarments. She pulls her ripped Gore-Tex shell tighter around her. "Don't be ridiculous. You can't go. What about other animals?"

"Deer's our mainstay. They breed like rabbits. If their population is off, then chances are the other ungulates are down, too. It's been bad for a while. I was hoping it was just our altitude on the ridge, but now I don't think so."

"Richard says it's fine, that it's just a seasonal lull. Are you sure it's not just… your…" Natalie doesn't finish. She doesn't want to say it.

Joe looks at the porch. Natalie wonders if she's pissed him off. "Nat, I know I can't see as well as I once did, but the other men can, and I'm not the one doing the shooting. I've found that Richard can be a bit overly optimistic about some things."

Natalie wants to say something snide about Richard's perpetually cheery outlook, but criticizing Richard usually just garners her frowns of disapproval. "Okay, we'll have to talk about it more tonight. I have to get to the fields."

Joe nods and moves aside.

No game, and potentially no potatoes. They truly are in trouble. She pushes through the blinding torrents of rain, her legs drenched before she even reaches the field. Groups of pickers move slowly down each row with pitchforks and shovels, turning over the mounds. They thrust the potatoes into tarp-covered wheelbarrows that are pushed up the rows next to them. A pile of sliced-open potatoes sits at the edge of the field, their insides laced with the brown of blight.

Natalie grabs a shovel and joins a crew. Her gumboots sink up to her ankles in mud. Solomon looks up, his hooded, bearded face and long hair making him look like a grim Jesus. Olivia, Joanne, and Patricia barely glance at her. Siobhan shivers in her shirtsleeves, her dreadlocks dripping water down her back in streams.

"How bad is it?" Natalie says to Solomon.

"We have no way of knowing," he says. "I've stopped cutting them open. We're just trying to get them out of the ground now. It was about a third of the sample I checked. But they can look fine and then disintegrate into mush in storage; we'll just have to hope for the best."

"Can't we use the horses?" Natalie thrusts her shovel into the sopping soil, snatches up the two potatoes that tumble off the side, and plunges them into the wheelbarrow.

"I've sent Daniel to hitch up the team. We're going to try, but I don't think they can pull through this shit."

Natalie falls into a rhythm of dig, grab, thrust. The rain trails under the collar of her jacket and drips off her nose and hair. Daniel arrives with the team, but their hooves sink deep in the mud and the horses panic and buck left and right trying to throw off the plough. Daniel yells and cracks the whip around them, but they just work themselves deeper into the mud, forcing Daniel to unhitch them and pull them out separately. He looks at Solomon and shakes his head as he leads the horses back to the barn. A few minutes later he returns and joins a digging crew. Natalie looks around at the other crews for the first time.

"Where's Richard?" she says.

"He's in the barn with Alfie, clearing a space to dry the potatoes," replies Solomon. Natalie clenches the shovel. Of course he is.

The rain pounds into the field all afternoon, until they're soaked to the skin. Anneke and Joe deliver tea and soup at lunch, but the food barely takes the edge off the cold as they huddle in clusters for body heat. Solomon dismisses some of the early crews to go and get warm. Natalie's arms start to shake as the afternoon wears on. Her fingers are numb and violent shivers pass over her body every few minutes. She feels a stupor come over her as she continues to dig. Solomon tells her to take a break, but she ignores him. The men wheel the last of the loads to the barn in the late afternoon, and Natalie picks her way through the puddles to the edge of the field.

Leon looms out of nowhere, his weathered face cracked open in a frightening grin. "Goodbye my friend, we're all going to die," he sings, making a slicing motion with his finger across his neck. He's high or drunk or both, Natalie realizes with a shudder. He spits a green sleet of pot from between his teeth. "Not so sure of yourself now, are you, Miss High and Mighty?" He makes his voice all high-pitched. "Of *course* we can feed more people. We have to help them. I'm just going to invite *all* my friends to the farm."

"Cut it out, Leon," Olivia says. But Natalie sees nothing but accusing eyes in the faces of the other drenched and desolate farm members on the edge of the field.

Natalie stumbles past Leon to Daniel's cabin and starts to peel off the layers of wet, mud-caked clothes, her hands stiff and uncooperative. The cabin fire is out, and a chill fills the interior. Natalie begins to shake so hard that she can't even remove her jeans. She sinks to the bed and wraps the quilt around her naked upper body.

The cabin door opens, and Daniel walks in. He stops when he sees her.

"I'm sorry," she manages to say, her teeth rattling together. "I'm so cold I can't move."

Daniel strips off his own wet outerwear and tosses it on the floor. His rain pants are caked with mud, but he's dry except in the places the pants are ripped and the rain has snuck through the neck of his jacket. He grabs some kindling and tosses it into the stove, then kneels and scrapes the steel across the flint.

"You've got to get those jeans off. They're soaked," he calls over his shoulder.

"Can you, please?" Natalie trembles so uncontrollably she has trouble speaking.

"I should get Richard."

The spark jumps this time, and the kindling ignites. Natalie starts to feel drowsy, and then Daniel is above her yanking her sodden jeans down and off. They catch on her chafed red skin and then slap to the floor. Of all the ways she thought of Daniel undressing her, this was not one of them. He rolls her up in the quilt like a mummy and then throws more wood on the fire, setting the kettle on top. He locks the door, then rips off his own shirt and lies beside her, wrapping his arms around her and pulling another quilt over himself. He entwines his hands in her hair and pulls her cold nose against his cheek. They lie there for several minutes. She slips her hand out of her quilt and into his, pressing it flat against his warm chest, feeling the brush of his chest hair. He winces at the touch. Her hands, she realizes are still ice cold. But he frees her other hand and then pulls her closer so they are chest to chest, her breasts pressing against him. She huddles her head into the warmth of his neck. The kettle starts to whistle, and after a few seconds Daniel detaches himself, tucking the blanket tightly around her, and removes the kettle from the stove. He pours the water into the teapot and throws in some tea leaves. Natalie watches his broad muscled back in a vague state of shock. She wants him back in the bed with her.

Boots clomp on the porch and the doorknob rattles. Richard. Natalie rolls herself back up in the quilt and pulls Daniel's blanket over top of her. Daniel yanks on a shirt as he crosses the floor to unlock the door. Richard peers in, a puzzled look on his face. A blast of damp air rushes in the open door.

"What's going on in here? Why was the door locked?" Richard steps inside. Raindrops cascade to the floor in his wake.

"Nothing," Daniel grunts. "Natalie got hypothermic, and I'm just trying to warm the cabin up." He steps around Richard and shuts the door, then strides over to the fire and tosses in another log.

Richard's eyes flick over Natalie's pile of wet clothes on the floor, Natalie's shivering form in the bed, the pot of tea on the counter, and Daniel's rain clothes crumpled by the door.

"And the door was locked because?"

"Because we're old enough that you don't need to see me change," says Daniel.

"And my wife does?"

"She hid her eyes. Sorry. She needed to get warm. We've got some rather tight living arrangements here." Daniel's voice is blasé, challenging. He pours himself a cup of tea and sits at his desk.

Richard plunks down on the bed next to Natalie. Droplets of rain from his jacket and hair fall on top of her. She wants to tell him to get off the bed, stop dripping on her.

"Dropped your core body temperature, huh, buttercup?" he says. He grabs her leg, squeezes it hard, and gives it a shake. It's meant to be affectionate, she's sure, but it hurts.

"The potatoes?" Natalie manages.

"They're all laid out and drying in the barn loft. We've stuffed the wood-stoves in the barn, hoping to get the temperature up. Now we just have to wait and see."

"I guess we better schedule a Farm Council for the day after tomorrow."

"What for?" Richard removes his wet coat and throws it over the back of a chair. Pools of water gather on the floor beneath it.

"To discuss what to do, of course." Natalie almost sits up, then remembers that she's topless. "We have to make some plans. I think we need to plant some winter wheat, and try to trade something for some potatoes or grains at the community gathering on Remembrance Day."

Richard cracks a half smile. "You're kind of putting the cart before the horse. We don't even know if the potatoes are bad yet. I checked them out. I think they'll be fine. And you know I'm leaving the day after tomorrow for Vancouver."

"You can't! I just assumed you'd cancel. We have a crisis here, and Alan thinks Leon might be hoarding."

Richard laughs and rolls his eyes. "The potatoes might be fine. I'm sure nobody's hoarding, especially not Leon. Stop worrying so much. Nothing's going to go off the rails in a month."

"Yes, it will. Are you *nuts*?" The words snap out of her.

Richard pulls back, wide-eyed and baffled. "I have to go. People are expecting me."

Natalie wants to slap him hard across the face, to see his skin indent and his head recoil sideways from the force of her blow. For not understanding; for *never* understanding. For once again putting his political career and ego ahead of everything else. But she can't. For Richard, it would be an unforgivable act. And what would Daniel think, to see her so unhinged?

"Can you *please* just talk to Leon?"

"Fine. But it may have to wait until I get back."

Daniel sits watching them. Natalie wants him to step in and help, to say something. But he doesn't. Perhaps his loyalties to Richard are stronger than she thinks. She wonders if it will always be like this. This constant battle of loyalties among the three of them.

"Can you both please leave?" she says. They look at her as if she has screamed *get the hell out*, as if being asked to please leave is unacceptable. Her face crumples. "Please. I need to get dressed and go to the kitchen. I can't do that in front of an audience. Please. Just let me get dressed." She stares at the wall while they rise, put on jackets, and file onto the porch silently, almost reproachfully. She hears them talking on the porch, their darkened figures visible through the slit between the curtains, and then they head off together toward the farmhouse.

———

TALK OF THE POTATO CROP dominates discussions—in the outhouse lines, in the dinner line, and now at the dinner table. The newcomers, including Craig, sit together at the end of the table, heads lowered over their food. A slight space on the benches marks the transition between the newcomers and the old farm members.

Andrew ladles himself some stew. The soups and stews have grown thinner and the servings more restricted since the arrival of the ridge people. Faint hunger pangs pull Andrew out of sleep at night now. Nobody's starving, but the fat comfort of fullness is a less frequent occurrence. Andrew's fantasies have turned from Siobhan and Elena to steak and donuts.

Christopher, Andrew's cousin, looks up as Andrew takes a seat. "Oh, it's the outhouse attendant who thinks we have too much to eat around here," Christopher says. Andrew winces. Christopher's not the only farm member who's become hostile since Andrew's actions on the ridge. Andrew's Uncle Leon, Christopher's dad, keeps talking about do-gooders that don't have a fucking clue. Andrew would sit with Craig, but that would only provide more ammunition regarding Andrew's questionable loyalties. He wonders if his detractors are right. Without the potato crop, things could go bad pretty fast.

Few people talk, aside from Richard, who cracks jokes about the Irish Potato Famine at the end of the table. Only Alfie and a few of the other men laugh. The smell of wet clothes and body odor wafts around the room.

Liz joins Andrew by the fire after dinner, her gray hair plastered in rain-soaked clumps around her face. The tents are sodden, and most of the newcomers now sleep on the barn and shed floors.

Maybe he *has* made a mistake. Maybe the farm is over capacity.

⸙

NATALIE AND RICHARD RETURN TO Daniel's cabin after dinner. They argue in hushed, hissed tones about Richard's inappropriate dinner jokes and his plans to leave the next day. Daniel ignores them and reads in his armchair.

"I'm not delaying my trip. Unlike you, Natalie, I don't feel a sense of responsibility for every dipshit that shows up on this farm. If it comes down to it, you, the boys, and I can go and live in Vancouver, and I can work for the government. Alfie says it isn't that bad there. It might be a hell of a lot safer and more comfortable than it is here. I don't know why I have to keep putting my ass and career on the line for everybody else."

"You don't care about anybody on this farm?"

"They have to take responsibility for their own lives." Richard's eyes are flat.

"They do, but we are all in this together. I can't believe you would just abandon everything we've worked for."

"What do you expect from me, Natalie? I don't even know. This whole farm thing wasn't my idea. It was yours. I have some things that I really want to achieve in my life, and staying here on the farm is not going to get me there."

"I can't believe you would say that! We *agreed* to do this. And you have no idea what Vancouver is like. Why are you doing this? How can you leave us like this? They listen to you. They don't listen to me."

Daniel closes his book, rises, and walks out of the cabin. Shock and disappointment stream through Natalie's limbs. She hadn't forgotten Daniel was there, but she somehow expected him to agree with her, or even step in.

Richard chuckles at Daniel's departure, and as if it signifies the end of the argument, the decision of the jury in Richard's favor, pulls off his pants and climbs into bed. "It'll be fine. I've been down to the cellar. There's oodles of food. I can probably buy more grain in Vancouver, once I start collecting a paycheck, and bring it back."

Natalie barely hears what Richard says. She stares after Daniel. But she can't run after him and demand that he explain himself, explain why he would abandon her, why he didn't back her up. She blows out the candle, undresses, climbs into bed, and lies in the dark, her heart throbbing. She hears Daniel return and settle on the couch an hour or so later.

THANKSGIVING DAWNS COLD AND DRY. The pig for the feast hangs in the barn. There had been talk of canceling the feast, and portioning out the pig to last for several days. But they decided that everyone needs a rest and some celebration. Chores will proceed as normal, but everyone will stop in the early evening for a group dinner. They need it.

Daniel digs around in his desk. He acts like nothing happened the previous night. Richard has already departed the cabin with a smirk.

"Hey, have you seen my binoculars?" says Daniel. "I can't find them, but I'm sure I left them on the table there."

Natalie shakes her head. Richard probably took them. But to say that would add to the countless betrayals Daniel probably thinks she heaps upon her husband. She slips out the door and heads for the kitchen.

She spends the morning with Siobhan and Solomon, weeding and trying to revive some of the struggling greenhouse crops. They have to decide how many seeds they can risk without jeopardizing the summer crops. Natalie heads to the kitchen mid-morning to help with the dinner. Her hands bleed at the knuckles, and she tries to shrug off the harried feeling creeping up her spine.

Laughter emerges from the shed as she passes. She opens the door and looks in. Richard and several of the men stand around the blacksmith forge, drinks in hand. Daniel sits off to one side, holding a mug. Richard bangs a piece of metal on the anvil, his back to her. "Those union women were hell to work with. They'd have their grievances typed up and filed before you could even get the change implemented. Don't piss off the army of hens. They'll peck you to death." Richard puffs himself up and parades around the shed flapping his arms like a chicken. He stops when he sees Natalie in the doorway.

"Hi, sweetie!" Richard says, too loudly. "What's up?"

"What are *you* doing?" Natalie says.

"Just having a little drinkie. It's Thanksgiving! Want one?" The other men chortle around him like little boys; only Daniel looks uncomfortable.

Natalie feels the tears that she didn't shed last night collecting in her throat. "I have to work. Can't you see the rest of us need some help around here?"

The room goes silent. Richard looks at the roof of the shed and shakes his head. Natalie casts a look of despair at Daniel, and runs out of the shed.

Richard is not far behind her. "Nat, do *not* talk to me that way in front of the other men."

"It's not fair. Some of us are working our butts off, and you're sitting around having a drink, doing who knows what." This is a mistake, and Richard slams his open palm into the shed wall.

"Why do you always have to have such a stick up your ass? Are you suggesting that I don't pull my weight around here? Is that what you're suggesting? 'Cause you better not be."

Natalie hunches her shoulders. Maybe she does have a stick up her ass. Maybe this *is* her fault. "I'm sorry. I'm just tired and overwhelmed. So when I see you and Daniel standing around doing nothing, it upsets me. I'm sorry." Another mistake.

"What the fuck does Daniel have to do with this?"

"Nothing." She wants to scream. Maybe Daniel is just the same as Richard.

"You saw me doing nothing for five minutes."

"Well, I don't know what you've done for the rest of the day."

"Are you asking me for a list of what I've done today? Is that what you're asking?"

"Forget it. Just forget it. I'm sorry, I was just trying to explain to you how I'm feeling."

"When is it going to matter how *I'm* feeling?"

Natalie pulls her arms tightly against her sides. How can things possibly be so murky all the time in terms of who's right and who's wrong? The only thing possible when Richard is this angry, this self-righteous, is to retreat and tell him he's right, even as every twitch of her body says that he's wrong. It's a scene they've played out over and over again until the words themselves have become meaningless, merely a declaration of continued war.

"It just upsets me when I see you not working. I'm sorry. I'm just scared."

"Whatever, Nat." Richard turns and starts to return to the shed. He will never depart from the script, never tell her that he understands her fears, that he'll do his best to take them away.

"Do you think, maybe, it's time we call this quits? This marriage? Maybe you should just stay in Vancouver for awhile," she calls after him.

"I think you should think about what you are saying," he says without looking back.

Daniel emerges from the shed a few minutes later, and she follows him to the barn. They rest their arms on the walls of two stables and look at each other, an empty stall between them.

"You think I overreacted too," she says.

Daniel's face is flat. "People need breaks. And men will be men. You can't expect us all to be working every second of every day."

"The women do," she snaps.

Daniel maintains his bland affect. "No, they don't. Have you watched Colleen do the wash?"

"Well, *I* do." She tries to pout, but her lips flip into the quiver that precedes tears. She doesn't want Daniel to be angry with her, cold with her. She wants him to hold her and whisper and kiss away her fears.

"I know you do. But maybe you should stop. Or ease back just a little bit." Daniel's mouth turns up in a tiny hopeful smile, a small anchor.

"Richard doesn't know I do. You think Richard pulls his weight around here?"

"Richard doesn't know what anyone does. And I know he fucks the dog sometimes...a lot of the time. I know it's irritating. But that's Richard. It shouldn't be any surprise to you."

"So I should just accept it."

"I don't know what you should do. But you being angry at him seems to be hurting you. He isn't going to change."

She flinches in anger. Richard is never expected to change. They're all expected to maneuver around him, recognize his manhood, his basic Richardness. "Why did you leave last night?"

"I can't stand listening to the two of you fight."

"You don't agree with me?"

"I do agree with you, mostly, but I really don't want to pick sides. He's my brother, and your husband."

"You aren't going to pick sides even when it comes to the survival of the farm?"

He looks down and kicks at the cement floor with his boot. "I don't know. I didn't say that. We just need to tread carefully. Richard has a lot of pull, especially with my parents and Leon and Krissy, and most of the men. If there's any suggestion of an alliance or a relationship between us, not that there is, we would be in big trouble."

The stupidity of wanting him strikes her. Maybe Daniel naïvely thinks that he won't have to pick a side. And realistically, how can she ever expect him to side against his brother? But how can he ever really support her if his loyalties are always divided?

"Please don't just march out like that again. It was awful."

"Sorry, Nat. When you fight with him though, some of the things you say... It seems like you're still committed to being married to him. And then I feel like a fool, hanging around here waiting for someday. And I start to think that I should just forget about it."

This pronouncement almost upends her. She wants to close the distance between them, take his hands and press them to her face, while her lips trace the skin beneath his eyes to the curve of his cheekbone, but she can't, for there are too many parts of what he says that she fears are true. "No, Daniel. Please, no. I'm not. It's just hard. You spend so much time with your life wrapped up in someone else's, for good and for bad, and it's just hard to even start to let that go. Besides, I'm terrified that, without Richard, we don't know the first thing about surviving."

This last must have hurt him. She wonders how often it's been suggested to him that he's weaker, less competent, lesser than his twin, but aside from a flick of something fleeting and unreadable in the set of his jaw, he doesn't show it.

"I think you need to stop being so afraid all the time. What's the worst that can happen?"

She feels a collapsing in her face at this, a disappointment, and an edge cuts through her voice. "You don't understand. You're not a mother. I don't care about my own life, except that my survival affects theirs. Everything is about Andrew and Justin. I wish it wasn't. But when you have children, and you're a woman, that seems to be what happens. And there are a lot of bad things that can happen, especially now. I'm sorry."

Daniel inches a bit closer, takes her hand in his, and holds it against the curve of muscle that lies over top of his heart. His half-assed gimpy heart. It's a simple touch, and yet it sends shudders down her body.

"You don't have to be sorry. I'm sorry. I know. Or maybe I know that I don't know. I guess I'm just used to living as if my number could come up at any time. Used to having all my family look at me with goodbye in their eyes. It changes how you live." He lets his fingers brush lightly against her hand as he releases it. "I just want to see you smile sometimes. I'm here for you, whatever you decide."

Footsteps startle them, and they both jump away. Daniel grabs a pitchfork and starts turning hay. Natalie turns, her heart a skein of wool, the final thread being wound ever tighter and tighter.

Leon saunters by with a malicious smile. "Oh, who's on a break now, huh?"

DESPITE THE POTATO SITUATION, THANKSGIVING dinner is festive. Everyone seems to be on his or her best behavior. Richard pats Natalie's leg and smiles and nods while she speaks. His way of forgiving and forgetting. Paul gives a sermon on thankfulness, community, and living together. Everyone looks hopeful, until

Richard cracks a joke about dying together.

Natalie has submerged her fears in a few glasses of moonshine by the time the music starts. Alan has his guitar, Solomon his violin, and Joe bangs on the old piano. Natalie listens as the men sing and play. Hans slips an arm around the back of Patricia's chair. Natalie almost smiles. The possibility of starvation doesn't stop the most basic of human drives. Richard plans to announce his departure tonight. She doesn't think she can listen. She sneaks out of the dining room to the den.

Natalie hears Richard's words drift down the hall. He speaks of making history, rewriting the constitution, and making Canada a stronger place than before. She sits at the desk and writes lists of potential foods that can get them through the winter, lists of things they can trade for grain or potatoes, and lists of chores that have to be done.

Before Richard finishes his speech, Natalie has tacked a notice of tomorrow night's Farm Council meeting on the bulletin board. She returns to the desk and logs on to the Internet to check for any sign of the online trading post that Hans indicated is coming soon. She doesn't hear the person approaching from behind until his hands are on her shoulders; she looks up to see Daniel's worried face looming over her, the gray of his eyes dusky in the dim light.

"Are you okay?" he whispers.

"I'm scared," she says.

"I know. Me too."

Despite her fears, or perhaps *because* of them, she lets him stand there with his hands on her, and she leans back into him, resting the back of her head against his stomach.

CHAPTER 16

THE MAGICIAN

NATALIE AND ANDREW

You are ready to become a conduit for power.
The only limits are the ones you impose on yourself.

Natalie lies in bed as Richard and Alfie leave the farm for Vancouver. Correction: Richard, Alfie, and *Virginia* leave. She does not want to see Richard smile as he canters off. And she especially doesn't want to see him smile as he canters off with another woman.

Richard told her about Virginia after dinner, sheepishly, saying that she wants to return to her family in Kamloops, and that he and Alfie can take her there. That's where they have to catch the train anyway. Natalie had nodded curtly, not asking questions, not suggesting that Virginia might be too troubled, not questioning the nature of Richard and Virginia's relationship. There probably is no relationship. Women like Virginia love Richard, throw themselves at him, and he likes to flirt with them. But Natalie's sure that's all it is. Richard is probably just doing a good turn. But still, the prospect of seeing the three of them ride off together makes the muscles in Natalie's chest tighten until they hurt.

Maybe she should have been firmer with Richard the previous day, about ending it. He always assumes she doesn't mean it. Maybe she doesn't.

But she has no idea why he doesn't just let her go.

She pulls on her jeans. She has a lot to do before Farm Council this evening, and she feels the stress massed in a bundle between her shoulder blades. Richard said nothing about her staying in Daniel's cabin during his absence, and now that Alfie's gone, Natalie intends to kick Claire out of the master bedroom and move a bunch of the newcomers in there. Spending the night alone with Daniel in the cabin hangs in the back of her mind. The prospect is somewhat thrilling, but mostly terrifying.

She heads to the barn after breakfast. Potatoes sit in all corners: brown russets occupy shelves and tarps at the front of the barn, reds are strewn about on tables in the back, and the Yukon Golds sit atop tarps over the straw in the loft. They all need to be stored. Siobhan and Solomon picked through them the day before, removing the ones that had already rotted. The cull pile outside the barn emits a foul smell and will have to be buried deep to try to avoid passing the blight to next year's crop. Natalie notes the gaps between the potatoes, and hopes that it reflects careless placement by Richard, rather than the number of potatoes that have already been tossed—or someone coming through and taking some. Someone like Leon.

The potatoes can't be stored in sacks in the cellar, as one blighted potato could ruin the whole sack. Alan and Ranjeet are adding shelves to the cellar so some can be stored without touching each other, but the rest will have to be dehydrated to reduce storage rot.

Natalie, Siobhan, and Solomon spend the morning bagging and counting. Half for storage and half for dehydration. Natalie presses her fingers against the skin of each potato, feeling for firmness—that crisp finish on the exterior that provides some promise of protection against rot. By the end of the morning, twenty-six bags line the inside of the barn: about sixty potatoes per person. Even with the wheat and corn, it won't be enough to feed the humans and animals and still save enough for seed the following spring.

Siobhan, green with early pregnancy, starts to retch, and Solomon guides her away, his hand pressed tenderly against the small of her back. Natalie wants someone to take her away and comfort her.

Natalie knows that she needs to be more like Richard and trust that the food will come, that they will find more wild game, butcher more of the cattle herd, or eat the farm cats or horses. That they will survive. But she's always driven by the fear of what will happen to them, what they might become in the dead of winter when the cellar is empty, when there's not a leaf to be coaxed out of the greenhouses, and when the game is as thin and withered as they are.

Daniel has been watching Natalie every time he's passed by: to milk the cows and goats, shovel out the stalls, and help the pig birth four piglets—tiny slippery masses of pink that seem too helpless to butcher. Natalie's sure Daniel counted the number of bags of potatoes each time. At first he just looked, and gave her a hopeful upturn of his lips as he strode past. Later in the morning, she could see him running figures in his mind just like she was doing.

He strides by again as they finish the count, slows as he passes, runs his boot gently against the bags, as if he can make them multiply by touching them. Then he stops and comes to stand next to her. He's worried, too. She can see it in the chalky undertone of his skin, the way he looks down into her eyes, the brim of his hat almost touching her forehead. He needs her reassurance as much as she needs his.

"Ideas?" she says.

Daniel shoves his hands in his pockets and shifts his weight to his heels. "We find something to trade, and hope someone has a grain or potato surplus."

"What about winter wheat?"

"Yeah, sure. We can plant it, but it won't be ready till early spring. Do we have enough food to get through the winter?" Daniel walks a few feet away and sits on a hitching post. Natalie wants to go and stand close enough to smell him, as if his scent can provide her with the strength she needs, or maybe just numb her to the situation. But Karl and Christopher muck out stables just a few feet away.

"Maybe, but it would be the beginning of a slow dwindle," Natalie says. "It would be risky to start the spring with a low seed stock and an empty cellar and barn."

"We've got the cows to trade. That was part of our plan when we got them. We're not going to be able to feed them all anyway at this point."

"How many can we afford to give up?"

"I'd say one bull and four steers or cows. We'll probably eat ten cows or steers a year with our new numbers. Five cows need to be kept for dairy. If we butcher only steers, that leaves a bull and nine cows and heifers for breeding for next year."

"Could we just eat the cows?"

"Pretty meat-heavy diet, and we might be able to get more calories in potatoes or some other grain in trade for the cows."

"So, someone takes the cows to Jerry for the community gathering and tries to trade them, or should we send someone to Tanner's Ridge?" The prospect of going back to Tanner's Ridge terrifies her. Who would volunteer for what might be a death mission? Or worse, who could she ask? Before today, she would have asked Richard to go. Richard, her crutch and reluctant protector. Perhaps that's one of the reasons their relationship is in such disarray.

Karl and Christopher have moved on to the chicken coop, and Natalie allows herself to edge into the triangle of floor space between Daniel's legs. Daniel tenses and straightens up, putting more distance between them.

"Yeah, or you try to find someone that wants to trade over the Internet."

"Richard changed the password on the email address."

"Get a new one."

"All right. We'll see what they say at Farm Council."

"Don't give them a choice," Daniel says.

Natalie bunches her lips in frustration. He thinks it's so easy. As much as she'd like to impose her preferences at Farm Council, it wouldn't fly; but Daniel doesn't seem to get that.

When Siobhan returns to the barn, the soft footfalls of her worn Birkenstocks don't alert Natalie or Daniel. Siobhan lowers her head in a sweep of dreadlocks as she passes.

Daniel heads back to the new piglets. Richard has been gone for six hours. Already the farm seems subdued, as if he's the bearer of the psychic energy that keeps the farm going. His sureness and his optimism may be irritating, but as much as Natalie scoffs at them, they are also reassuring. She tries to shake the feeling of vulnerability that haunts her when Richard is away.

Natalie heads to the farmhouse for lunch. Leon and Terrence wait for her by the shed. They look like caricatures of hardened ranchers, in their old Wranglers and ball caps, their lips pouched with their homemade whiskey corn snuff. As the two men draw nearer wearing sly grins, Natalie realizes that Richard's absence might be more problematic than she had expected.

"We were just talking about who's gonna chair Farm Council now that Richard is gone," Terrence says.

Natalie stops. She had just assumed there wouldn't have to be a formal Chair, that she would lead the discussion. She called the meeting, and she knows the issues best. She hadn't even thought of anyone else chairing the meeting.

"I thought I would," she says.

"Really?" Leon says with a silky smile. "We were thinking it would be more appropriate if someone with experience chaired the meeting."

"I've run meetings before," Natalie starts.

"We don't want you to be in over your head," Terrence says. His words sound concerned, but his blue eyes, so like Richard's, gleam with victory. "We might want to consider the Farm Code. It says that in the absence of the Chair, the Deputy Chair will take over, not the Secretary. I know you're more involved in the day-to-day, but we should probably stick to the Code and let Leon chair," Terrence says with a breezy upturn of his lips.

Natalie feels defeat closing around her. Leon was chosen Deputy Chair four years before, to appease Terrence, Brent, and Colleen. As long as Richard was around, it was a figurehead position with no real duties, which was just fine, since half the time Leon was drunk or high and the rest of the time he was just stupid.

"Okay," Natalie says. "Do you want to send me your agenda items?"

"No, I'll do up the agenda. I have some ideas that I'd like to throw out there. I think we're going to do things a bit differently now," Leon says, giving her a quick dismissive wink.

"Well, we need to decide if we're giving the newcomers a vote, if anyone's going to the Remembrance Day gathering, and what we're going to do about the potato crop."

"You let us handle it," Leon says. He and Terrence have already started walking away. She wants to call after them, to tell them that they have to post the agenda, but she's been outmaneuvered.

Natalie drags herself the rest of the way to the kitchen. She collects her bowl of roasted parsnip soup and slinks into a hidden corner of the pantry to eat. Anneke bustles around her. Anneke hates Leon, but she might not support Natalie as Chair. Anneke has always wanted Paul as Chair, claiming he is the most neutral of everyone. Natalie could threaten to expose Anneke if she doesn't support Natalie, but that seems too dirty. Joe still doesn't have a vote. Daniel won't speak against Leon publicly, but might support her in a secret ballot. Mike and Joanne will support her, as will Siobhan and Solomon and Paul and Cyrus. But that leaves a lot of people whose loyalties she's uncertain of. She should have forced Richard to hold the meeting and re-elect a new Chair before he left. She hadn't even considered this problem. Damn Richard.

Natalie crashes into Liz on her way out of the pantry to wash her bowl. Liz follows her to the sink.

"Bad news about the potato crop," Liz says.

"Yes."

"Is that going to affect us newcomers?"

"I don't know, Liz. I can't say for sure. I don't know what's going to happen tonight. Leon will be chairing the meeting." Natalie flicks her head over her shoulder to where Leon preens by the fireplace between Terrence and Brent.

The crow's-feet around Liz's eyes widen and separate. "The drunk woman-hater?" Natalie looks around, concerned that Liz's words were overheard, but the buzz of discussion at the table is loud, and Elena's baby squawks in the corner.

"Yes," Natalie replies in an undertone. "He's the Deputy Chair. Farm Code says he gets to run the meeting."

Liz drops her dishes into the soapy wash water. "I've been reading your Farm Code. It says that an Executive member can be removed by a majority non-confidence vote of the entire Council or of the Executive. As Secretary, if the Deputy Chair is removed, you're next in line to chair. Who's the Treasurer?"

"Olivia. But she won't vote Leon off. He's her son-in-law." Natalie starts washing the lunch pots and dishes.

"You're her daughter-in-law."

"That doesn't mean much. Not in this family. Not on this farm."

Liz tilts her head pointedly toward Leon. "Do you want *him* in charge? You get us newcomers a vote and we'll support you."

"But then Leon will hate me, and he'll just turn around and call a non-confidence vote on *me*."

"As Chair, you get first shot at tabling the agenda. Any additional votes have to be added as a motion to amend the agenda. You'll know right away if the crowd is with you if your agenda is approved."

"And if the crowd isn't with me?" Natalie says.

"At least you tried," Liz says.

Easy for you to say, Natalie thinks. Trying to take Leon out, if she fails, could get her exiled. The pool of dread that always sits fallow and waiting in her stomach leaps through her veins.

NATALIE FINDS OLIVIA IN THE barn kitchen cleaning the beeswax cappings for candles. The milkweed strings are laid out carefully on the counter next to her.

Olivia's words are rushed and nervous. "I know what you're here for. Terrence and Leon have already been here. Don't ask me to do it, Natalie. I don't want to get involved."

"I know, but by not getting involved, you're de facto supporting Leon."

Olivia gives the strainer with the cappings a shake. "Oh, don't say that. I don't want to get between you and Leon. Can't the two of you talk?"

"Leon hates me, Olivia. He thinks I'm dumb as a post and can't run this farm."

"Oh, he just thinks that of all women."

"Right, and we want someone who thinks women are idiots chairing Farm Council?"

"I'm not good at this kind of thing, Natalie. I only agreed to be Treasurer because I used to be a bookkeeper." Olivia tips the strainer and dumps the cappings into the sink. "Oh, no. Look at what you've done. You've made me so nervous I can't even think."

"What if I were to convince Daniel to take over as Chair?"

"He wouldn't," Olivia says. But Natalie sees a strand of hope in Olivia's eyes. "Though it would be good for him. I worry about him."

"Let's say I could convince him. We get Leon out, and I call a vote to get Daniel in. Come on Olivia, Leon is a drunk and a fuck-up. You know that."

"Do you really think you could convince Daniel to take over as Chair?"

"I could try. Promise me you'll do it, and I'll call an Executive meeting for ten minutes before Farm Council."

"NO WAY!" DANIEL'S VOICE CONTAINS a level of horror that would suggest she'd just asked him to run naked through the farm kitchen.

"We don't have any choice here. It's either Leon or you."

"That is *not* our only choice."

"He's going to fuck it all up. He'll put forward a motion to get rid of the newcomers to save our food supplies, and who knows what else. He's a lunatic, Daniel."

"You don't know that. What you're asking me to do, I can't."

"Why not?"

"Because I'm a private person. I'm not good with people. I don't have people skills. I would screw it up. You should be Chair, not me. I just can't. I'm not Richard."

"For me?"

Daniel groans. "No. Don't ask me to do it for you."

"You have to."

"No. I don't. Find someone else." There's a finality in Daniel's voice, and his eyes tell Natalie not to press any further. "You can't ask me to be like Richard."

"Thanks a lot." A bitter disappointment underscores her words. She breathes shallowly to hold back the tears. "Fine, if you won't do it, promise me you won't say anything to your mother until after she votes Leon out. She'll get over it." Daniel starts to pace about the barn like he's wrestling with a wild animal in his mind.

He stops and stares at her. "You're going to trick my mother?"

"Does that bug you?" Something about his tone buoys her, like he's perversely proud of her. A small ray of possibility pulls at her.

"Nope. I'm okay with it. I actually think it's a bit funny."

He yanks her against him and squeezes her tight against his chest, causing his hat to tumble to the floor. Then, realizing who might be watching, he lets her go, so she almost stumbles backward. But only the horses stare out of their stalls, their placid eyes offering no judgment.

ANDREW CONSIDERS HIS OPTIONS. CONTINUE his rather ineffectual efforts to woo Elena, continue to moon over Siobhan—who has become less appealing now that she's barfing and showing, three months into her pregnancy—try to chat up one of the two remaining traumatized pregnant girls, which seems like a bad idea, or wait until the gathering on Remembrance Day. The decision with regard to who's going, if anyone, should be tonight. At least Alfie and Virginia left this morning. Andrew hasn't been able to forget the noises that he heard that night in the office.

Andrew is finally off shithouse duty. He's been assigned to washing with Claire, a woman's job, according to his Uncle Leon, but at least it doesn't involve human excrement. Claire stoops over the washtubs when he arrives. She wears a long pink tunic with frills over top of black leggings, a rather dressy outfit for washing, but it accentuates her long legs.

Andrew feels the beginnings of a hard-on. He's never considered Claire as an option. Too old, too high-maintenance, and married to Alfie. But with Alfie gone and clearly fucking Virginia, maybe Claire is fair game. He wonders if Claire has any idea about her husband's extracurricular activities. Perhaps she could use some consoling and a shoulder to lean on. With his Dad's favorite song about nice legs starting to unspool in his head, Andrew plasters a smile on his face and goes to take a closer look at what Claire might have to offer.

The first thing he notices is that her face is red and folded into a pout. And not a cute little vixen-like one, but the full-on pout characteristic of a three-year-old. Her features aren't half-bad though: a little wispy and delicate perhaps, but all normal-sized and in the right places without any detracting accentuation like a mole or something. Breasts small, but appropriately rounded and perky, unlike Elena's, which are always engorged and drenched with milk. Andrew searches his mind for Claire's age—younger than his mother, he knows. Finding no clear reference points in his memory, he settles on thirty-three, just over double his age.

"Hey Claire. What's up?"

Claire extends her sour look. "Does everybody on this farm just roll around in the dirt every day? Look at this water. It's disgusting."

Claire's hands glow brilliant red from the scalding water, which has already degenerated into a filmy brown pool.

"'Fraid so," Andrew says. "Do you want me to dump that and get you new water?"

Claire focuses on Andrew for a few seconds. Her eyes are glassy, with a trance-like quality, as if she's not all there. "I guess. Andrew, right? I could never keep you and Justin straight when you were kids. You were such adorable little boys. Everyone thought your mom was nuts for having kids so young. But she was the smart one. Now it's too late for me."

Andrew does some recalculations in his head about Claire's age. She still has her hands in the water, and Andrew's hesitant to rip the washtub out from underneath her.

"May I?" he says, placing both hands on the washtub handles. Claire obediently removes her hands and starts wringing out the clothes she's placed in the next tub with small half-squeezes, not the knuckle-busting wrenches that Andrew knows are necessary. Andrew dumps the tub outside and refills it from the kettles on the woodstove. He lathers up some of the clothes lying beside the washtub and starts scrubbing.

"Alfie left today, even though I start ovulating next week. And now I've missed another opportunity." Claire stares at the ceiling. Andrew's not sure if she's even addressing him. Her pose makes her look almost ethereal, but that and her talk give Andrew the alarming sensation that she might be as batty as his father always said.

All right, so: not bad-looking, but needs to work on her filters, possibly crazy, and needs to smile a bit more, Andrew thinks.

"So Claire, tell me about what it's like in Vancouver now."

Claire's hands close around a shirt in the rinse basin, twisting it into a thin rippled snake of red.

"It's horrible. Unimaginable. People and human waste everywhere. Gunfire and fights at night. Dead bodies in the streets every morning before the street keepers come to pick them up. Going out at night is just asking for it. Alfie got us into a group home with a bunch of hippies that were pretty much work Nazis. We had to share a garden and a kitchen. That's how everyone lives there now. But everyone in our home hated me for not working hard enough. Kind of like here. Except there they just let me stay in bed."

Andrew adds *possibly in need of antidepressants* to his mental list. "I don't think everyone here hates you, Claire. I don't." He smiles his most sincere and charming grin, and considers just how far he would go for the possibility of getting laid.

A slow smile blooms across her face, and she laughs. The tinge of distrust or wryness that's laced through her smile only adds to her appeal.

"You are a funny boy, Andrew."

Andrew isn't sure if being called a boy is progress, but he decides he wants to find a way to make her laugh again.

NATALIE'S HEART POUNDS UNCOMFORTABLY. SHE can't believe she's allowed things to go this far, been the architect of them going this far. She's been a fool. She told Leon to meet her and Olivia in the den at quarter to six. But for all her bravado with Daniel, she's not sure she can do this. Leon has to know what Natalie's thinking. She just hopes he doesn't bring Terrence. She doesn't want to lead. She just wants things to be fair and right. If she lets Leon take control, he'll destroy the farm and everything she's worked to create.

Daniel hovers out in the hallway. Natalie wonders if this is his way of supporting her. Olivia will probably view Daniel's presence as a sign that he wants the Chair position. Joe and Liz sit just inside the dining room, waiting for Natalie's nod. Natalie feels bad about deceiving Olivia, but Olivia never stays mad for long; otherwise there would be no way she could have stayed married to Terrence for forty years.

Olivia and Leon arrive at the same time. Olivia brushes past Daniel, all stiff and skittery. Leon dwarfs her as he towers down the hall. He punches Daniel in the arm as he passes, too hard, sending Daniel veering into the wall.

"Hey, buddy. Look alive. What're you doing hanging out here? You don't want to get involved in this shit, do you?" Leon stops to study Daniel for a second. "Or do you? Just make sure you've thought good and hard about where your bread's buttered and the hand that feeds you, if you know what I mean. Karma, my friend, karma."

Daniel regards Leon coolly. "No Leon, I'm not sure I know what you mean." But he turns and heads down the hall, and Natalie is alone with Leon and Olivia.

Leon seems somehow bigger than usual as he turns to face Natalie and Olivia in the den. "So, Nattie girl. What's the deal? What was so urgent that you had to see us before Farm Council?" He wears an innocent smile, but his creepy blue-brown eyes are dark and hostile.

Natalie's entire right leg shakes. "According to the Farm Code, the Executive can have a majority vote of non-confidence for any of the Executive positions. I would like to call that vote right now for the Deputy Chair position." She wonders if Leon can see her jiggling leg and quivering hands.

"Oh," he says. "We don't have to do that. We're all friends here. Aren't we, Olivia?"

Olivia flinches slightly. They have to do this quick. If Leon keeps talking, Olivia will lose her resolve. Natalie focuses on a spot on the wall instead of Leon's murky eyes. "Yes, Leon. I'm afraid we do. I'd like to call that vote now. All in favor of removing Leon as Deputy Chair due to non-confidence?" Natalie raises her hand, pleading with all the gods she knows, and after an interminable few seconds, Olivia raises hers too. She holds it low, not even elevating her elbow, just extending her fingertips skyward, but it's enough. Leon looks at Olivia in stupefaction and then leans into Natalie.

"You'll be sorry, you little *bitch*. I'll just deny this vote ever happened. Nobody's going to believe you, and Olivia isn't going to speak against me in public." His words and his proximity make Natalie's stomach explode in a spray of fear. He could so easily kill her, twist a knife into her side in the dark, whispering his hateful words, on any night on the farm.

"I don't like the way you're talking to us, Leon Gunn," Olivia says.

Natalie holds up a piece of paper with the words confirming the non-confidence vote, which she carefully wrote out in advance. She signs it and passes it to Olivia.

"So, you're going to side with the little whore, are you? You know what she's doing? She's using your sons to gain power. It's the oldest trick in the book." Natalie's face flushes with the white-hot fury of shame and righteousness. She is not using Daniel. But the denial, even within the confines of her own head, has the bitter undertone of untruth. If even *she* can only take the darkest perspectives on her own motives, what must other people be thinking?

Olivia looks at Natalie and pauses. "Natalie wouldn't do that."

Leon rolls back his head and lets out a blast of laughter. "That's what you think. You don't know anything. What did she promise you to vote with her?"

Olivia's eyes sharpen in Natalie's direction.

"Think about it, Livvie. First, she brings her ex-boyfriend and all his buddies here, and drives her own husband, your son, away. Then, when she can't control poor Richard anymore, she gets all doe-eyed and who knows what else with your second son in order to take control."

"None of that is true," Natalie declares.

But the seeds of doubt have been sown, and Olivia looks at Natalie with new eyes, the lines on her face, etched by sun and age, more pronounced than they were a moment before.

"Do not sign that piece of paper, Livvie. Think about what she's doing to the farm."

"Please, Olivia. Don't listen to him." Natalie hears her voice, almost a whisper.

Olivia's fingers curl around the pen. Leon lunges forward in his chair and jabs the air in front of Olivia. "Your husband does not support this." Olivia pulls away and the back of her chair knocks against a framed painting that Andrew did in kindergarten. The painting falls to the ground, and the glass shatters. Natalie suppresses a scream.

The door to the den flies open and Daniel rushes into the room, his hands balled. Leon snaps out of his chair, his broad shoulders squared, ready to snatch back a fist and launch into Daniel. The two men circle each other, glaring. They're the same height, and Daniel packs more muscle, but Leon is ganglier, with a longer reach, and has years of bar-fighting experience.

"What's going on in here?" Daniel says.

"Your mother and I were just talking about your special relationship with your brother's wife," Leon says.

Daniel visibly chafes, but then tightens his lips. "There is no relationship. You're making things up."

"And what did she promise you?" Leon says. He mimes sex in a graphic fashion.

Daniel shifts to his bland look, a tell that he's nervous, but maybe Leon doesn't know that. "Nothing, Leon. I've decided I want to be Chair of Farm Council, and Natalie agreed to help me."

"That's a lie," Leon spits.

"Richard's not the only one in the family with ambitions. And just so you know. Farm Council is starting. Everyone's assembled." Natalie realizes that Olivia has been scrawling her name on the piece of paper.

Leon looks at Olivia with a sneer. "Well, now you've done it. You think you're supporting your son. Well, you're not. You've just made *her* Chair." He thrusts a finger at Natalie. "Effin' great. We're all dead now. Might as well bring out the cyanide and have a big effin' party. But don't worry. Karma'll get you." He separates his lips into a frightening grimace of yellowed teeth. "It's coming for you tonight, Miss High-and-Mighty." Leon marches out. They can hear the clump of his boots down the hall.

"Thank you, Olivia," Natalie says weakly, although she's not so sure she's thankful at all. It might have been better—safer—to let Leon win.

Olivia rises and fixes them with a pointed stare. "I hope you know what you're doing. Both of you."

Natalie just wants to collapse into Daniel's arms, but she forces herself to head to the door. Olivia precedes them down the hall.

"Do you really want to be Chair?" she murmurs to Daniel.

"No. I want to punch Leon between the eyes." Daniel's lower lip is thrust out, and he glares down the hall with a scowl. He grabs Natalie by the shirt and pulls her hard against him, and she can feel his breath on her neck and the solidity of his body. "We can't do that again. I'll be Chair if I have to, but it won't be pretty because my first action will probably be to shove Leon's head in the pig trough. See what else you can pull off in there. But if it comes down to it, I'll do it."

Natalie makes the slow walk to the front of the dining room, where most farm members have already assembled. The newcomers cluster along the edges of the room, not yet permitted to take a seat at the table. Daniel remains in the back, away from Natalie. It's calculated, and probably necessary, but she wants him by her side. Terrence and Leon are absent, likely outside strategizing, or planning her lynching. This is her chance to call a vote on the newcomers. The room buzzes with chatter, the news of Leon's ousting whisking around the table in shocked exclamations and undertones before she even reaches her spot.

"I would like to call this meeting to order." Her voice is too quiet, and the noise continues. "Let's get started," she says, raising her voice and extending her arm into the air. The room quiets, but whispers still reach her. Leon and Terrence enter and stand at the foot of the table facing her, wearing cool smiles. She passes around the single copy of the agenda she wrote on the back of a piece of scrap paper. "I'm chairing because we have had a non-confidence vote on the Executive. We'll hold elections for a new temporary Executive tonight. That Executive will operate until Richard returns. Can we have a motion to approve the agenda?"

Mike raises his hand, followed by Siobhan as seconder. Farm members glance from Leon and Terrence to Natalie and back again. Waiting.

"Discussion?" Natalie says. Her right leg vibrates again, and she wonders if she might faint. Leon raises his hand. He has remained standing, and stares down at her from the end of the table. "Leon?"

"We would like to change the order of the agenda items. The elections for the new Executive should be first, followed by the vote regarding the newcomers."

Natalie finds her voice and discovers it to be firmer than she expected. "Perhaps some of the newcomers would like to stand for election, but they won't be able to until we have voted them in. We have a motion on the table to approve the agenda as written. Are you making a motion to amend that motion?"

"Yes. I move to amend the motion to state that we accept the agenda with the order of those two agenda items reversed."

"I second that," says Terrence.

"Okay, we have a motion on the table to amend the motion to accept the agenda as written, and instead accept the agenda with the order of items one and two reversed." Natalie pauses. She has no idea what to do next, suggest discussion, or call the vote immediately. Better to not even give Leon the floor if possible. "I would like to call a vote on the motion to amend. All in favor?" Leon elevates his eyebrows in challenge, and slowly, but deliberately, raises his arm. It punctuates his body like a threat, and the room teeters a bit around Natalie.

Other hands rise. Natalie counts. Anything over thirteen will be a victory for Leon. Twelve hands stand in the air around the table. "Opposed?" Fourteen hands rise. "Motion defeated." Leon mouths the word "fuck," and smacks the table with both hands, his face angled and ugly, but he takes a seat at the table. He knows the game. He still has more chances to defeat her on the other motions, and on the election of the new Executive.

She puts the motion for the newcomers to be accepted as voting members on the table. She has to allow for discussion on this one. "There will be a two-minute time limit on each person wishing to speak to this motion," she says, and scans the group.

Leon rises without waiting for permission, his hawk nose a sharp jagged gash on his supercilious face. "I will be voting against this motion. We do not need to dilute our current voting structure with people who aren't even supposed to be on this farm according to our no-refugee policy. What? If we give them the vote, are they going to vote on their own acceptance onto the farm and then vote us down the totem pole in terms of who gets to eat? That could be the laughable outcome of this motion. We don't know them, we don't know where they're from, and we shouldn't trust them. But that is beside the point: this motion is out of order because it's against the policy."

"Might I remind the speaker that farm policies are just intended to provide guidance for our consideration?" Natalie says. "They are not the same as bylaws or Farm Code. Therefore this motion is not out of order."

Leon sinks into his chair with harsh laughter. "What's the point of even setting policy then?" he says to the people sitting next to him. Terrence shrugs and thrusts his palms upward with exaggerated emphasis.

Leon rises again. "When countries used to take in refugees, they would evaluate each refugee on their merits. So great. Let's take the dentist and the computer programmer. The rest can find another farm to invade, or they can individually make the case for their own acceptance. I certainly don't recall countries ever giving refugees the opportunity to vote on their own status."

The red flush of anger creeps up Natalie's chest.

Hands rise all around the table. Natalie nods at Anneke and starts a speaker list. Anneke stands and speaks quietly, but firmly. "There are eight of them potentially eligible to vote. Not quite a voting bloc compared to the twenty-six of us. We do know some of them, and they've been working hard to demonstrate their commitment to living with us. It's only right, if we're going to expect them to work here, to afford them the democratic privileges of the farm."

The speakers grind away at each other for the next half hour with the expected parties rising to express support, or lack of support, for the motion. Natalie lets the words blur into each other, not caring what each person has to say, knowing she should focus and keep count of who is voting which way, but she just wants it to be over. They're all the same arguments they've already rehashed over and over. New people bring new ideas and diversity. New people can't be trusted. New people have rights. New people should have to prove themselves. The tics of all the farm members clamor around her. Paul presents his thoughts as if he's the only person who's ever thought of them. Jane fluffs her hair and juts her face at the ceiling while she speaks. Karl says "um" after every third or fourth word. Leon and Terrence applaud and stamp their feet on the floor for every speaker they agree with.

Natalie knows she should speak herself, but she doesn't think she can add anything that she hasn't already said year after year. They all know what she thinks. Even though she created this structure for debating farm issues, and believes fervently in the democratic process, the constant requirement for this stilted grandstanding to resolve issues exhausts her.

When they have worked their way through the speaker's list, Natalie calls the vote. She is so drained by being the center of attention and having to manage everyone that she's on autopilot, and wants to slink to the backmost bench in the room. She cannot understand why Richard relishes the role of Chair.

A jungle of hands rises into the air to oppose the newcomers getting the vote. Natalie is almost too taken aback to count. The motion is defeated. Leon cracks a victory grin. Natalie's knees start to wobble.

"Can I just say something?" Natalie tries to turn her attention to Ramona, who has risen. "I voted against giving the refugees the vote. I think we would all feel more comfortable if the refugees were evaluated on a case-by-case basis as Leon suggests, and then we revote on giving them the vote."

"Noted," Natalie says.

She announces that they will move to the Executive elections and calls for nominations. When Leon rises to indicate that he will stand for Chair, Natalie feels no surprise.

She stares at Daniel. He takes a deep breath and presses his lips together. She sees his arm start to rise.

"I want to be Chair." Anneke's voice startles Natalie, and Natalie shifts her gaze to her friend, who stands with her arms folded across her chest, face patchy red. Natalie recognizes the signs of rage in Anneke's complexion. Anneke wanted the refugees to get the vote. Natalie flicks her eyes to Daniel. Anneke and Daniel would probably split the vote and allow Leon to win. She twitches her head slightly in Daniel's direction. He dips his chin in agreement. This is not a good turn of events. Daniel would have stood a better chance of winning against Leon than mercurial shut-in Anneke.

"And I am standing with Anneke as Co-Chair," Paul says. Natalie wheels around in shock. Anneke nods as if this had been decided long ago. Clearly everyone and their dog wants to be Chair of this goddamn Council. But Paul and Anneke as a team stand a chance against Leon. Perhaps a better chance than she or Daniel would have. She allows each of the candidates two minutes to state their platform, and then calls for a secret ballot.

Leon smirks in a corner while Siobhan and Ramona count the votes.

Siobhan writes the results on a piece of paper, her dreadlocks tucked behind her ears, her face drawn.

Natalie reads the name on the paper. It feels like the world is falling away from her. She has lost. "The new temporary Chair of Farm Council is Leon Gunn," she says. Terrence and Leon slap each other's backs at the other end of the table. Anneke's nostrils flare and her eyes become dangerously slitty. Daniel widens his eyes helplessly at her. She feels an irrational fury toward him. "As per the Code, Paul and Anneke will be co-Deputy Chairs and will step in as Chair, if something happens to Leon." Natalie finds herself wishing for something, anything, to happen to Leon. Like a wild dog attack, or a random strike of lightning.

Leon swaggers to the front and gives her arm a squeeze that's a little too tight. "Thanks for the floor, Nattie. No hard feelings about what happened before, right?" His eyes are flinty though, and there's no mistaking the self-satisfied threat that lies behind them.

Leon turns and addresses the room. "All right. I'm not a big fan of process. Not like some folks." He winks at Natalie. "So I'm going to run things a bit differently. I'll just have to rely on Miss Process here to let me know when I get totally out of line." His smile at Natalie suggests that informing him he's out of line would be dangerous at best. "It seems to me that we have a problem. Not enough food. Too many mouths. Now, I'm not a heartless man. Seems to me, these new folks here ought to be given a chance to prove their worth. I can see the case for taking in a dentist and a computer programmer." He nods at Hans and Carson. "But we still need more food. Now I've heard talk about trading cows for grain at the upcoming gathering or at Tanner's Ridge, and I say, that's not a bad plan. The question is who would volunteer for such a dangerous mission—and I would say, it should be the people who got us into this situation. Which would be you, you, and you." Leon jabs his stubby finger at Natalie, Joe, and Liz. "Anyone opposed?"

"Hold it a second," Mike says. "You can't just volunteer someone for a trip like that."

Leon shrugs. "Didn't see anything in the Farm Code that says you can't, as long as Farm Council agrees by vote. I would argue that if Joe and Liz want their people taken in, and Natalie wants to invite her friends to the farm, this is their responsibility to take care of. I'd send some reliable men with them, of course, to make sure the mission is a success and they don't make off with the cows. You're welcome to go yourself, Doctor."

Natalie reels at Leon's words, but shockingly some of the other farm members are nodding in agreement. Leon turns to her and gestures at Liz and Joe. "Now, I'm not going to give those two a choice because, if they don't go, they're out. But rather than a vote, I'll just ask you. Will you take responsibility for your actions and go and try to fix this problem?"

Natalie automatically lifts her hand to where the bullet pierced her shoulder in Tanner's Ridge, then shifts her eyes to Justin and Andrew, her children who might starve this winter while her husband attends political events in Vancouver. Then she looks at Anneke. She could turn her friend in and potentially absolve herself of responsibility. Or she could suggest that they simply turn the newcomers out. She doesn't like any of the options.

"Fine. I'll go," Natalie says.

"I'm going too," Daniel says.

"Of course you are," Leon replies. "Any other takers?"

Mike raises his hand, followed by Ranjeet, one of the newcomers.

"Excellent," Leon says. "That should make for a nice, well-rounded party."

"DID I DO THE RIGHT thing?" she asks Daniel for the fifth time as they sit on the couch in the darkness of his cabin. Her bag is packed. She's going back to the farmhouse to sleep on the floor of Justin and Andrew's room. Now that Richard is gone, it would be inappropriate for her to stay here. But she and Daniel can sit alone for a couple of minutes.

"I don't know what else we could have done. Bastard. I can't believe they voted for him," Daniel says. "Still, we had planned to consider this mission anyway, and I'm not unhappy with our choice of people to go. Except for maybe crazy Liz. It's a death mission, maybe, but if I have to die with you and Mike… Well, I can think of worse people."

"That's the spirit. Leon probably just hopes Liz and I are the red-shirt guys and that we'll get killed. And Joe. You didn't have to volunteer to go."

Daniel slips his arm around her. "What, you think I'm going to let you go by yourself?"

"I'm not your responsibility. But, thank you."

"You *are* my responsibility," he says. "Although generally speaking, I think you're fairly responsible for yourself. I'm just here to help when you need it." His hands shift over her back, massaging her shoulders, tracing the contours of her muscles. She allows her body and mind to absorb each stroke, each pressing of his fingers into her skin.

"I'm going to kiss you."

Natalie almost jumps away from him. A kiss would shift them into a whole different category of deception and guilt. There could be no pretending that they had not crossed a line.

"Seriously. If we're going on a death mission, I'm going to kiss you. At least once." She has no time to make a decision before he slips his hands around her waist and pulls her into him. His lips are soft and gentle, almost tentative, but still her knees shake with the gravity of it. Her fingers curve into the silk of his hair, and she tastes his tongue and his mouth and feels the press and warmth of his broad chest. He releases her, his gray eyes uncertain, his lower lip trembling slightly, and studies her. She wonders if that will be it, but he reaches for her again with the finality and certitude of fully giving himself over to desire.

This time his tongue invades her mouth, flicking over her teeth and lips, and her body leaps with hope. After years of kissing the same man, it's shocking to kiss someone else. Richard's kisses are polished and gentle, almost chaste. Daniel's kiss is demanding and carnal. Yet his fingers, as they rove her body, are precise and tender, slipping into places and drawing responses from skin that make her almost whimper with pleasure. He pauses to inhale her neck and hair, his eyes wild but delightful gray pools, before his lips take hers again.

Her hands slide from his back to cup the curve of his buttocks and pull his groin square against hers, feeling his hardness against her pelvic bone. She feels his lips curve into a smile at this, while he continues to tease her with his tongue and slips his hand into her jeans. His lack of inhibition sweeps Natalie down an unfamiliar path, and she allows her own fingers and lips to brush those parts of him she has ached to touch for so long.

Their clothes become a tangle of entry points to flesh, and their movements start to elicit moans and sighs. With a groan, Daniel lets his arms drop, his breath coming in raggedy fits. "We better stop, or we won't be able to. Death mission or not."

Natalie resurfaces with reluctance. She doesn't disagree although every part of her body howls in argument. Daniel takes her hand and places it against his breastbone as he kisses her softly. His heart ricochets wildly against his skin, and her hand rises and falls with it. They lie in the dark with their lips meeting forehead and cheek and eyelash in tiny brushes.

"I love you," she says.

"I love you too." She hears the rush of his syllables—his need to get them out, to reassure her, or himself.

"What are we going to do?" she says.

"I don't know."

"I have to go."

"I know."

CHAPTER 17

THE HERMIT

—⟨∞⟩—

DANIEL AND ANDREW

Listen to your inner voice and create your own light for others to follow.

Daniel grips the reins tightly. He's thinking. He doesn't like distractions when he's thinking, especially noisy distractions. But there is no lack of noise around him today.

Natalie sits next to him on the front seat of the first wagon. Joe, Ranjeet, and Mike ride off to the side, their horses' hooves clattering on the pavement. The second wagon, intended to carry any grains or potatoes they're able to purchase, skitters along behind them, and the cows plod and moo behind that. The Clydesdales, Catherine and Heathcliff, unused to walking on pavement, can't seem to get their gait, and Daniel finds himself having to correct and reassure them verbally, his own voice adding to the cacophony. Only Liz is silent, staring out the back of the wagon, watching almost expectantly it seems—for what, Daniel can't tell. She clutches her tarot cards, and every half hour or so flips a card over to scrutinize it.

It's all making it impossible for him to think.

Their party is probably not the best for defensive purposes. Leon decided that Daniel would lead the mission and informed Daniel that he was counting on him to make the mission a success. Daniel is somehow supposed to miraculously find a way to trade the cows for enough grain or potatoes to get them through the winter. Worse, Leon decided that, since they're going to be in the area anyway, they should go to the gathering in Jerry and see what information they can get, and what else they can trade—and Natalie agreed. The wagon contains a whole mishmash of probably worthless household items, such as clothing, silver, and tools.

Daniel carries his leadership responsibilities like a queasy shiver that runs through his body every time he thinks about it. He hopes that Mike, Joe, or Ranjeet have some negotiating skills so he can just play the veterinarian, assuring the buyer of the quality of the cattle while the other men do the talking. Natalie found some potential traders on the Internet, and they're scheduled to meet them tomorrow outside of Jerry. Daniel runs the figures again. Young, well-bred shorthorns should fetch a thousand dollars a head. Or at least they would have, before the peak. At pre-peak prices, that would allow them to buy three thousand pounds of potatoes, which might get them through the winter. But who knows how much potatoes or cows are worth anymore? Before the peak, Daniel researched each purchase with care, comparing prices and going only to reputable stores. The thought of trying to function in an unregulated, unpredictable market brings on the shiver again.

Daniel decides to shelve this fear for now and focus on his other issues. It's best to think about his problems sequentially, he decides, and he'd rather not think about that one until tomorrow. He lets his mind shift to his other major problem. Natalie.

"I love you." Every time she says it, the words explode in his body like crazy-assed fireworks, jumping from nerve ending to nerve ending, illuminating every center of feeling he has. If he wanted her before, it's now been replaced by a whole new level of want: an acute one that throbs through him.

But every time he thinks about it, his mind reels forward to the disaster that would accompany them trying to have a relationship, telling his parents, telling Richard, Richard's reaction.

He tells himself that the night he kissed her in his cabin is the one time he will touch her. That he just had to know. To know how much he loves her. And now, unfortunately, he knows.

Terrence and Olivia hadn't been strict parents. But there was always an unspoken family code. Homosexuality, interracial marriage, drugs, being a hoity-toity, microbrew beer, and flaunting your education, or even getting one for that matter, were not cool. Of course they were just fine with bigotry, misogyny, and acting like a general a-hole when drunk. Family loyalty and the general wondrousness of Richard were also promoted. Daniel wonders where stealing your brother's wife falls in the family code.

Kristen and Richard were always his parents' favorites. Kristen because she stayed home and married stupid Leon, and Richard because he was Richard. Daniel had contented himself with being the quiet one, never stepping over the line, while Richard partied and boozed it up; although, truth be told, it had never really occurred to Daniel to step far over the line. Now he's blown the line all to shit.

To make matters worse, he's going to trade cows. Somehow the damn cows keep creeping back into his thoughts. They're taking the deserted highway, a concession to the fact that they have the wagon and the cows. A deserted highway where there are probably raiders and travelers and dozens of other kinds of ne'er-do-wells. He can't shake the feeling that there is someone following them. He hasn't seen anyone, but his ears, used to analyzing the clop of horses' hooves, keep registering another, more distant, echo of foot-falls. But every time he turns around to scan the roadway behind them, he sees nothing.

He feels exposed in more ways than one. The wagon lurches slightly, as Catherine and Heathcliff once again get themselves off pace. He corrects them and wonders if they're pushing the animals too far. The horses are used to short, hard pulls, not long distances. Daniel's mind continues to turn like the wheels of the wagon, as thought upon thought grinds away at him, wearing him down until he's desperate for the solitude of his cabin on the farm.

She loves him. *Him.* At first he thought there must be some mistake. But she seems sure, and there is the way she looks at him with softness in her face and crinkliness around her eyes. A look she always reserved for Andrew or Justin.

He had waited for love, dreamed about love, eschewed all those women that Richard tried to berate him into dating because he wanted to be *in love.* But he understands now that the love he had imagined was a fiction, created by a mind that hadn't yet grappled with the realities of love. And now he's in love with his brother's wife.

Daniel's hands tighten on the reins. His own mother was unable to handle the stress of his childhood heart operations and abandoned him in the hospital as a toddler to the care of nurses, appearing only during visiting hours. "That was just the way it was then," Olivia always says brusquely. "I had two other children. I couldn't live at the hospital."

If asked, Daniel would say he's taken it all in stride, that it hasn't affected him. He just became used to being independent. As much as he imagined being in love, he liked not needing anybody. The happiest people are those who can be alone—that was always his motto. He even seriously considered becoming a monk. His friendships were always superficial and his relationships brief: in the past, he would say that he just hadn't met the right person. Richard would laugh and say he was too picky and completely incapable of relating to women. Until Natalie.

Daniel is sure that he loves Natalie. The surge in his heart when he thinks of her tells him that he does. The fact that his half-assed gimpy heart can even surge at all is a hell of a bonus. But what does loving her mean? He feels a hardening in his cock just thinking about it. But if anyone finds out, they'll both probably be shunned, or worse, run off the farm.

Leon pulled him aside before they left, to say that whores never change and Daniel will be sorry for his choices. He mumbled a whole bunch of shit about karma and said that Daniel still has a chance to redeem himself if he walks now. Of course, it was just Leon talking, and he's often full of crap, and nobody ever calls him on it. He could have just been plying Daniel for information. But it rattled him. Most farm members seemed to be behaving normally toward him and Natalie, but since Leon's comments, Daniel has turned every whisper and murmured word he's heard into some sort of conspiracy or plot against Natalie. And against him.

And what of Richard? Daniel's boundaries—his need to remain loyal to both his brother and to Natalie—have become blurred beyond recognition. He loves Richard. He doesn't always agree with how Richard does things, but he loves him, and now he might have to choose between his brother and the woman that he wants more than anything, and he has no idea what to do about it.

But deep inside him, with every turn of the wagon's wheels, Richard's voice reverberates harshly as if in an echo chamber. Traitor. Traitor. Traitor.

ANDREW PERCHES ON THE CHAIR in the den and tries to hack into his father's email account for the third time. He *should* be doing the washing with Claire. But he's become obsessed with what he found in his dad's email account—before his dad changed his password. Emails about clubs being opened in Vancouver to take advantage of the fact that vice never goes out of style; the types of clubs in which his father might be interested in investing. There were emails from political friends in Vancouver, talking about the need for real leaders, and emails about a new start-up hydro company in Nelson looking for supporters. Andrew had no idea his dad was so connected. The emails were like Andrew supposes newspapers once were: information from the world outside after years of silence. His father's replies were enthusiastic, talking about things getting back to normal after his years in purgatory, and setting meeting dates.

But Andrew has had no luck in cracking his father's new password. He's tried every derivation of the old one he can imagine, every saying he associates with his dad, and every word or phrase scrawled on the scraps of paper on his dad's desk.

Andrew decides to log into the address he set up for his mother. She gave Andrew permission to check while she's gone. The emails pop up on the screen, the list of email addresses, the trading post list, and Natalie's exchanges with potential buyers of the cows, all opened and read. A new email pops up, dated a few days ago, from Richard T. Johnston. Emails now have a way of taking a few days to get to their destination.

The message is brief. "Possible flu pandemic in Eastern Canada. No need to worry. You get upset when I don't tell you things. Nevertheless, I think I'll come home soon."

Andrew closes the computer lid with trembling fingers. He knows his mother and Mike have talked about the flu. Have said it could be only a matter of time.

He goes to find Claire in the laundry room. He doesn't want to die without at least having sex once. Yesterday was her shower day, and her hair floats around her in a gauzy cloud. She wears a gray tunic dress. Someone's cast-off office attire. Too fancy for the task at hand as usual, but it suits her quirky style. She's already filled the tubs with steaming water and moved the first batch of clothes over to the wash table.

She smiles when Andrew enters. "You're late." It's an observation, not a reprimand. The skin under her eyes is puffy and pink, and her movements are slower than usual.

"You didn't sleep again last night."

"No, I didn't, and I'm afraid I might not be too much use here today. I'm so tired. I'm sorry, Andrew. I'm not much of a workmate."

"Nonsense," says Andrew, forcing a bright voice. "You're a great workmate." Andrew searches his mind for a way that Claire is great. "At least you know when your effort level sucks. A lot of other people on the farm, they don't even know. They think they're going all out when really they're not."

His remark is lame, Andrew knows, so he pats her arm. He doesn't want her to think he's saying this because he wants to sleep with her.

"You're funny," she trails off. "This life… I'm really not cut out for it. I kind of planned to be a society wife with a couple of kids and a nanny. I know it sounds pathetic, but I really don't like hard work." She draws her hands out of the foamy water. "Look at me, I have old lady hands and I'm only thirty-five."

Thirty-five, Andrew thinks. Okay, a little older than he'd hoped, but workable. Besides, if maturity level is taken into consideration, Andrew feels far older than Claire. He glances at Claire's hands. Her long, tapered fingers are chapped and reddened. But her fingernails still form neat ovals, and she holds her hands with the graceful extension of a dancer.

"I think your hands look fine, Claire. And you're doing fine here. Look at how far you've come since you got here."

Claire wrinkles her nose. "We're behind on the washing, and Anneke says if we don't catch up today, we'll have to stay here until we do. I don't know why she hates me so much."

"Get used to it. Anneke hates everyone."

"It just doesn't seem like anyone here really understands my migraines and insomnia. They're really debilitating."

"I know how hard it is." His words are not entirely untrue. He's seen Claire stumble through her days like a zombie often enough to know that she's not making it up.

"Last night I tried so hard to fall asleep for hours. I just kept trying to go to my happy place by imagining I was holding my baby in my arms."

Andrew ponders an appropriate response, and it occurs to him that Claire's baby obsession could be problematic. He doesn't like the idea of a flu pandemic with a baby. He doesn't like the idea of a baby, period. He'd best make his way to the infirmary at lunch to find out what kind of prophylactics are to be had.

To Claire, he says, "Why don't you go talk to Elena if you want to hold a baby? She seems to like to have other people hold Eve." Andrew glances back out of the washing water to see Claire staring at him with a slightly speculative look.

THEY MAKE CAMP AT DUSK, having used up the last of the horses' energy. They pick a spot well off the highway, by a creek in a secluded clump of trees, but the cows are hard to hide and the creek may draw other travelers in search of water. Daniel hopes nobody comes by. They'll be in Jerry midday tomorrow—plenty of time to try to trade the cows before the community meetings. Daniel will be glad to offload the cows for something easier to transport.

His ears buzz and his body aches from the constant rattle and grind of the wagon. He sees to the cows while Natalie hustles about preparing dinner. The others pitch tents and set up camp. Natalie will sleep with Liz tonight, continuing the charade that he and Natalie are playing, while Daniel can't help but wonder if everyone already knows.

Mike comes to help currycomb Catherine and Heathcliff, while the other men discuss a perimeter guard. Heathcliff's right front leg shudders, and he's favoring it. Daniel checks for swelling and curses once again his decision to bring the Clydesdales. He should have brought the quarter horses, but eight thousand potential pounds of potatoes would be a shitload for the quarter horses to pull. He finds nothing along the length of Heathcliff's muscled leg, then checks for a misplaced nail in the new shoes he pounded into place himself the night before. He hopes it's just fatigue. They don't have far to go tomorrow, but it could be a long and heavy pull home. He could dope Heathcliff up on painkillers to get through the trip, but if the ligaments or tendons are damaged and he pushes him, he might permanently wreck a good horse.

Mike watches Daniel's routine with respectful interest. Mike is the kind of man Daniel wouldn't have expected to have been friends with before. Mike would have been a popular guy before the peak. The kind of guy that played rugby or ultimate frisbee with his buddies on Saturday. But also a man of substance. Someone who Daniel would have admired, but wouldn't have been able to get past superficialities with because he was just too shy and socially awkward. The kind of man that might have seemed interested in being friends with Daniel, but that Daniel would have frozen up around.

"So, how are you with trading cows?" Daniel asks Mike, hoping to strike up a conversation, but also hoping to assess where they're going to be tomorrow when it comes down to business.

"I can't say I have a lot of experience with cows," Mike says. "And before the peak I had a portfolio manager who managed to bankrupt me, so can't say I have a lot of experience with trading, either. But I'll have your back in any discussion we get into."

"Yeah, great, the monk vet and the broke doctor trading cows. Think Ranjeet or Joe have any experience?"

"A laborer and a chef? They might have more."

"Richard would know how to handle it." Daniel regrets his remark as soon as he says it. It's part of his mental script that he never lets into the open, but apparently his decision to try to become friends with Mike has removed all his filters. If he keeps going, soon he'll be blubbering in Mike's arms.

Mike gives him a speculative look. "I dunno about that."

"You don't like Richard?"

"Well, God knows where we'd be if he wasn't so willing to shoot things. But he's not my type of guy. There's always some sort of weird fraught kind of energy around him, like we're in a stage production and he always needs to have the best line. But he's Natalie's husband and your brother, so I'm just going to shut my big fat mouth."

Daniel tenses. He wonders if Mike thinks something similar of him. Sometimes as he lurches through his day trying to interact with people, he feels like it's all a performance, except that he's forgotten half his crappy lines. But Mike doesn't seem to notice that Daniel needs a prompter.

"Besides," Mike continues, "Natalie's better when Richard's not around."

"What do you mean?"

"Nothing. I shouldn't have said anything."

"What was she like," Daniel hears his voice asking, "…before Richard?" He tries to make the sentence sound casual, as if he's just making general conversation. Clearly all the filters are off now.

Mike peers at him with a perplexed look, the way one stares at a car engine when one has no background in mechanics.

"Normal, kind of fun, pretty confident. Natalie was the top of her class in poli-sci at UBC. She got accepted to Yale for law. It was a pretty big shock when she gave it up to marry Richard."

"Are you saying she made the wrong choice?"

Mike shrugs. "I'm just saying she's different now."

Daniel realizes he's been combing the same spot on Heathcliff's back for several minutes. He wants to keep talking to Mike, but they should rejoin the rest of the group and help out. He places the comb back in the saddlebag. "I guess we should go talk to Joe and Ranjeet and come up with a strategy for tomorrow."

"Righto," says Mike. Richard would have ribbed Daniel about not wanting to go into tomorrow with his pants down. But Mike just agrees with him and follows his lead.

⁂

ANDREW DIGS THROUGH THE DRAWERS of the infirmary cabinet. The beds beside him are empty for once. Elena and baby Eve moved into one of the new cabins last week, and the farmhouse has been blessedly peaceful. Andrew pulls out packets of gauze, bandages, ointment, steri-strips, saline, sterilized rags. Why the hell wouldn't his mother and Uncle Mike have stockpiled condoms? Do neither of them have sex? Andrew experiences a slight twinge of the heebies at the idea of his mother or uncle having sex. Of course the condoms would be past their expiry date now, but an expired condom would be better than no condom.

Justin pokes his head through the office door. He wears the heavy-lidded look of a cat woken from a nap. He's been given special dispensation to study his uncle's medical books twice a week in order to increase their medical preparedness.

"Can I help you, Andrew? Are you looking for something in particular?" Justin's tone is sardonic as always.

Andrew considers lying, but nothing pithy comes to mind. "Just wondering if there are any condoms here."

Justin's face becomes more alert at this. "Condoms? Are you looking to protect your hand from an unwanted pregnancy?"

"Very funny."

"Seriously, who are you planning on having sex with?"

"Isn't there some sort of doctor-patient privilege? You're not allowed to ask that."

Justin raises his eyebrow. "I'm not your doctor. Condoms were rationed to the married couples, and then someone came and stole the rest of them last month." He cracks his usual know-it-all smile. "You could try the rhythm method. With effective application, it can be up to ninety percent effective. You have to know your partner well enough to be able to discuss her menstrual cycle and cervical mucus with her, though." Justin wiggles his eyebrows and winks, as if to suggest the likelihood of Andrew discussing a menstrual cycle with anyone is about zero. "And you have to hope they're not a double ovulator."

"Thanks, textbook man. Any other methods?"

"Aside from the withdrawal method, which isn't effective at all, so don't try it, or a vasectomy, which I expect you're not interested in, no."

Andrew shudders at the thought of any sort of knife near his balls. "What about making condoms? Didn't they used to be made from sheep's intestines?"

"Sure, you go explain to Uncle Daniel that you need the intestines from the next sheep that gets butchered."

"Who the hell stole the condoms anyway?"

Justin shakes his head and starts closing the drawers that Andrew left open. "I dunno."

"Maybe it was Alfie."

"Alfie? Why would you think that?"

"Did it happen after he arrived?"

"I don't know. It's not like we take inventory every day. I doubt Alfie would need them. Claire's infertile." There's a moment of silence. Justin presses his lips together. "This doctor-patient privilege stuff is harder than I thought. Forget I said that."

"Sure." Andrew turns to leave, but then stops. "How bad would something like, say, a flu pandemic be?"

"What are you talking about?"

"Nothing. I'm just asking a question."

"Well, it would totally depend on how virulent the virus is. But potentially really bad. The Spanish flu had a mortality rate of ten to twenty percent of those who got it. Why are you asking?"

"Can we do anything to prepare for one?"

Justin is squinting at him again and then cocks his head. "Not really. Other than minimizing contact with anyone from off the farm."

Great, Andrew thinks. Half the people from the farm are off having contact with people from off the farm right now.

"Do you think someone here has the flu?" Justin says. His voice has taken on a panicked edge. Justin may be just too much of a stress-case sometimes to be a doctor.

"No. Everyone is fine." No need to get everyone upset, Andrew decides. His dad said possible, and not to worry. His dad will tell everyone when he gets here and make the appropriate decisions. "Forget I said anything. Thanks for the birth control advice."

Justin calls after him. "As your doctor, it's my responsibility to tell you that I think you're about to make a bad decision of some sort."

"Good thing you're not my doctor then." Andrew heads down the hall to lunch. No need for condoms then. That would explain why Claire doesn't have a baby after all these years of trying. Why wouldn't she mention that though? Andrew scoops a pile of collard greens and cornbread onto his plate and goes to find a seat next to Claire.

Ten to twenty percent. That would be like ten people on the farm. Andrew just hopes he's not one of them.

<hr />

MOONLIGHT FLOODS THE WALLS OF the tent, painting the shadows of the trees in ghostly form. Daniel rolls around for the eighth time in his sleeping bag. He has woken early, in the middle of the night really, and he knows he won't be able to go back to sleep as he thinks about all the potential ways the cow trading could go bad. He curses his lifelong sentence of insomnia that leaves him cranky and stupid half the time. Ranjeet slumbers next to him. Joe is on watch. Daniel rises. He might as well relieve Joe of duty. No point all of them going sleepless.

DANIEL HUNCHES ON A ROCK near the small glow of the fire and stares at the huddled cows. Joe didn't argue with the suggestion that he get a few more hours of sleep. The moon disappears behind a cloud, and Daniel's eyes adjust to the darkness. One of the cows starts to stray from the group. Daniel watches it for a few minutes hoping that it returns. But it continues its slow meander away from the rest of the herd in the direction of the creek. The animal must have escaped its picket. Daniel leaves Mitch and Daisy guarding the camp and makes his way over to the herd.

He stuffs his gun into his pants, grasps the picket rope, and starts to haul the beast back. The cow, annoyed that someone has decided to interrupt her midnight stroll, plants her feet in the mud. Daniel pulls harder, but the damn animal remains where she is and refuses to even turn her head in Daniel's direction. Daniel approaches her from the side and gives her a firm push on the rump. "Get going, you pinhead." She ignores him. He's going to have to get Mitch. Or, he reflects, he could just leave the beast where she is and drive the picket back into the ground here. He bends to plunge the stake into the dirt, his damn rickety heart clawing uncomfortably in his chest as he does.

Daniel sees a set of tattered black boots and feels the cold tip of a firearm against his ear. He straightens slowly. The clouds drift away from the moon, bathing the clearing in white brilliance. The man's hair is longer now, a crop of matted dark curls, but the black tattoos that snake up his neck are instantly recognizable.

Rafe. Not dead.

Rafe smiles, revealing a mouth full of blackened stumps. Daniel finds himself thinking inexplicably about the decline of oral hygiene since the peak and runs his tongue over his own intact teeth. The sleep deprivation must be affecting his judgment.

"Give me your gun," Rafe orders.

Daniel hands over the weapon. "What's your plan here, Rafe? There's a lot of us and only one of you."

"Yes, but I have a hostage," Rafe says.

"What do you want?"

"A more useful hostage, for starters."

"Who do you want?" Daniel asks, wondering what uses Rafe has in mind.

"None of your business. Let's go give some folks a little wake-up call."

Rafe presses the muzzle of his rifle into Daniel's gut and pushes him in the direction of the tents. Daniel considers wrestling the gun out of Rafe's hands. This would likely result in him getting shot and dying. But it would alert the rest of the campers, who would emerge from their tents armed—and with him dead, Rafe would no longer have a hostage. This is, after all, his fault. Daniel tries to evaluate his willingness to get shot. This is a complex equation, and the fact that the whole scene seems to be unfolding in double time isn't helping.

Daniel decides to walk as heavily as possible and ask Rafe questions loudly. Maybe the noise will alert the camp and someone will figure out a better goddamn plan.

"So, what have you been up to since we last saw you?" Daniel affects something resembling a smile.

Rafe looks at Daniel as though he's just proposed a sexual encounter. "Shut the fuck up."

"Have you found a place to live? Maybe we could help you."

"Shut the fuck up or I'll shoot you."

There's been no sign of recognition from the tents, but Daisy and Mitch have smelled the new arrival and start to growl.

"Silence your dogs."

"I can't," Daniel says.

Rafe shoves him hard in the gut with the rifle. "The hell you can't. You have perfect control over those dogs. You know it, and I know it."

Daniel flicks his wrist, extending his palm flat to the ground. Daisy and Mitch drop into down stays, alert for their next command. Mitch's lip curls back over his teeth, but he remains silent. Rafe and Daniel reach the small sphere of light of the campfire. A trickle of sweat slips down Daniel's back.

"Call the women," Rafe whispers in his ear, his breath ripe with the foul stench of rot. "Tell them you need them to get up."

The women. Why the women? What does Rafe mean by *a more useful hostage*? Daniel should end this now; he should get shot while he pounds Rafe between the eyes and hopes that Mike can sew him back up again. He's in the process of making this decision when he hears a tent zipper, and Natalie and Liz crawl out of their tent, guns in their hands.

Rafe lifts Daniel's gun so it's pointed at the two women. Daniel could still try to wrestle the gun away from Rafe and get shot, but what if Rafe fires both guns at once? Natalie is not a great shot, and he has no idea about Liz. Rafe must want to kill Liz for orchestrating the death of his men, and he could easily hit Natalie. Daniel braces for the moment when Rafe shoots Liz and him—the moment where, bullet in his gut or not, he will jab his elbow into Rafe's neck. But it doesn't come.

"Put down your guns, ladies, or our friend here is dead." Natalie and Liz both slowly lower their weapons to the ground.

"Rafe," Liz says.

"I've been following you," Rafe says.

"I know." Liz flashes a tarot card. Rafe nods as if this is sufficient explanation. Daniel glances sideways at Rafe. Perhaps Rafe's not so smart. Rafe turns and ejects a thin sleet of green from between his teeth. Or he's high. But if Liz knew Rafe was following them, why the hell didn't she tell anyone? Then again, Daniel had thought someone was following them and he hadn't said a damn thing, and now he's screwed things epically on watch.

"I'll need you to come with me," Rafe says to Liz.

"Only if you don't kill anyone."

Rafe's fingers dig harder into Daniel's arm.

"I need a horse, some food, and a cow," Rafe says.

"Take them," Natalie says. "Just leave us alone." She squints her eyes at Daniel though. He's not sure if she's telling him to do something, or to not do something stupid. Rafe can have Liz for all Daniel cares, but there's no way he's taking one of Daniel's horses.

Rafe's stumps flash. "You're a cute little thing. Maybe I'll take you too."

Liz steps in front of Natalie. "You don't want her, Rafe. She's bad luck and too old. We can find someone better for you; someone younger." Daniel experiences a ridiculous twitch of anger at hearing Natalie described this way.

"Shut up, you lying old bitch," Rafe says, but the words seem to have twigged something in him, and he no longer looks at Natalie. "Now, let's go get my food and my horse."

Daniel finds himself escorted to the place where they hung the food from a tree the night before. They have more food in a steel drum in the wagon, but Rafe appears happy with the pail of food from the tree. They move on to the horses. Rafe selects Mike's horse, Spock. The best horse, of course. The only goddamn Rocky Mountain trail-riding horse on the farm. He will not turn over such a loving and gentle horse to a monster like Rafe. There are several humans on the farm Daniel would rather hand over first. He tries to convince Rafe that Cain is a better horse, but Rafe just laughs, careful to keep one gun firmly pressed between Daniel's ribs, and the other pointed at Natalie.

Rafe has Natalie load the food into the saddlebag and orders Liz to mount. Then Rafe has Natalie lead Spock over to the cows. Based on Rafe's horse selection, Daniel isn't surprised when Rafe instructs him to tie the bull to Spock. The best horse, the best cow.

"All right, we're going to walk away," Rafe says. "Don't even think of following us, or I'll shoot Liz." Daniel tries to evaluate whether this might be worth it to get Spock back. "And then I'll shoot the horse," Rafe concludes, placing the muzzle of Daniel's pistol against Spock's rump. "Oh, don't worry, Mr. Horse Dog Whisperer, I know what makes you tick."

Daniel watches Rafe move into the darkness, Spock's creamy mane and the white coat of the bull marking their location. Spock looks over his shoulder as they go, as if to question whether he's doing the right thing. Daniel could take out Rafe now and get the bull back, but it would be at the expense of Liz's and Spock's lives.

"Damn it all to hell," Daniel says. He clenches his fists and makes as if to punch at something.

CHAPTER 18

THE THREE OF WANDS

NATALIE AND ANDREW

Move fearlessly into new areas. Accept your vision and achieve it.

Natalie pulls Daniel back through the maze of tents and supplies to the small campfire. His gait is stilted and slow. He's analyzing his choices, thinking that he screwed up on watch, wondering whether some heroics could have saved Liz, the horse, or the bull, trying to decide whether they should go after them.

"Should we wake the others?" Natalie says. Daniel stands with his back to her, staring at the fire.

"I don't know."

"Should we go after them?" She can't imagine chasing Rafe and Liz through the night. Someone would get shot.

Daniel sinks to one of the logs by the fire. "Better the horse and bull than one of us. But we're not going to be able to get as many potatoes now. Rafe must have let the cow off the picket, and I fell for it. I'm such an idiot. I should have taken one of the dogs. None of this goddamn wrestling guns out of people's hands and deciding what to do in the moment is as easy as it used to look in the movies. Richard would have handled it better."

She sees the ache of self-condemnation in the shadows beneath his eyes. "Richard would probably have done the exact same thing," she says.

Daniel adds a small piece of birch to the fire. Natalie shivers in her heavy riding jacket and fleece pants. They have been lulled by long hot autumns, but this year the air has a deep chill around the edges.

"Did you and Liz hear me?"

"Liz did. She didn't seem surprised Rafe was here, said she was okay going with him. Maybe she saw him following us, but I can't believe she wouldn't tell us."

She puts her hand on Daniel's thigh to reassure him that he didn't screw up. The moon hangs higher in the sky now, and Natalie guesses it must be around three in the morning. They can sit like this for a bit. She wouldn't be able to sleep anyway.

"Why did she think he wanted her? Revenge?" Daniel says.

"Liz said Rafe had always talked about taking her to Vancouver with him to gamble in the new clubs because he thinks she's psychic. Apparently they've set up a bunch of new clubs in Vancouver. I heard Alfie telling Richard about it. It's the new thing: ghetto gambling. Of course, Alfie and Richard were all excited about it. I can't believe people still gamble when most people can't even eat." Natalie watches the firelight play across the lines that mark Daniel's face.

Daniel stares at the fire. "People have always gambled while other people couldn't eat. It was just that the people who couldn't eat were mostly in other countries. Do you really think Liz is a psychic?"

Natalie shrugs. "The newcomers swear by her predictions. I guess it's theoretically possible that some people are tapped into some greater knowledge. I don't believe it. But I wish I did."

"People's beliefs make them see things that aren't there." Daniel's words are flat.

"You don't believe in anything at all, then?" These words hurt her slightly. As much as she claims not to believe in anything, maybe she does because for some reason she wants *him* to. Or maybe she just wants Daniel to carry her along with his beliefs like Richard always has even though she thought Richard was wrong half the time.

"I believe in us. But I don't believe in psychics."

I just want you to tell me it will all be okay, she thinks. She sees it in Daniel's eyes though. He doesn't know if it will all be okay.

They sit together in front of the fire in silence. Natalie realizes how much of her world, her sense of security, has been for so long built on Richard's faith or his willingness to lie to her and say what she wants to hear. Without that, she is adrift in a strange and uncomfortable way. And yet despite all the gravity of their circumstance, feeling her shoulder pressed against Daniel's, her hand on his warm leg, is the most tenuous of fragile perfections, a bubble of happiness that she wishes could be suspended in the air around her forever.

THEY TELL THE OTHERS ABOUT Rafe and Liz when the early streaks of dawn mark the sky. They stand in a circle, their breaths puffs of white air. Eyes widen, but Mike, Joe, and Ranjeet nod, as if these kinds of things are to be expected. Nobody suggests that she and Daniel should have done anything differently.

Natalie pulls Ranjeet and Joe aside as they pack. "Are you upset? I don't want you to think we sacrificed Liz because she's a newcomer."

Ranjeet fixes her with his earnest stare. "If Liz believed that was the thing to do, then that was the thing to do. Last year she forecasted the death of some of the men in our group in a mudslide, and the next day half the mountain came down and took them out."

Natalie's mind flits back to the tarot card reading Liz did a few weeks ago: illness and death, two kings, and Natalie following her shadow impulses. Guilty thoughts of Daniel enter her mind. She's skipped right over shadow impulses and gone all the way to the depths of deception. Karma will probably find a way to make her pay.

They strike camp and hitch up the horses. They're due to meet the potential traders on the outskirts of Jerry at noon, and still have a long ride. Daniel hurtles between loud good cheer and brooding silence. She pulls him aside just before they leave.

"You're acting really strangely."

"It's this trading thing. Sorry. Nerves turn me into a lunatic."

She climbs into the wagon next to Daniel and hopes that driving will calm him down. They depart into the brisk morning with a rattle of wheels and clatter of hooves, the cows plodding behind them. Natalie yearns for a Starbucks, a bucket seat, and the sun beating in the window. Catherine and Heathcliff inch along, and Natalie wonders if Daniel is trying to save Heathcliff from further injury, or just delay their arrival at the trading meeting. She looks over at Daniel, but he has glued his mouth closed and stares straight ahead.

Once they turn right at the highway junction that goes to Jerry, they see a few parties on the road heading the same direction as they are, probably going to the gathering. But the other travelers are way ahead and quickly outpace them. As the day progresses, a few people overtake them—men mostly, on horseback, traveling in pairs. The men tip their hats and carry on. Some of the men give the cows and the loaded wagons an appraising look. The peak has muddied the protocols of social engagement: everyone fears strangers now, and nobody is sure what to say anymore. Daniel doesn't help matters by keeping his hat low and ignoring everyone.

They had agreed to meet the potential traders at the old Jerry Volunteer Fire Department Hall that sits just outside of town. Daniel turns down the old lumber mill road that runs parallel to the highway. Jerry had been a nothing town, just a general store, gas station, church, and a cluster of run-down houses for the former millworkers. The mill shut down a few years before the peak, due to the downturn in the US housing industry and the influx of cheap lumber imports from overseas. The town persisted though, even when there were no more jobs. EI, pensions, and people willing to travel elsewhere for work must have held it together. And so it became an almost creepy place, with a silent mill and decaying houses decorated with tin-can men, rail tie planters, and wagon wheels.

Now the old lumber mill looks like it may have had recent activity. Fresh sawdust lies on the ground, and a small stack of cut lumber is piled next to the light blue metal exterior of the mill building. They hurry past. No sense attracting unwanted attention, especially when they're laden with the cows. Daniel pulls into an old turnout a few miles past the mill. The trees are overgrown, and the group is somewhat sheltered from the road.

The men dismount, and Natalie unfolds herself from the wagon seat, her legs stiff and bunched. Daniel seems to have calmed down a bit, but still seems to be vibrating at an accelerated frequency. Natalie finds herself jumpy and tense in response.

Daniel calls a huddle to discuss the trade. He pushes his hat back on his head as he speaks. "I figure Mike and Ranjeet can stay here with two of the cows. Joe, Natalie, and I take two of the cows to the meeting place for them to check out until we agree on price. That way, if they have anything funny planned we only lose two, and hopefully get out of there with our lives. If it all looks good, we'll come back and get the other two. It'll take longer to do the exchange, but I think we have to be careful. The loss of the bull is going to be a problem. I just hope it doesn't tank the whole deal. Sound good?"

Everyone nods. Natalie is relieved. Daniel still looks tense, but he has a plan.

The men unhitch the back wagon where the supplies are stowed, and Natalie finds herself wedged between Daniel and Joe on the way to the trade. At the last minute, Daniel decides to leave the dogs behind in case they scare the traders. They cut back out onto the highway, and the boxy gray corner of the fire hall swings into view within ten minutes. The parking lot sits empty. Natalie had said noon. But few people have the exact time anymore unless they have a windup pocket watch or wristwatch. Natalie checks the sun. Its outlines appear blue-black against the cloud cover. The low angle of incidence makes it hard to tell the time though. Natalie hopes they're not too late.

Daniel guides the horses around to the back of the fire hall. Fireweeds and dandelions push up through the pavement, still holding on deep into the fall. The parking lot is strewn with piles of fallen leaves and branches that have blown up against the cement staircase and retaining walls. The cicadas, emboldened by the afternoon warmth, kick up a racket on the blacktop. Daniel climbs out of the wagon and loosens some of the leather harnesses that hold Catherine in place. He turns back to Natalie and hands her his pocketknife.

"If anything goes wrong—if they pull guns on us or it looks like it's going bad—cut here and here." Daniel shows her two parts of the harness. "And then get on Catherine and ride like hell. Go get the others and go home. Don't even think about trying to come and help Joe and me. I packed the spare one-horse harness with the supplies. Catherine can pull the wagon alone. Turn the cows out to graze."

"Oh, Daniel, no," Natalie says.

"We need to have a backup plan."

"So the backup plan is that you and Joe get shot?"

"No. The backup plan is that you *don't*," Daniel says.

Natalie turns to Joe, but he just nods and gives her a small smile of encouragement like he agrees with Daniel. His hair is growing back more silver than black. Joe has been quiet since the Farm Council meeting when Leon took over. That night he reiterated his offer to leave the farm with the other men. But Leon scoffed and said Joe would have to take the whole lot of newcomers if they didn't manage to make some successful trades. She suspects that Leon intends to try to turf the newcomers anyway. She curses Richard once again for leaving, and she curses herself for not being able to hold things together after Richard left.

The surreal nature of her new life grasps at her. She is standing in a deserted churchyard with her old friend, a pair of cows, and her husband's brother, whom she loves—and they are potentially about to be shot, to ensure that she lives. She feels the weight of karma beating against her back.

A bald man in camouflage gear with a semi-automatic weapon steps out of the bushes, followed by two identically dressed men with rifles. They stop at the edge of the parking lot, their guns out and ready, but not yet pointed at Natalie, Daniel, and Joe. Daniel and Joe whip their pistols out, but also keep them aimed at the ground. The men must have been waiting and watching in the trees. Natalie wonders how much they heard. The men wear neutral expressions, but the little guy on the right looks scared shitless. His hands tremble and his expression is oddly gaping. Natalie realizes he's just a young boy, maybe only eleven. There's something wrong with the way he stands. He hunches his shoulders and holds his legs too wide apart. Natalie tries to breathe. The men look scary with their camouflage gear and shaved heads, but in a peak world where hunting is a necessity and lice common, these could be practical choices. Anyone surveying Daniel and Joe, with their dirty clothes, scruffy beards, holstered hunting knives, and pistols and rifles, would probably be scared too.

"Gabriel?" Natalie says.

"You promised four cows and a bull," the man, presumably Gabriel, says.

"I'm sorry," Natalie says. "We still have the four cows. They're in a safe place. But the bull was stolen on our way here."

Gabriel swears. "We need a fucking bull."

His words seem to prod Daniel into action. "Three of the cows are pregnant, due in the spring. You might get a bull out of one of them. The other cow has been recently freshened so you'll get milk right away."

This appears to assuage the man slightly. "All this variety?"

"Breed," Daniel corrects. "They're all Whitebred Shorthorns. Hardy and good for beef and dairy."

"We'll need to check them out."

Daniel, Natalie, and Joe look at each other. They hadn't planned out how to do this. "Yes," Joe says. "But we'd like to see your potatoes."

"We brought potatoes and corn. They're offsite. There're two bins in the wagon in the trees there."

"Guess we're not the only ones with a trust issue," Daniel says with a flippant tone. Natalie flinches, but to her surprise Gabriel barks out a laugh.

"Can't trust nobody these days," Gabriel says. "A five-year-old kid would skin you alive in your bed after you gave her shelter. So how are we going to do this?"

"How about we each choose one person to go check out the merchandise? The rest of us stay here and watch each other in case anyone gets any ideas," Joe says.

"Works for me. Five minutes each?" Gabriel says, stepping forward.

"I should go," Natalie says to Daniel. "I know the most about potatoes."

"You can't, it's not safe," Daniel hisses.

"It's no less safe than standing here," she says.

"Yes it is. They could have men in the bushes waiting to jump you."

"They need our cows as much as we need their potatoes and corn."

"That's what I'm afraid of, except I'm afraid they might not *have* any potatoes and corn," Daniel mouths in her ear.

"Is there a problem?" Gabriel says.

"No, no," Natalie says. She squeezes Daniel's hand. She starts walking toward the men. The boy's gun still rattles in his hands. Natalie hopes her knees aren't similarly shaking. She and Gabriel pass each other in the middle. She attempts a small smile, but he looks straight ahead, and his features are arranged into a fierce expression. As she gets closer, Natalie realizes that the boy's legs bow out slightly and his jaw is offset. Rickets. They need these cows.

She makes her way over to the wagon in the woods. There's no horse. Unhitched, probably, so she can't drive off with the goods. Two wooden bins made from container pallets sit in a heavy plank wagon with the wheels of an old truck. They never tried to use the wheels of the abandoned vehicles on the farm. Richard always said they would break the axles. Natalie risks a peek underneath the wagon. Steel rods hold the wheels in place. The part that attaches the wheel to the axle is like nothing she's ever seen before and looks like it's been created just for the wagon. These guys must have access to the waste of a city to strip for parts—and a welder.

She climbs into the wagon. Russet and red potatoes fill the bin. Dry potatoes with a firm skin. Natalie digs into the bin and pulls out potato after potato, pushing her hand right down to the bottom of the bin to make sure they're okay. She sifts her fingers through the corn. It looks fine, the kernels a pale yellow hue and slightly shriveled. She examines the germ. It's a pale creamy color like it should be. It all looks okay. But she can't be positive.

They also have no way of knowing precisely how many pounds of potatoes or corn are in a bin. A cow is a cow, but one of the bins could contain anywhere from seven to nine hundred pounds of potatoes. Natalie tries to imagine how many bags of potatoes would fit inside the bins.

"Time," Gabriel yells.

Natalie walks slowly back out into the open. Daniel watches her exit the woods and walk across the parking lot, his features settling into a more relaxed state once she reaches him. This worry for her is a strange new thing.

They agree to each discuss their own terms before reconvening.

"I don't know," says Natalie. "It looks legitimate."

"Then let's just do it," says Daniel.

"Are you sure?" says Natalie.

"No, I'm never sure, but I don't think we have a choice."

They meet Gabriel and his camouflaged partners in the middle of the parking lot. The inspection of the goods seems to have established some degree of trust. The sun escapes the clouds and the cicadas go into overdrive in the afternoon heat.

"Four hundred pounds," says Gabriel.

"Are you kidding? Four thousand," says Daniel.

"That would be out of this world even if you had the damn bull," says Gabriel. "I'll give you fifteen hundred pounds. You couldn't even transport more anyway."

"The transportation is none of your business. Three thousand, or no deal," says Daniel.

They settle on two thousand pounds. Richard would have done some theatrical hard-nosed last stand to get another two hundred fifty pounds, but Daniel doesn't. Natalie oscillates between relief that they've reached agreement, and worry that it may not be enough to get them through the winter. Daniel and Gabriel shake hands.

The boy's tremors have grown more intense as the negotiation has proceeded. Natalie realizes that his shakes are probably because of the rickets, too. They discuss how to exchange the remainder of the goods, and agree to exchange the first load now and meet back in half an hour for the second. Daniel and Joe pull the wagon up to Gabriel's, and the four men lift the bins of corn and potatoes from one wagon to the other with grunts and heaves. Gabriel assures them that each bin contains five hundred pounds.

"Are you going to the gathering?" Natalie asks Gabriel as they prepare to leave.

"Nah," he says. "Sounds like a crazy bunch of shit. We don't need a new government, and we don't have time to waste at meetings that'll strike a committee to strike a committee."

"You prefer this to how things were before the peak?"

"Nah, I'm not saying that. We just don't see how government is going to make things better. We had too much government before the peak. Bloody bureaucrats with their hands in everything. If we had government now, they'd have their hand out takin' a quarter of our trade. That'd be a cow. No thanks."

"But what about medical services, hospitals?"

"Ain't nothin' of value we ever got out of the medical system. It was just a holding tank for old folks who were past their time anyway. I mean, how much did it cost to replace a hip? Fifteen grand? And why were we doing it, so some old codger can push himself around on his walker for a couple more years or die two weeks later from the surgery? And when we did need it," the man flicks his head in the direction of the boy, who has sunk to the ground on the hot pavement, the effort of standing too much for him, "it wasn't there for us."

Daniel nudges Natalie in the side. "We should probably get moving," Daniel says.

Natalie pauses. She wants to offer Mike's assistance to the family. But after what happened in Tanner's Ridge, she decides against it.

Daniel borders on euphoric as they return to the pull-off for the next set of cows, repeating again and again that he's just glad to get that over with. Natalie frets. Joe stares at his tattered and hole-filled black boots. They all know it isn't quite enough.

———∞∞∞———

ANDREW WATCHES AS ANNEKE DISHES out seconds of the chicken stew. Anneke has taken to controlling the servings, and those wanting more must line up for what she deems their fair share. Andrew understands the food situation is tight, and he understands he's not starving to death, but what Andrew *doesn't* understand is why Craig always gets more seconds than him. There's little disputing that Craig could stand to put on some weight. When he arrived in August, he looked like a stick bug. But he's rounded out somewhat since then, and Anneke's preferential treatment mystifies Andrew. Andrew's taken to lining up for seconds even when he's not hungry, just to compare his and Craig's takes.

Anneke screws up her eyes at Andrew when he reaches the front of the line. She's been making more effort with her appearance in the last two months: selecting more flattering outfits, wearing makeup, and combing her hair. Not that it helps, really. Anneke always reminds Andrew of some sort of androgynous farm animal in clothes—with her blotchy skin, big pores, flat feet, and tank-like figure. Now she just looks like a farm animal with lipstick.

"Back for more again, Andrew?"

"Yup," Andrew says, rubbing his stomach. "I'm a growing man." He says man instead of boy in case Claire is listening. But Claire pushes her food around on her plate and stares vacantly at the wall. Then Andrew feels like a damn fool. Anneke sees him staring at Claire and her mouth angles into a half sneer.

A half spoonful of stew splats onto his plate, and Anneke has already redirected her attention to the person behind him in line. Andrew scurries back to the table, aiming for the spot next to Claire, but Leon plunks himself down next to her before he can get there. Andrew wonders if he should tell Leon about Richard's email—but what would his uncle even do? Richard will be home soon enough.

Andrew parks himself next to Craig, who's working his way through a much more generous second helping. Andrew glares back at Anneke as if to ask what gives, but Anneke's attention is completely fixed on Craig. Bits of stew drip from her ladle onto the hardwood floor.

She notices Andrew staring at her and pulls her lips into a narrow line. Then she flicks her eyes to Craig and Claire and then back to Andrew. She gives

Andrew a faint nod, with an elevated eyebrow. She's suggesting some sort of alliance. Andrew hesitates and then nods back. He has no idea what he's agreeing to. Sometimes his life is so fucked.

At the very least, perhaps he'll start getting more food.

CHAPTER X
THE FOOL

—⊶⊷—

RICHARD

*High ideals and the possibility of a brighter future through choice
and personal effort.*

Richard sips his tea by the heavily curtained parlor windows that look out
onto the drive. The rain cascades out of the sky in a continuous stream,
saturating the lush green yard and creating a chain of muddy lagoons that will
pool together into a massive lake by morning. He can hear Alfie's and Virginia's
voices, loud and rough, in the office—drunk already, no doubt. Climate change
has not been kind to Vancouver. The clouds never seem to lift, and the air hangs
thick with moisture even when it's not raining. The crack and howl of the wind
and storms over the open ocean and past his bedroom window would be exciting, if it weren't for the fact that sometimes Richard wonders if the house won't
just lift off its foundations and be thrown out to sea.

But otherwise Vancouver is almost everything that he hoped for. Alfie
calls it the Wild West, but to Richard it's more like the Wild West on amphet-
amines, and the adrenaline rush is mind-blowing. Squatters occupy empty
buildings, offering whatever marketable skills they possess in exchange
for food. Doctors and dentists are in demand of course, as is anyone with
skills in sewing, smithing, or sex. Gangs, predisposed to violence first and

questions later, rove streets populated by abandoned vehicles and vacant high-rises. High-stakes fly-by-night gambling casinos and brothels set up shop in empty buildings, only to vanish and appear across town three days later. The police hired by the provisional government are little better than a gang themselves. Raging blazes taking out entire city blocks are common. People build fires in the streets and buildings to keep warm and cook food, but when alarms are sounded and cries for help raised, nobody comes to save them.

The nauseating stench of sewage in the streets is irritating, of course, but tolerable. The house that the provisional government put him up in, a massive heritage number in Shaughnessy with a flirty Latino maid, while perhaps a bit dreary with the wood paneling, is befitting of his rank. But most importantly, Richard gets to spend his days with men. Powerful men, hard-talking men who are reestablishing the government with none of the pussy-whipped affirmative action that allowed incompetent women and men to infiltrate the government ranks. It's a relief to be back to the merit system and scrap the everyone-deserves-a-chance shit. Thank God they decided the new seat of government should be in Vancouver—where it always should have been—not stiff, plaid-curtain, slow-moving Victoria. With the ferry service only intermittent, Victoria has pretty much ceased to exist anyway.

His arrival a few weeks ago was met with suitable excitement, immediate acceptance, and a mid-level position in the new provisional government: Minister of Revenue and Gaming. Richard's stomach muscles automatically tighten as he says it, as if photographers might be in the hall ready to capture his image while he stares out the window in a pensive state. It is a bit concerning, of course, that the provincial government is already in a deficit situation due to the heavy costs of policing, and that the primary source of revenue is the casinos, in which the provisional government has part ownership; but as soon as they reestablish taxation, Richard feels certain that the financial situation will be turned around. He had hoped for something slightly higher up, of course, like Minister of Trade, or Minister of Foreign Affairs. But pickings were slim, and the veiny-nosed provisional leader, Ron Merlo—who doesn't quite understand the range of skills that Richard has to offer, and reminds him of Mr. Rogers with a drinking problem—already had his inner circle in place. No matter. The guy's so tightly wound, it's only a matter of time before he snaps—and by then Richard will be ready to step in. And even if Merlo doesn't crack up, the elections are in a year, and Richard plans to start campaigning quietly through his new links in the casinos long before then.

Richard adds a splash of homebrew brandy to his tea. Virginia's bray grates on him tonight. Perhaps they should have left her in Kamloops as originally planned. But Alfie had insisted, and Richard capitulated. Virginia had set her sights on Richard initially. Richard strung her along a bit, all in good fun of course. She's a live wire, and he got a charge out of joking around with her. Anything more than that would give him the heebies. Why big women seem to think he likes them, he'll never know. Alfie was only too happy to step in and take advantage of the situation. And now Richard's stuck with their carryings-on. He thinks he preferred it when she was shaking her hooters at him and throwing him come-hither looks.

The dark form of a sedan pulls into the drive, its headlights illuminating the puddles and flashing brilliant on the wall behind Richard. Peter. Only Peter Hilton can afford gasoline these days. Richard wonders where he gets it—if he has a secret stash somewhere, or if the rumors are true, that the Chinese are still producing and have tankers floating off-shore, selling to the highest of bidders.

Richard scurries to the door and ushers Peter in, in a spray of wind and rain, Peter's butler holding an umbrella above his employer. Richard cries greetings, hoping that he's put the right amount of hearty in his voice, and takes Peter's coat, a butter-soft black leather car jacket completely unsuited to the weather. He glimpses Alfie hovering ghost-like in the hall outside the entryway, his eyes wide.

Richard ushers Peter into the dim parlor, wishing that he were deeply entrenched enough in the inner government circle to qualify for electricity, but he isn't—yet. At least a fire crackles in the grate, and a selection of reasonable brandies sits on the desk. Peter sinks into a wingback chair, his limbs rustling with impatience.

"Can I offer you a sip of brandy? I have a fine one from the new distillery in Ladner." Richard cringes at the eagerness and the nerves in his own voice.

Peter makes a brusque flick of his hand. The image of the fire splays across the lenses of his round glasses and his shiny bald forehead. "I only drink cognac. I'm not staying. We need to talk about your new Manager of Gaming." Richard pours himself a large tumblerful of brandy.

"Silas?"

"He's been asking questions about the regulations. Making himself an irritant."

"Well, he's new to the job. Serious fellow. I'll talk to him."

"He was asking questions about the table limits. Citing some new regulations."

Richard forces a hearty laugh. "Oh, the new regs are just Merlo being an ass. Thinking that we have to get control over things. Doesn't have a clue what side his bread is buttered on. He can't enforce it. Don't even think about it."

"I thought we agreed that you would handle things on that front." Peter's tone is unpleasant. "Isn't that what I'm paying you for?"

Richard's own temper licks at the sides of his skull, but he keeps his voice steady, as his eyes travel down Peter's body searching for signs of a firearm. "I *am* handling things."

"I need you to deal with this new employee of yours."

"I'll talk to him."

"I'd rather you just got rid of him. Characters like that—I know them. They're like a dog with a bone. They don't stop."

"You mean fire him?"

"No, I mean get rid of him. For good. He already knows too much. He's doing the math on the take. He'll try to take you down too. We don't need the hassle."

Richard finds himself about to squeal out something about Silas having a young family but thinks better of it. He takes a gulp of the brandy and lets the amber liquid burn at his throat. "I don't want that kind of exposure. I thought we agreed that I need to stay clean for the election. You shouldn't even be here." This last is a risk, and Peter's eyes rake over him.

"Don't you *dare* tell me where I should or shouldn't be. Have your little friend do it if you want. But see that it's done."

"Can't *you* do it?" The brandy has made Richard's eyes water, and he sets the cup down on the desk.

"I could put a bullet between *your* eyes right now if I wanted, and nobody would even knock on my door to ask a question."

Richard's eyes flick to Peter's hands, which thankfully remain empty, and then to the drawer in his desk where his own gun sits. Peter smiles, the firelight tracing the skeletal lines of his gaunt face. "The point is, Richard, that we can still do whatever we want. The police are completely ineffective. I want to see what you're made of. Consider Silas your pre-test because Merlo is next on the list."

"You're going to take out Merlo? Tell me you don't want me to take out Merlo." Richard pulls his hands through his hair.

"What kind of organization did you think you were joining here? The Ladies Auxiliary?"

"It would be way too risky. My career. My family. You said profit and information-sharing." Richard starts to pace around the room, but then considers which angles and vulnerable fleshy parts he might expose to Peter in doing so, and decides to remain perched on the desk. Like a big sitting duck.

"Relax. Panic doesn't become you. Makes you look old and fat. I didn't say we were going to do it any time soon, and I didn't say *you* were going to do it. But we *will* need your help. Deal with Silas. Keep on working like you've been doing, and when we need you, we'll let you know. We won't put you too far out there, Richard. You obviously don't have the stomach for it. But you'll have to find other ways to make yourself useful."

Peter rises and gestures at the door. Richard marches out obediently; Peter always walks behind. Richard sits in the dark of the entryway for a while after the hum of the Audi fades into the distance. Alfie and Virginia have gone silent. After a bit, Richard sees Alfie peering around the corner of the curving staircase that leads to the second floor. Next to the massive stairs, Alfie looks diminutive, like an imp or an elf.

"What'd Peter want?"

"Nothing. Just sharing some news on profits."

"That man is like…the Grim Reaper or something. You sure he didn't rough you up?"

"No roughing. Just some suggestions on how I should run some operations."

"Okay. Well, Virginia and I are heading to bed. You don't need anything, do you, buddy?"

"Nope. You go ahead."

The clouds break slightly, and a sliver of moon glimmers in the hall mirror. He should have guessed that this arrangement with Peter, while financially rewarding, could lead to some hassles. But he had no way of knowing that not all of Peter's business dealings were on the up-and-up when he first agreed to part ownership in the casinos. Perhaps the fact that he had to be a silent partner should have been a tip-off. Besides, compared to some of the other crime lords in town, Peter should be citizen of the year. Everyone's running their casinos the way Peter is—with massive buy-in minimums, stacked decks, and ringers who work for the casino at every table—and still the stupid buggers come and lay down their cash, or their horse, or a crate full of chickens, all for the hope of what, Richard isn't sure. He likes a good gamble himself, but he'd never put his money on the table of any casino in town. He flinches a bit at the thought of Suicide Alley, the new name of the street that runs in front of the downtown club, the most upscale of the casinos. At least Peter's casinos don't accept women and children as payment. Yet.

Well. He'd known there would be some compromises in his rise to the top; there always are. And Peter will be a generous campaign donor. And once Richard is Premier, he'll clean up the city and the casinos.

By the time Richard goes to bed, he has himself so convinced that Peter really is a good guy that he wonders if perhaps Peter was just joking about taking care of Silas.

RICHARD BROODS ON THE SKYTRAIN the next morning on the way to his office. The security guards stand by the doors with drawn looks on their faces, checking and rechecking Richard's security card and photo ID, even though he rides the same train every morning. There must have been more incidents overnight. He fucking hates the SkyTrain—even though it's government transport only now—with its unreliable service and the shitload of looters clamoring around outside the terminal. Still, it's safer than riding his horse through the streets. He needs to talk to Merlo about getting a personal guard.

Alfie and Virginia were still asleep when he left. Alfie barely turns a wheel these days, and he's racking up quite the bill at the tailor. He pops into the office bright as a button at around two each day, shakes a bunch of hands, talks about all the people he's going to talk up about Richard, and then he fucks off. Richard's never sure if he actually goes anywhere or talks to anyone. As far as he knows, Alfie feeds ducks for the rest of the afternoon. Then again, most of the ducks in town were eaten long ago.

Silas is waiting outside Richard's office when he arrives. Bonnie takes his coat and hands him his coffee, and rolls her eyes over in Silas's direction. Richard considers slipping silently back down the hall, but Silas sees him and scrambles over to him, bobbing and flailing like a golden retriever.

"Sir, I've had a very interesting first few days."

Richard feels a momentary flash of satisfaction that Silas remembered to call him sir. But it's quickly replaced by the irksome reminder that he's been instructed to kill Silas. It's not that he has a problem with killing, per se, or that he thinks he won't get away with it. Peter can think that if he likes. It's better at this point if Peter underestimates him. But Richard kills raiders, murderers: bad guys. Silas, with his affable demeanor, earnestness, and evident worship of Richard, is nowhere near the "bad guy" category. Richard isn't entirely certain what the consequences are of not following Peter's orders, but he's also not too keen on being one of the bodies they fish out of the Burrard Inlet every morning. Or the Fraser River, for that matter.

"You don't say."

"Yes, sir. Do you have a minute?"

"Actually I don't. I'm very busy," Richard says. Silas's face crumples. "Why don't you come to my house for dinner tonight? Six o'clock. We can talk about things. Get the address from Bonnie."

Silas looks like he might be about to leap up and lick Richard's face in gratitude, and Richard quickly backs into his office and closes the door. *Premier*, he repeats to himself. He just needs to stick this out for a bit longer, and then he'll have the corner office and call the shots. He pictures himself in the new legislature at the former Vancouver Art Gallery, in a navy wool suit with a bright blue dress shirt. He'll need a car, of course—an energy-efficient one, for optics. He'll convince Peter to tell him where he gets his gasoline, and then Richard can begin to move the province forward again, out of these stinky horse-trodden dark ages.

International relations will have to be the first priority. He feels a slight wobble of stress at the prospect. He's honestly surprised Vancouver hasn't been invaded yet. But maybe China and the US spent the last few years digging themselves out from under. Maybe it's just a matter of time. He's sure Merlo knows more than he's telling. He needs to ingratiate himself more with the Minister of Foreign Affairs and find out what the hell's going on instead of sitting in his office managing casinos and figuring out how to reinstate taxation.

"SILAS, HOW DO YOU FEEL about taking a little trip into the interior?"

Richard savors his steak with blue cheese sauce. His flirty little maid can definitely cook. He struggles vainly to remember her name—Esme, Esmerelda? He'll have to ask Alfie. He doesn't miss the gruel on the farm at all.

The candlelight flickers against Silas's wide, eager face. "On assignment, you mean? Are there casinos in the interior?"

"No, not yet. I need someone to take a message to my wife, near Tanner's Ridge. Since we don't have the post anymore and all. Consider it a new avenue of work. We could reinstate the postal service together." Richard gives Silas an encouraging grin and eye-blink.

Silas's face scrunches up a bit. "Can't you use the new Internet?"

"Connection on the farm is down, I'm afraid."

Silas's eyes work nervously in his head, flitting from Richard to the wall, back to Richard. "Well, sir, you know I have a wife and child. It sounds like an awfully long trip."

"Work with me here, Silas. It's a very important message."

"Okay. I'll talk to Nancy. How long do you think I'd be gone?"

"You have to go tonight, direct from here."

"But I have no stuff."

"You can borrow some of my clothes. Virginia here will drive you to the train station in Mission."

"Mission? Why not the Vancouver station?"

"Full of drunks and vagrants. You don't want to go there."

"But Nancy…"

Richard grits his teeth. "Silas, are you putting up roadblocks on me? Road-blockers don't get promotions. It's a very urgent message. The train leaves in a couple hours. Do as I ask, and you will have a lovely bonus waiting for you when you get home. I'll go talk to Nancy tomorrow, myself. Let her know you had to go. I'll even check in on her while you're gone."

Silas looks tremulously around the table at all of them. Alfie and Virginia nod. They have a limited idea of what's going on, of course, but they've agreed to participate in *Operation Get Silas Out of Town*, as Alfie is calling it. Virginia was quite cranky about having to take Silas all the way to Mission, but when Richard made some observations regarding her free rent and food, she decided to play ball pretty quickly.

"Okay. I guess. Will you return my bicycle to Nancy? We only have one. "

Richard wipes his lips with his napkin, rises, and stretches. "Of course. Well, let's move along then. I already have the team hitched to the wagon."

Richard almost pushes Silas out the door and into the front seat of the wagon. He wants to ask the younger man to lie down in the back under a blanket, but that would set off all sorts of alarms, he's sure. He just hopes that in the dark streets, nobody will recognize Richard's team and the man that occupies the wagon, his straw-colored hair a beacon in the half light.

"There's a bag of clothes in the back. The farm address, an envelope of money, and the message are in there. Take the train as far as Kamloops. You'll have to rent a horse when you get there and make your way to the farm."

"Sir?"

"Yes."

"I've never actually left Vancouver. How will I know the way?"

"Ask directions, for Christ's sake."

Silas nods his head, and Richard gives him a big thumbs-up. Virginia yanks the reins, and the wagon scuttles off down the drive, bumping and heaving on the rutted mossy pavement with Silas clutching the bench seat.

Alfie watches them depart. Richard turns away and starts to head back to the house, his armpits greasy with sweat. The fucking kid will probably get himself killed before he hits Vernon; that's assuming he even turns the right direction after he hits Kamloops. But at least Richard didn't have to shoot him.

"Okay, buddy, what's he got on you?" Alfie says.

"What's who got on me?"

"Silas. He must have something. You hustling him out of town and acting as jumpy as a cat on a flaming roof."

"Nothing, Alfie. Everything's fine. Just make sure you amp up the campaigning, got it? No more of these half days. The election's in less than a year, and you need to make sure I win. I'm going to bed."

RICHARD IS AT HIS DESK the next morning, his head throbbing with exhaustion, trying to determine the best structure for the new tax network. Virginia didn't come home last night, which means his team of Arabians is missing, and he got no sleep lying there waiting to hear the rattle of the wheels in the drive. She could have just fucked off, sold the horses, and run. Or worse, knocked Silas out of the wagon and taken the money and run. But Silas would have shown up here to report in if that had happened. She probably took the horses. His body feels heavy and dopey.

Richard is launched out of a dream of dark horses in a raging river, and Virginia and Natalie looming on the horizon like massive inflatable figures, laughing at him. A sharp knock on the door repeats itself, and he jerks his head up to see Peter's round glasses peering through one of the clear swirls on the frosted glass wall of Richard's office. Swirls that match the five-circle insignia of the provisional government engraved on the wood paneling on the wall opposite. Merlo says it's supposed to be waves and breakers, signifying BC's ocean connection. Richard thinks it's a dumb insignia; it reminds him of some sort of bastardized Olympic logo.

He leaps up from his desk and yanks open the door.

Peter enters silently, and Richard leans out the door and looks both directions. How the hell did Peter get inside? The hallway is deserted, and Richard has a sudden image of all of his employees slumped over their desks with bullets through their heads. He closes the door. Peter settles into one of the leather chairs in front of Richard's desk. Richard feels rather like small creatures are delicately chewing his insides to bits.

"Silas didn't show up for work today," Peter says. Richard almost curses aloud. He forgot to go tell Silas's wife about her husband's trip, and Silas's rusted bicycle still leans against his front porch. Richard prepares to launch into some sort of theatrical behavior to suggest that he already knows this, that he in fact killed Silas. The whole scene seems tired to him though. He just wants to be done with the posturing. He nonetheless collects his features into a buoyant expression and is about to comment when Peter continues in a bland tone.

"Tell me, Richard. What does political life mean to you?"

"I don't know what you mean."

"How badly do you want to be Premier?"

"Badly…ish." Richard shakes his head and squints his eyes. He tries to smile, but he's fairly certain it's more of a sneer. Where is Peter going with this?

"You might want to work on your speaking skills and word choices, then."

Anger snaps Richard back into himself. He will not let himself be controlled by a little man like this. His fingers brush the cool metal of the gun he has taped beneath the drawer of his desk. "What do you want, Peter?"

"It seems I have a lovely pair of matched Arabians in my stable."

Richard lets out a laugh. "Really? That's funny. I was wondering where they'd got to."

Peter cocks his head slightly at Richard's reaction, assessing. "You didn't do as I asked."

"Nope. You're right. I didn't." Richard keeps his words flat, even though his skin vibrates with electricity, and the adrenaline kicks through his veins.

"That little whore of yours couldn't wait to tell us all about it."

"You don't say."

"She's dead now."

"I figured." Richard feels a small flash of remorse at Virginia's death. But he puts it out of his mind easily. She was a non-entity to him, an extra who popped out of existence once she exited Richard's stage. He hopes Alfie doesn't make a stink about it. He hooks his forefinger into the trigger of the gun. "And Silas?"

"He got away," Peter says. Richard contains a small smirk. "But it's not like he'd be hard to find."

"I wouldn't waste my time," Richard says.

Peter's stubble adds dark contours to his face. His small delicate nose seems almost skeletal. "I could have you killed this afternoon."

"And I could shoot you right now," Richard says. Peter's eyes drop to Richard's hands resting under his desk.

Peter's smile is faint and cool. "I'm beginning to appreciate your style."

"You need me."

"You aren't that hard to replace."

"Do it then."

Peter's face tightens, and he scowls. "All right. Since you're feeling so confident in your own value-add, you can start working on Merlo a bit more, find out what communications he's having with the Chinese. If you want to start calling some shots around here, Richard, you'd better get your ass in gear and prove your worth because I'll be watching and evaluating. Nobody's irreplaceable."

"Yup." Richard savors the hit that winning brings. At least, he thinks he's won. He should go retrieve Silas and make the young man his assistant, but that would probably be too in-your-face. His own inclinations give him pause sometimes.

Peter rises and waits, expecting Richard to walk him to the door. But Richard simply stands. Peter turns and leaves. After he's sure Peter's gone, Richard rushes out into the hallway. Bonnie stands by her desk, clutching a paper bag. The chatter and rustle of the interns and his staff echoes up the hallway. They were all probably in the lunchroom. Richard wonders if he shouldn't perhaps shorten their lunch hour.

Bonnie stares down the hall where Peter was. "I just went out to get your lunch. Who was that man?"

"Nobody," Richard says.

The first bullet shatters the exterior window and glass wall of Richard's office. Richard plunges to the ground. Bonnie shrieks, drops the bag, and crumples next to Richard. The interns and staffers leap for cover under desks. Five shots follow, each one landing in the wall opposite Richard's office.

They remain on the floor for several minutes. Bonnie trembles and whimpers, and the paper on the brown bag, which she has inexplicably drawn into herself as if for protection or security, crinkles in her hands. Richard rises, his own knees a bit flaccid, and examines the pattern of shots, each one centered in one of the five circles on the provisional government insignia. Perfect shots. The bullets wouldn't have hit him as long as he remained sitting at his desk. It's a warning. He looks out his broken window to the building across the street, and almost smiles.

The fucker's got style.

CHAPTER 19
STRENGTH

⟨⟨⟨⟩⟩⟩

DANIEL AND ANDREW

Master your fear and emotions; let go of your lower self.

Daniel drives the wagon around the bend into Jerry. Tents, horses, and people surround the green-shingled church. There must be at least a hundred people present, and most are men. Drinks pass among the men leaning against wagons, weapons prominently displayed on their hips—and the talk, while still subdued, could so easily slip out of control as the day wears on. Everyone eyes everyone with open distrust, or at least appraisal. Pairs of men with guns—standing back to back, one facing outward and one inward—stand in a circle around the perimeter of the camp. Security guards, Daniel assumes. He doesn't feel much comfort. Attackers could already lurk within the camp, ready to rip them apart from inside when night falls.

Mike and Ranjeet have agreed to camp back near the mill with the potatoes and corn, leaving Daniel, Natalie, and Joe to carry on. Daniel proposed just going home after the trade, but Natalie insisted on sticking with the plan, arguing that they need to make more contacts and find something else to trade to get through the winter, which he didn't disagree with. But he's not sure this is the place. He just let himself be convinced.

Daniel spots Ilene's white head at what appears to be a check-in table at the outskirts of the camp, and guides Catherine over to her. He left Heathcliff, now officially lame, with Mike, hoping that the horse will be better and ready for the trip home after two days' rest. He has his doubts though, and he runs through scenarios for how he's going to get a lame horse back to the farm.

Ilene greets them with an enthusiastic wave and rises to hug Natalie as she disembarks from the wagon. The older woman has her hair tied in a knot on her head. She's aged over the past few weeks, and darts occasional looks behind her at the accumulated men.

"We need you to write out the password," Ilene says, passing a pencil to Natalie. "It's just a formality because I know you, of course, but we need everyone to do it. I'm so glad you made it." She looks over her shoulder again and lowers her voice. "We had hoped for more families and women. But I guess we have to go with it. We have an initial Town Hall kind of meeting tonight. Tomorrow we'll all divide up and go to the meetings of your choice from this list." Ilene flutters a list in their direction. "If you could sign up now, or if you see something that's not on the list that you think we need to discuss, let me know."

While Natalie writes out the password that Ilene gave them so many weeks ago, Daniel scans the list. Nearly a dozen topics are written in a shaky but legible script: local vs. provincial government, regional hospital, postal service, taxation, legal system, trade, militia/policing, regional boundaries, orphans, refugee camps. Each topic has a list of names jammed beneath it and curling up into the margins. Daniel's head starts to spin. He's never liked these kinds of meetings. The idea of having to establish these things from scratch is even more daunting. He wonders if they'll also have to wear "Hello, my name is" stickers.

He looks around at the groups of men gathered in the churchyard, with their scraggy clothes and hats pulled low, their glances shifting to Ilene's table and then back. There's no way all these men can be here to discuss setting up a postal service or legal system. Half of them have guns slung across their backs, and a few carry what appear to be quivers of arrows or spears. He hopes most of the guns are for show and not loaded, but he can't be sure. Someone is probably making bullets by now. Daniel instinctively reaches back and touches the safety on the compact Smith & Wesson that he retrieved from the holster he attached to the bottom of the wagon after Rafe took his Sigma.

He passes the list to Natalie.

"I'm going to sign up for trade. What are you going to do?" she says. Daniel is taken aback. He just assumed they would stick together.

"Are we splitting up?"

"It's better that way," Ilene says. "Allows for more sharing of ideas." Daniel's brain starts to cycle in horror at the twin prospects of having to participate and of Natalie being alone in this crowd of all too eager and almost feral men.

"And one of us should go to the regional hospital discussion. Mike needs to know what's going on. Scott needs treatment, and others will too, I'm sure." Natalie says.

"Fine," Daniel says, "I'll go, but Joe is going with you."

He watches as Natalie adds his name and places Joe's next to hers. This whole gathering is half-baked. Order will be reestablished with guns and tanks. Not group meetings. Not at this point.

"Um, what are we hoping to get out of this?" he says to Natalie as they take the wagon to their designated camping spot, which—Daniel observes with relief—is on the edge of the camp. Several men have already eyed Natalie with more interest than Daniel likes.

"Before the peak you always complained about the government and the bad decisions they made," Natalie says. "This is our opportunity to decide how we want things to work on a regional scale, rather than have someone dictate to us. You can bet Richard and others are making plans in Vancouver to tell us how things are going to be run around here."

"Yeah, but we barely have any semblance of civil society," Daniel says. "Don't you think we should reestablish the rule of law first?" Things could go so wrong here, and all this community-building stuff is for extroverts and people with political savvy. It's way out of his comfort zone. He knows how to take care of animals, not create a legal system. He doesn't argue that it needs to be done, but getting some of these things off the ground will require more energy and discourse than he can even imagine.

"Maybe this is the way we do that. I think we have to give it a try. Besides, we have to try to make some trades anyway," says Natalie.

Or maybe this is the way we all end up getting shot, Daniel thinks. He tries to picture himself singlehandedly reestablishing the postal service, kind of like Kevin Costner. But it's a stupid vision, and he ends up feeling idiotic for romanticizing it.

"We should sleep in the back of the wagon," he says. He'll leave Catherine hitched; that way if they need to make a quick getaway in the night they can. He sees other horses remain hitched and at the ready.

Natalie shrugs as if to say this is fine with her. They make a quick meal of leftover venison, apples, and bannock, eschewing a fire in favor of haste. They've arrived late because of the trade, and the town hall meeting is due to start. The day-old venison with its congealed gamey juices almost makes Daniel vomit and will surely give him the shits. The day has been chilly, and the venison has been stored in an old cooler beside a pail of crisp creek water. But the lack of refrigeration doesn't thrill Daniel. He cranes his neck around looking for the latrines. A cluster of coffin-sized huts stands at the edge of the field: shallowly dug pit toilets that will reek of too much spoiled food and bear meat before the end of tomorrow. He'd rather take his chances in the trees. But that would be bad etiquette.

At around seven o'clock, the church bell clangs, and Daniel, Natalie, and Joe join the line of people filing into the church building. *Lambs to the slaughter*, Daniel thinks, but he tries to replace this with positive thoughts. Sad-looking sacks most of them, in dirty, ill-fitting clothes, faces lined with dust and worry. Their shoes alone could be a study of the fall of modern society. Homemade wood-carved clogs and leather slippers next to dilapidated old riding and hiking boots stitched together with pieces of twine and duct tape. Some men scuffle along in beat-up, uncomfortable-looking black dress shoes—their wedding and funeral shoes, probably, tucked into far corners of their closets until they became the only shoes they had left. One man has crammed his feet into women's sandals, his toes hanging ignominiously over the end. A few women stand among the men. Some wear white caps covering their hair, and keep their heads bent. A new religious movement, Daniel wonders, or the revival of an old one? Stale-smelling bodies press under and around him as he huddles against the wall, hoping that lice aren't leaping onto his shoulders from the heads that pass below his chin. He's got to hand it to Natalie, and perhaps Richard: the folks from the farm look a hell of a lot better than most of the people present.

They sink into pews or stand at the end of rows and in the back. Daniel finds himself pressed against a thick-paned stained-glass window, Natalie and Joe squished into each of his fragrant armpits. In an emergency, he could shatter the glass. He tries to recall how far off the ground this window is situated.

Ilene rises to her feet at the front of the room, her shroud of white hair—she's released it from its bun—making her look like an aged angel.

"Thank you for risking your personal safety and putting aside your doubts to attend this important gathering. We are in dark days. We know they're rebuilding government in Vancouver. We know almost nothing from the rest of the world. We don't know how long it will take for any rebuilt government to reach out to us here in the hinterland, to help us, or even if it *intends* to bring help. Some of us here think we don't need any Vancouver government telling us how we should live. We think we should rebuild parts of our society on our own. So when, and if, the government does arrive, we can negotiate on our own terms."

The audience responds with a smattering of applause, polite acknowledgement. But Ilene has not yet won them all over. Headshakes and suspicious looks are exchanged in some of the pews.

Ilene passes the floor over to a man she introduces as Reverend Casey McDermid. He's a youngish, skinny man with floppy brown hair that he keeps whisking out of his face. *Too young to impress this crowd*, Daniel thinks, although he guesses the reverend's at least thirty. Great, he's become a grumbly old man who thinks a thirty-year-old is a baby.

The reverend speaks passionately about the importance of community and trust at times like this. He moves around the floor and speaks with apparent comfort, waving his hands for emphasis. He talks about the past four years in Jerry: the huge initial death toll, the number of people who just vanished, the scourge of raiders and the trickle of refugees, and the slow rebuilding that has occurred. The resurrection of ancient wild fruit orchards, the conversion of the small golf course to agricultural land, the new mill operation, and the reestablishment of some trade. Thankfully he doesn't bring God into the speech, although Daniel is convinced that references to God twitch at his lips on many occasions.

"Now for what we need in Jerry. We need a doctor, or several doctors; salt, antibiotics, ammunition; and young people of marriageable age, especially women. I'm pleased to offer my own hand in marriage to a hard-working, healthy woman, preferably under the age of thirty," the reverend concludes with a wink. This draws laughs from the crowd and a few men wave the arms of their daughters.

Ilene gets to her feet again. "Now I would like to introduce the people I've asked to lead each discussion to come to the front and tell us what we know with regard to each area, and what some of the major challenges are."

Daniel recoils when Natalie steps out from under his shoulder and weaves her way through the crowd to join the row of assembled men up front. She didn't tell him that Ilene had asked her to lead a discussion. Daniel tenses to have her so far away from him. If anything goes wrong, it's no longer a matter of breaking a window and hoping the fall is mercifully small. Now he would have to push his way to the front, probably shoot a bunch of people, try not to get shot, grab her, and take a leap out one of the larger windows at the back, which he's certain are positioned higher off the ground. If he tries to inch toward her now, someone will notice and wonder what he's doing.

The men begin providing updates on what they know. In general, not much. Few people even have a handle on the remaining population of the area, although most guesses place it at a third of what it was before the peak. The need for salt, antibiotics, and medical care is a common theme throughout the presentations. The idea of establishing some sort of regional system rather than waiting for the provincial government surfaces many times. Daniel wonders what Richard would think of that.

Daniel tries not to cringe when Natalie's turn comes. He doesn't know why watching her speak makes him so nervous. Several of the men hoot as if the long-awaited stripper or boxing-ring girl has arrived. Daniel scans the crowd, wanting to clobber each and every one of them, but he tries to concentrate on what Natalie is saying.

"So, assuming that we're all agreed on the proposition that we need to increase trade, the questions I would like to explore revolve around how much trade we really require within the region and external to the region. Do we want to allow ourselves to specialize in the manner that we once did, whereby some farms produce only one item? Or do we want to try to keep ourselves as diversified as we've had to be? Then there's the issue of whether it would be most effective to pass our trade items through a storefront or broker, or keep it more informal just between the seller and buyer; and what kinds of systems we can set up to facilitate that. Some of you have heard about the new Internet, but what other approaches can we use to determine who has items to trade and who wants them?" She speaks well, and Daniel sees a flash of what she might have been capable of—still could be capable of—if she had made different choices.

Many of the men in the audience lean forward with hungry looks on their faces. She no longer wears her wedding ring, having given it up in trade in Tanner's Ridge. Daniel feels a sheen of sweat between his shoulder blades. She's too beautiful to be drawing attention to herself in this crowd where civility barely teeters on the edge. "And of course we're going to have to talk about having some sort of currency, or just keeping it a good-for-good barter system," says Natalie.

She slips back into the lineup of men at the front, and a grizzled man with a buzz cut, tanned skin, skinny awkward limbs, and lots of age spots steps forward. The man introduces himself as Earl, and is about to start talking when another man from the audience stands and pushes his way to the front, waving his rifle in the air. There's an instant ripple through the audience as at least a hundred guns and bows are snatched from pockets and laps and trained on the man—and, Daniel realizes in terror, Natalie.

The man steps onto the platform next to Earl and turns to the crowd. "Don't shoot!" he yells. He looks about forty, and has a giant weeping tumor on the side of his neck. "I just have a question." Nobody lowers their gun.

"You could have raised your hand at any time," Ilene says, her voice quavering. "What is your question? Everybody, please, put down your guns." Nobody moves, and the man with the tumor stands slack-jawed, staring at the rows of guns pointed at him. Daniel cringes. If someone opens fire, it's going to be a bloodbath, and he has no way of getting to Natalie. Smashing the window would be too noisy. Someone would pull a trigger. He sees a few men slipping out the front door of the church.

Earl puts both his hands in the air. "Stop, everyone. Stop right now. I know what's going on. This is a trick. This guy," he gestures at the man with the tumor, "and whoever he's working with, *want* you to open fire. He's a sacrifice. He's dying anyway. There are some doctors here who have deliberately kept their identities secret because there are folks here who would abduct them and force them to try to save lives. If you open fire and injure or kill half of us, they figure the doctors will tend to the wounded and can then be identified. Don't do it. We're setting up a field hospital tomorrow under guard. We will help you. Please don't do this."

"How do we know that's the truth?" a bearded man with glittery blue eyes in a ripped and stained camel trench coat calls from the back of the church. "You've kept yourselves hidden away, refusing to treat anyone for years, or charging ridiculous sums like selfish bastards, while we all lie dying around you."

Earl blazes slightly at this. "What would you have us do when there are people willing to turn us into slaves, or camp all around our homes, lined up day and night, oozing disease, when we have no supplies, no instruments, and no help? We're here to help now. You should let us." Eyes swing around to look at the bearded man. Daniel wonders whether, if he took him out with a clean shot, this would be over, or if it would just cause pandemonium.

The bearded man does not reply.

"What about as a show of good faith, I have all the doctors come up here so you can see how many of us there are? Then you can work out your potential chances of getting treatment tomorrow. Which won't happen if we all get shot today."

The man with the beard hesitates and then nods. "All right."

Earl makes a gesture to the audience, and one by one three men and a woman inch their way up the center aisle and hunch low on the floor at Earl's feet. Daniel shoves his gun into his pants and pushes his way to the front as well, to Natalie. Earl glances at him in surprise and then nods, assuming, probably like everyone else, that Daniel is identifying himself as a doctor. The number of gun barrels aimed at him makes Daniel's stomach lurch, but at least he could now grab Natalie if necessary.

"Put your guns down. You won't get treated if we're dead," Earl orders. "The field hospital opens tomorrow at nine a.m. We will be expecting payment, but rates will be set at a reasonable sum. Disperse now," Earl barks.

Guns and bows are lowered slowly, and there's a massive jostle toward the door.

"We'll have the group meetings tomorrow," Ilene calls out as people leave.

Then suddenly the meeting is over; the church hasn't burned and nobody has opened fire. Daniel stands almost crumpled at the front and feels Natalie's hand snake into his from behind.

Earl eyes him up and down. His eyes linger on the long scar that marks Daniel's forearm from his wrist to the center of his hand. A bad encounter with the horse-pulled combine. The purple line still bears the tick marks of Mike's tidy stitches.

Earl thrusts out his hand, "Earl."

Daniel provides his own. "Daniel."

"You a specialist?"

How does he answer this? "Not exactly." Now that he has Natalie, and they're alive, he plans to pack up the wagon and depart as soon as they get out of this goddamn church.

"Are you experienced in surgery?"

Daniel nods yes. This is in theory true.

"Good. I'll put you on general surgery assist then. The rest of those pansies there are used to treating sniffles and earaches. Meet tomorrow at eight at the field hospital." Earl turns away and starts talking to Ilene. Daniel pulls Natalie down the aisle and out of the church, Joe trailing behind them. They stride back through the wagons and tents where people cluster in groups, talking in urgent tones. Some wagons are already pulling out. Everyone stares at him as he passes.

"We've got to get out of here," he murmurs to Natalie. "It's too dangerous."

Natalie stops and pulls her lips tight over her teeth, not convinced. He holds her gaze, hoping to God they don't have to fight about this. "Fine. I should tell Ilene. I promised to help tomorrow," she says.

"You don't need to tell her anything," he starts, but relents when he see's Natalie's face stiffen. "Five minutes," he says. "Take Joe. I'll have the wagon ready." Natalie and Joe turn back to the church.

He's so focused on getting out of there and identifying the points of egress where he won't have to steer around too many other wagons that he almost doesn't notice the queue forming by their wagon until it's ten people deep. Daniel nearly jumps out of his underwear at the sight of it.

"We heard you're a doctor," the first woman in line says, thrusting a teen-aged girl in front of her. She wears one of the white lace bonnets that he noted in the church, and the girl keeps her eyes downcast. Grime marks their clothes, and gray strands thread through the woman's dark hair. Her left canine is missing. She's probably only forty-five, but she looks fifty-five at least. "I was hoping you could look at my daughter. We can offer apples in trade."

"I'm not a doctor," he barks, turning his head automatically to gauge the distance between him and the woods, as if he could flee. Nobody in the line moves. They all just continue to stand and watch him, like a row of walking corpses with guns, prepared to wait him out. He starts to repeat his statement about not being a doctor and that they should all go away, but they ignore him. The people at the end of the line simply sit down, their faces set and silent. They stare at him, their eyes cradling some small and strange gleam of hope that unnerves him. What blind faith or sheer desperation is this? How the hell is he going to get out of here? Run them down? Maybe when it's evident that he doesn't know what he's doing they'll all go away. And yet their eyes tweak at him. He wants to be able to help them.

He turns back to the woman. "Fine, I'll look at her. I have no medications and I'm not promising anything."

Natalie arrives back at the wagon. The look of abject horror she gives him would almost be funny if the situation weren't so bad. She beckons him over with her finger.

"What are you doing?" she says.

"Treating people. They wouldn't leave and they have guns. I already told them I'm not a doctor. Let's just get through the lineup quietly, give them some reasonable diagnosis—it's not like I have no clue—and direct the ones we know are really sick to the field hospital and get the hell out of here." Natalie's eyes burn with indecision and stress, but she nods.

The next half hour brings several festering wounds, askew limbs that should have been set months ago, probable cases of gout, heart disease, and tuberculosis, and a mass on the stomach that he guesses is cancer. He explains some possible diagnoses, suggests dietary changes, and recommends some people consult the field hospital doctor. All the while the line keeps growing.

Word of what he's doing must have spread because Earl appears on the scene with three of Ilene's security guys and marches over to Daniel and Natalie.

"We agreed we wouldn't provide services outside the hospital and that we would charge a set rate, not offer our services for free. What are you trying to do?" Earl says.

"They wouldn't leave," Daniel says.

Earl squints, and Daniel waits to be strung up by his toenails. "I'll have the security guys bring you and your wagon around to the field hospital."

"That's not necessary. Just make them disperse."

"It's for your own protection," Earl says and turns to the lineup of people. "All right, folks. Show's over. Do not shoot at us. As I said before, the hospital opens tomorrow morning. If you want treatment, we need to keep this nice and civil."

Daniel, Natalie, and Joe find themselves escorted to the field hospital. Daniel curses inwardly the whole way. He should just tell Earl he's a vet—then maybe they'll be allowed to leave. Or maybe he'll be thrown into jail for pretending to be a doctor. Or they'll be followed by a horde of people desperate for treatment. The field hospital is heavily guarded by a circle of security guys to keep folks out—or perhaps to keep the "doctors" in. Daniel isn't sure.

Earl tells him to be in the surgical tent at eight a.m. sharp and warns him not to even think of treating anyone else until then.

They eat in silence, vacillating about what to do with mute looks and whispers.

"I think you should just tell him you're a vet. You can't do this. How are we going to set up any trades?" Natalie says.

"They could throw me in jail, Nat. Besides, I can help. I'm better than nothing. Earl said he'd put me on surgical assist. I'll just need to hold clamps and stop bleeders. If I'm not sure about something I'll say so. I won't get in over my head. Besides, I think they're going to pay me." He doesn't know why he's being so dogged about this. This could go wrong in so many ways. But something about helping these hollow-eyed, scared people drives him along. He'll make sure he does no harm.

THE SKY IS GLOWING A deep-reaching black when Andrew herds the sheep to the barn for the night. No moon, only the spatter of a thousand stars. Andrew's breath puffs out before him in a heavy cloud, the clarion call of the coming winter.

Leon waits in the sheep pen, his head bent, the orange glint of his cigarette visible beneath the rim of his Budweiser cap. He unfolds and straightens as Andrew approaches, his eyes dark and hollowed, his limbs lanky and almost disassembled-looking.

"We're going to get rid of Joe and his band of Pakis. There isn't enough food for the real farm members, and there's no reason they should sponge off us. We'll let the dentist and the computer guy stay, but that's it. I need to know, when the time comes, if you're with us," Leon says.

"I think Ranjeet is a Sikh…from Canada," Andrew says, grasping for an appropriate response.

"Whatever," Leon says. "Which side are you going to be on?"

"I don't know," Andrew says, his voice almost a squeal. "I need to think about it."

"Well, don't think too long. We need to act as soon as they get back from the gathering."

"What are you planning to do?"

"You only get to know the plan if you join us."

"My dad is on his way home," Andrew remembers suddenly. "Maybe you should wait."

"How do you know that, boy?"

"He emailed a few days ago. Said he was on his way home." Andrew leaves out the part about the flu pandemic. He doesn't even want to think about what Leon would do with that news.

"All right, that's good information. You have three days to give me a sign that you're with us." Leon leans over to whisper into Andrew's ear. "Otherwise, we might assume you're against us." Andrew tries not to recoil from his leathery uncle, etched with too much sun and hate. The acrid scent of tobacco fills Andrew's nose.

THE NEXT MORNING DANIEL FEELS out of sorts. A trip to the hospital's now-putrid latrines does nothing to improve his mood. At least the camp didn't explode into violence last night. He should just tell Earl the truth, but he's too embroiled in this now. He spent the night in the field hospital tent helping Earl sterilize surgical instruments in a pressure cooker on a woodstove, while the four other doctors sorted meds, drank whiskey, and kibitzed about the good old days in nervous voices. Earl told Daniel about his stints years ago with Doctors Without Borders in war zones, and the children with limbs and faces shattered by landmines. Then the two men's talk turned to whether they had an obligation to treat people or not, and Earl's tone turned dark.

"I don't know where the other doctors are. Dead or hiding out. Those four are just babies. Interns when this thing started. They may not even know their ass from their left ventricle. I don't know where you've been, but it got pretty dangerous there for doctors for a few years. People demanding treatment at gunpoint, people showing up with multiple gunshot wounds, babies dying left, right, and center. The regional hospital is defunct. Without electricity, supplies, nurses, or money, the few doctors willing to treat people were overwhelmed and the working conditions became too unsafe. Nobody has any medical instruments. People are dropping dead from parasites, rickets, bacterial infection, malnutrition, and tuberculosis. I don't even want to talk about the cancer situation. We need pharmaceuticals to the point of desperation. I managed to get some antibiotics and pain meds, but I know it won't be enough."

Earl went on to talk about setting up field hospitals and publicizing them in the hopes that doctors will come out of hiding and start to provide services in the hospitals for a few weeks out of the year. Kind of a "build it and they will come" approach. He indicated that, if they establish a field hospital in Jerry, he'll work there for the first month. He just needs to find a second doctor and nurse to agree to stay and assist in surgeries.

Then Earl had jerked his head at Daniel. "You obviously have access to a surgeon." Daniel started to shake his head, but Earl pointed to the scar on Daniel's left hand. "That would have required tendon repair."

"It was before the peak," Daniel said.

"Not faded enough, and the stitches are too tidy to be the work of a hack. Convince him or her to come and help me. We can't go on like this. Restoring medical services is a key step to restoring civil society."

"I'll think about it," Daniel said. Would Mike be willing to expose himself to this kind of danger? Probably. He seems heroic in that kind of way. But could Daniel ask it of him?

Now Daniel watches the people jostling in the queue outside the perimeter of security guards. Most of them slept there last night on the cold ground in huddles of stiff, frozen blankets. If he just helps for two days as he promised, maybe they'll be able to leave with their lives.

Natalie, too, is a collection of nerves. He can see it in the jerkiness of her movements, her refusal to make eye contact. "I'm going to go and participate in my discussion. I'm not going to let Ilene down, and it'll be a good way to figure out what people have to trade," she says.

"You can't. Most people have already left anyway, except the people waiting to see a doctor," Daniel says.

"I agreed to do it. We came here for the gathering. We need to establish trade contacts, and I believe in what Ilene is trying to do."

"It's not safe." He wants to add "for a woman" but he clamps his lips hard around his tongue on this. It would not go over well with Natalie.

"Joe's coming with me."

"No."

She scrunches her face slightly. "You could be coming with me too, if you hadn't pretended to be a doctor yesterday."

"I wouldn't have *had* to if you hadn't decided to lead a discussion." This is not fair, he knows, and his tone is too snappy.

She looks briefly like she's been struck before her forehead creases into anger. "Ilene asked me to. This is important. I have skills to offer too, and you're not my boss."

She walks away without another word. The security guards allow her to leave the circle, the perimeter of safety—or their prison, depending on how you look at it.

Daniel looks at Joe, who stuffs pemmican and dried fruit into a pack to take with him. "Keep her safe." Joe nods and follows Natalie without a word. Daniel tries not to feel the reproach in Joe's silence. Maybe Joe would be a better match for Natalie: supportive of her interests, yet still capable of protecting her. He's surprised Joe isn't in the hospital line to get those cataracts of his fixed. He should talk to Earl about doing them later.

The stench of wood smoke, moldy canvas, and sweat assaults Daniel at the door of the field hospital. The other doctors already lurk in the gloomy shadows, taking up posts at the examining tables that will serve as their offices, stethoscopes dangling around their necks and wide-eyed jangled looks on their faces. Security guards occupy each entrance.

"You're with me," Earl grunts. "We'll be taking the surgical cases." Daniel goes and stands beside Earl, relieved that he won't be working alone.

When Earl announces it is eight a.m., they open for service. Daniel finds himself wearing a facemask and assigned the job of triage. Infectious diseases to Drs. Lapena and Christiensen. Minor trauma and chronic illnesses to Dr. Albert. Babies, pregnant women, and immunizations to Dr. Moran. Cancer, severe trauma, heart disease, and other organ-failure issues to Earl. At first, Daniel doubts every choice he makes in sending patients shuttling off to wait in another lineup inside the tent. Oozing wounds, maternity, and babies are easy. Potential cases of cancer are not. But there's more crossover than he expected, and as the morning wears on he becomes more confident identifying cases of congestive heart failure, Parkinson's, pneumonia, and cataracts. The fruity smell of diabetes on the breath of a scrawny six-year-old child sends him into a panic and he pushes the child to the front of Dr. Albert's line amid the grumbling disapproval of the other patients. He guesses at a few cases of Lyme disease with reports of a previous bull's-eye rash and complaints of fatigue and muscle aches. With the warmer winters and summer heat, the ticks are a multiplying scourge. Once Daniel's done with triage, Earl assigns him to help him with the minor surgeries and look at parasites under a microscope.

By what feels like eight p.m., they've worked through the day's queue, dispensed most of the minuscule supply of meds, treated people as best they can, and racked up a number of people who need surgery. The next day's lineup has already formed, but it is blessedly smaller. Bins of apples, potatoes, beets, and carrots cover the ground in trade for their services. Daniel has had no chance to leave the tent all day, and he prays that Natalie is okay. But despite his worries, he feels almost pumped about his day's work.

"So, what happens to them?" Daniel says, pointing to the surgical patients Earl has assigned to beds in the tent.

"Them? They're tomorrow."

"What happens tomorrow?" Daniel asks, fearing he already knows the answer.

"Tomorrow you scrub in."

Daniel considers this for a few moments. He stares at the vials of ketamine Earl has lined up in the surgical tent. He's injected it into more horses than he can count. But he can't imagine using it on a human. Earl proposes to remove cancerous masses and do heart surgery. Some of these people are going to die on the table. Earl would be damn well better served with a real surgeon helping him. Daniel knows he'll hold himself and his clumsy veterinary fingers responsible for every last person who passes away on that table tomorrow. His operating days had long been dominated by the mantra of "no heroic measures." If the animal is too sick, or the surgery too risky, the animal is put down. But the people in the tent *need* heroic measures, and Daniel fears that his hands do not have the stamina, or his brain the patience and focus, to deliver. He should go get Mike.

"Can't one of them help instead?" He flicks his hand at the other doctors, who mill about other rooms of the tent finishing up with patients.

"They're already booked doing the minor surgeries and seeing patients."

Calls for help fracture his thinking.

It's a woman. Natalie. He thunders from the tent, followed by Earl.

Natalie emerges from the dark into the pool of light cast by the tent lantern. She drags a horse by its halter. It's Spock, his gray fur matted with blood. Not the horse's blood, Daniel realizes quickly—it's the blood of the figure draped over his back. Liz.

"She barely has a pulse. She's bleeding from so many places," Natalie says.

They lift Liz's limp figure from the horse and carry her inside. The front of her pink tracksuit is a rusty red. Earl cuts open her shirt to reveal multiple stab wounds to the papery white skin of her abdomen. The side of her face is bruised and swollen and a flap of skin hangs down on her temple, exposing what appears to be her skull. Daniel teeters at the sight and grabs the tent post to steady himself. This is his fault. He let her go with Rafe. He stumbles out into the night air.

"Where are you going?" Earl yells. "This woman needs surgery."

"Get her prepped. I'm going to get you a real surgeon," Daniel says, grabbing Spock's halter. "I'll be back in thirty minutes." He points at the perimeter guards. "Tell them to let me go." Earl cocks his head in confusion. "Look, I'm a vet. I can't do this. Let me go get someone who can."

Earl's face contorts into disbelief and then irritation. He waves his hand at the perimeter guards. "Let him go."

Daniel runs his hands over the expanse of Spock's body. The horse seems unharmed and nuzzles Daniel. Spock's fur, where not covered in Liz's blood, is dry, and his heart rate is normal. Daniel guesses they weren't riding hard, but from how far did they have to come?

"I'm sorry, buddy," he whispers into Spock's ear as he mounts. "You're going to have to go a little farther." Daniel runs with Spock to the wagon to collect

Joe, ignoring the faint numbness in his left arm that always accompanies a sprint, and then both men ride into the darkness. The people in the lineup just watch them go and don't attempt to swarm him as he had feared. Perhaps the establishment of some reliable form of medical treatment has restored some modicum of civility already.

Mike waffles a bit about exposing himself to danger because of Joanne and the girls, but agrees fairly quickly. Joe stays behind with Ranjeet, and Daniel and Mike ride back through the bleak November night. Spock still lifts his feet gamely, but Daniel is sure it's only devotion driving the horse at this point.

The camp is subdued when they arrive—just a few bodies moving around wagons with small fires glowing beside them. The hospital perimeter guards let him in, apparently still under the impression he's a doctor. He leads Mike into the hospital tent; Earl and one of the other doctors are bending over Liz, while Natalie passes them instruments. The other doctor doesn't seem to be helping much. Mike introduces himself, scrubs in and joins Earl. The other doctor steps back and motions for Natalie to leave, and then Mike's and Earl's hands dance around each other as instruments flash and twist in the lantern light. Natalie steps away and starts to wash her hands at the small sanitizing station.

Feeling a bit useless, Daniel steps outside and stands alone beside the canvas tent. Natalie joins him several minutes later.

"It doesn't look good. She's lost too much blood. She was conscious for a few minutes when she arrived, babbling. Rafe stabbed her. Something about him trying to sell information about the farm in Vernon. She tried to stop him and he lost it. Left her for dead and then passed out. But she managed to haul herself on to Spock. She said we have to get back to the farm. Made me promise we'd leave at first light. She kept saying that they're coming. I don't know if she even knew what she was saying. She was pretty out of it. It could be the ketamine. But we better go home just in case."

Daniel nods, processing what this all means. Will they even be allowed to leave?

Natalie continues. "We can go. Mike's staying here. He and Earl struck a deal. Mike's going to help with the surgeries and spend a week working with Earl to get the hospital set up. Earl's going to give him a quarter of the food they get in payment. It'll get us through the winter." Daniel feels a thud of disgust for himself. Mike has saved the day, and he has been dismissed to slink away like a liar.

They're ready to leave within a half hour. Mike and Earl are still operating on Liz. Mike steps out for a few seconds to say goodbye. Natalie has gone to say goodbye to Ilene, with instructions to pick her up just past the church. The perimeter guards part to let them through, and they pull away from the hospital, Daniel almost clammy with shame. At the last second, Earl emerges from the surgical tent and tips his fingers in salute. Daniel lifts his hat in reply, his heart hammering in relief.

Natalie stands with two young children by the church, a boy and a girl—about six and eight, Daniel would guess. Forlorn-looking dirty wraiths with dark curly hair and small bags clutched in their tiny hands.

"They're orphans," Natalie announces when he stops the wagon. "They have no place to go. I told Ilene we would take them." She lifts them into the wagon and then launches in after them before Daniel can sputter any sort of response. She introduces them as Charlie and Rebecca, and settles them in the back of the wagon before returning to sit beside him. "I'm sorry. I couldn't say no." He decides not to reply. What can he say?

It doesn't take long to get to the camp where Joe and Ranjeet guard the potatoes and corn. Daniel walks Heathcliff around the camp. The horse still favors his right front leg. Daniel checks the other horses and swears. The roads are tearing the shit out of the horses' hooves, but they can't get the wagons back unless they stick to the roads.

Natalie is helping Ranjeet and Joe strike camp when Daniel pulls her aside.

"I think Ranjeet and Joe better go back ahead of us. The horse's hooves are shot. Heathcliff and Catherine can't get the wagons back unless we go slow."

"Joe and I should go," she says. "Not Ranjeet."

"Why?"

"Because you need Ranjeet to guard the potatoes. Serendipity and Cain are the faster horses. We can be there in twenty-four hours."

"It's a bad idea."

"Why?"

Daniel searches for something sensical. He wants to tell her it's too dangerous, but really it's just a flip of a coin as to whether Natalie, or anyone, gets shot at with him or with Joe. He directs his thumb at Charlie and Rebecca, who hunch down in the back of the wagon and watch everyone with scared eyes.

"They'll be okay," Natalie says. "You can deal with them. I just met them tonight. It's not like they're attached to me any more than you."

Just call me Uncle Daniel, he thinks. But he relents and nods. What else could she have done?

"We should go," she says. She waits, looking at him. He should tell her that he loves her, but he freezes. What if someone hears? He can't quite get the words out. He would rather take her in his arms and kiss her. But he can't do that either.

"Be careful," he says.

"You too," she says. Sadness, or disappointment perhaps, flits across her face, and then she mouths what looks like "I love you" and walks away and speaks to Joe.

Joe bends in to Natalie, ever attentive, unconcerned about being in her space, their bodies arched together in the comfort of long-term connection. Joe nods, and they start to shove supplies into Cain's and Serendipity's panniers.

Daniel walks back to stand with Heathcliff and Catherine, taking refuge, as always, in his goddamn animals. Maybe animals are all he's suited for. Then Natalie and Joe are on horseback, and within seconds they ride away.

ANNEKE AND ANDREW MEET IN the pantry. The plan is to discuss their alliance of sorts, although Andrew has no idea what the nods they provided to each other a few days ago really mean, and he's still trying to figure out what to do about Leon's proposition.

Anneke thunks a ball of dough down in front of Andrew. "You might as well learn how to make bread while you're here," she says. "Are your hands clean?" Andrew considers the recent locations of his hands, and none of them being too bad, nods. "We're kneading right now," Anneke says, pressing her fists into the pliable dough. Andrew follows suit.

"So," he says.

"So," she says. "Tell me about Craig."

"Craig? What?" Andrew wonders why everyone on the farm seems to think he knows more than he does.

"You hang out with him. What does he talk about?"

"I dunno. Not much."

"I need you to make friends with him." Anneke flips her head at his dough and glares. Andrew starts kneading again, pressing his dough into as small a ball as possible. "I'll make sure you and Claire continue to be on wash duty together. God knows that's all that woman can do anyway."

Andrew considers telling Anneke about Leon, but Anneke shuffles him out of the pantry. Shit. His hands are beginning to look as wrinkled and cracked as an old lady's, but his groin draws him back to the laundry room.

Claire stands with her back to him, up to her elbows in the wash water. She wears a man's shirt today, an old dress shirt of fine quality, too fine for working in the fields. It hangs to mid-thigh, and she's belted it at the waist and wears pilled yoga pants underneath. Stains mark the collar and it's ripped at the elbow, but the silhouette is all Claire, gangly and shapely at the same time. Her shoulders convulse in shudders. She's crying again. He's become used to her crying spells, so he just stands and does the washing next to her. Eventually, she lifts her hands to wipe away the tears on her cheeks, but her hands are wet from the wash.

"Sorry. You must think I'm crazy."

"No. I just think you're sad."

"I don't know why I want a baby so much, considering how awful our lives are. I just feel like if I had something to love, it would be better."

Andrew shrugs. "We all want things. It's okay."

They scrub the clothes in silence for an hour or so, until the tips of Andrew's fingers are raw with the texture of fabric.

"Do you think they'll come back? Your dad and Alfie?" Claire says.

"Yeah, I do."

"Oh."

"You were hoping they wouldn't?"

"I don't know."

She looks so vulnerable standing there in the laundry room—with the front of the old men's shirt soaked from the water and her fine hair curling around her face—that Andrew kisses her. He forgets that he's never kissed a girl before, never mind a woman, and has no idea how—that he's not sure whether to open his mouth, or add tongue, or press hard or soft. Her body is like a quivering bird's in his arms, and his heart rate skyrockets as he feels the imprint of her body on his. Her lips part, and Andrew slips his tongue delicately into her mouth. A trial slip. The rush is mind-blowing. She tastes like salt and tart apples and smells like lavender. Her tongue brushes his for a second, and then she sags in his arms and pushes him away.

Andrew had been so engrossed in the moment that he feels as though he's been thrust out of an airplane. Then Claire bolts in a flash of shirttails.

CHAPTER 20
THE DEVIL

———⬦———

RICHARD AND ANDREW

Accept the shadows within yourself, or your actions will bring only harm and misfortune.

Richard wallows in his own peevishness outside the deserted house in the blackened woods. They're still several hours from the farm. What could Alfie be doing? Honestly, the man is so fucking slow. Richard would leave him behind if it weren't for the fact that Alfie, when he focuses, is the best campaign manager around, and one of the slickest thieves that Richard has ever met, which has its uses. Just last week, Alfie lifted documents right out from under Merlo's bulbous nose, all while imitating one of the feral cats that roam the streets of the city. So dramatic were Alfie's contortions that Richard barely even saw Alfie take the papers, even though he was watching for it.

But now Richard wants to get to the farm, get into some dry clothes, have a warm meal, and make sure the newcomers know who's in charge. He doesn't trust Joe one bit, and he's sure the bastard will be putting the moves on his wife. Waiting here in the quiet of the forest with just the hum of mosquitoes bugs him, and heading back into rural buttfuck-nowhere gives him the creeps. He can almost hear the twang of banjo music.

But the briefs that Alfie took revealed not only that the provisional government is negotiating with the Chinese, which they have vehemently denied, but that there's a deadly flu outbreak in the eastern part of the country. Richard passed the papers about the negotiations on to Peter and burned the briefs regarding the flu. Then he decided he ought to head home for a bit, let the flu outbreak subside, and work on Natalie. She'll be a political asset in the run-up to the election, and he misses the boys. Perhaps Natalie will be better away from that farm where she's constantly burdened with having to run things. The boys could go to a proper university, which Richard has heard could be up and running as early as next fall. But it might be a challenge. Natalie becomes hysterical at the slightest suggestion of danger, and if he's completely honest with himself, she hasn't seemed too fond of him lately. But she's too dependent to make a true break, and he's sure that if he lays it out for her in the right way, she'll come.

With any luck, the flu will fell Merlo and perhaps Peter too, and Richard will have a clear path to being Premier. Peter's been keeping him on a tight leash since the Silas incident, and Richard is done being ordered around. Peter auctioned off the Arabians, then found Silas wandering around Kamloops like a lost dog, and ran him and his wife out of town. That's what Richard was told anyway. He hopes Peter didn't kill them.

Richard drums his fingers on the saddle horn. Alfie, who had always relied on narcotic cocktails before the peak, took Virginia's disappearance hard, and has taken to stopping at every abandoned farm to comb their medicine cabinets. They're close to home now, and Richard is not sleeping another night on the ground.

Clearly this farmhouse has yielded results because Alfie has yet to emerge. Either that, or Alfie has run into trouble. Some farmhouses aren't as deserted as they look. Good riddance perhaps, Richard thinks, imagining Alfie speared in the spleen with a cheap Henckels paring knife from Zellers. Richard feels a momentary pang of shame for his uncharitable thoughts. But as his friend stumbles closer to becoming a full-time junkie, he could become a liability.

Maybe he should go in and get him. Better yet, Richard turns to his new bodyguard, Erik, who sits in the gloom on his horse several yards away. Merlo finally caved on Richard's request. Finally, an acknowledgement of his importance. It sends a frisson of electricity down Richard's legs, almost as if someone is sucking his cock. Erik seems to take his job seriously. In Richard's fantasies of leading the province, Erik thrusts his body in front of Richard's to protect him from a shower of bullets, although Richard can't help noting that ever since they got off the train in Kamloops, Erik has been twitchy and stiff with strange rapid eye movements, as if he's scanning each bush for potential assailants. Maybe the boy just wants some action. He should send Erik in to get Alfie.

But Alfie traipses down the steps with a jauntiness that indicates success, the ridiculous topcoat with tails he took to wearing in Vancouver fluttering out behind him. *Christ, the man's starting to look like Willie Wonka.* The last thing Richard needs is an obvious association with a dandy. "A whole cabinet full," Alfie crows. "And a full bottle of these." He holds up a little blue pill.

"Oh, for fuck's sake, you hardly need that. You're already half cock with almost nothing between the ears. If you take that, you'll cut off all the blood flow to your fucking brain." Richard digs his heels into his horse.

"You'd know it," replies Alfie, vaulting onto his horse. "Can't a guy have a little fun?"

"Your *fun* is wasting our time."

"Come on, Richard. Everybody needs something to bring them up."

Richard surveys Alfie with irritation. "God, Alf, you're so high right now, I'm not even sure you knew that was a double entendre."

"Come on, buddy. I just need something for the pain."

"Yeah, well keep it up, and I'll need something for the pain too."

"Look, there's the big dipper." Alfie's voice has taken on a singsong quality.

"For Christ's sake, Alfie, watch where you're going. You better clean up before you get to the farm, or Claire'll have a bird."

"Ha ha. Claire's so wrapped up in herself she wouldn't even notice."

"Well, Natalie's not quite so tolerant."

"No, man, she's like a drill sergeant. You are, like, *castrated.*" Alfie elongates the word as he makes snipping motions in the air with his hands. His horse veers into Richard's.

"Watch what you're doing. And can you stop making reference to me and castrated in the same sentence?"

"Not that the literal snip-snip is bad. It saves you a whole shitload of trouble."

"Are you ever going to tell Claire why she can't have a baby?"

He expects Alfie to capitulate at this, or at least back off. But the drugs have emboldened him. Alfie's laugh has an edge to it. "You're funny, Richard. I guess we all have some skeleton bones in our closets. Or should I call them boners?" Alfie chortles at his own joke.

Richard grinds his molars together and feels his cheeks pulse. He doesn't like to be questioned or mocked, even by Alfie. "What? You're so fucking stoned I have no idea what you're talking about." Alfie shouldn't joke in front of Erik. He doesn't need rumors of any sort surrounding his campaign. He doesn't know what Alfie seems to think Richard has in his closet, but he suspects Alfie is referring to those political parties from years ago, when the wine flowed and interns threw themselves at anyone they thought was a hopeful. He'd always been shocked at how quickly a cute young thing would unzip his pants and service him in the elevator, while he stared at the smoky mirrors on the ceiling, trying to keep his balance and figure out how to put her off. But he never really cheated, even if Alfie thinks he did.

"Right, right, of course not." Alfie mimes thrusting on his horse, then charges ahead.

Richard counts to ten under his breath. *Forgive them, for they know not what they do,* he tells himself. *Because most of them are too stupid,* he adds. But Alfie's not. He pulls it together when he needs to. Richard kicks his heels into his horse to catch up. "The farm's only about a few hours away, you know," says Richard. "I say we ride on through the night. Surprise them."

"Righto, buddy. Shall we make it worthwhile? Put some money on it. Best jump and fastest riding. Make Erik the judge? I'm on fire tonight!"

Richard's stiff forty-six-year-old body rebels at the notion of keeping up with Alfie's wiry, forty-year-old, drugged one. But he'll never admit it. He takes a few swigs from his own flask of whiskey. "All right. Betcha we can make it to the farm in three hours."

⸺◦◦◦⸺

THE SOUND OF THE DOGS barking washes through Andrew's dreams. He drives a fire-engine-red Corvette along a wide freeway packed with traffic, weaving in and out of the other vehicles, chased by a pack of dogs. Claire sits beside him, naked, wearing a lascivious smile and red lipstick. He needs to find a place to pull over, to take advantage of the opportunity, but the dogs won't go away. He accelerates, hoping to outrun them.

Andrew awakes with a shudder. The dogs are going berserk outside. Alarmed human voices can be heard in the hall.

They've experienced nighttime raids before, but this is the first without Richard and Mike. Andrew hopes that Justin has reached the section on gunshot wounds in Mike's medical journals. He leaps out of bed and looks out the window.

The waxing moon, a brilliant thumbprint in the sky, casts cool shafts of light all around the courtyard. Terrence, Leon, and several other men hustle to the armory in a swarm with untucked shirts and over-the-shoulder looks. The nighttime watch party already sits in position in the western pasture. Andrew can make out Solomon's dark head, a rifle in his hand, stealing across the west fields to where the dogs stand barking into the darkness. No sound of shots yet. Or even screams. Just the dogs.

Andrew snatches up a shirt and pants and descends to the dining room. Everyone knows the drill well. Anneke marshals the children, who will be dispatched to the cellar. Women mill about the room in nightshirts, workpants, and wool socks, organizing blankets and food, clutching children, and staring out the windows into the night sky. Claire flits about in a filmy white negligee, looking completely useless. She's ignored by the other women. Where the hell does she get her clothes?

Andrew pushes through the cluster of women out onto the farmhouse porch. He should tell Leon about the flu, about not having contact with people from off the farm. Not that Leon would. Leon will shoot first. But he should be told not to touch the bodies. His dad had said not to worry. But just in case.

It's still quiet outside. The chill November air bites into his skin. Most of the men have assembled near the barn. Andrew spots Scott and Leon, almost at the edge of the woods now. Then he sees it: a patch of white that doesn't belong, deep among the blackened trees of the woods. What is it? A tent, a screen? It's too far, and too dark, to tell. It looks like a white elephant or giant puffball mushroom. Andrew wonders if he's still dreaming.

As Andrew makes his way across the courtyard, Paul and Hans, guns in hand, escort the last of the women and sleepy-eyed children to the main farmhouse. Everyone speaks in hushed tones, and the silence is more ominous than the usual gunfire that accompanies raids. Shadow the cat laces through Andrew's legs, purring idly. Andrew resists kicking the cat away. He realizes he has tensed every muscle in his body, waiting for an explosion, shots, something. The purring seems foreboding, like the quiet orchestral tones in a minor key that used to precede death in the movies.

Solomon, Scott, and Leon stop walking.

Two men stand in front of them at the edge of the woods with their arms in the air. They walk slowly toward the farm group, careful to keep their hands up. It looks like the five men are talking.

Andrew says, "no" under his breath and starts running across the field. But within seconds, Leon waves his gun at the men and backs away yelling something, followed by Scott and Solomon.

—————

"GOOD ONE, MAN," SAYS RICHARD as Alfie executes a deft jump over some shrubbery. "Not as good as mine over the old stump, but good."

"In your dreams, buddy. In your dreams," Alfie says. "Hey, I recognize that tree. Are we almost there?"

"You'd think you'd know the landmarks of the farm a little better than that, Alf. We've been almost there for fifteen minutes."

They ride in silence, slowing their pace a bit to let Erik—who seems a bit uncomfortable in the saddle—catch up. Richard makes a mental note to tell Erik that he needs to work on his riding. They proceed together into the last expanse of trees before the west field.

Richard sees it first: a large white object in the trees, like a tent fashioned out of bedsheets. Richard has some vague thought that a circus has come to town, or a hot-air balloon has descended upon the farm. He stops abruptly, almost causing Alfie to go headlong as his horse stops when Richard's does.

"What the fuck? Richard!" Alfie says. Richard places his finger to his lips and points.

"What is that?" Alfie says. "Some new thing of Natalie's?"

"I'm not sure," says Richard. "Her emails didn't mention anything. I can hear the dogs barking. Whatever that thing is, it's not right. Let's tether the horses and get a closer look."

They weave through the trees, their guns drawn. The provisional government may not be good at getting food to the people, but it *is* good at procuring bullets, and Richard had helped himself to a generous cache before leaving. Alfie, still high—or high again—steps on twig after twig, and Richard wants to strangle him. He motions for Alfie and Erik to stop. They crouch behind some trees, while Richard peers through Daniel's binoculars.

It's a covered wagon. One of the old-fashioned, little-house-on-the-prairie covered wagons. Two men with crossbows sit outside it. Richard counts six horses grazing in the trees. So with two horses to pull the wagon, there are probably at least four other people in the party.

"What is it, Richard? Can I have a look?" Alfie tugs at his sleeve.

Richard passes him the binoculars. "Looks like we got ourselves a raiding party. And we can pen them in on both sides, assuming the folks on the farm have any wherewithal at all in my absence."

"What are we going to do?" says Alfie. "Just go in there with guns blazing?"

"Ambush." Richard likes the way the word sounds. He repeats it under his breath.

"How does that differ from going in with guns blazing?" Alfie says. "Shouldn't we try to go around to the farm and see what the plan is?"

Richard feels the irritated disappointment slip through his body. Why does Alfie always ruin his moments with his questioning? Why can't people just appreciate his leadership qualities? He's like a soccer ball with a slow leak, still rolling along, but gradually sagging under the repeated questioning. He needs to get back to Vancouver, where he can still impress and excite. "If you're going to be that way, I'm not going to tell you the plan."

Alfie rolls his eyes and elbows Erik in the side. "All right, sorry, Rich. What's the plan?" Alfie's response is even worse in terms of respect. But whatever. Alfie's a lost cause. Richard focuses his attention on Erik.

"Erik is going to run around to the south and catch their attention, and then when they're looking that way, you and I will sneak up from the north and take them out. And make sure you shoot the wagon too, in case someone's in there."

Alfie nods, but Erik looks a bit skeptical in his beanie cap with his carefully clipped blond goatee. Richard wonders why he's never noticed the precision with which Erik trims his beard. "And what happens when the men with the crossbows shoot me?" Erik says.

Richard scowls. Maybe the kid wouldn't take a bullet for him, after all. "Oh, come on, don't be a big pussy. What are you worried about? We'll be right there shooting once the men look your way. They probably won't even get a shot off."

"Right. Seems like a great plan," Erik says.

Richard scowls more. Everyone has something to say these days. Everyone has to be a smart ass. "What did you do before you joined the provisional government security detail, Erik? And you should call me 'sir,' by the way."

"I was a grad student at UBC…sir."

"Right. In what?"

"In English literature…sir."

"Right. And why didn't that come up in the interview?"

"With all due respect, sir, you were a bit distracted during the interview. There was that guy there. Some big guy in the government. You were talking to him. Saying you could read someone just by looking at them. That you always went with your gut on interviews. You were impressed by the fact that I had survived in the city for three years. You said anyone that had the street smarts to live that long must be smart. You didn't ask about my background."

"Great. Masters or PhD?"

"Um, PhD, sir. Does it matter?"

"Yeah," Richard snaps. "Because it means you were a lifer, and you never spent any time in the real world. Which is why you're questioning my plan." The kid definitely needs to be replaced as soon as he gets back to Vancouver. English Literature? Good Christ, who did English Literature anymore? "So are we down with the plan? Erik, you wait until Alfie and I are in place. And then draw their attention by firing at them. If you're a good shot you might even be able to take one of them out so they can't shoot you."

"Um, just a couple of questions, Richard," Alfie says. "What if the wagon is full of a whole bunch of other guys that can shoot at us? Or women and children? And what about the rest of the folks on the farm—shouldn't one of us circle around and tell them our plan?"

"Is everyone a fucking critic these days? If we circle around and tell them what we're going to do, we'll waste time and lose the element of surprise. We've already wasted half a fucking hour talking about grad school. If you circle around, Shakespeare here will have enough time to finish his dissertation before we make a move. If there are other men in the wagon, we'll shoot them when they come out. If there are women and children, then we'll stop shooting and take them hostage. Now can we just get on with it? Are we men or are we grad students?"

"We're men, I guess," Alfie grumbles. "But I think I'd rather be a grad student." Erik squints his eyes at Richard, but he doesn't say anything. With a nod, Alfie and Richard head off to the north and Erik to the south.

⸻

"I TOLD THEM THEY HAVE an hour to clear out. I would have shot 'em, except I want them to have the manpower to pull their fucking wagons out of here," Leon concludes. Leon's face is drawn tight and his eyes are unblinking. Andrew feels the fear gather like an avalanche and cascade through his body, coming to rest deep in his gut. Influenza right on the border of the farm. A pandemic that has already devastated the eastern provinces and is working its way west. A twenty percent mortality rate. It had seemed so theoretical in his dad's email. Something that was far away. Something that might potentially make its way to the farm, eventually. But, he reflected, his dad was prone to underestimating risks.

"Oh my God," Anneke says. "Oh my fucking God."

Everyone stands around Leon, Anneke, and Paul except for a few men that had been left on the perimeter of the field to keep watch. They all wear the same pinched and frightened looks, mouths agape, eyes darting to the woods every few seconds as if something might be floating toward them. Claire has managed to find a trench coat that makes her look like a flasher. Andrew tries not to imagine a cloud of viruses stretching its tentacles out from the forest behind him.

"They say they aren't leaving until we help them," Scott says. "They know we have a doctor and a stocked infirmary. They seem pretty determined. What if they sneak up on us? It only takes one contact. Driving them away would be risky in and of itself."

Paul stares at his feet and strokes his forehead with his thumb and forefinger.

"Shoot them all from a distance," Leon says. "And burn their camp."

"They have children with them," Anneke says. The light drizzle mists her glasses, making her look like a sightless specter.

"Then they should leave, if they know what's good for them," Leon says.

"We should have a Farm Council meeting and decide how to handle this," Paul says.

Leon whirls on the smaller man. "We can't let them camp here. Who's to say they won't sneak up on us in the night?"

"We'll put a guard on them for tonight," Paul says. "You may be Chair, but that doesn't mean you call all the shots."

"In emergency situations, the Chair is in charge."

"Emergency is very clearly spelled out in the Farm Code as an armed attack, fire, flood, shots fired, or some other clearly emergent issue."

Leon lifts his large hand as if to wrap it around Paul's neck, but then withdraws. "Desperate people do desperate things. What's to stop me and a couple of other men from riding out tonight and taking care of them?" Leon says.

"That would be a breach of your precious Farm Code," says Paul. "We'll set up a double watch, equip them with the facemasks that are in the infirmary, and decide what to do in the morning. We all need time to think about it. We're not just going to burn innocent people."

Leon steps closer to Paul. "And what are you going to do if I take matters into my own hands? Shoot me?"

Paul inches back, but his fingers brush the metal of his rifle. "I might." Leon's usual supporters—Terrence, Brent, Bob, and Karl—all crowd around him, while Anneke, Solomon, and Alan stand behind Paul. Andrew wonders if a full-out brawl is in the offing.

"We'll have you removed as Chair," Anneke says.

Leon lets out a booming guffaw. "Fine then. We'll do it your way. Farm Council in the morning." He calls out the names of the second-watch group and goes to talk to them by the armory. The rest of the crowd disperses, casting long looks at the wagon in the woods.

ANDREW IS STILL IN THE courtyard when Leon is done with the watch people. When he sees his uncle striding toward him, he turns and starts to scurry back to his room.

"Hey, you, boy." Andrew turns, feeling like a squirrel in a snare.

"Your dad's got some gasoline hidden away in the shed. I say we manage this problem pretty quick and head out there as soon as everyone settles in.

The men on watch will let us slip past. I arranged them all proper so there's a hole to the south. Our do-gooder Paul thinks he's got the most important spot in the east. We can make it look like an accident."

The thought of charred bodies makes Andrew shiver.

"Think of it, boy. Drowning in your own phlegm, bleeding out your ears, your asshole; dead, diseased bodies all over the farm." Leon looms suddenly closer to Andrew, the wrinkles in his leathery skin shadowed in the moonlight. "We can't let that happen. It's what your dad would want, and it's your way to make up for what you did up on the ridge."

He wouldn't actually do it, Andrew thinks. But then again…Leon might just be crazy-assed enough to torch people.

<hr />

"I can't see him. Can you see him?"

Richard stares through Daniel's binoculars at the patch of forest south of the covered wagon. A light rain has set in, and the bushes where he and Alfie crouch shed droplets of water on him every time he moves. His stomach grumbles with hunger, and his riding boots are sodden. Discomfort always makes him reckless.

"If you'd hand over the frickin' binoculars, I might be able to tell you." Alfie hiccups.

Richard turns to Alfie. "Christ, how much have you had to drink?"

Alfie hiccups again. "Just a little. It was cold," he says.

"Yeah, well just make sure you don't shoot me. Preferably not Erik either, but definitely not me." Richard peers through the binoculars again. "He must be in place. It wouldn't have taken him any longer than us to circle around. Why the hell hasn't he started shooting yet?"

"Maybe they took him hostage. Maybe we should go and check." Alfie starts to inch his way out of the bushes. Richard grabs his shirt.

"And lose our position? And risk getting caught ourselves? We need to assume he's in position and start executing the plan. Maybe this will jar those pansies on the farm into action." Richard creeps off through the bushes.

"We are *so* going to get shot," Alfie mutters, but he follows Richard nonetheless.

THE TWO MEN IN THE camp hear them coming and leap to their feet, their cross-bows drawn. Richard is fast on the trigger, and both men fall to the ground, blood oozing from the wounds in their chest. Screams come from the wagon. Several of the men are black. Richard hadn't expected that. Not many black people in these parts. They must be American. Richard has heard rumors that things are even worse south of the border, and the provisional government has feared the possibility of an unorganized invasion for months.

Shots come from the south. Thank God Erik is finally getting with the program, and then from the east, the direction of the farm. Richard feels a wave of relief; everyone is working together now, and this should be dealt with in no time. He might even get in a few hours of sleep before sunrise.

Freaked by all the gunfire, Alfie starts firing wildly in all directions. Richard now sees that there are actually two covered wagons side by side. Richard opens his mouth to yell at Alfie to stop, that he might be firing at Erik, or at some of the farm members, when two more men run around the side of one of the wagons, crossbows in hand. An arrow whistles past Richard's ear, barely missing him. He fires automatically, hitting one of the men as two more arrows pelt at him. He's in the middle of the camp now. A man jumps him from behind and tries to wrestle him to the ground. The man is strangely weak, and Richard knocks him in the head with his rifle. The man sags to the ground, and Richard lurches back to his feet. The screams from the wagon are too high-pitched. They have to be children. They should stop shooting and take the people hostage. The shooting from the south and east has stopped, but Alfie still shoots randomly into the darkness. Richard grabs Alfie's arm to jerk him back and stop him from shooting, but he trips and falls, taking Alfie down with him. Alfie's shot goes wide to the south.

Then there are more screams. This time from the south. "Help! Help!"

Richard knows that voice. Natalie.

CHAPTER 21

JUSTICE

<small>⟶❊⟵</small>

RICHARD AND ANDREW

Everything will come back to you eventually.

Richard staggers to his feet. The shrieking from the south has turned into cries for help. This time the sound of Natalie's voice is undeniable. Richard heads in that direction. In the dim moonlight, past the bodies of the men he has shot, Richard can make out dark figures approaching with guns. They stop well before they reach the clearing, their guns trained on the camp. It's Solomon and Scott, with one of the newcomers, the computer programmer, just behind them. Richard sees Paul a bit farther off, talking to some of the other men. The men approaching the camp wear facemasks and gloves—the expensive facemasks that Natalie had insisted on buying and he had laughed at. He doesn't have time to think about facemasks now. "Thank God," Richard says reflexively. "What took you so long? You stay here and deal with these people. I have to get to Natalie."

"I'm afraid not, Richard," Solomon shouts across the clearing, his voice muffled by the mask. "You and Alfie need to stay where you are. Someone else has gone for her."

Richard feels his back stiffen with anger when he realizes that Solomon's and Scott's guns are pointing at him. "What are you talking about, stay here? I have to get to my wife! You don't know what you're talking about. Get the hell over here."

Solomon doesn't move, but he looks like a big scared Great Dane, almost unable to make eye contact with Richard. "Richard, you've just exposed yourself to the flu. These people are really sick. They came to us for help. We've just been discussing what to do about it. And now you've walked right into the middle of it. So, sorry, but Paul says you're going to have to stay there."

A few women have crawled out of the wagons and weep over the dead men—the men Richard has shot. One of the women takes a run at Richard, but stops when Richard lifts his gun toward her and shakes his head. She's pale and clammy and looks like she wouldn't have made it the fifteen feet or so anyway. She crumples to the ground and lies there. Richard begins to feel like perhaps he's made a mistake.

"Don't be ridiculous!" Richard yells. "Paul? Paul's not in charge here. I have to go see what's wrong." But Solomon doesn't move or lower his gun.

⸺∞⸺

ANDREW AND LEON HAD BEEN lurking in the fields to the south of the sick camp when the shooting started. Andrew had talked Leon into doing recon instead of proceeding immediately with his planned torching. Brent, obviously one of Leon's men, standing sentry, had let them past. They hit the ground at the first shots, Leon muttering that this is what he'd said would happen, that nobody ever listens to him. But then Leon spotted Richard and Alfie in the camp, and popped up, declaring *"Finally someone knows what they're doing,"* then took off into the trees firing his own gun.

Andrew stared after him. Alfie was firing maniacally into the trees all around them. A few shots also came from the east, from the direction of the farm, and then frighteningly from the south, right behind Andrew, and then from the west. So he lay there listening to the horrifying cries of the children in the camp, as the mosquitoes, undeterred by the shooting, pelted him with bites.

CRIES OF "HELP!" FIFTY FEET to the west of him launch Andrew to his knees. That was his mother's voice.

A few last shots ring out. Leon is nowhere in sight. Andrew starts crawling in the direction of his mother's cries.

He finds her on the ground next to Joe, hair falling into her face, pressing her hands against Joe's leg, yelling for help. A strange man with a blond goatee kneels beside her, pulling clothes out of a daypack to hold against the wound. Wailing from the wagons still pierces the air. Joe writhes about in pain, his mouth agape. Andrew approaches, still on his knees, and tries to help by holding Joe still.

Brent lurches out of the bushes a few seconds later, gun flailing at them all. Sees Joe. Sees Natalie. "What are you doing here? Where are the others?"

"They're way back," Natalie says. "Heathcliff's lame. Quick. Get the stretcher and get Joe to the house. He's going to bleed out."

Leon strides into the clearing and takes in the scene. His eyes gleam in the faint light. "And who's this? Your new boyfriend?"

Natalie gives Leon a look of utter loathing, but beneath it is a flinch of fear. "I don't even know. He was just here."

"Where're Mike and Daniel?" Leon says.

"Mike stayed in Jerry to help at the field hospital. Daniel's with the potatoes. Joe and I rode ahead to warn you about someone who might be coming to the farm." Natalie grabs another bundle of clothes from the goateed man and replaces the crimson one that she'd been applying. Andrew tries not to faint at the amount of blood. His mother turns and looks at him. "Can you please get the stretcher and Justin, right now?"

"I need the boy here," Leon says. "Get Justin and the stretcher," Leon orders Brent, who heads off back toward the farm. Then Leon turns to the goateed man. "Now we need to figure out just who *this* fellow is, and how he got here."

Karl arrives at a run, interrupting Leon. "Alan's missing. He was on watch. He hasn't checked in."

Andrew turns and jogs through the burned stumps and hollowed trees of the southeast part of the wood. Alan had been on watch near the big alder log just in front of where he and Leon had been hiding. Karl crashes through the dry underbrush behind him.

They find Alan's prone form a hundred feet from the log. Andrew blanches at the size of the stain on Alan's chest, and the whiteness of the man's face. Whiter than his hair.

Alan's eyes are unfocused and his breathing is shallow. The bloodstained grass beneath him forms a dark halo around his crumpled form. Karl steps on a twig, and Andrew shifts his glance away from Alan. They look at each other. They both know that Alan doesn't have a chance.

RICHARD IS IN THE MIDST of hurling a string of expletives at Solomon when Paul emerges from the trees to the south.

Paul simply stands and looks at Richard until he stops swearing, the way one would treat a small child having a tantrum, except for the fact that Richard is still at gunpoint. "Are you done?" Paul says. "How many people do you think you've killed tonight with your little stunt?" Richard looks around at the bodies in the clearing, and feels a prick of discomfort and panic. Have he and Alfie killed someone from the farm?

"Get that fucking gun off me, you bastard! You're not in charge here, and there's no fucking way I got infected with this much contact!" Alfie sits on a rock, his head in his hands, moaning. Richard starts heading off into the woods in the direction from which he heard Natalie's calls.

Solomon circles around to head him off, keeping his distance. "Stay right there, Richard," Paul warns, the remains of the campfire glinting off his bald head. "Or we *will* shoot you. You're quarantined until Farm Council meets. Set up camp here for the night. Maybe you should try to help out some of the people you've attacked. Show some of that Christian charity you always claim to believe in. We can drop off some medical supplies. You'll be under guard for the rest of the night."

Rage climbs Richard's neck. This is so fucked up. Influenza. He can almost feel his lungs heavy with fluid, and his head throbs with imagined fever. Diseased people repulse him even at the best of times.

"No fucking way are we staying here. Where's Leon?"

"Busy."

Suddenly, the bluster in Richard's voice shrivels. "Did someone from the farm get killed?"

"Alan. And Joe's on his way."

Richard's stomach feels laden with boulders. "What? Not by us."

"I don't know who else was shooting like a lunatic. We were firing warning shots."

"That's crap. It could have been anyone. It was a shootout." Richard pushes away the swells of guilt tugging at his feet like a riptide. This is not his fault.

"A shootout that *you* orchestrated."

"That's bullshit."

"I'm not arguing with you."

Richard's rage returns with a vengeance. Paul has always been too sanctimonious for his own good anyway. Richard forces his words to be calm. "Please, tell Anneke I'm sorry for her loss. Alan was a good man. Can you send my wife or Leon here? I'm not staying out here tonight."

"I'm afraid they're both busy. You'll have to stay put for a while."

⸙

THEY MOVE ALAN TO THE infirmary anyway, barely conscious, his pulse weak and erratic. They elevate his feet, give him shots of antibiotics and morphine, and offer him some moonshine. Justin stands at the other bed racing to close off the bleeders in Joe's leg, Natalie awkwardly moving clamps and handing him instruments. Anneke hovers by Alan's bedside, her hair threaded with blood spatter, haunted circles under her eyes. Nobody has suggested operating on Alan. Justin has already repeated several times in low panicked tones that if they open him up he won't be able to control the bleeding, and he's not even sure how to sew up some of the perforated organs. They need Mike. Justin isn't ready for this. And even *with* Mike, it's a virtually impossible case.

Andrew edges out of the infirmary. He should leave Anneke alone with her husband. He's just reached the door when she gives her head a shake, emits a low wail, and presses her forehead against Alan's chest.

Blinded by his own tears, Andrew stumbles out into the empty dining room, which by this hour is usually fragrant with the smell of morning bread and lively with the chatter of farm members. The children and most of the other families were dispatched back to their beds two hours ago with orders to stay in their own rooms as much as possible, to reduce the risk of contagion. Armed guards have been set up around both the sick encampment and Richard and Alfie's camp. Leon hustled the goateed man, Erik, who claims to be Richard's bodyguard, off to the barn earlier, stating that he needs to be questioned.

Andrew enters the pantry. He has no idea how to make bread, but he shuffles through the cupboards looking for Anneke's recipes. Someone needs to make bread.

The rattle of wagon wheels breaks the silence. Andrew looks out the pantry window. Heathcliff limps past, pulling a wagon filled with bins of potatoes. Ranjeet sits in the front wagon with Daniel, and the dogs follow behind, leaping and bounding in joy. Two children crouch in the back like filthy vagabonds. Daniel pulls the wagon in and gets out, looking around in puzzlement at the covered wagons in the woods, the deserted courtyard, and the armed guards in the fields.

Andrew watches as his mother crosses the courtyard and rushes toward Daniel, stopping only inches from him, her arms half-extended. She pulls her arms back to her sides and then they stand there, poker-straight like soldiers, faces bent to each other as they talk.

⁂

RICHARD SITS IN THE CLEARING where he and Alfie have made camp. The sun has slipped over the Scarecrow Mountains, igniting the valley in the ochre swell of an autumn morning. Scott stands watch in the woods wearing a facemask. He stands as far away as he can get, but close enough to shoot Alfie or Richard if need be. Paul made Richard and Alfie leave all of their guns in a pile in the woods.

Alfie snores in the tent, in a drug-induced slumber. Richard throws a rock hard against a tree. It ricochets off and rolls into the woods. Scott leaps to attention in the woods in response. Richard lobs a rock in Scott's direction, making sure it falls short. Richard wants to kick the tent where Alfie lies. Kick Alfie. How could Alfie have been so stupid, shooting like that?

Richard throws another rock, and then a whole bunch more. His destiny cannot involve a pathetic death from the flu and the ignominious shooting of sick people and a friend. Not now. It had to have been Alfie who hit Alan. Why didn't fucking Erik warn Joe and Alan to stay down? That was his job. Fuck. He can't believe he has to sit here doing nothing. The likelihood that he and Alfie picked up any germs is minuscule. Where are Terrence and Leon? Why aren't they talking any sense into Paul? How has *Paul* taken over his farm?

Richard watches the farm through his binoculars as Daniel pulls up in the wagon. He watches Natalie and Daniel stand together. From a distance, he can see that something in the air between them has changed. Their years of comfortable indifference has been replaced by an exaggerated carefulness. Richard almost laughs. Daniel has probably confessed to some soppy feelings for Natalie. But Daniel could never handle Natalie and would never betray him. And Natalie would never find Daniel attractive. Not for long, anyway. They would fall immediately into a pit of their own fears, tempers, and irrationalities. Richard must be seeing things. Natalie follows Daniel into the barn. Alfie sleeps on, oblivious.

Leon shows up half an hour after sunrise, his lanky, loose-limbed body veering through the trees. Clouds have rolled in, and an almost oppressive humidity makes the farm seem as if it's enveloped in a sulk. The mosquitoes surge about in a frenzy, taking advantage of their few more days of life before the fall of winter.

Richard's relief at seeing Leon evaporates when he realizes that Leon, too, wears a mask and seems oddly skittish, keeping careful distance from Richard, after sending Scott out of earshot.

"Richard, man, bad times."

"When are you going to get me out of this ridiculous quarantine?"

"I'm working on it, man. Don't you worry. But you know, on this crazy farm, nothing's that easy. You're holding up, though?"

"I'm fine, Leon."

"Feeling okay?"

"I'm fine, Leon. Just get me out of here. And tell me why Paul suddenly thinks he's in charge."

"He's not. That's all you need to know. We need to deal with these sick people right away. Now that your wife is back, she'll have all the bleeders stoked, and we'll end up hand-feeding the sick people chicken soup. You need to talk to her."

"Got it."

"Bet you wish you'd never laid eyes on that ass."

"I don't know what you mean."

Leon stares at Richard for a few seconds, then makes a motion as if he's zipping his lips. "Right, oh right. Well, I hope she's good in bed for all the shit you have to put up with. You better talk to your brother, then, because he's about to fall right into her trap. I'll be back as soon as I know more and have a plan. I know you'll know what to do when the time comes. But it'll be tonight for sure."

Know more about what? Richard wants to ask Leon's retreating back. But the taller man has already ambled away across the field in his bobbing, disjointed gait.

NATALIE COMES TO SEE HIM next. Richard watches her walk across the fields, her tiny, graceful form still impressive after all these years. The power of a truly beautiful woman is almost ridiculous in his opinion. He would have thought his social nitwit little brother immune. She arrives at the edge of his camp. Unattractive red welts cover her face from crying. She, too, stays well back, but she doesn't wear a mask. "What were you thinking?" He can tell she would slap him if she could come near him. He's glad she can't. Her slap might upend him. He can see her clench her teeth, trying to suck in her emotion, to not cry in front of him. He pushes away his guilt over Alan. He needs to focus.

"I'm sorry. I thought they were raiders. How was I supposed to know you were all milling around on the other side of their camp?"

"We weren't milling. Alan was on guard, and Joe and I were heading back to the farm. You need to think a little more about these things, Richard."

Richard feels the hatred and hurt balling in the back of his brain. Why is he expected to take the blame for something that was an accident? He didn't even shoot Alan. It was probably stupid Alfie. And he doesn't even see how Alfie's bullet went that far. He's sorry of course. Horribly sorry. But he's not going to apologize for trying to defend the farm against potential raiders. She couldn't possibly be sleeping with his brother. Or could she?

"Don't talk to me like that. Can you please get me out of this idiotic quarantine? We need to do something about the sick camp."

"No, you're potentially contagious. You need to stay right there. We're going to deal with the sick camp."

The corner of Richard's mouth pulls into a partial sneer. "That's not constructive. I'm not going to apologize for defending the farm, and I'm still Farm Council Chair."

She crumples a bit. Pushback always works with Natalie. "Why can't you just say you were wrong?"

"Because I wasn't wrong."

"I don't believe that. Did you ever talk to Leon about the missing food and lumber, by the way?"

Richard gives her a big smile. "I sure did. I did that before I left. I told him that Alan noticed the missing lumber. Leon didn't know anything about it. I bet it was one of those newcomers, or Anneke. I'll track it down as soon as I'm out of detention here."

"Ugh." She shakes her head at him again, and he doesn't know what he said wrong. Then she turns and walks away, leaving him trapped with only his rocks to throw.

Going back to the farmhouse. To Daniel.

"You're making a mistake," he calls after her. "A huge one."

"Joe's going to make it, by the way," she throws back over her shoulder.

Richard tosses a rock far and wide so that it thuds into the damp sod ten feet to her right. She doesn't look back.

CHAPTER 22

THE EIGHT OF SWORDS

———◦◦◦◦———

It is coming, quickly.

Natalie marches back across the field, bristling with fury at Richard for his foolish attack. Yet somehow, inexplicably, she pities him at the same time. She doesn't understand how her emotions toward him can be so complicated and unclear, how one person could cause her to question so much of what she thinks she believes in. Even if they part ways, she'll always have this horrible feeling that he's out there mocking her, that he was right about everything all along. About the raiders, about her, and most importantly, about Daniel. She wants an omniscient judge to review their case and outline all the various ways Richard has failed her. But then again, maybe the ruling wouldn't be in her favor.

She must find Craig and Elena, and tell them about Liz, but she needs to talk to Anneke first. Farm members and newcomers drift from the cabins toward the dining room, with backward glances at the covered wagons that still occupy the woods. Andrew inexplicably occupies the pantry, making bread with the assistance of Claire. There's something in their movements, a nascent flirtatiousness, that concerns Natalie, but she doesn't have time to deal with it now.

Natalie finds Anneke in her room, her face taut and shiny. Katie and Steven sit on the bed, folded into their mother, shuddering with muted sobs. Natalie gestures to the hall, and Anneke extracts herself and follows her to the door.

"I'm so sorry, Neke. So sorry." Natalie doesn't know what else to say. She considers going on about what a wonderful person Alan was, but that seems trite.

"Sorry? Sorry that your husband did this? That he has no judgment and is a fucking psychopathic lunatic? That he killed four men, including my husband, and created potential suicide bombers out of sick people?" Anneke's hostility borders on unhinged. Natalie shrinks away from her friend. Perhaps Richard has finally done the unforgivable.

"I know," Natalie says. "Richard was doing what he thought was right. Alan's death was an accident. Richard is as devastated as the rest of us; he made a bad choice, a very bad choice. I'm sorry. So sorry…" She trails off.

Anneke makes a slicing motion in the air. "What do you want?"

"I hate to bring this up right now, but you heard about Liz?" Natalie says.

"Yes," says Anneke. She presses her lips into a tight line and stares away from Natalie at the floor, her face rigid.

"Someone has to tell Craig and Elena," Natalie says. "I was going to get Joe to do it, but he can't, and Liz kept saying your name over and over before she went in for surgery." Natalie lets the words, and her suspicions of her friend, hang in the air between them.

Something snaps to life in Anneke's eyes—some small fleck of fire, but the gaze that meets Natalie's questioning one is as impenetrable as ever. "I'll tell them," she says.

Natalie feels weariness pulling her down. She should pursue this, but she's too tired right now. Farm Council is at noon. Leon deferred the meeting. Natalie's sure it's because he's going around and lobbying for support. And now she must do the same. "Daniel, Joe, Paul, Justin, and I are meeting in the infirmary at ten to discuss what to do. You can join us if you want."

Anneke nods curtly, dismissing her, and Natalie retreats to go and start canvassing support.

"I TALKED TO THE SICK people," Daniel says.

"What?" says Natalie.

Justin, Paul, Anneke, and Andrew sit in the infirmary at Joe's bedside. How Andrew sidled in on the discussion Natalie isn't sure. Even Andrew's normally effortless nonchalance is strained; his freckles stand out in a stark mosaic on his white face. Anneke's eyes look swollen, and she's plastered greasy bear-fat moisturizer all over her face, making it glisten. Natalie's head is spinning from trying to decipher oblique medical journal articles. Exhaustion, grief, and fear wash over her in successive waves, each one threatening to capsize her.

Daniel continues. "I delivered some hay for their horses, so I asked them a few questions." He removes his hat and sets it on the desk. "Apparently Rafe is in Kamloops, selling information about the location of doctors. That's how they found their way here."

Natalie closes her eyes. "Oh my God, who else is going to arrive on our doorstep?" She turns and looks at Justin. He bites his lips and his skin looks almost gray. Alan's death shattered his confidence. This is too much pressure for him; they need to get Mike back to the farm. Solomon and Cyrus rode out in the middle of the night to try to retrieve him. It's probably sixteen to twenty hours' hard ride each way, with a whole host of potential hazards along the way, and that's if Mike is allowed to leave at all.

Natalie turns back to Daniel. "What else did you find out?"

Daniel consults some notes on a piece of paper. "There are twelve people sick in total: three men, four women, and five children. There are two older women tending to them who haven't gotten sick yet, and two men who have recovered but are still weak, and seem to have relapses. The three men that Richard killed never got it. They were older men. It seems to be hitting the children and younger adults the hardest. They've lost eight people already. Some people die within the first forty-eight hours."

Everyone is silent at this. Natalie can hardly imagine a virus that can cause enough damage to kill in forty-eight hours. She pictures it sweeping through their bodies, splintering cells and liquefying organs. She wants to lock her sons in the cellar for the next year.

"So not everyone gets it?" Justin says. "Then it may be related to the 1968 flu, which would explain why the older people aren't getting it: perhaps they have some immunity. Incubation for influenza is usually two to three days. At the outside five days. If it's a new strain—which it probably is, given the mortality rate—we'll have no natural immunity to it. If it progresses at the rate that some influenzas do, some of us could be dead within a week or two."

"Well, that's a real upper," Andrew says. "Is there any good news?"

"Most of them are probably dying from secondary infections, so we do have some antibiotics to deal with that, which could reduce our mortality rates."

Justin turns back to Daniel. "Did they say how the people died?"

"The man said most of them turned blue—so cyanosis, I'm guessing."

Justin nods. "Probably from viral or bacterial pneumonia. Antibiotics would help some of them, and oxygen support, but we have no way of giving them that. We could make mist tents."

"Do we have enough antibiotics?" Natalie asks.

"To treat a major flu outbreak? Not even close."

"Could we *make* antibiotics?" Natalie says.

"If you're thinking of growing mold on some bread, forget it," Daniel says. "When they started making penicillin, a lot of the molds they grew killed bacteria, but were so toxic that they would also have killed humans." He turns to Justin. "Do you have any way of knowing whether the pneumonia is bacterial or viral?"

"No. Even before the peak, with the ability to test in a lab, the results were usually inconclusive. The practice was to start giving antibiotics anyway if the patient was critical because it took too long to wait for the lab results."

"I hate to say it," Joe says, his voice weak, "but if we leave them, won't they all just die soon? And if we help them, won't most of them die anyway? And then we've risked ourselves, to do what, save a few of them? I know that sounds callous and awful, but…"

"Great, so we're inhumane murderers, as usual," Anneke says.

Joe glares. "Are you suggesting going in there like Florence fucking Nightingale and dispensing all of our antibiotics?"

"We took you and your people in, so I wouldn't be the one to start casting stones," Paul says. "I beg you to remember Deuteronomy 15:11. *For there will never cease to be poor in the land. Therefore I command you, 'You shall open wide your hand to your brother, to the needy and to the poor, in your land.'*"

"We appreciate that Paul, and we want to help them, but the Bible doesn't exactly offer guidance with regard to totally putting our own selves at risk," Natalie says.

"Even if we don't help these people, there'll probably be others if this pandemic is just beginning," Justin says. "It takes at least a year for a pandemic to run its course. The Hippocratic oath says that I should help these people. I could go and talk to them, get their symptoms, and at least give out some antibiotics. I could keep my distance and wear a facemask. There really is no other treatment for influenza—just rest, analgesics to control fever, and liquids. And antivirals of course, which we don't have."

"No way," Natalie says.

"Richard and Alfie are going to be a problem," Paul says. "Terrence is already arguing that quarantining them is unfair and is trying to marshal support, and who knows what Leon's doing."

Daniel shakes his head in disgust. "Sometimes my dad is totally obtuse. They only have to be quarantined for eight days."

"Richard and Alfie can keep their asses parked in the woods till next summer," Natalie says. "Leon is our big problem. He'll be gunning to burn the camp down, today. We need to buy time to think."

Daniel flips his hat up and back onto his head. "I'll try to find out what Leon's up to. We could probably convince him and the others to wait until Mike gets here. He knows dick all about medicine. We could convince him that the germs could spread from the ashes. It'll buy us a day to decide."

⚬⚬⚬

RICHARD WATCHES THE FARM THROUGH the binoculars. They've come in quite handy. It looks almost like a regular day on the farm. Smoke emerges from the farmhouse and greenhouse chimneys. Siobhan and Solomon tend the gardens. Other farm members go about their duties. He spies Natalie, Daniel, and Paul heading to the farmhouse. They're having a fucking meeting without him. It is like nobody even cares or has noticed that he's being held at gunpoint on the edge of the farm. Leon had better get his ass in gear. But Leon was a little too jittery for Richard's liking.

Richard shifts his focus to the sick camp. Most of them must be in the wagons. Maybe they'll all die and cease to be a problem for the farm. It would just be easier. The flies have already settled on the dead bodies in a seething mass. Two skeletal women huddle by the single fire. Richard sniffs the air. He almost expects to catch a whiff of antiseptic laced with the sweet dull stench of decaying bodies—the smell of sickness in hospitals. But he inhales only the fresh peat of the forest.

He shudders every time the wind picks up, imagining germs falling through the trees like bits of volcanic dust, settling into his hair and lungs, marking him with death.

He snatches up the binoculars again and turns them on the camp. He can see the flies bounding from spot to spot on the bodies. He doubts the sick people even have the ability to crawl the full distance to him. As long as he didn't pick up any germs last night, he's okay.

A fat fly swoops lazily overhead, plowing through the air like a bulbous water tanker. Richard feels the brush of movement on his cheek as it passes. The flies.

Richard stands and starts to yell. "Hey!" He directs it at Brent, who's on guard duty.

"Morning," Alfie says, as he emerges from the tent and rifles through his pack, looking for drugs to quell his morning tremors. "What are you yelling about?"

"Don't bother," Richard says. "I threw them out. Hey!" Richard waves his arms. But Brent still looks out over the fields. Brent always was an incompetent dud.

"You what?" Alfie says.

"I got rid of your drugs. You need to get off them." Richard hears the sanctimony in his own voice. In actual fact, Richard isn't sure of his own motivations in disposing of the drugs. He went through Alfie's pack looking for bullets— anything to reassure himself that Alfie had been shooting a .45 the previous night—the .45 that had hit Alan. Finding the drugs was incidental. Richard studied them, feeling the coatings and casings of each individual cheerily colored pill, each one promising some happiness, some relief from something. And then he decided he wanted to see Alfie go through withdrawal, to shiver and shake, to throw up, to rip his crawling skin off, to wish himself dead. He wanted to torture Alfie for shooting Alan, for getting him into this situation, or for just being Alfie. Or maybe he just wanted Alfie to act sane for once, to be a reasonably reliable friend so he has someone to talk to.

Brent finally notices Richard waving and moves into a spot where he can hear.

"The bodies," Richard says, "in the sick camp. They need to be moved. The flies are going to infect us all."

Brent looks from Richard to the bodies and then back to Richard. "Who's going to do that?" Brent says.

304 | JENNIFER ELLIS

"I don't know. Since you won't let me leave, that's a *you* problem, not a *me* problem. Just have the bodies dealt with."

"Well, it'll have to wait until I change shift. I'm not supposed to leave you unattended," Brent says, looking over his shoulder at the sick camp.

"I guess you should watch for flies, then." Richard offers a terse smirk before returning to the rock he'd been sitting on. Brent starts to examine the air around him.

Alfie has emptied the contents of his pack. "You really took them all?"

"It's time you took control of your life and started taking responsibility for your actions."

"You fucking bastard! Give me back my fucking pills! You're the fucking asshole that got me hooked. Feeding me cocaine fifteen years ago. Saying a little bit wouldn't hurt. Did you even take it yourself? Or was it all a big joke to you, you fucking cocksucker?"

For a second, it looks like Alfie might take a run at Richard. But Richard is larger, and heavier, and, in a non-hung-over state, faster. Alfie knows it, and is not agitated or out of his mind enough to risk it. The younger man sits down hard and bursts into tears. "Please, please, please. Just give me a couple of them. I'll wean myself off, I promise."

"You killed Alan last night," Richard says. "Because you were high as a kite and had no judgment or self-control. I yelled at you to stop; I grabbed your arm. But you didn't stop."

Alfie lets his head fall into his hands. "Richard, I need those drugs. Give them to me and I'll do whatever you want. Anything. I promise."

Richard considers the possibilities associated with this, but says nothing in response. He'll let Alfie hang for a bit.

Alfie retires to the tent after half an hour in a delirious state of half consciousness. Brent waves his rifle at imaginary flies in the air around him. It's only a matter of time before one of them crumbles.

Richard sees a woman headed his way. Natalie? No, Claire, he realizes, wisping across the field like a ghost. Heading toward him, or Alfie probably. Except damn Alfie is indisposed, so Richard will have to deal with her. At least she can take a message back to farm headquarters that they have to deal with the bodies, 'cause useless Brent isn't doing anything.

Claire reaches the edge of the clearing and waves at Richard, as if he might not have noticed her. "Where's Alfie?"

"He's in the tent…resting."

She blinks several times and her nose tinges red. "I need to talk to him."

"Can I pass on a message?"

She turns away and then turns back. A tear trails down her cheek. "I'm ovulating. I know it's not the best timing, but at my age every missed cycle reduces my chances of getting pregnant."

Richard squints his eyes, trying to make sense out of what the woman is saying. Only a complete lunatic would think about babies at a time like this. Maybe that's why Alfie takes so many drugs. "Claire, in case you hadn't noticed, we're in quarantine."

"I know. But some of the farm folks are saying you won't last in quarantine."

Richard ponders what they could possibly mean by *not lasting in quarantine*. Does that mean they expect him to drop dead? Or that Leon is expecting to spring him from this crazy lockdown? Maybe the woman really is loony enough to be of assistance. Richard checks to see if Brent is listening, but the nitwit is fully absorbed in fly swatting. "If you really want to have a baby, we need to get out of this dumb quarantine, and get rid of these sick people. I need you to keep your ears and eyes open and report everything that's going on at the farm back to me. Everything."

Claire's eyes narrow a bit and her lips frame into a pout. "Nobody tells me anything."

Richard decides this isn't surprising. "Just watch, and try to listen in on people's conversations. I need to know who's talking to who, who's in charge, what's going on. Tell Leon anything you find out, and then come and tell me. And have them send someone to remove the bodies. The flies are going to kill us all."

Claire nods and turns back to the farm. As she leaves, Richard second-guesses his decision to have Claire tell Leon everything instead of just coming directly to him, but she's already too far away to call back.

Nobody shows up for the next few hours, but he feels the eyes of the other farm members on him as they move about their tasks. He watches Leon striding around like he owns the place, looking in Richard's direction every few minutes, but despite his repeated glances, the stupid ass does not come to tell Richard the plan. Even Natalie emerges from the farmhouse several times to stand in the field staring in his direction.

He feels like a monkey in a cage.

But Richard can't help but notice that every time Daniel passes from the barn to the farmhouse, or when he's checking on animals in the field, he keeps his back turned to the wood. The wood where Richard sits watching.

Alfie crawls out of the tent, retching and puking. When he's done, he scrabbles over to where Richard sits and curls up on the ground beside him, like a dog. Richard can feel Alfie's warm breath against his exposed ankle. Richard stands abruptly. "I'm going to have a nap in the tent," he says loudly, to nobody in particular. He leaves Alfie where he is.

—ooo—

NATALIE PULLS DANIEL INTO HIS cabin, away from the sight of the white wagons in the trees, away from the pall of death that lingers in the valley around the farm.

"I need to talk to you," she says.

With Leon's surprising acquiescence, Farm Council agreed to put the decision regarding the sick camp off until the next morning, or until Mike arrives, whichever happens first. But now the farm hangs in limbo. Nobody is doing chores, not really. A few people move around the farm, halfheartedly sorting vegetables, mucking stalls, or framing the new cabins. But mostly they remain in their cabins or cluster in groups, their chatter low. Except Leon, who scuttles about with purpose, moving from group to group, and giving Natalie a toothy sinister grin every time she crosses his path. And still she has no plan, no idea what to propose with regard to the sick camp. Razing the camp to the ground, or driving the people away, seem too horrific to consider—but so, too, does the alternative.

Daniel, ever trusting of her, follows and stands inside the threshold of his cabin waiting, believing that she's brought him here for good reason. She draws him into her and kisses his lips. He seems startled but doesn't pull away, and she breathes in his hay smell and feels the solid press of his body against hers.

"Sorry," she says. "I just needed that." She pulls away from him, but takes his hands in hers. "We could die within the next forty-eight hours."

"It would seem so," he says.

"We might only have today. Now."

He edges slightly closer, and his face shifts from attentive to faintly hungry. "And how do you want to spend your today, now?"

"You know how."

"We can't," he murmurs. She knows. There are too many eyes. Still, she risks pressing her lips against his neck and running her hand up his leg, over his groin. This jolts him, and his lips take hers while his fingers rove her body with deft caresses that leave her breathless. She pulls his hat from his head and drops it to the bed, while he pulls her shirt and bra aside and his lips and teeth fall to her nipples, his tongue dancing delicately on the tip of each before returning to her waiting mouth. She slips her hands inside his pants and strokes him until he thrusts into her hand and bites her lip. Daniel slides his fingers into her gently but insistently, his gray eyes never leaving hers, until she's almost begging. Then his lips take hers again.

"We should stop," he says, but instead of stopping, she sinks to her knees and takes him inside her mouth, tasting his saltiness, feeling the smoothness of his skin against her tongue. His breath catches, and for a second he seems staggered as he grabs the bedpost and murmurs "Oh my God" before entwining his hands in her hair.

"Your heart?" she says.

"My heart is just fine." His voice is ragged.

She rises and pushes against him, demanding now. He pulls away for a second to smooth the hair out of her eyes and kiss her, and then, the decision apparently made, they both scramble to remove their jumble of clothes. She trembles when he enters her, and then they pause fractionally, as if their bodies are exhaling a joint sigh of relief and shock. Then Daniel starts to move, and she matches his movements, carried by the sweet wrenching intensity of feeling him inside her. His final thrusts and the sound of his release push her over the edge, and she falls to the bed throbbing and shaking.

She feels the damp of his tears between her breasts. And she cries too.

"I'm sorry. This was wrong. I just wanted you so much," she says.

He gathers her in his arms and burrows his face into her neck. "It's okay. I wanted you too."

"Do you think we could have this forever?"

"Well at this rate, forever might just be till the end of the week."

Her laugh comes out as a sob. "That's not funny. Richard has let me down so many times. Maybe I've let him down too. I just want to believe again, in something."

He draws away and looks in her eyes. "I can only say that I want us to be together when we're old, that I picture it, that I long for it, and that I'm building my life around it." Hope twists in Natalie's heart. And still a thread of doubt maintains its stranglehold on her. Taunting her.

What is this bitter diffidence that always frames her heart? Was it watching her mother disintegrate into the dark territory of her mind, her illness rendering her almost unlovable? The accidents that took Scott's wife from him and Natalie's father away from her mother? The possibility that she might have to watch a lover waste away from disease, or worse, be the one watched? Or just the grind of life and inevitable fading of passion, leaving them with nothing but their own mundanity? Her mind pursues all of these possibilities relentlessly. Are those not the potential paths of all but a few lucky lovers? Perhaps, as Richard has always claimed, she is just genetically inclined to melancholy. The black dog of depression may not walk beside her, like it did her mother, but when she turns, she can always catch it with her eye, flitting stealthily in and out of the shadows behind her.

Or does it just come down to Richard and their failed marriage?

She nods and drops her eyelids to hide her tears. She draws the inside of Daniel's forearm to her lips. "Can you go talk to Richard? Find out what he's up to, what he thinks we should do. I know Leon and Terrence will be out there lobbying him, but as much as I complain about Richard, he's not a bad person. We need his input."

—◦∞∞◦—

AS HE APPROACHES, DANIEL SEES Richard watching the farm through binoculars. Alfie is nowhere to be seen. Daniel assumes he's in the tent. Typical of his brother, Richard doesn't put the binoculars down, even when Daniel stands in front of him only twenty yards away. Daniel wonders if Richard was watching when he and Natalie went into his cabin, and then when they both emerged a few minutes ago. The barn would have blocked Richard's view. But Leon had seen them come out. Leon will use it against them. None of anybody's business, but everyone will think it is.

Daniel speaks to Brent. "Why don't you go have lunch? I'll relieve you for a while. I want to talk to Richard anyway."

Brent nods in assent and makes off across the field like he's being pursued by a pack of wild dogs. Daniel sits down on the rock that Brent had occupied, and lays the rifle across his lap. Shadow the cat has followed him, and sits on the ground cleaning himself with long, even strokes, the pupils of his eyes just slits in the afternoon sun. Richard continues to ignore Daniel and study the farm, focusing the binoculars with deliberateness on the barn area.

Daniel clears his throat. Richard puts down the binoculars and regards his brother with affected equanimity. "So. It's come to this," Richard says.

"Oh fuck, Richard, quit being so melodramatic. You did something stupid, and now you're quarantined for a few days. Don't make it into any big personal affront. Your "Poor Richard" routine may work on Mom and Dad, but you would've quarantined anyone else that did the same thing…" Daniel catches a glint of sunlight off the binoculars in Richard's lap. "Hey, are those my binoculars? I've been looking for them for a month."

Richard has the grace to give a sheepish smile. "I borrowed them. You didn't seem to be using them."

"Richard, 'borrowing' is when you ask someone permission to take something. They were in my house, on my bedside table. When are you going to quit taking things that aren't yours?"

"When are *you* going to quit taking things that aren't yours?" The tone is taunting.

Daniel feels his neck flush. His underwear is still damp and his fingers smell of Natalie. "I don't know what you mean."

"Really?" Richard's voice is flat. Daniel has no clue how much Richard knows or has guessed. Frustration courses through Daniel's veins. He feels like a marionette in a play. Richard pulls the strings, and Daniel hasn't received a copy of the script. His only defense is to slump over and do nothing, a defense he has employed too effectively for most of his life, especially where Richard is concerned.

"Richard, even if I did know what you meant, which really, honestly, I'm not sure if I do, do you really care? I'm tired of this game."

"What game?"

"You know what game. The game we've played for years. The game where you pull my strings and make statements that may or may not be true, to get me to do what you want, and I have no clue what the hell you're thinking."

"I have no idea what you're talking about." Richard affects a look of genuine confusion.

"Fine. I didn't come to talk about this anyway. I came to talk about the situation, see what you think."

"Oh, you're actually interested in what I think? It didn't seem like it when you and Nat were holding your special little meeting. Point of order in holding meetings, Daniel: if you want your people to feel heard, consult them *before* the meeting."

"It was a discussion, Richard. Nothing is decided. Natalie specifically sent me out to get your thoughts. Why do you always have to be such an asshole?"

"Well, has anyone considered how I'm going to participate in Farm Council tomorrow?"

"We're going to set up a videoconference line, Richard, what do you think? That's why I'm here. To get your input."

"How am I going to read the crowd, go with the flow, come up with synergistic ideas on the fly?"

Daniel takes off his hat, scratches his scalp, and replaces his hat. "You're not. And I guess you should have thought of that before you started randomly shooting people last night."

"I was protecting my land and family," Richard says. "But no matter, I have no input. It's a tough decision, you guys. I'll just be sitting out here on my little rock waiting for the results when you're done."

"No input," Daniel repeats blankly. It's impossible for Richard to have no input. Input is Richard's middle name. Richard offers input into naming the calves in the spring. But here his brother is, smiling benignly on his rock, with glittery eyes, claiming no input. "Are you sure?" Daniel asks.

"I'm just going to stand aside on this one. I don't know why someone hasn't dealt with those bodies though. The flies are getting bad."

"Who the hell is going to do that?"

"Well, I'd get some ropes tied to them and haul them into a grave with the horses, but I guess that's your problem now. I'm feeling a little tired. I'm going to head in for a nap. Looks like a regular round of afternoon chores for you. Can't say I miss my time on the chain gang."

"But I have to wait for Brent to come back," Daniel splutters.

"Enjoy your time in the sun then," Richard says, heading to the tent. "Oh, and Danny boy, just so you know, I know you. I know how you think and how you cope. I know you better than you know yourself. You're not up to the pressure. You'll fall apart. It's coming. You've made a big mistake."

"How many times do I have to tell you not to call me that?" It's Daniel's turn for his voice to be flat. Richard's words have dug in, but the sound of the tent zipper drowns out Daniel's words. And so he sits, Shadow curled up beside him, thirty yards from the tent that somehow mocks him, until Brent returns.

"HE'S UP TO SOMETHING," DANIEL says, holding his hat in his hands.

"What?" Natalie looks up from the medical journals.

"Richard. He's up to something," Daniel says again. "I went to talk to him like you asked. He's acting all wrong. He wasn't interested in providing any input into the Farm Council meeting tonight."

"Richard. No input," Natalie repeats slowly, as if Daniel is speaking some sort of a different, nonsense language.

"He's got to be working with someone," Daniel says. "Probably Leon and my fucking dad. And he knows about us, I think. What should we do?" Daniel feels as though his world might be sinking away from him, leaving him in this unknown terrain of limited allies and unlimited exposure.

Natalie rubs the spot between her eyes. "I have to go talk to Paul, Joe, and some of the others before Farm Council tomorrow, see if we have a plan to propose… Can you deal with Richard? You're going to have to get him to talk."

Daniel nods, not really feeling certain at all that he can deal with Richard. "Don't you think he might tell *you* more?" he says, wondering if he sounds pathetic.

"I doubt it. He doesn't tell me any more than he tells you." She rises and kisses him, almost absently, on the cheek, and squeezes his hand. "Just go confront him. Try to scare him a bit. He's not invincible. You're just as important to Richard as I am. Maybe more important. And then go talk to Leon."

Natalie leaves the infirmary office and Daniel finds himself alone in the white-walled room. One quick, albeit good, fuck, a few I love yous, and he's suddenly expected to take on the duties of, well, Richard. *You're not up to the pressure.* Richard's words clamor in Daniel's ears.

He knows he can do this. He knows it was more than just a fuck. Way more. He fucking loves her. But deal with Richard and Leon? Christ. He would have used his half-assed gimpy heart as an excuse in the past. But he's not sure he can do that anymore.

CHAPTER 23
THE THREE OF SWORDS

Listen to your inner voice. The people around you are not what they seem.

Andrew heads to his hidden place in the hayloft after lunch. He has chores to do, of course, but he's very tired all of a sudden. He supposes it's the two nights with almost no sleep. And then the stress of Alan being shot and this whole flu thing. He'll just have a little nap before hitting it hard. Nobody has seen him slouch off. He wonders if Daniel even knows about his hayloft retreat.

Andrew is amazed at how soft and enveloping the hay seems today. It's always been so scratchy and irritating before, nestling into places he didn't want it. But today it's cushiony and inviting. And his body feels so heavy.

Claire indicated that she wants to talk to him. She went off to see Alfie earlier. She said it was important, that she needed his advice. He'll just sleep for a bit and then go and find her. He thinks about what Justin said, when they were alone, after everyone else except Joe had cleared out of the infirmary: that he couldn't be sure, but he thinks Alan was shot from behind. Which doesn't make sense because surely Alan had been facing the sick camp, and only Andrew and Leon had been behind him.

His last thought, before he drifts off to sleep, is that his throat is strangely dry, as if he swallowed a bunch of entangled threads, and they run down his throat and he can't clear them.

JOE HUDDLES ON A BENCH on the farmhouse porch, his leg elevated and bandaged, his face puffy from the pain meds, a stubby cigarette clenched in his fingers. The acrid smoke curls up and around him. He used to smoke only when he was drunk. He shouldn't even be out of the infirmary. She sits on the bench next to him and feels the slight warmth of his shoulder in the chill fall air.

She asks her question without preamble. "Who's Craig's biological mother?" She already knows the answer. She's seen it in the curves and angles of Craig's face and the yearning look in Anneke's eyes when she watches him.

"It's not my business to tell you, but I suggest you go talk to your best friend." *My best friend wouldn't have kept this from me*, Natalie thinks, but then reconsiders. What truths has she herself kept from Anneke?

"What do you think we should do?"

Joe takes a deep drag on the cigarette stub. Natalie examines the shadows that fall across his face. "We can't help them, Natalie."

Paul joins them on silent feet, his bespectacled face puckered in stress and worry. Natalie thinks his look betrays a hint of disdain when he glances at Natalie—over Richard's actions, her relationship with Daniel, her position regarding the sick people. She's not sure, but the judgment cuts into her just the same.

Natalie wonders if the flu has also hit Jerry, and so Mike can't leave, or worse, he's already dead. She tries not to think about it.

Paul pushes his glasses up on his nose. "We agreed to think about it, and my view is that we have to help these people. I know Cyrus would agree, and Siobhan is also on my side. Even if Farm Council goes against me, I think I'm going to have to be a conscientious objector."

"You might not be allowed back on the farm if you do that," Natalie says.

"What are we becoming if we privilege our own survival over everything else?"

"I don't know," Natalie says. She thinks of the many generations of humans that quarantined and exiled the sick long before them. *Quarantine*, from an Italian phrase that means forty days. And influenza was considered a quarantinable disease. But in recent history, people in quarantine usually received medical care.

"We should take Leon into custody," she says.

"On what grounds?" Paul says. "And who would support us?" He's right.

With Alan dead, Mike gone, and Solomon and Cyrus sent to retrieve Mike—and the newcomers still unable to vote—the balance of votes now probably lies with Leon. Even if some of the others, such as Bob and Ramona, wouldn't actively engage in burning the sick camp or driving the sick people away, they would probably tacitly allow Leon to do so.

"What about a coup? We get the newcomers on side. We would slightly outnumber them then."

"Pretty risky," Joe says. "Half of us would probably get shot, just so we can what? Die of the flu?"

Joe's remark is met with only silence, and then the three of them part ways, Natalie into the farmhouse, Paul in the direction of the bunkhouse, and Joe left behind on the porch with his cigarette—a sudden turning away of bodies with nothing left to say, no clear answers, and their own disparate opinions.

"CRAIG'S MY SON. MINE AND Joe's, so what? It doesn't make any difference now," Anneke says. Piles of diced peppers, chard, onions, and chicken sit on the counters around her with no apparent destination, like she has done nothing but chop for the last several hours. Her face is drawn and grayish. "Liz adopted Craig when he was a baby. Liz and I stayed in touch. Joe didn't know. He didn't give a crap about me anyway. He was just looking to get laid, as usual."

"Why didn't you ever tell me?" Natalie says.

"The more people you tell, the more real things become. If you tell nobody, then it's almost like it didn't even happen. So I went to France for a year while I was pregnant and told nobody. When things started to go bad, I sent Joe a letter telling him about Craig. Then I sent him the letter, ostensibly from you, telling him about the farm. I thought he would be more likely to come that way, as I figured he'd be pretty pissed at me. I didn't think it would take him five fucking years to get here."

"Are you going to tell Craig?"

"I don't know. He's an adult. He doesn't need parenting. He doesn't even like me." Anneke flicks her wrist slightly. Light flashes off the tip of the knife.

"You deliberately fed the dogs inside, the day of the second attack?" Natalie's voice is mild but thin, almost shaky. Why does confronting Anneke rattle her so much?

Anneke bows her head and bunches her lips. "Yes, but I didn't know about the attack. Joe and Liz had set up a meeting time if Joe could get away. I went out to meet him instead of Liz, but he never showed."

"Pretty risky considering that you didn't know anything about the rest of them. What if Liz knew about the attack and tricked you? Why else would Rafe let her come down here?"

"I'm sorry. They were slaves. Craig is my son. What wouldn't you do for one of your children?"

"Why didn't you tell me? I thought you did it because you had a thing for Joe."

Anneke turns on her, her eyes wild and her face distorted. "You really think I would do this for a man? Just remember my husband is dead because of this damn farm and your damn husband, who is a murderer. Now please leave me alone." Anneke slams the knife into the onion she's already diced into bits.

Natalie stands and stares. Richard, a murderer. It would be so convenient to go this direction, to tell everyone that she left Richard, and is now with Daniel because Richard is a murderer. But she doesn't quite believe it.

She turns and leaves, banging the door into Claire's face as she goes.

ALFIE IS STILL SNORING WHEN Richard emerges from the tent and picks up the binoculars. Ranjeet, Solomon, and Karl skirt the sick camp and farm with guns. They twitch like a pack of squirrels ready to skitter away in terror at the slightest provocation. Daniel exits the farmhouse and walks over to the barn, his footfalls slow and reluctant. His donkey walk. Daniel is feeling the pressure. Richard almost feels sorry for him. Daniel is the weaker twin in so many ways, so burdened by everyday life. It's pathetic, but good news for Richard. Natalie still hasn't come to see him. That's her style. Always avoiding difficult conversations. But she'll come. She needs Richard, and Daniel is no substitute.

Richard puts down the binoculars. This quarantine is ridiculous. He isn't sick. Do they really think they can shut him out like this? That he'll just sit in the woods like a good little boy, while they make him an outsider on his own farm?

He considers packing up and leaving, heading back to Vancouver. But he refuses to leave in a cloud of shame with his tail between his legs. He has to take back control. Tonight.

DANIEL STEWS ABOUT THE BARN, slamming down tack, shutting stable doors with an excess of force, and swearing. The horses turn their heads away, and Mitch retreats to the farthest corner of the barn to curl up in a ball, afraid that it's his fault, or perhaps just disgusted with his master's behavior. Great. He's embarrassing himself in front of his own dog.

Why the fuck is he scared shitless of confronting his own brother? His own brother, who is under armed guard and cannot touch him. What is he afraid of? That Richard is going to say something? Do something? Withdraw his brotherly love? His brotherly support and alliance? Not that Richard had ever been a particularly reliable ally. Ensure that Daniel is exiled from his own family?

Probably all of the above. Richard has always had a way of getting under Daniel's skin, of twisting him one way or the other, of keeping him in line. Richard always seemed to get the best of everything and emerge the victor, while Daniel was forced to walk away and lick his literal and figurative wounds.

And it had never been any other way. The literal wounds had started in utero—where Richard acquired better placental real estate, forcing Daniel to emerge tinier and weaker and with Ebstein's anomaly, a heart problem that required two surgeries and forever barred him from any playing field. In grade three, Richard's reckless choice of bike paths had landed the less-agile Daniel in the hospital with a broken arm. And Daniel's left knee still bears a white scar from the knife wound he received when Richard got into a scrap outside the Coyote Club, Richard's favorite bar in the nineties.

The figurative damages were worse. Daniel had spent much of his life waiting for Richard while he engaged in some pick-up, had another drink, or just took his time. And he'd spent virtually all of his life being compared to Richard—by Richard, if nobody else. The quieter twin, the less athletic twin, the less popular twin, the less attractive twin, the less ballsy twin, the single twin, and—in Richard's famous mocking words—the gay hermit twin. The twin with the half-assed gimpy heart.

Richard's shadow.

When they were young, it was Richard who'd decided which paths they would ride their bikes on, which TV shows they would watch, which Halloween candy was the best. In high school, Richard made the friends, found out about the parties, and got the beer. Later, the decisions got even bigger. Where they would go to university, which apartment they would rent, which girls they would chat up—although Richard did almost all the talking. Richard was always confident enough for the both of them, and Daniel was always carried along by it.

The list in Daniel's brain grinds at him as he paces. The internal and external scars that mark his relationship with his brother bind him like a netting.

Going to veterinary school had been the first line in the sand, Daniel's first departure from Richard. His first independent decision. And even now, at age forty-six, he has miserably few such independent decisions under his belt.

Confronting Richard feels like another line in the sand, one that may divide him forever from his twin. Of course, sleeping with Natalie also has the potential to do this, but Daniel still harbors some strange hope that his affair with Natalie will never be discovered, that Richard will somehow transition out of Natalie's life, realize their marriage is a failure, and graciously step aside, and Natalie and Daniel can be together, after a suitable time has passed. He knows this is probably magical thinking, but still he clings to it. Because, for whatever reason, he still needs Richard.

Daniel slams his fist into his desk, sending papers flying; they flutter slowly to the ground, slipping soundlessly beneath furniture. His fist lands next to his book on Saturn's moons: Tethys and Calypso, the twins. Tethys, the large, perfectly formed one; Calypso, its smaller, irregular brother, trailing behind. The Trojans. Daniel knows he's Calypso. Everyone knows he's Calypso, even if they've never heard of the moons. He studies his hand. The half moons at the base of his nails are tinged slightly blue—a reflection of his chronic circulation problems. Dirt that will never wash off weaves its way through the cracks in his skin.

His is a hand that has only ever held two hands, for his mother's hands were always too full of groceries or laundry or Kristen. One hand held his when both were chubby and soft and pink with youth. Held his until it was something that they were too old for, something that only sissies did. But it had been a fairly reliable hand until then. Helping him over the rocks and brambles of life. Sometimes letting go at the wrong moment. Sometimes sweaty. Often sticky.

And the hand that holds his now. A hand that is like his, marked with sun and hard work. A hand that has become reliable in its own right. And now he has to choose.

He looks up and sees Leon watching him like a skeletal wraith, a wild look in his mismatched eyes. Daniel almost jumps back.

Leon sidles over and whispers, his breath thick with pot. "We're making a plan to spring Richard and deal with the sick camp. Help us. Help your brother. Everyone else in our family is on the same side."

Daniel remains silent, mute. What the hell are they planning?

Leon continues. "Natalie's using you. She's a controlling little whore. She's probably sleeping with Joe too. Look at the way they sit together. The way he looks at her and does what she asks. That's how women get power, by spreading their legs. You know she's duping you. It's only a matter of time before she leaves you for someone better." His indictment slaps Daniel like a sickness. Is this what the other farm members think of Natalie, of him? He hates Leon, knows he's full of shit, but Leon's words find an edge and stick under.

Leon laughs softly at Daniel's expression, and his raspy wheeze seems to pound in Daniel's ears. "I can see I'm right. Richard is already plenty pissed at you, and he doesn't know the half of it. When the people on the farm find out what you've done, how you've betrayed your brother, you won't be welcome anywhere, and your brother will never speak to you again. You'll be a fucking outcast, and you better believe Natalie won't go with you. No way. She likes to fart in silk and be taken care of, that one. You'll be alone. Break it off now. Help us and I'll keep your secret."

"What's the plan then?" Daniel hears himself say.

Leon spreads his lips in a yellow-toothed smile. "You can't be trusted yet. I just hope that when the time is right, you'll do the right thing." Leon wheels about on his heeled cowboy boots and swaggers out of the office.

Forever. Whore. Outcast. Alone. The words grind through Daniel's brain in sequence. Where is he going with this? He loves her. But is he willing to give up everything for her? His fingers, with their blue half moons, are slick with sweat.

———⦵———

RICHARD GOES TO CHECK ON Alfie just before dinner. He finds him still and silent. No breath warms Richard's face as he leans in to Alfie, and there's no reassuring throb at Alfie's wrists, no matter how hard Richard presses. His skin is cool, and when Richard props open his eyelids, his pupils remain unfocused and almost cloudy. Alfie's mouth smells of vomit, and chunks of his lunch are caked on his chin and neck. With shaking fingers, Richard clears Alfie's airway, hurling pieces of spew at the tent walls, and pumps furiously at Alfie's chest. He brings himself to press his lips against Alfie's, and fills the man's lungs with air. But there is no response. A fetid aroma emanates from Alfie's pants. Richard almost doubles over at the stink. Overdose probably. Or the flu…?

Richard lurches outside and grabs his water bottle. He pours water over his hands and lips and scrubs them violently. He follows this with a splash of the last of the whiskey.

He returns to his rock. There's little point in calling for help at this point. He goes back into the tent to check.

Still dead.

Now what is he going to do? Reporting Alfie's death would bring all sorts of questions that he doesn't need. Not tonight, especially if, as Leon has intimated, the plan is coming down tonight. Leon seemed sufficiently rattled about the flu to cut Richard out. But if he waits too long, rigor-whatever-mortis will set in, and some frigging bright-ass, probably Mike, will know that Richard didn't report Alfie's death when it happened, and then he'll not only be implicated in Alan's murder but probably Alfie's as well, which is complete bullshit. But Richard could just say he hasn't gone into the tent all afternoon or evening. That he let Alfie sleep off his withdrawal symptoms.

It has to be an overdose. He let Alfie take too many pills when Alfie begged a third time and Richard just wanted to shut him up. And then there was the moaning and thrashing that had emerged from the tent an hour or so ago. Richard had ignored it, assuming it was some drug-induced hallucination. He had been watching Scott and Daniel maneuver the dead bodies into a trench with the horses and plow. But it could have been Alfie in his death throes.

Maybe it's for the best. Alfie's behavior had become increasingly erratic, making him a liability. But they'd had a lot of good times and pulled off a lot of schemes.

Perhaps he should say some sort of liturgy or mass, or whatever it's called, for his friend. Fuck. It's hard to come up with high-impact, piquant words without a speechwriter. He settles for a quick "Goodbye, Alfie" under his breath. But this seems a bit stupid because nobody can hear him, and there's still the matter of Alfie's body in his tent. Richard is certain he won't be sleeping in there tonight. When this is all over, he'll ensure Alfie has a proper burial. Paul can make the speeches, and Richard will play the bereaved best friend.

Now all he has to do is wait, and hope nobody notices Alfie's absence before tonight. He spots Leon headed across the field. Finally. Leon relieves Brent from guard duty and gives Richard a conspiratorial wink as Brent leaves. Then he makes a dramatic show of standing with his back to the tree, facing away from Richard.

"How's it going, buddy?" Leon mutters, barely moving his lips.

"You mean aside from my incarceration? Fine, Leon, just fine."

"Just wanted you to know that everything is in place for tonight." Still no lip movement.

"You know, Leon, nobody's here. Nobody can hear you, or see you really for that matter."

"Oh… Oh, right. Okay. Well, we're all set."

They're both silent for a few seconds.

Leon speaks again. "The little do-gooder Christian and the cheater have no idea what's coming. I think I've convinced Daniel to join us."

"Daniel, really?" Richard says. Perhaps his spineless brother has a backbone after all, but it almost makes him squirm to hear Natalie talked about that way.

Leon continues somewhat cautiously, "But you're feeling fine, right? No sore throat or aches or pains or anything? You'd tell us, right?"

"Leon, if I was feeling sick, don't you think I would tell you? Don't you think I would quarantine myself for the best of everyone? I'm totally fine. Healthy as a horse. Got the immune system of a tank." Richard wonders whether he's trying to convince himself, or Leon.

"But what about Alfie? Where is he?"

Richard forces his voice to be carefree. "Alf's sleeping off a tear. You know him, always partying."

Leon laughs, but there's a tinny sort of forced conviviality to his laughter.

"Can I ask what exactly is the plan?"

"I don't want to give too much away, but it's going to involve gasoline and matches." Leon gives a dramatic eye-blink and head thrust. Richard almost recoils.

"You don't mean you're actually going to *burn* them?"

"No, no. Not unless they resist. We're going to make them leave. Then we're going to decontaminate the area." Richard considers this. He's not sure if this is the best plan. Leon could end up torching the whole farm. But he needs to be sprung from quarantine. Then he'll be able to wrest back control, once he's allowed to actually talk to people and convince them of the right plan...even though he's not sure what that is just yet.

Claire arrives, her face flushed, carrying Richard's dinner. "I have news," she says, her voice barely above a whisper, darting a meaningful look, with a funny head tilt, in Leon's direction.

Richard sighs. Do all of his helpers have to be so melodramatic? Surely that's not how he appears when he's engaged in a covert mission. "It's okay, Claire, Leon is on our side."

"Oh, right. Wait until you hear what I overheard..." she pauses for effect. Richard waits. Leon waits. Richard is just beginning to squint his eyes in exasperation when Claire finally speaks. "Anneke is the traitor, and Natalie knows all about it. They were in the pantry talking about it."

"Anneke?" Richard says, rising from his rock and starting to stride around the campsite.

"Bitch," Leon says.

Richard looks up from his striding. "Why? Why would she do it?"

Claire's face crumples a bit. "I don't know. I didn't hear that part."

Richard makes his voice soothing. "It's okay, Claire. Good job. Go back and see what more you can hear. Don't tell anyone until I figure out what to do about it."

Claire nods. Richard is about to make some speech about working together when Claire interrupts. "Where is Alfie anyway? I want to talk to him," she says.

"He's sleeping. He's pretty tired from the trip."

But Claire doesn't move. "He's been sleeping all day. Surely he could come out and talk to his wife for a few minutes? Go wake him up."

Cold beads of sweat start to form on Richard's neck. Shit. What is he going to do? He walks toward the tent. "I'll just go check on him, see if he's stirring." Richard makes an exaggerated show of unzipping the tent flap.

"Nope, still dead asleep." The words freeze on Richard's lips. They'd come out before he'd even thought about it.

Claire stomps her foot. "This is ridiculous! He needs to get up." To Richard's horror, she starts yelling at the tent. "Alfie! Alfie! It's me! Claire! Get up! I want to talk to you. Alfie!" Claire continues hollering at the tent for a few seconds before glaring at Richard.

"What's wrong with him?"

Richard shrugs. "He's just really tired. You'd be surprised how little sound travels across the clearing here, and how soundproof the tent is." He speaks too rapidly. "When I'm in the tent I can barely hear a thing," he adds for good measure. He's starting to sound deranged.

Claire looks at him funny. Even Leon is looking at him funny.

"Let him sleep it off, Claire. I know Alfie, he'll be totally testy if you wake him up now. Trust me. He'll be far more receptive to your plan if he's well rested and not hung over."

"Fine," Claire says. "Just be sure to let me know when he wakes up."

Richard almost starts panting in relief when Claire turns and marches across the field.

Leon's face is greenish through his tan. "Alfie isn't...sick, is he?"

"No, no, no. He's probably just avoiding Claire. Can you blame him?" Richard makes a circular motion around his temple with his finger. "A few bricks short of a load, that one."

"I guess," says Leon.

"Who's getting me a horse?"

"Don't worry, your dad's got that one tied down."

⸎

THE SUNLIGHT THROUGH THE SMALL window has shifted by the time Andrew awakes. The rays have that deeper, more resonant midafternoon quality. His brief nap has gone on long beyond what he had intended. As he opens his eyes a crack, the light impales him, and he snaps them shut with a shudder. His head pounds, and his body is engulfed in the heavy ache of fever. The hay is damp and uncomfortable around him, sticking to his face and arms, and he realizes his clothes are soaked too. His stomach gives a sudden lurch of nausea. As he vomits in the hay beside him, Andrew feels the entrails of fear thread around him.

Nobody knows where he is.

But even moving fractionally to vomit makes him see spots, black fuzzy spots that dance across his line of vision. He sinks back into the hay in a dizzy haze. He'll just rest and work up his strength for a few more minutes, before trying to navigate the ladder out of the hayloft.

NATALIE WALKS THROUGH THE ORCHARD searching for Andrew. She has Paul looking through the eastern pasture. It's too silent, and there's no movement around any of the cabins or tents. Natalie wonders if people are packing, planning to sneak out in the middle of the night, away from the threat of disease and death. She has to find Andrew. She knows he goes off to nap and do Andrew things sometimes, but she can't believe he would sneak off at a time like this.

Alone in the orchard, circling the trees, yelling for Andrew, she lets a few tears fall. Alan's body lies under a sheet in the shed. People are dying on the edge of the farm. Leon wants her dead. Her best friend seems to hate her. She has utterly betrayed Richard. She has let things with Daniel go much further than she should have. She had not at all wanted to live her life this way. In the eyes of most of the farm members, it's not Richard who's done the unforgivable by murdering Alan. It's her. Richard was defending his farm and family. She should go to Richard, ask his forgiveness, and live her life as a marked woman.

But a small edge of fight rises up in her and catches. She will not do that. No matter how much everyone else thinks she should.

Natalie reaches into her pocket for her handkerchief. She doesn't have time to wallow in emotion. She must find Andrew and figure out what to do about the sick camp. Her hand bumps against the edges of a card. One of Liz's tarot cards. She took them from the woman when she went for surgery, intending to give them to Elena. The remainder of the deck lies on Daniel's dresser, but this card must have become separated from the rest.

She removes the smooth, cool card from her pocket.

The Star. A naked woman pours water into a pool beneath a starry sky. The stars look almost like the mosquito constellation that Daniel showed her. He had joked about praying to it so they wouldn't get eaten alive by mosquitoes. Mosquitoes that are thriving in a climate-changed world.

Mosquitoes.

She turns and heads back to the farmhouse at a run.

CHAPTER 24

THE SIX OF SWORDS

—————

A balance of head and heart is needed.
Use your intuition and analytical mind.

Natalie speed-walks through the kitchen and pushes into the pantry to find Anneke and Joe engaged in a hissing discussion.

"Come to the infirmary!" she orders. "We don't have much time."

They follow Natalie through the kitchen and down the hall to Mike's office. They burst in on Justin, who launches out of his chair like there's a grenade under it.

"What if it's malaria?" Natalie says.

Justin looks blank. "What if what's malaria?"

"The sickness." Natalie waves her hands at him. "The mosquitoes have been so bad this season. I saw a map once of zones likely to experience increased malaria as a result of global warming, and one of the zones was right here. Aren't the symptoms of malaria like the flu? I'm sure I've read before that they're often mistaken for each other. Daniel said that some of the people got better, and then got worse, which matches the cyclic aspect of malaria. And the fact that the older men didn't get sick. They're African-American and possibly recent immigrants, which means that they may have already been exposed, and have so much in their blood that they are, relatively speaking, immune.

We have medication for it. We could treat them!"

Justin frowns. "I want to believe that's possible. But it's still probably influenza. Occam's razor."

"Occam's what?" says Joe.

"Occam's razor," says Justin. "The explanation requiring the fewest assumptions is the most likely. And in this case it's influenza."

"But we can test for malaria," says Natalie. "All we need is a blood smear from a finger prick; we can look at it under a microscope."

"Yes, but we need someone willing to go to their camp and potentially expose themselves to influenza to get the blood smear, in which case they're probably going to have to stay there. And the specimen could carry the flu virus," Justin says.

"We could use gloves," says Natalie. "Get them to prick their own fingers, put it on a slide. Wipe it with disinfectant."

"If we're wrong, it could be a death sentence for the person who goes," Justin says, his eyes pinched and desperate.

Joe looks up from the infirmary cabinet that he's been leaning against. "If we're doing it, we better do it soon, before Leon makes his move."

"I'll do it," Justin says.

"No," Natalie says.

"I'll do it," Anneke says.

Natalie considers this. Anneke has three children. "Neke, you can't."

Anneke turns to Natalie and squares her shoulders. "Leon has already been in to threaten me. Apparently it's now common knowledge that I put the bullets out for Joe and that Craig is my son. Leon says I'll be out on my ass as soon as this is dealt with." Anneke's accusation is clear, and Natalie blanches. It has to have been Joe—or, she reconsiders, Claire. At the door.

"I'm going," Natalie says. "Please though, someone needs to find Andrew."

———— ✧ ————

DANIEL APPROACHES RICHARD AND ALFIE'S camp. Shadows dance around him in the woods, making him jump. Mitch trails him.

Richard is on his rock as usual. Ramona is on guard duty. Daniel wonders if she's in on Leon's plan.

"Oh, you're back. Missing me, dear brother?" Richard's normal irritation and sarcasm seem underscored by a fragment of nervousness. He leaps to his feet and starts circling around.

Daniel takes a deep breath. "What is Leon planning? I know you're in on it. I need you to tell me. You're about to do something."

Richard's face curves into his dewy-eyed look of innocence, as if God himself is shining a light on him. To this Richard adds his usual little chuckle. His "I have no idea what you're talking about" chuckle. Daniel has heard it many times. When Richard was booby-trapping his room. When Richard was conning Daniel into writing an economics paper for him. When Richard was convincing their parents that they had been at the library studying all night. But even knowing Richard, the look is enough to wedge some doubt into Daniel's mind.

"Do something like what?"

"Do something like you do?" Daniel says.

"I don't do things." Richard shifts to a more aggressive look.

"Yes, you do."

"I don't." Back to the chuckle and the innocent expression. Richard throws his arms up into the air for good measure. Daniel feels his exasperation rising. It's a bulletproof defense. Never ever admit to anything. If you never allow a single chink in your armor, people begin to doubt themselves, doubt what they've seen, doubt their interpretation of events. Unless he's caught red-handed, Richard always seems to be able to walk away leaving people uncertain whether he's done anything wrong. And since Daniel usually walks away the enraged one, punching walls and knocking over chairs, Daniel seems to be the unstable one.

Richard speaks again. "Do you really think I would plan something and not tell you?"

"Yes, I do."

"Oh, come on Daniel, when have I ever done that before?"

"Too many times to count. I can't believe we're even having this conversation. Leon told me you're planning something. Can you please tell me what you're up to because I think you're about to rip this farm apart."

Richard laughs again and shakes his head. "I have nothing. You're barking up the wrong tree." He affects a stretch, raising his arms into the air like the conversation bores him. His grin, though, seems plastered on, and his eyes are blue-green pools of accusation.

Daniel feels the sweat of fury creep across his skin. He knows that under his jacket his neck and chest are mottled red. Should he beg? Shake Richard? They would be evenly matched in a fistfight, but Mike has been explicit with Daniel about the risks of getting into a fight, and he'd be potentially exposing himself to the flu, too. Threaten to shoot him? What can he do to get through to his brother? He stands in the clearing, uncertain. Thinking.

Richard breaks the silence. "Hey, it's cold out here, can I borrow your hat?"

"My hat?"

"Yeah, the one on your head. You have lots. Can you lend me that one?"

"It's mine."

"Daniel, it's a fucking hat. Help a guy out. I'm cold. You have other hats… Exactly the same, unless I'm mistaken."

"It's mine, though."

"Fine, don't worry about me. I'll be fine, then."

Daniel feels a twist of rage. He tosses the hat at Richard. "Take the fucking hat."

Richard gives his preening little smile and places the hat on his head.

"What do you think?" Richard says.

"What do I think of what?"

"The hat, on me, does it look good?"

Only Richard would think about how he looks on a night like tonight. "It looks great." This is fucking pointless. Daniel turns to leave. He turns back. "Where's Alfie? I haven't seen him all day. He's not off doing something, is he?"

This jolts Richard in a way that Daniel has never seen before. "He's in the tent. Sleeping. Really bad trip."

"I don't believe you."

Same look, same chuckle, same arm flail, except now Richard is starting to look like a crazy cartoon character. "He is. I swear it. Where else would he be?"

"Let me see him then. Now!" Daniel orders.

"You wouldn't want someone disturbing you if you were sleeping."

"I haven't seen him all day."

Richard starts walking toward the tent. "Here, I'll let you peek in on him, while he sleeps."

"What are you talking about?" Daniel says.

"You go over there where you can see the tent opening. I'll unzip it and you can look in and see that he's there."

"This is ridiculous. Just wake him up. I don't have time for your games." But Daniel nonetheless walks over to where Richard gestured.

Richard ceremoniously unzips the tent. Daniel can see Alfie's prone form on the sleeping bag face down. Then the wind shifts and the stench hits him. "What is that smell?" The smell is followed by the shock of understanding. "Oh my God! He's dead!"

Richard starts sputtering. "It was an overdose! His own fault. Not the flu. I'm sure of it. He only died this morning."

Daniel is incredulous. "But why... Why didn't you tell anyone?" He pauses. "You don't want Leon to know."

Red-handed in the cookie jar. "No, no, no. Not true. I just didn't want to panic anyone."

Daniel yells now. "Your best friend is dead in your tent, has been dead for hours, and you didn't want to *panic* anyone?" An audible gasp emerges from the trees. Claire stands with her mouth open. They all freeze for a second before Claire turns and runs back to the farmhouse.

"I just realized he was dead. Just a few minutes ago," says Richard.

"But you just said he died this morning."

"Oh right, well, I didn't want to panic anyone." That was the thing about Richard. He never gave up. Never technically knew when the game was up. And maybe for Richard, that was why the game never was up.

"So you're lying? Fuck, whatever, Richard. What makes you so sure it was an overdose?"

"He just kept taking pill after pill. I couldn't stop him." Richard seems earnest this time.

Richard's words are drowned out by gunfire that pierces the air near the sick camp. Daniel turns to look. Ramona is gone.

Daniel whirls back to Richard. "What the fuck is going on?"

Richard pulls a gun out of his pants and heads across the clearing. Daniel realizes that like a bloody fool, he's unarmed. He follows Richard at a trot.

"Sorry. Nobody was dealing with the sick camp problem. It's nothing personal against them, we just can't take the risk that some of the bleeding hearts would take it upon themselves to be charitable. It's just too risky."

"So you're going to exterminate them?"

"Oh, little brother Daniel. Always thinking the worst of me. You're welcome to join us at any time." Richard gets on a horse that had been hidden in the bushes. Shadowfax. Daniel's horse.

"Stop. Please. Wait!" Daniel yells.

But Richard is gone, riding off on Daniel's horse, in Daniel's hat, leaving Daniel speaking to the clearing. More shots join the first one. Daniel starts running. Running as fast as he can back to the farm, his heart pounding, his breath coming in labored gasps.

CHAPTER 25

THE TOWER

━━∞∞∞━━

The Tower is the card of sudden change, chaos, and crisis. It is about changes in fortune, and sudden releases in energy, anger, or truth.

Natalie is in the sick camp in a facemask and gloves—ladling out the soup that Anneke thrust at her before she left the farmhouse—when the first gunshots shatter the still. She's already collected the blood samples and set them in the woods, and Paul has come to retrieve them. Her heart starts to jerk around painfully in her chest. They're too late. Leon has already started. She couldn't find Daniel or Andrew to say goodbye before she headed into the camp.

Shadowy figures with guns now stand in the clearing west of the wagons.

The sick women grab children and huddle behind the wagons, too weak to scream, and the two remaining men snatch up crossbows.

Leon emerges from the shadows of the clearing on horseback, pointing his gun directly at them. Brent and Terrence follow with drawn guns. They make certain to keep their distance.

"What the hell are you doing?" she yells.

"Dealing with a problem," Leon says evenly. "Protecting my wife and kids. We don't owe these people anything. They've put us in danger, coming here with their germs."

"But Leon, it might not even be influenza. We're testing for malaria. That's why I'm here."

"Malaria sounds just as bad as the flu."

"But it's treatable."

"Oh yeah. That's why everyone in Africa was dying from it before the peak. We don't need some darkie disease around here," says Leon.

Natalie raises pleading eyes to Brent and Terrence, but they won't even look at her.

Leon lifts his head to the assembled group. "All right everybody. We're done being sentimental little soup dispensers. You have five minutes to pack up and get the hell out. Please go *that* direction." Leon points southwest, the direction of the old country road that leads away from the farm. "Come back and you're dead on sight. Stay behind and you'll get to see what it feels like to be a marshmallow." Natalie catches the faint whiff of gasoline.

Leon flicks his reins as if he's about to head off.

"Wait! Please don't do this. You'll burn the farm. And what about me?" Natalie says.

Leon cocks his head. "This seems like the right place for a traitor who can't keep her legs together. I'm sure your poor husband would approve. Just to be clear, almost nobody is on your side here, not your husband…" Natalie sees another horse gallop up to join the others in the woods. The hat cuts a swath against the trees, and the silver horse is unmistakably Shadowfax. *Daniel.* Leon gives a jubilant crow. "…and not your lover," he says, then disappears back into the gloom, Brent and Terrence behind him.

What is Daniel doing with Leon? Her heart feels like it might rupture. Daniel would never do something like this…or would he? Especially if he knew she was here. But perhaps he doesn't know.

She can't make out the other figures in the woods. Some remain in the clearing on horses, while others seem to be skirting the perimeter of the camp, pouring gasoline. The sick people have already started loading their wagon and hitching up their horses.

Natalie can't stop trembling.

ANDREW HEARS THE SHOOTING. SHIT. He's still in the hayloft. He'd intended to climb out to safety, to alert someone. To tell them he's dying. But his limbs won't move. The smell of his own vomit envelops him, the sticky chunky coolness of it against his cheek. He braces as his stomach turns inside out again. More shots are fired.

Maybe they're all going to die. He hardly knows if he cares.

———

DANIEL ALMOST TRIPS OVER CLAIRE, huddled behind a roll of hay in the field, weeping uncontrollably. Mitch pulls to a dead stop when Daniel does, waiting, his ears pricked for an instruction.

"Come on, we've got to go. I've got to get back to the farm. You can't stay here."

"But Alfie's dead, and the shooting and—"

Daniel grabs her by the arm and hauls her to her feet. She's heavier than she looks—or maybe he's weaker. "I know, we can talk about it later. We have to get back to the farm."

"But Alfie and my baby."

"Claire, you don't have a baby. Get on your goddamn feet."

"Richard promised he would help me."

"Did you have something to do with this, Claire?" She doesn't reply. Daniel digs his fingers into her arm. "Just so you know, Alfie had a vasectomy years ago. He joked about it all the time with Richard, and Richard told me. I told him he should tell you, but I guess he didn't. My brother lies, Claire. Lies to get what he wants. And if there's any other part of this plan that you know of, you had better spill it now while we get our asses back to the farm. Now move."

Daniel's breath is coming in wheezes and chokes by the time he reaches the barn. Claire has gone mute except for frequent moans. Droplets of sweat run down Daniel's face. He pushes Claire into the barn office.

"Stay there and don't do anything stupid."

He saddles up Sherlock with shaking hands. His left arm seems inexplicably heavy and useless. His breathing evens. He'll be fine. He's always fine. He mounts up and heads toward the sick camp, circling around wide to come in from the other side. The soft thud of Sherlock's hooves in the muddy field rings in Daniel's ears. His heart hurts in a way that it never has before. Kind of like it's in a vice grip. The cool air pricks against the sweat on his skin. He has no real plan. He needed the horse because he wouldn't have been able to make it to the camp on foot. And Richard is on horseback—on Daniel's horse, who's probably terrified. He should find Natalie. But he doesn't have time.

He sees Joe, Anneke, Paul, Scott, and the rest of Joe's men milling around to the southeast, uncertain what to do. He wonders if that means everyone else is with Leon, or hiding out in their cabins. Where are Natalie, Andrew, and Justin? Daniel veers to the north, Mitch a streak of white and black ahead of him. There's a goat trail through the trees that will get him to the sick camp faster. Here he is, the apolitical hermit, riding right into the middle of a total shit show where he'll probably get himself killed. He'll tell Richard and Leon that he's joining them. Leon will believe him.

DANIEL NAVIGATES BY THE LIGHT of the torches. He can hear cries from the children in the sick camp. Leon, Brent, Bob, Terrence, and Kristen sit on their horses in a circle in a clearing just west of the camp. Richard is still on Shadowfax. Daniel notes that everyone has given Richard a rather wide berth. Flames jump from the wooden torches in Brent's and Bob's hands.

"This isn't right," Kristen says. "They're children. We can't do this."

"Go back to the farmhouse, Krissie," Leon says. "This is a man's job. We'll take care of this. They're dying anyway. We can't help them. All they're going to do is infect us."

Richard's voice is uncertain. "I think we should just stick with Plan A."

"We should just burn the camp," Leon says.

"Where is everyone else, anyway?" Richard says. "I thought you said most people were on our side. I wanted to talk to everyone."

"Everyone that's important is here."

Daniel digs his heels into Sherlock's side to guide the horse into the clearing. His heart feels like it's being shoved into a box about half its size, and it hammers in rage against the sides. His eyesight seems wonky, cloudy, but maybe a mist has fallen.

He's almost to the group when gunshots cut through the night from the trees east of the sick camp, behind the wagon. Daniel looks back in alarm; is it one of the sick people, someone from the farm, or part of Leon's plan?

Fingers go automatically to triggers, and shots ring out from Leon and Richard and the rest of them, pelting the camp with bullets. They're too far away for clean shots with handguns though, and the men kick into their horses to close in on the camp, or at least as close as they're willing to get. Daniel sees the red circle on Shadowfax's rump as Richard wheels the horse around and Shadowfax tries to launch into a gallop.

Shadowfax veers directly into the middle of the camp—and then crumples beneath Richard, toppling him, Richard's mouth stretched wide open in shock.

Sherlock, already in motion and startled by the gunfire, jolts forward, and Daniel finds himself in the middle of the camp next to the fallen Shadowfax before he even knows what's happening. He has a vague thought that surely his own brother, father, and sister won't shoot him. The nausea and pain are overtaking him though, and the sweat dripping into his eyes blinds him. Daniel has the feeling of falling. Has he been shot? But his foot is caught in the stirrup and he's being dragged.

He can hear Joe yelling behind him. "Stop shooting! Please! They have malaria, not influenza! It's not contagious, you idiots! Everybody stop shooting!" Daniel's head is being pulled along the ground at a reckless pace. Dark shapes careen past his skull. Mitch barks.

Then his father. "Oh my God, it's Daniel!"

Then silence, and darkness, like he's sinking and waves are washing up and over him.

———— ⟨✦⟩ ————

RICHARD SEES HIS BROTHER CRUMPLE. He tries to disentangle himself from Shadowfax. His foot is twisted under the horse's rump, and waves of pain travel up his leg. His ankle feels broken. Shots still come from the east, from behind the wagon, but they fly high and wide. Terrence and Leon return fire cautiously from the west, trying to fire over Daniel and hit the wagons. Joe yells like a lunatic from the woods that it's malaria. They have to stop firing. They might hit Daniel.

Richard wrenches his foot out from under Shadowfax. The horse shudders now, dying. Blood coats Richard's leg. Horse blood. The agony in his foot is searing.

"Go around and stop the shooter. Stop the shooter! Get control, you ass-hole!" Richard yells at Joe. Joe stares at him, then turns and hobble away. The bullets fly over Richard's head from both the east and west as he crawls over to Daniel's fallen form. Leon and Terrence continue to cautiously return fire. Richard hopes to God they have the sense not to hit *him*. Daniel lies on the ground, one leg extended from being pulled by the horse. Richard scans his brother's body for blood, for a bullet wound, but finds nothing. Daniel's lips are gray. Shit. It's Daniel's heart. He doesn't even know how to apply chest compressions. Doesn't know the first thing about pulmonary resuscitation—he'd always meant to learn, of course, but there was never time—and now there's no ambulance to call. He looks at Terrence and Leon. They don't know anything either. Mike had tried to teach them once, but they had joked that it was unnecessary because Mike never left the farm. And now dumb Leon let Mike leave the farm.

He turns to the people in front of the wagon. "If one of you knows CPR, help me. Help me, and we'll help you. He has a heart condition." They stare back at him and then turn to speak among themselves. Heads shake. "Please. Help him, and we'll help you, I swear," Richard says. "We'll stop this. If you have malaria, we can help you. We have the drugs." Nobody moves. Heads press together in discussion. "Please," Richard repeats. Then louder, "If you *don't* help me, we *won't* help you."

A gaunt, filthy blond woman detaches herself from the group and crawls over to Richard. She pushes Richard aside—a little harder than required, Richard thinks. "You," she says to Richard, "shield them from the bullets, and get your people to stop shooting or I stop." She places her palm on Daniel's chest, and two of her fingers against his wrist.

You've got to be kidding is Richard's first reaction. But he grits his teeth and drags his body so it's between the people by the wagon and Leon and his dad and everyone else, like a big sitting duck waiting to be shot. His dad and Leon won't shoot him, not on purpose anyway. His vision seems to be tunneling, and Richard wonders if he's going to pass out. Joe better hurry, and whoever it is behind the wagon better continue to be a shitty shot. The woman still isn't applying chest compressions, and leans in to press her cheek against Daniel's mouth. Richard can almost see the cloud of germs spilling from her mouth.

"Wait! No," Richard says. "You might be contagious. He needs chest compressions."

The woman looks at him. "Do you want me to do this or not?"

Malaria, Richard reminds himself. He just hopes Joe knows what the hell he's talking about and it's not some bureaucratic fuck-up. But Natalie's got to be behind it, and Natalie doesn't make mistakes. "Just do it," Richard says.

She leans back in. "His heart is still beating. He doesn't need compressions yet. Does he have aspirin?"

Richard grinds his teeth together. Terrence, Leon, and Bob are still shooting, and nobody has come to help. "In his inside jacket pocket," he says.

⸎

NATALIE CRAWLS THROUGH THE LOW-LYING burned-out remnants of the bushes that used to occupy this part of the woods, cringing with every gunshot. She started moving toward the shooter behind the wagon as soon as she heard Joe claim that the sickness was malaria. She hears Joe yelling for them to stop shooting, and then nothing but the echo of gunfire.

The rifle fire is almost on top of her now, and Natalie risks looking up. Claire stands in the trees holding a rifle with two hands. She can barely manage the recoil and her shots are going high.

"Stop. Get down! What are you doing?" Natalie says. Claire eyes are unfocused like she's in a dissociative state.

"Richard lied to me," Claire says.

Natalie feels like her brain might explode. "Get down and stop shooting, or you're going to get shot and be responsible for the deaths of half the people on this farm."

Claire drops to her knees and starts to cry. Natalie snatches away the rifle. Ranjeet crashes through the bushes, followed by Joe, struggling on his crutches. Both of them are crouched low.

"Is it really malaria?" Natalie says.

"It really is," Joe says. "Paul was just coming to get you."

"We've got to stop them before they kill everyone," Natalie says. "Can you get her back to the farmhouse?"

"You take her. I'll stop them. Daniel's hurt," Joe says. The gunfire west of them has slowed now that there are no longer any return shots from this side of the wagon.

"Daniel's hurt?" Natalie's palms start to sweat and the panic seeps through her limbs. "How badly?"

"I don't know. He fell off his horse. He must have gotten shot, but I didn't see him get hit."

"No," Natalie says. "It's his heart." In her mind, she can already see Daniel lying on the ground. Unresponsive. Fragile. "Get the stretcher. I'll take Ranjeet."

———

THE SHOTS EAST OF THE wagon seem to have stopped. Richard sees Leon looking at him, aiming his gun low, and pointing at the people in front of the wagons with his other hand. He's asking whether he should start shooting the people in front of the wagons, Richard realizes—make it look like an accident. Richard shakes his head violently *no*. Richard tries to rise. Perhaps he could carry Daniel to the infirmary, but his foot is useless beneath him. The pain makes him want to vomit. It must be broken. Daniel moves his head to the side and looks like he's trying to talk, but his words are slurred and low.

"Get help!" Richard yells at Leon and Terrence. The two men start approaching, but then begin arguing with Kristen and Brent about the need for a rear guard. Richard waves violently at his father.

———

NATALIE WEAVES THROUGH THE TREES with Ranjeet behind her, the light cast by Brent's and Bob's torches pulling her through the darkened trunks, the scent of gasoline heavy in the air. Daniel and Richard lie in the middle of the clearing. A tiny, ratty blond woman sits beside Daniel's prone form, her fingers on his pulse. A huddle of white and black lies near him. Mitch. Sherlock pokes his head out of the trees not far beyond them. Leon and Terrence make their way toward Daniel and Richard in some sort of militia formation, crouched low with their rifles trained on the sick camp. The sick people cower by the wagons. Natalie feels as though the ground is falling beneath her.

Richard stares at his foot, his face the color of fresh snow. Daniel's hat lies on the ground between them, and Shadowfax lies crumpled to Richard's left, a stain of red covering his beautiful white coat. Even in her haste to get to Daniel, Natalie scans automatically for Andrew, but sees no sign of him. She tries to contain her shaking. He might be fine, she reminds herself, but where the hell is he?

Leon and Terrence jerk their rifles in her direction when she enters the clearing, but resume their advance on the camp when they see it's her.

"It was Claire, you idiots. Shooting. There's nobody else. Just stop," she yells.

The relieved expression on Richard's face when he sees her is heartbreaking. She dares not look at him. She sinks to the ground next to Daniel. His eyelids flutter, and words with elongated guttural vowels and missing consonants emerge in a slur from his mouth.

"Daniel, it's me. Natalie. What's happening?"

Daniel tries another unintelligible sentence, then shakes his head and lets his eyes drift closed again. Leon and Terrence stop several feet away and stand there as if the whole lot of them have the bubonic plague.

Natalie drags her emotions under control and looks at the woman. "What happened?"

"His pulse is slightly elevated. I'm not sure if he's having a heart attack, or he knocked his head on a rock, or both," the woman says. "Or, it could be a stroke."

Natalie closes her eyes. She wants to scream her fury and fear into the night. She grinds her teeth together in determination. "No," she says to herself. "No," she repeats. "Why are you just sitting there?" Natalie says over her shoulder to Richard. "You should have sent someone to get Justin! Where's Andrew? We need to get Daniel to the infirmary and find Andrew."

"We gave him aspirin. I have no idea where Andrew is." Richard is silent for a few seconds, then addresses her in a voice she's never heard from him before. "Natalie, I need help."

Natalie turns just in time to see Richard's eyes roll into the back of his head, and then he crumples. A stream of blood oozes from a hole in his boot, a bullet-sized hole.

"Leon! Terrence! Help!" Natalie screams.

Leon scuttles over, looking askance. "I sent Bob for the stretcher," he says. "How do we know we're not all going to be infected? We should have burned this camp hours ago."

"Richard's shot. Help me get his boot off," Natalie says.

340 | JENNIFER ELLIS

Leon looks at her and then at Richard, and tightens his lips into a ragged crack. Then he kneels to wrench at Richard's boot, keeping his nose and mouth turned as far away from them as possible, while Richard lets out semi-conscious moans. Natalie applies pressure to Richard's foot, but the blood quickly seeps through and turns her handkerchief crimson.

The woman snatches at Leon's sleeve. "He promised he'd help us. He better keep that deal." Leon flinches away from her.

"We will," Natalie says. "We have malaria drugs." She looks wildly around for the stretcher, for Andrew, for anything.

Finally, Ranjeet and Bob crash through the underbrush with the stretcher. Joe trails behind them. They lay the stretcher beside Daniel to transfer him. Daniel's eyes open momentarily.

"Wait!" shouts Leon. "Take Richard."

"What?" says Bob.

"Take Richard. He's hurt worse."

"He is not," Natalie almost retorts. But stops. How can she choose between her husband and her lover? What was Daniel doing with Leon anyway? She can't let Daniel die, but she'll never forgive herself for letting Richard die. And nobody else will either.

Leon sees her hesitation, and she sees the judgment in his eyes, then she sees the sick people huddled in front of their wagon.

"The wagon," she says. "Put them both in the wagon. Drag it over to the farmhouse. Hurry. Come with us," she instructs the woman still standing beside them. "I'll get you the drugs if you help." The woman studies her and then nods.

Leon grabs her by the wrist and squeezes it tight. "You better be damn sure it's malaria," he says.

They move the sick people away from one of the covered wagons at gunpoint and heave the two unconscious men into it. Then Leon orders Bob to guard the sick camp, and they push the wagon through the woods and across the fields. Farm members join them as they approach the farmhouse, and the wagon picks up speed.

"Have you found Andrew yet?" Natalie asks Paul when they're halfway to the farmhouse.

"No."

"You need to put more men on it now. Please. We need to find him."

Paul drops his voice to a whisper. "Don't they need to be taken into custody of some sort?" He gestures at Leon, Terrence, and Kristen.

"Later," Natalie hisses. "You need to find my son. Take Joe and Ranjeet. Please."

Paul pauses for a few seconds, assessing, and then he runs off.

Olivia goes tight-lipped and grayish when she sees her sons side by side in the wagon. Hands grasp the two men and haul them into the farmhouse, through the maze of hallways, to the infirmary.

Justin stands in the infirmary with the defibrillator paddles ready, a syringe of medication laid out on a tray, and an IV bag hanging from a pole with a drip chamber and tubing already attached. But his eyes almost glaze when he sees the body of not just his uncle, but also his father. The two men are deposited in the hospital beds, and bodies scurry out of the infirmary, leaving just Natalie, Justin, Leon, Terrence, Olivia, and the woman from the sick camp.

Justin looks from Daniel to Richard.

"Treat Richard first," Leon says. Justin looks to Natalie.

The room seems to be rising and falling in waves, taking Natalie's stomach with it. She can't ask her son to treat his father last, and she can't ask him to choose. Daniel's still got a heartbeat. He might make it. She nods.

A flurry of activity jump-starts around Richard. Justin starts an IV, while Terrence dabs Celox on the bullet wound and Leon elevates Richard's feet.

Olivia grabs Natalie's arm. "We have to help Daniel. What can we do? It's his heart, right?" Her gray hair is wild and scattered, and she has a pincer hold on Natalie's arm.

"I don't know. He hit his head." Daniel rolls over and his eyes open a crack, squinting against the light.

"Daniel!" Natalie says. "Is it your head or your heart?" She's almost yelling at him.

His words lurch together. "I don't know." And then a faint "both." She snatches up a stethoscope and presses it against his chest. His heart rate seems too fast, too uneven, but with all the noise in the room she can't tell. She turns to watch Justin hook the heart monitor to Richard, who's pasty-faced but conscious. The heart monitor will draw power. The power that might be needed for the defibrillator. Her eyes fall on the syringe of medication on the tray.

She yells above the din of voices. "Justin, Daniel's heart rate is elevated! Should we give this to him?"

The monitor belts out Richard's heartbeat. Justin looks up, flustered. Leon is thrusting his arm at Justin, insisting on a transfusion for Richard. "I don't know. It's adenosine. It's all we have." Leon jabs his arm at Justin again, and Justin returns his attention to Richard. He pushes his uncle aside. "Stop. He doesn't need a transfusion. Not yet. Let's cauterize the wound, let the IV work, and see if his pressure comes up."

Natalie turns to the blond woman. "Can you inject it?"

"I want the malaria medication first."

"In the medicine cabinet, bottom drawer. There's ten bottles. You can take four. But please stay. He might need chest compressions."

The woman squints her eyes at Natalie. "I have a five-year-old daughter back at the camp. She needs medication now. I'll give him the medication, but don't ask me to stay."

Daniel's face is now a light pewter. Natalie's hands vibrate with fear. "Just do it then," Natalie says. "Give him whatever's in that syringe. Then take the drugs and go."

The woman injects the medication.

"Please, please, please," Natalie prays. "Please stay with me." And please someone find Andrew, she thinks.

The woman opens the medicine cabinet and pulls out four bottles of artemisinin, reads the labels quickly, looks at Natalie one last time, then slinks out of the room. Back to her people. Back to her child. Natalie has to get to her own child. She hears a commotion out on the porch, the clamor of footsteps in the kitchen. She hopes nobody's stopping the woman from leaving.

She focuses on the thump of Daniel's heart. *Thump, thump, thump.* It's slowed a bit. It just needs to keep beating till Justin finishes with Richard. Maybe just a few more minutes. Then she has to go and find Andrew. *Thump, thump, thump.* Natalie own breathing is shallow. Daniel's heart just needs to keep beating. Richard has joined the argument over whether he needs a transfusion or not.

Fingertips graze her upper arm. Daniel.

She's about to say his name. Then the stethoscope goes silent.

CHAPTER 26

THE LOVERS

—⟨∞⟩—

It is time to make a choice.

There is a sudden blinding, cracking jolt. Daniel fights his way up through the water. His breath comes in short, painful jabs. Voices. He can hear voices. Maybe he's dead.

Mike's voice. "Idiot, idiot, idiot! Don't you fucking die on me, you fucking idiot. How many times have I told you not to run? I don't have enough for another charge. You better fucking live."

"Is he okay?" His mother's voice.

"Shush. I'm trying to listen," Mike says, and then a pause. Something cold moves around on Daniel's chest. And then a jubilant, "I have a heartbeat!"

Daniel's eyes flutter open. He's in the infirmary, with IVs attached to both of his arms. Three faces hover over him. Mike, Natalie, and his mother. People cluster around the patient in the bed next to him, and Daniel can see the back of Justin's white blond head.

"What…" he says, his mouth like a dried corn husk.

"Don't you dare try to talk," Mike orders, continuing to move the stethoscope around on Daniel's chest. "Nat, go, find Andrew. I've got him now." Natalie races from the room.

"Natalie…" he begins again.

Mike glares. "I told you not to talk." Mike studies the heart rhythm on the monitor and cranks the sound up.

Daniel raises a feeble finger toward Mike. "How…"

"I got back just in time to save your sorry ass," Mike says.

"The sick people…" His chest feels tight, and it's still difficult to breathe.

"Stop talking. I need to get your pressure and do a neurological exam. Then I have to go help with Richard."

Daniel closes his eyes. He feels encased in pain. A series of images flows across his vision. Andrew with Claire. Claire and Andrew. He opens his eyes once more. It takes significant effort. "Claire knows," he murmurs, "where Andrew goes." And then he closes them again.

⁂

NATALIE SCRABBLES THROUGH THE HAYLOFT, clambering over bales and slipping on shiny loose pieces of creamy hay. Paul and Ranjeet stumble after her. She reaches the dark, cool wall of the back of the barn and turns left. A wall of hay bales greets her, but Paul and Ranjeet move in and haul them out of the way. Andrew lies in a small crevice between the barn wall and the stacks of hay, chalky and covered in vomit. His eyes are slitty, and he burbles something about gunfire as Paul and Ranjeet lower him down the ladder. But seeing him breathing, no matter how shallowly, is a profound relief after all the possible outcomes Natalie had imagined.

It's got to be malaria. They have the drugs. He'll be okay. She repeats this over and over to herself as Paul and Ranjeet carry him to the infirmary. Two fires burn at the sick camp, and Bob has moved around so that he sits between the camp and the farm. Most of the other farm members have drifted away, ostensibly to snatch a few hours of sleep.

In the infirmary, Natalie's eyes flick to Daniel. He still lies on the far bed, his eyes closed. But his chest rises and falls. Olivia sits next to him, but she stands when she sees Natalie, and goes into the office. Natalie tries not to imagine that she sees accusation on Olivia's face. What was Daniel doing helping Leon? Mike rushes to the door to place his fingers on Andrew's pulse and gestures at the third infirmary bed wedged against Daniel's. Justin races around, sterilizing instruments and checking the solar surgery lights.

Joe and Ranjeet deposit Andrew in the bed. He rolls over and bats at the light, muttering something incomprehensible. "Where's Richard?" Natalie says to Kristen. Leon and Terrence are also absent, Natalie notes.

"In the office, waiting for his surgery. He could really use some support from his wife."

"I can't leave Andrew."

Kristen narrows her eyes and marches through the door that leads to the office. Mike already has his stethoscope pressed against Andrew's chest.

"I'm going to start an IV and the malaria drugs right away," Mike says. "Then Justin and I need to grab a couple hours of sleep before we operate on Richard's foot. Andrew will be okay, Nat. We found him in time, I think."

"You think?"

"No. I'm sure. I've got him. Don't worry."

"How did you get here? Where are Solomon and Cyrus?"

Mike shakes his head. "I don't know. Earl shut down the field hospital as soon as he got word of the flu pandemic. We were only four hours into surgeries. He paid me for the work I did, as well as Daniel's work from the day before, and I headed for home as fast as Spock could drag the wagon. Solomon and Cyrus will come back when they see the hospital has been abandoned. Liz didn't make it. I'm sorry. She lost too much blood before she got to Jerry." His eyes are tired; he barely suppresses a yawn. "Do you think you can hold down the fort here while Justin and I sleep? I've been up for more than forty-eight hours now. And please go see Richard. He's supposed to be sleeping in the office. I don't know if it's the morphine because morphine doesn't usually cause significant cognitive impairment, but he seems agitated."

"What about Daniel?"

"I'm watching him. He's stable. I'm just going to be in the den. Call me immediately if anything happens. And Nat, you should know, Alan was shot from behind. Justin suspected and had me check it out. I don't know who shot him, but given what Justin told me about what happened that night, it couldn't have been Richard and Alfie." Natalie tries to process this. The shots east of her and Joe. Andrew and Leon had been hiding in the bushes there. *Leon.* The missing lumber, the missing potatoes. Leon hoarding.

And then she's alone, with Daniel. She makes her way over to the side of his bed and sinks into the chair that Olivia vacated. She takes his hand, and

346 | JENNIFER ELLIS

his fingers curl automatically around hers. His eyelids flutter.

"How do you feel?" she says.

"Okay." Then he appears to realize where he is, and his hand loosens on hers. He pulls his hands together and folds them over his chest. She feels a faint shock.

"I was so worried about you."

"I'm fine."

"What were you doing with Leon?"

Daniel looks away, his jaw tight. "Do you really need to ask that?" The defensive tone in his voice jars her.

"No. I don't know. I'm sorry. I just wanted to know what you were doing. Why are you acting so strangely?"

"I'm not. You should go and be with Richard."

Natalie feels the drop of her heart. "What do you mean?"

"He's your husband. He needs you."

"What about you?" She barely dares to breathe the words.

"This thing between us, Natalie. It was a mistake. I don't think I love you. I just wanted you. Go be with Richard. We can't be together." Daniel turns away from her and stares at the infirmary ceiling.

Natalie realizes her whole body is shuddering. "You can't mean that."

"Please, Natalie, just go. Leon isn't always all wrong, you know."

Natalie draws herself up, and her features go rigid in an effort not to weep. "Yes, he is." Hurt shapes itself around every one of her words.

The door to the office opens then, and Kristen stands there, imperious as always. "Richard is asking for you," Kristen says. "I'll watch Daniel."

Natalie stumbles through the door into Mike's office, her heart throbbing and leaden. Richard lies on the couch, his foot wrapped in yards of gauze and elevated on cushions. Olivia hovers over him.

"Oh, look. It's my wife." Richard wears a bright smile and speaks too loudly, his pupils tiny pinpricks. "Come here, wife, and sit next to me." Richard pats the two inches of couch next to his torso. Natalie tries not to flinch away.

"There's not really room, Richard."

"For your skinny little ass? There's lots of room." He pats the couch again, and she relents. She perches precariously on the edge, trying not to touch him. "So. Leon and I were just talking about you." Richard catches her wrist and squeezes it as he speaks.

"How so?"

"Oh, just your tenacity. You don't let things go." Richard flutters his knuckles in the air as if he's about to give her a noogie. "Kind of like a pit bull."

"I see," she says. Danger signs pulse all around her. Richard's too-jovial demeanor, Olivia's pinched lips.

The words come involuntarily, and she clenches her fists. "I can't believe you and Daniel helped Leon tonight." She emits a faint sob.

Richard immediately switches to a more earnest expression. "I swear I didn't know what Leon was planning. I was trying to stop them. There's no way I would have torched that camp. I just wanted out of goddamn quarantine." He pats her leg. "Good catch on the malaria, by the way. That's my wife, always such a smarty-pants. I really could use someone like you on my staff. As for Daniel, I don't know why you would have expected any different. He's always been a follower, and when he gets scared, he always looks to save his own ass. He may claim otherwise, but when the chips are down, he folds like a cheap suit." Natalie wishes Richard didn't always have to speak in mixed metaphors. She's not sure he even knows what he's saying sometimes.

"Anyway, I was thinking maybe you need to get away for a while. Why don't you and the boys come and live in Vancouver with me? It'll be a nice change of scene. Vancouver's not so bad. A bit lawless, but no worse than here. I have a nice house and food allowance. You could relax a bit. You've been working too hard. I think I could be Premier in a few years. Really. We can leave Leon in charge here. The boys need to go to university and get off this godforsaken farm. We'll wait for the pandemic to be over first, of course." Richard delivers all of this with a wide-eyed expression that borders on excitement. His cornflower blue eyes, made even more electric by the narcotics, look as youthful and earnest as they had on the autumn day when they first met.

Natalie shakes her head in confusion. Richard has gone from seeming mildly angry to wanting her to come to Vancouver with him. Does he not think she's been sleeping with Daniel, or does he not care? Is this an olive branch, or a trap, or both?

"I don't know what to say." She finds herself almost smiling at him, her relief at having him look at her this way, not hating her, is so profound.

"You should say yes," Olivia puts in.

Natalie considers what *yes* would mean. Could they go back to the way things were a long time ago, when they had a clean slate and no guilt? Loving Daniel has haunted her for so many years. She has retold the early history of Richard and her relationship in her mind so many times that she's no longer sure which version is more revisionist than the other. Were they happy? Did she love him? Did her body yearn for his then the way it does now for Daniel's? She no longer has any sense of the facts. The only small, tenuous truth that keeps clawing its way back into her mind is Daniel.

Daniel with the half-assed gimpy heart. Daniel the hermit. Daniel the vet. Daniel, Richard's twin. Daniel, her lover.

Daniel, who helped Leon and told her he wants nothing to do with her.

The room has fallen silent. But Richard still looks excited at his proposal. How can she hurt Richard yet again by saying no?

Give up the beliefs that are no longer serving you, Liz said. Follow your intuition. Her intuition is shot all to hell. Richard would be the safe path, the comfortable path. Maybe. Daniel doesn't want her, doesn't love her enough to fight for her. Or perhaps doesn't love her at all.

A triangle is the strongest shape. Or is it her fault? Is it that she's tried to have them both?

Which one of them is Vega in the Summer Triangle, the star around which the others appear to rotate? Maybe it's Richard. Maybe it has always been Richard. And she and Daniel just follow along and play their parts. Maybe that's the way the heavens want it to be. She opens her lips to say yes to Richard. Yes, she will come to Vancouver. Olivia and Richard already smile with the expected answer.

There's a knock at the office door. Joanne pokes her head in. "You better come. Paul, Joe, and Anneke have decided to take Leon, Terrence, Brent, and Bob into custody. It's not going well. We've moved all the kids back into the cellar again. The sick people have left. I guess they didn't want the kind of help we dispense anymore."

Natalie rises while Richard sputters, "Idiots. Can't anyone manage on their own around here? Does everyone always have to be getting their knickers in a knot? Tell them to cool their jets, we'll deal with this in the morning. At least the flu problem is dealt with."

"It was malaria, remember?" Natalie says. Richard has a habit of getting these kinds of important details wrong. It occurs to Natalie that, like Mike, she hasn't slept in the last forty-eight hours. She presses her fingers between her eyebrows and follows Joanne out to the porch.

"Leon and Terrence went out to see that the sick camp had all cleared out. And that's when Joe, Paul, and Anneke moved in on them. Joe's got his men helping. Bob and Ramona were already out there, as was Brent. Paul had this idea they could do it peacefully, but I don't know what he was thinking."

The mountains hint at the edges of morning when Natalie crosses the field, and a few birds offer hesitant trills, but the woods are still sheathed in shadows, and only the light of two torches cuts through the indigo air.

Leon, Terrence, Bob, and Brent stand with their guns drawn facing Joe, Paul, Anneke, Ranjeet, Hans, and another of Joe's men. Joe leans heavily on his crutches. Scott and Karl stand away from the two groups, clearly unattached to either side. Torches in Bob's and Brent's hands cast trembling orange light onto faces dirtied from soot and blood. Everyone looks feral and half-insane from exhaustion, and the cloying smell of gasoline still cuts through the pungent earth of the forest.

"You can see that this is not going to end well," Paul says. "Why don't we just agree to all put down our guns."

"What, so we can hand over our farm to a bunch of newcomers? People *she* brought here!" Leon extends a long finger at Natalie.

"No, we're not handing the farm over to anyone. We're just going to go in and have a talk." Paul's glasses form an eerie mask in the darkness, and he holds one hand palm to the ground, as if he can soothe Leon the same way he calmed congregations before the peak.

"Talk, talk, talk. That's all we do around here." Leon flaps his hand in the air, miming someone talking. "The problem is solved. Thanks to us. Terrence, Bob, Brent, and I here were just going to do a final clean-up. I see no reason to talk."

"You'll incinerate the farm, you fools," Anneke says.

"How much time have you spent out in the bush, little miss prissy? This forest has already burned. There ain't no fuel left to catch. That's why we need the gasoline, to clear up the camp area."

"If there was gasoline, it should have been reported to Farm Council. It could have been put to far better use," Paul says.

Leon snatches one of the torches from Bob. "Farm Council this. Farm Council that. I'm sick of Farm Council. We need to just start dealing with problems."

"We have a democratic process on this farm, and if you don't like it, you can leave," Paul says.

"Or, we can do things *our* way," Leon says cheerfully. Too cheerfully.

"Please. We don't want anyone else to get hurt here tonight," Paul says.

"Then you should have just let us carry out our business."

"So you can run the farm like a bunch of fecking vigilantes?" Anneke quivers with rage.

"Why not? Seems like that's what other folks do. Every time we turn around, that one's inviting more mouths to feed." Leon jerks his head at Natalie. "Now it's a pair of ratty orphans. Probably carrying the plague, and who knows what the two of them will teach our children. Don't think we'll be standing for that. Now move along, leave us to our business. Nobody is taking nobody into custody."

Natalie looks at Paul, Joe, and Anneke. Shitty shots, all of them. She doesn't know about Joe's men. But she's not liking the odds.

"I need to talk to Leon, alone," she says. "Everyone else should just calm down and go back to their rooms."

Leon cracks a smile. "And why would I be interested in that? I can't be influenced the way you seem to think you can tow other men around, by the nose—or the cock."

"Because I have a few things to say to you that I think you'll be interested in hearing. It's about some missing wheat."

"Fine, then. Your folks leave first."

Natalie nods at Paul and Anneke, who squint their eyes at her.

"What are you doing? What missing wheat?" Paul says.

"I'm not sure, but we don't have any better options right now," she says.

Paul gives her a grim look like he doesn't totally appreciate her intervention. "If you're wrong, then they'll have a hostage," he says. But he and Anneke file away, followed by the others. Leon gives a nod to his men, and they clear out as well, leaving Natalie alone with Leon.

"So…what brings us together tonight, cute stuff? Karma? I'd sleep with you myself if you weren't such a slut. Missing wheat, you say? Someone should be hung," Leon says, fondling the trigger of his gun.

"I know you killed Alan."

Leon's gaze sharpens. "You don't know *anything*. You haven't got any proof, and even if it was my gun, you'd never be able to show it wasn't an accident. Everyone was shooting everyone."

"Not from behind. Not someone who suspected you of hoarding. Alan had no enemies around here. If word gets out you shot him in the back, you'll have no friends."

Leon lunges so close to her that she can see the seething of the torch flames in his pupils. The oil-dipped cloth wrapped around the end of the stick has almost burned through, and the torch is starting to spark more now that the flame has reached the wood. Natalie watches each spark fall.

"Are you blackmailing me?" he says. "What about word about your relationship with your husband's brother? How would Ms. Perfect look then? You want to see who'll end up with no friends?"

"Step down as Farm Council Chair," Natalie says firmly. "Turn yourself in for your actions tonight, return the food over the next few weeks, and we won't go through your cabin with a crowbar."

"You still seem to think you're calling the shots, honey. All it would take is a couple of words to Richard and you'd find yourself out in the cold."

"Maybe, Leon. But you know damn well we'll be out in the cold together, and I don't think we'd make good campmates."

Leon starts to back away from her slowly, his face twisted in a strange smile. It takes Natalie a few seconds to realize what he's doing.

"I don't think we'd make good campmates either. I hope you like the heat as much as you seem to be willing to brave the cold. Karma, baby. Karma." He smiles and then makes as if he's wincing.

"Ouch. The sparks are hurting my hands."

Leon dramatically throws his arm into the air as if he's been burned, drops the torch, and gallops with long strides away from her. The flames find the gasoline, and the dry, partially scorched grass ignites. Natalie swings around to run in the other direction, but the fire sails through the trail of gasoline, and she's quickly surrounded by a ring of fire, an ever-rising wall.

The flames rip across the grass, closing in on her with alarming speed, and she starts to scream, the hairs on her arms singing and the sparks catching in her hair. The heat sears her mind and she can do nothing but fall to her knees and cover her head with her arms. She'll be burned alive. She cowers, nearly sick with terror of the approaching pain. Perhaps this is her karmic end. She grieves for her motherless sons, the perfection of their still hopeful faces, warm cheeks, and easy love. She grieves for everything she has never said or done, and then the flames are upon her.

Through the fire she hears the rattle of a wagon and the pounding of hooves and suddenly she's being doused with powerful stream of water. It soaks her, but it puts out the fire around her, and after a few seconds she crawls out from underneath the shower. She looks up to find Anneke and Joe pumping Richard's crazy water-machine invention, Paul aiming the hose, and Joanne supporting a sagging Daniel at the reins.

Natalie kneels on the forest floor, drenched, and takes in the marvel of it.

Scott emerges from the darkness and places two curved fingers to his lips. Two curved fingers: the black dog, the sign from their childhood, stay out of the way. Natalie drops all the way to the ground; Ranjeet, Hans, and Scott point their guns at Leon, who hadn't quite been fast enough to escape his own ring of fire.

"Help me for God's sake, you idiots," Leon yells. Flames burn all around him. They haven't quite reached him yet, but he's trapped.

"Put down your gun first," Scott says.

"No fucking way."

"Do it," Scott says.

"Fuck you. You are *not* going to take me into custody," Leon yells through the flames.

"We can't wait. We have to help him," Paul says, flipping the handle on the hose to send a blast of water at Leon. Water shoots out of the hose, but Paul can't control the jerk, and it goes wide before he finally brings it under control. Before he can put out the blaze around Leon, Leon turns and vaults through the fire, his long lanky limbs carrying him high into the air. He almost makes it, but the flames catch on his pant cuff and fly up his loose trousers, and suddenly his clothes are entirely aflame.

"Get on the ground, man, and roll! Turn the hose toward him!" Scott yells. Paul tries to veer the hose in Leon's direction, but Leon runs howling in an erratic and wild circle for what seems like minutes, with everyone trying to close in on him to throw him to the ground and douse the flames. Finally he falls and Paul launches gallons of water on him.

Once the flames are out, the men approach cautiously, but it's quite obvious that there's nothing that can be done. They look away.

"I'm the one who invited the newcomers to the farm." Anneke says loudly to nobody and everybody.

Daniel has staggered from the seat of the wagon toward Natalie, and she travels the few feet to him and catches him in her arms. He falls forward into her, and they both fall to their knees, but his arms fold around her more tightly than she expects, and he buries his face in her shoulder. "Don't ever do that again," he says, and then as quickly as he was in her arms, he pulls away and leans against the wagon.

They take Leon's body to the shed and place it next to Alan's. Natalie and Joanne help Daniel back to the infirmary, with the assurance that Scott will unhitch and look after the horses. They pass Mike, Karl, Craig, and Patricia, who seem to have managed to take Bob, Brent, and Terrence into custody. Kristen has rushed, hysterical, to Leon's body, but everyone else walks around tight-lipped and mute. Has everyone become numb to loss, united in their permanent post-traumatic stress, or was Leon many people's ally, but nobody's friend? Leon's children will be traumatized of course, but right now, they're still down in the cellar, unaware. Natalie feels a thud of guilt and grief for a man who brought her nothing but trouble.

Daniel weaves as he walks, and seems completely spent. Natalie is terrified he'll have another heart attack. But when he reaches the infirmary, he settles back into the bed.

Richard is wild as a pack of feral hyenas that he had to remain in the infirmary during "the showdown," as he's calling it, having already heard reports from Justin regarding the events.

Other than Kristen, Richard seems to be the most upset by Leon's death, saying that he was a good old codger, and that nobody deserved to die that way. The thrill of farm drama plays around the edges of his pupils though, and Natalie can't tell if he's truly upset.

She just nods and murmurs apologetic words. She can't go with Richard to Vancouver. She can't be with Richard ever again. But she'll wait until after his surgery to tell him this. She may not be able to have Daniel. But she wants to live in the world of hopes again.

Mike opens the other door to the infirmary. "We're ready for you, Richard." Justin pushes a tray of sterilized instruments on a cart behind him.

"Can you give me a few minutes?" Richard says.

"The sooner we get that foot sewn up, the better," Mike says.

"Fine. Proceed," Richard says.

Mike moves over to help Richard to his feet. Richard wraps his arm around Mike's shoulder to hop to the infirmary. When he has his back turned to Natalie, she sees the slight indent in Richard's hair that encircles his head. She knows that indent. It's a hat indent, like the one Daniel always has. But Richard never wears a hat. Images juxtapose themselves in her mind. The man in the hat on Shadowfax in the dark. Sherlock in the woods. Richard cussing Sherlock for being jumpy and unreliable. Richard would never ride Sherlock. The hat indent.

Richard was wearing Daniel's hat last night, riding Shadowfax.

Daniel wasn't helping Leon. Why had she ever doubted him?

MIKE ASKS HER TO STAY in the infirmary during Richard's surgery. Richard had a paranoid out-of-body hallucination due to the ketamine anesthetic the last time Mike operated on him, and only Natalie had been able to talk him off the metaphorical ledge. Richard doesn't look at her. He seems strangely subdued, his face gray and turned in on itself, as Mike and Justin prep him.

Ranjeet wheels Andrew's and Daniel's beds into the office, where they'll stay during the surgery. Joanne has agreed to sit with them, and Daniel—after receiving a tongue-lashing from Mike for leaving his bed—seems to have fallen asleep anyway. Natalie watches the rise and fall of Andrew's and Daniel's chests, ever alert for any cessation of movement, of breathing; and then, satisfied that they might be okay for an hour, gently shuts the door to the office. Richard closes his eyes as the ketamine sinks into his veins.

When Richard is out, Mike's hands twist and arch instruments gracefully through the air around Richard's foot. Justin assists with careful attention, his blond hair pulled tight off his face, always ready with the right instrument, always following his uncle's movements with his eyes. Mike provides a blow-by-blow description of what he's doing as he goes. Natalie's heart aches with pride for her brother and this wondrous child of hers.

The surgery lights flicker and dim by the time Mike is almost finished suturing up Richard's foot. They have run down the farm's small supply of power. Natalie hopes there will be no more need for it tonight. Her eyes flick automatically to the office door. She rises and lights a few candles so they're not left in the dark when the lights go off. Even under the anesthetic, Richard's face seems constricted in a flinch of pain or irritation, the expression he has always worn when asleep. She has watched it often, wondering what it means, this annoyance and impatience with the world that he carries into his dreams. She hopes that it is not disappointment with her, with their relationship, that he wears on his face each night. Despite the crushing guilt of what she'll tell him when he recovers, a small anchor of relief tugs at her. She will no longer have to lie to him. Perhaps once there is truth between them, she and Richard can rebuild a friendship.

Mike pulls the final stitch closed, loops the needle holders into a closing knot, and reaches for the scissors to cut the thread.

The rhythmic beeping of the heart monitor accelerates into a spiral of faster beeps, and then an alarm starts to sound. Mike jerks his head toward the monitor. He passes his needle holder to Justin and reaches for Richard's wrist. The beeps on the heart monitor speed up even more until the green line is a blur of rises and falls. Mike turns dials on the anesthetic IV frantically. Richard's skin has a creeping blue undertone.

"Turn off the lights," Mike snaps. "I need the power."

Natalie frantically switches off all three of the operating lights, her fingers clumsy and uncooperative.

The green line on the heart monitor gives one last frenzy and then flatlines. The heart monitor alarm drones through the room. Natalie wants to go over and pound it, or shake Richard until the line leaps again, tells her that Richard is alive.

Mike pushes Justin out of the way, flicks on the power to the defibrillator, and yanks the machine over to Richard's bedside. The green line on the heart monitor sputters and dies. Without the alarm, the room is ominously silent, and the candles sputter in the gloom.

"Damn it, damn it, damn it," Mike says, jamming the defibrillator machine out of the way with his hip and starting to pound Richard's chest with compressions. He presses his lips against Richard's, thrusting air into his lungs. Justin stands, still holding the needle holders, staring at his uncle and his father, motionless, in shock. Natalie snatches the needle holders from him and snips the thread with the scissors. This snaps Justin to action, and he takes his uncle's place in giving Richard mouth to mouth. Together the two of them count a terrible rhythm of air, listening for breath falls and hammering Richard's chest with compressions. Richard remains motionless, and different parts of his body—his foot, his nail beds, his arm—give way progressively to a deeper purple hue.

Mike's cheeks color from the exertion and a trickle of sweat runs down his temple, but still he keeps going, his face a grim mask of determination. Justin wears a look of disbelief, his eyes wide and dark. Natalie shakes and chokes on sobs that wrench her gut and spill over her hands.

After what seems like an eternity, Mike snatches up a scalpel and seems poised to crack open Richard's chest. Justin moves in to keep doing compressions. Mike moves the knife wildly over Richard's chest, from his heart to his lungs and back again. Finally, he puts it down and lowers his head.

"It's no use. Without x-rays, I have no idea where to cut him open. He must have thrown a clot. I can't do anything. I'm sorry. So sorry."

Justin increases the intensity of his chest compressions, tears streaking his face and falling onto Richard's exposed chest, until Natalie and Mike take him by either arm and pull him away.

WHEN DANIEL OPENS HIS EYES again, Mike is gone. Darkness shrouds the infirmary. Andrew lies in the other bed, hooked to IVs. Natalie sits between them, her face buried in Andrew's mattress, asleep. If he reaches out, he can touch her.

He doesn't, but that's enough. For now. He sleeps.

THE DREAM WASHES OVER NATALIE. It is a dream she has relived many times. Strings of reality and memory interwoven with skeins of fantasy. The night she met Richard and Daniel. A frat party. They had approached her and introduced themselves. Twins. She'd had trouble remembering which name was attached to which twin. She tried to string together some rational thought from the occasional word she could hear over the beat of the music and clatter of voices. The louder twin bounced around, jittery and giddy, throwing his arm around her waist and squeezing her. The quieter one seemed content to be his brother's foil, drinking his beer and listening to the music. She smiled at him and tried to start a conversation. A few times he edged closer so he could hear her. But then the other brother would swagger over and flick him in the shoulder and do some sort of fight posturing. They were, she established, living together and both taking economics.

They walked her home through the park together. The louder brother's arm was slung around her waist, fingers dangling carelessly into her back pocket. The quieter brother seeming to sink deeper and deeper into the shadows as the night progressed; or was that because the louder brother was moving into sharper and sharper relief?

When they reached the sidewalk to her apartment complex, the quieter brother hung back and waited, while the other escorted her to the door, wearing an engaging grin, his eyes the blue of an autumn day. He asked for her phone number. She gave it to him. How could she not? The blue-eyed one was so insistent, so sure of himself. She was charmed despite herself. She darted her eyes at the other brother. He had his back turned, staring out into the street, like an ever-present satellite.

⸻⁂⸻

NATALIE IS GONE WHEN DANIEL wakes in the chill darkness of morning. His head pounds, and he feels faintly like vomiting. The kitchen hums with the clank of pots on the stove and footfalls on the floor. Andrew sleeps. Daniel's hat, the hat that Richard took, sits on the nightstand next to him. Rain thrums on the tin roof. Shadowfax is dead. This pains him. But somehow Daniel had known when Richard rode off on his horse that it was the end. His whole chest feels bruised, as if he could pull aside the sheet and see big purple welts all over him. But he is still alive. And the farm has not, unless anything has changed in the last few hours, become a collective of mass murderers.

He tries savoring his aliveness, the breaths of air he consumes, the soft hardness of the infirmary bed. But after a few seconds, the potential state of the barn and animals rises before him like a specter, and he tries to sit up, only to be greeted by unnerving head spins and Mike pushing him back down, thrusting a glass of water in his face.

"Don't even think about it. Only *you* would try to get out of bed a second time with a head injury just after you had a heart attack," Mike says. "Erik and Scott are taking care of the barn and animals, and you are not moving. Not even an inch, until I say so."

"Natalie…" Daniel manages after a few sips of water.

"Is dealing with some things," Mike says, checking Daniel's pulse.

"Andrew?" Daniel says.

Mike moves on to blood pressure. "Should be fine. We found him in time. He had built a little room of hay in the back of the loft. You couldn't see him, and he'd made it so narrow that it looked flush with the wall."

"Erik?"

"Richard's bodyguard. Turns out he's rather handy and eager to please." Something flashes in Mike's eyes at the mention of Richard. Something that sets Daniel's heart skittering. What has Richard done now?

"We need to talk about your heart attack," Mike says, flicking a light in Daniel's eyes. Daniel recoils at the brightness. "I don't know how bad it was. I'm hoping it was mild, but I can't tell how much damage you did. The next forty-eight hours are the most critical. If you feel anything weird, call me immediately. I have a feeling you've been having arrhythmias and minor transient ischemic attacks for months and haven't told me. That's why you fell off the horse. Am I right?"

Daniel lowers his head in a faint nod.

"So, you were stupid then. That's great. I'm afraid I can't tell you your future prognosis. The heart could completely heal itself, and you could be at no greater risk than you were before. Or you could be living on borrowed time—especially if you don't tell me when you're experiencing symptoms."

Living on borrowed time. He's always lived on borrowed time. Now it's borrowed and mortgaged and still mostly unlived, especially after his conversation with his mother, and then Natalie last night. "What would you have done anyway, if I had told you?" He says it dully, reconciling himself once again to his own limitations.

Mike's shoulders droop slightly. "I don't know. What good am I really? Without electricity and meds, sometimes it feels like I can't do shit."

"What aren't you telling me?" Daniel says.

"Nothing." Mike doesn't make eye contact. He's lying, though. Daniel knows it.

DANIEL STARES OUT THE INFIRMARY window at the mist-covered mountains. What decisions does a person on twice-borrowed time make?

Natalie arrives with a flushed face and beads of moisture in her curls, her eyes bloodshot and puffy. She sinks into the chair next to his bed. "Thank you for helping us find Andrew," she says. "How are you feeling?"

Daniel can't stop the tears that brim in his eyes and stream down his face. She stares at him, and then she leans in and rests her head lightly near his heart. But there's a stiffness to her, a resistance. He's told her he doesn't love her.

Through the blur of his tears Daniel sees that Andrew has awakened. Instinctively, he wipes the tears away. Natalie rises and kisses Andrew's forehead.

"Sorry for leaving you this morning," she says. Daniel's not sure if she's addressing him or Andrew. "We're dealing with Terrence, Bob, and Brent. They're in custody, and Claire too. We're not quite sure what we're going to do about punishment."

"Where's Richard?" Daniel says.

Natalie pulls her shoulders up toward her ears and tenses. Her lips turn up and then down. Her voice comes out in a thin whoosh, her hand grasping for Andrew's.

"I'm sorry. So sorry. He died during surgery on his foot. Mike thinks it was a pulmonary embolism or a stroke. Maybe a heart attack. There was nothing Mike could do."

She breaks down then, her shoulders convulsing in heaves, and buries her face in Andrew's shoulder. Daniel reels in shock. Richard. Dead. Before Daniel. This was a possibility he had never entertained. Richard with the sky-blue eyes and sunny smile. His twin.

Andrew stares straight ahead, silent. Natalie's sobs occupy the space between them. Andrew pulls the bed sheet taut in his hands, bows his head, and starts to weep in big gut-wrenching gags, his voice quivering above and below its newfound baritone. Daniel's own tears come in a quiet flood that builds behind his eyes and seems like it might drown him.

"OKAY, SO YOU'RE GOOD TO go," Mike says. "Keep taking your beta blockers, but you know as well as I do that we only have another year's supply. I'm hoping, as I'm sure you are, that things will change in the next year or two and we'll be able to access more drugs. Let's hope Earl or someone makes it happen." Mike looks Daniel in the eye. "The key, or part of the key, is that you're going to have to learn to really listen to your body. If you feel the slightest twinge when exerting your-self, I need you to report back to me. Take it easy. And I mean *easy*. And if you feel anything, and I mean even if you fart funny, I want you back here pronto. Got that?"

Daniel nods. It feels strange to be back in his own clothes. His black hat, which Natalie retrieved from his cabin, on his head. He can't bring himself to put on the one that Richard wore. They wheeled him out in a wheelchair like an invalid for the funeral—a joint ceremony for Richard, Alfie, Leon, and Alan—where he had sat dry-eyed in a pit of self-recrimination.

Daniel turns back to Mike. "Thank you. Thank you for saving my life."

"It's my job, Daniel. But it's also a pleasure. Really." They both know he's thinking that he didn't manage to save Richard.

Before either man chokes up, Daniel walks out of the infirmary. Mitch greets him, alternately whirling in circles and prostrating himself at his master's feet. Daniel hugs his dog, feels Mitch's tongue on his cheek, and feels a second of relief from the grief that threatens to crush him. He'll go to the barn and ensure that everything is okay. Then he will find Natalie.

⟨≈⟩

PICTURES OF RICHARD HAD ALWAYS been strange, like the camera stripped away the swagger and left someone more vulnerable peering through Richard's eyes. Natalie wonders if she ever saw him without affectation. She's not sure if she ever tried to really know him. Not that Richard had been easy to know.

She had thought she wanted him dead because that seemed the only way to be free of him, free of his laughter and his scorn; but now that he is, she's almost destroyed by her own grief and guilt.

She has spent the last hour in their old master bedroom closet, looking through picture after picture of him. Looking for something. She's not sure what. His truths. The reasons why they couldn't make things work. The reasons he was Richard. His old shoes still sit in a jumble against the bedroom wall. Fancy black and brown Bostonians and Rockports. She holds her tears in a tight ball in her chest as she leaves the bedroom. She shouldn't be here. She has work to do. She should check in on Andrew and Justin. She should do any number of things, but she finds herself in the barn office instead.

Daniel sits at his desk with his head in his hands. He looks up when he hears her, his face impassive and pale, and the circles under his eyes deeply etched. She almost shrinks away from him, this man that she loves. His twin is dead. Will that be too much for him?

She stands alone on the other side of the desk. "The night…the night everything all happened, at the sick camp I mean. Where were you? What were you doing? I saw Richard wearing your hat on Shadowfax and I thought…" She doesn't finish this statement. "But where were you? Why were you in the sick camp, and why did you give Richard your hat?"

Daniel's features tighten further. "I was out talking to Richard like you asked. And then he fucked off with my hat, and so I ran back and tripped over Claire, and I told her about Alfie, which was obviously a stupid decision. And then I went and got Sherlock. I saw you and Joe heading around south of the camp. I didn't think I had time to come and talk to you, so I went north to stop them. And tried to save my goddamned horse." His voice is snappy, slightly defensive. His eyes flick from the ground to hers, to someplace over her shoulder.

She nods. "I'm sorry. I'm just trying to understand. And the hat. Why did you give him your hat?"

"I don't know. I guess I was just used to doing what Richard asked."

Her own anger rises in response to his tone. "When we first met at that party years ago, were you interested?"

"What? Nat, I barely remember the party. Maybe. I liked you. But Richard declared that night that you would make the perfect wife, and you seemed happy with him. He was absolutely determined. I wasn't going to get in his way."

"Why are you angry with me?"

"I'm not. It's just… My brother died trying to save me, and I was sleeping with his wife." He holds up his hand. "I know. I know he was the architect of us all being there in that ridiculous situation in the first place." His gray eyes are wide with entreaty. "But I'm ripping myself apart with guilt. So I'm sorry, but can you leave me alone for a bit?"

"Fine," she says. She rushes out of the barn office in a whoosh of hurt and steps out into the brilliant afternoon sunset. She closes her eyes and feels the final rays of the day's light on her face. As the sun slips behind the mountains, and the light shifts from golden to gray, Natalie heads down to the river. An icy breeze lifts off the water. Patches of ice pile on top of each other, snagged in sunken logs. Areas of frigid water pool ominously still. It's not yet time for ice fishing, but the thermocline—the breakpoint between the warmer oxygenated water and the cooler oxygen-depleted layers—has turned over. Every spring and fall, the layers overturn. If it were to happen too fast, or not happen quite right, the fish would be caught in the wrong place at the wrong time and they would die. And now, she thinks, it's as if the thermocline of her life has turned over, replacing one brother with the other, and catching Richard in the wrong place. The Wheel of Fortune. For one to rise, the other must fall.

Will Richard's death drive them apart? Perhaps she and Daniel are now just a triangle with a missing side. Unable to function without Vega around which to revolve.

She rises and scales the bank to the farm, following the path between the birch and poplars that dot the fields between the cabins, their graceful willowy shapes casting black outlines on the dirt before her. The cabins are quiet and dark. Most people are in the farmhouse having dinner or finishing up the last of their tasks for the day. Shadow scampers out of some bushes near Daniel's cabin and trails her back to her farmhouse, leaping and spiraling after some imaginary rat.

Daniel meets her in the field, his hands thrust in his pockets, hat pulled low over his eyes.

"I'm sorry," he says. "Richard's death. I'm not dealing with it too well. He died saving me. And maybe if I hadn't been angry with him, and told Claire about Alfie, she wouldn't have started the shooting. And who knows how much of his behavior was because he knew about us."

She looks up at him. His face is all shadows, and his gray eyes reflect the first sliver of the round white moon cresting Scarecrow Peak. "I feel sick with guilt too—don't think that I don't—but Richard died from injuries he sustained participating in an attack on innocent people. Who knows what would have happened if Claire hadn't started shooting, or if you hadn't had a heart attack? *More* people could be dead, including Richard. Even if he did know about us, that doesn't excuse his behavior." She's uncertain about this last statement, though. Maybe it *is* their fault. Maybe they'll always live with that.

Daniel takes her hand, and she feels the shaking of his fingers. "For all my years with him, I feel like I didn't really know him at all," he says. "Maybe if I had, maybe if I had tried to be something more than his fucking shadow, maybe if I wasn't consumed by guilt over *us*, I could have stopped him."

"Or maybe you couldn't have. Richard was complex. I don't think anybody really knew him."

She guides him over to a log by the orchard, and they sit next to each other in the cool night air.

Daniel looks straight ahead. Venus crests the rounded peaks of the foothills of the Selkirks. "My mother talked to me that night in the infirmary. Told me how much Richard loved you. Her message was clear that I should back off, that I had no right. Then she came and told me you were planning to go to Vancouver with him. That you had said yes."

Natalie's heart rails against the unfairness of this, but she knows that everything she has left unspoken for so many years has brought her here. When you say nothing, people fill the void with whatever matches their vision of the world, and you can end up carried along by it, living someone else's reality. "I didn't. I didn't say anything. I was going to say no. I was just waiting until after Richard's surgery. But your mother is right: until the fire, I did think about saying yes. You had destroyed me, and I thought maybe I could go back to Richard and rebuild. But then I almost died, and I knew I couldn't."

"And I almost died, and I still couldn't tell my ass from a hole in the ground."

"You just had more to consider. He was your brother." She almost chokes on the word *was*, and she hears him break down too, and they sit and stare for a few minutes at the emerging skiff of stars, each through their own haze of tears.

Daniel breaks the silence. "Us being together, maybe it's not fair to Richard, and this heart of mine—it's not reliable. My number could come up any day." Natalie closes her eyes against the thought of losing Daniel, and braces to be broken up with all over again. But after a pause, Daniel continues. "All my life I've been waiting—for what, I'm not sure. Waiting to feel like it's my time, to do the things I want to do or say, waiting to allow myself to love somebody. And now, according to your brother, I'm living on borrowed time."

"So, what are you saying?" Unrestrained and perhaps unrestrainable hope floods every spare corner of her heart. Yet she runs panicked after it, trying to pull it back into place; to tamp it down to a manageable ebb.

He removes his hat, sinks to his knees, places his hands on her thighs, and draws his body between her knees. His gray eyes, always so earnest, meet hers, and just this barest of touches makes Natalie want to launch herself on top of him, to kiss and bite his lips, to bury herself in his strong but gentle arms. "I'm saying I need to stop waiting. I'm saying that every piece of you makes me happier than I ever thought possible. And maybe it's time we allow ourselves a bit of happiness. Your smile is my favorite thing in the world—and the next time I almost die, I want to know that I've spent every second I had left putting that smile on your face."

"Do you really mean that?"

"Yes, I really mean that." He lifts his fingers to her face and draws it to his. His kiss, his tongue, and his hands entwined in her hair erase any doubts she might have had.

They sit there wrapped in each other's arms until the Summer Triangle stands out resolute from the rest of the stars, its vertices glittering in the deepening black.

THE NEXT FEW MONTHS ARE tense and silent, with many farm matters to be dealt with. Claire makes a teary plea for leniency, claiming post-traumatic stress. Terrence, Bob, and Brent fob responsibility off onto Leon, claiming that Leon bullied them. Natalie is torn between the truth about what they did and the reality of their lives on the farm. It's not as if there are judges to declare their guilt, or jails to lock them away in. The best they could do is exile them—and debates rage regarding the inhumanity of that and the risks associated with the enemy within versus the enemy outside. So they're all placed on probation and have to apologize publicly to the other farm members. And they're not permitted to carry firearms or vote at Farm Council for two years.

Natalie keeps a vigilant watch over Andrew and Justin, and tries to spend as much time with them as possible. They're remarkably stoic and solid despite their grief, and she delights in their company. Joanne and Mike ask to take in the two children that Natalie impulsively brought home from the gathering, and Natalie reiterates her gratitude so frequently that Joanne finally tells her to stop. Claire does her best to fit in and make amends, and spends an inordinate amount of time with Andrew.

The winter is lean, and angry words are exchanged whenever they can't find game. Winter turns into spring, and the spring freshet threatens to spill over the banks of the river and flood the fields. But it doesn't, and the harsh spring gives way to an exceptionally productive summer, with searing temperatures and lots of rain. News that a man named Peter Hilton assassinated the provisional government leader reaches them via the new Internet, and Natalie finds herself almost relieved that they may have more time to build their own community without interference.

And throughout it all, Daniel is her steadfast center—her personal North Star. She sleeps in the den alone for a few months, Shadow pressed against her side, rumbling with purrs whenever Natalie rolls over. She and Daniel are discreet, but eventually she doesn't hesitate to take his hand or kiss his cheek when she wants to, and he, despite looking over his shoulder the first several times, does not object.

The conversation sometimes stops when she enters rooms, and Jane and Colleen dish out snide remarks, but nobody shuns them outright. In fact, some people seem oddly relieved. She and Daniel find themselves at the center of burgeoning new friendships—with Mike and Joanne, and with newcomers Marta and Carson, the man that Daniel interrogated in the clearing the night of the forest fire, so many months ago. Olivia avoids Natalie for many weeks, and then finally settles for a curt "Do not hurt him" before resuming cordial relations. And eventually, Natalie moves her stuff into Elderberry Cabin, and finds a passion so deep that she finds herself shaken to the core every day.

IN LATE AUGUST, NATALIE FINALLY makes time to clear out the old master bedroom in the farmhouse, Claire having finally been banished to the bunkhouse. Natalie comes across old journals of Richard's in a banker's box in the corner of their closet. There is an odd self-conscious boosterism to the writing, like he preferred to keep secrets even from himself. Many of the entries are self-affirmations about being rich and powerful, tales of victories at work, and business ideas.

An early journal entry lists her good and bad traits, along with a written analysis of her suitability as a wife. Kind of like an employee evaluation. Her immaturity, career aspirations, and temper are contrasted with her attractiveness, intelligence, and malleability.

Entries about the boys follow. Richard goes into detail about Natalie's stability as a mother, and her possible depression and its potential impact on the boys. The writing is too clinical, too detached, and Natalie feels sickened. He never shared any of this with her. She's struck by Richard's calculation and sense of superiority, and yet there is a child-like quality to the writing that is unsettling.

An astrological chart falls out of the journal, showing the locations of the stars on Richard's date of birth: May 27, 1972. The words Gemini, twins, duality, and mosquito constellation are scrawled at the top of the page. Stapled to the chart is a printout of a story on artificial constellations in London. In order to allow urban dwellers to observe the stars, a French designer had created twelve fake constellations, each one a man-made duplicate of its heavenly counterpart. The mosquito constellation was among the twelve.

Two mosquito constellations. One for each brother. One constellation a symbol used by an early civilization to make sense of their world and plan their crops. The other a testament to her own civilization's glitzy and wasteful pre-peak lives. She tries not to feel that there is a fitting irony to this. That wouldn't be fair to Richard.

Natalie closes the journal and goes to the window. She can just make out Andrew's form in the fields, moving sprinklers. Justin, still recovering from the horrific night in the infirmary, and hoping to expand his repertoire, stands in the animal pens learning about veterinary medicine from Daniel, who has one hand on his hip and the other on his forehead, his black hat pushed up over his brow.

Justin, the accident, who had led her to marry Richard. Richard had been so gleeful at the prospect, while she groused and doubted, until her perfect baby had been born.

She looks out the window again and watches the three people she loves the most in the world—three people who wouldn't be alive if it were not for Richard.

CHAPTER 27

THE TWO OF CUPS

————⚭————

NATALIE

The synergy of a person with their soul mate is
like the synergy of two stars.

There is laughter, and there are flowers on one of those cloudless, blue, end-of-August days. The tomatoes ripen on the vines, and the scent of the upcoming fruit harvest hangs sweet in the air. The air will turn cold as evening descends, foretelling of the winter to come. But for now the sun is their comfort and safeguard, bathing shoulders and arms in its exquisite warmth and holding the mosquitoes in check, even if just for an afternoon. Natalie walks barefoot down the aisle in a borrowed white sundress, a white circlet of daisies in her hair, and a bounty of buttercups and anemones in her hands. Mitch sits at the end of the aisle, next to a man with a black cowboy hat who waits patiently, but expectantly. Andrew stands next to him.

Rachel, stunning in purple taffeta, sashays triumphantly ahead of Natalie, darting smiles at the assembled crowd, especially Craig. The two blond little twins that Natalie met almost a year ago have already bounced down the hand-mown green grass aisle—a temporary nod to the days of kept yards—tossing white asters. The rest of the farm members sit on dining room chairs and make-shift log benches. Natalie's eyes still search for Richard among them.

Anneke sits next to Joe and Craig. Although she will never be beautiful, Anneke's eyes, lined with blue kohl, are again alive with the fire and acuity that Natalie had first loved about her friend. Claire and Patricia are both pregnant, and Siobhan cradles her new baby boy. Claire won't tell anyone the identity of her baby's father, but Natalie has her suspicions. In the flush of pregnancy, Claire seems almost normal. Scott sits next to Mike and Joanne, gaunt and tiny. Even with the field hospital, there is nothing they can do for him. Natalie closes her eyes against the surge of sadness.

They had decided to use the wedding also as a fall gathering, to celebrate the new community that they're building. Several neighbors, including Fred and Ilene, sit on blankets in the grass. Lauren sits at the front, waiting to see her daughter and her husband come down the aisle. It is still a community fraught with danger and mistrust. But they are moving ahead, trying to establish bioregional governance, rather than one based on old political lines. A small hydro operation near Nelson now feeds the farm with intermittent power, and Mike goes faithfully to the regional hospital in Jerry for one week out of every month. The influenza pandemic has hit eastern Canada and the US hard, but has not yet made its way across the country, a benefit of their now-constrained lives. They're bracing for it, but enjoying their temporary reprieve, the conflicts that always simmer beneath the surface of farm life held in check by the abundance of late summer.

Standing next to Daniel, Justin waits for his soon-to-be wife. Natalie has invited Neil and Lauren to move to the farm with Hannah, for she cannot bear to have Justin move away. It's odd, this little community that they're building, filled with unusual personalities and so much loss. Natalie never pictured herself living surrounded by so many people at all times, and yet despite the constant frustrations and the endless work, she finds her days filled with reasonable happiness and camaraderie.

But today is Hannah's day, and when she arrives at the foot of the aisle on her father's arm, Natalie is struck by the raw lushness of her youth and the loveliness of her gown, hand-sewn by Patricia from bits and pieces of the old wedding dresses abandoned in the closets of their former neighbors. It seems strange to find hope in these fragments of beauty that she had railed against before the peak. Hannah will change out of her dress before nightfall and will don work clothes in the morning. But the mere fact that they are able to pause for an afternoon, that they are rich enough to celebrate this glorious day, and enjoy the play of light on faces and bodies that are ripe with health and at least temporary good will, fills her with gratitude.

"Do you want to get married?" Daniel had asked Natalie in their early-morning rumple of bedclothes, their skin still warm with sex, the sweet silk of sweat between them. The intensity of their physical connection still manages to shock Natalie every time they touch. Shadow, irritated at his exclusion, mewed quietly on the porch.

"I don't know," Natalie had replied in truth. "I don't know what that would get us."

"I have this half-assed gimpy heart," Daniel said. "We might not have that long."

"Everyone has a half-assed gimpy heart in one way or another," she replied. "Yours has just been mapped out."

Now, Natalie breathes in the waft of ripening fruit as the sun warms her skin, and watches her son greet his soon-to-be wife. The black dog no longer stalks her so industriously, and on days like this she can convince herself that he has fallen far behind and will never catch her.

Paul speaks. "We are gathered here today, to celebrate how life changes, how life goes on, and how life brings people together."

The tips of Daniel's fingertips brush hers, and Natalie marvels yet again at the continuing and odd perfection of this imperfect man.

ACKNOWLEDGEMENTS

Seldom does a book have quite so many hands in it as this one has. I'm quite sure that I have forgotten someone here, and if I have, my sincerest apologies. It has been quite the odyssey.

I started writing this book in 2007 when I spent a lot of time surfing peak oil and doomer sites. I had just read *The Long Emergency* by James Howard Kunstler and, given my environmental background, I was plenty concerned. Just like Natalie, I started searching for a back woods acreage and learned to garden. This book sprung from my imaginings of how we might live in a dystopic future, but a less dystopic one than many of those created by other writers. A kinder dystopia, if you will.

This book has been through the hands of many editors (really, I probably could have bought that acreage). For developmental edits, it went first to Claudia Casper, through the Vancouver Manuscript Intensive, then to Verna Relkoff of the Mint Literary Agency. Susan Swan edited the first 300 pages of it through the Humber School for Writers Correspondence Program in Creative Writing. Roz Nay of FreshEdit did a full copy and line edit, and cheered me on as I worked to improve it again and again. Individual chapters were reviewed and edited by countless kind and amazing writers as I shopped it out many times at the Fernie Writers' Conference. All of these writers and editors helped me to push this manuscript further and further.

I also owe my sincerest thanks to two of my great doctor friends, Karin Goodison and Adele Pratt, who kindly agreed to read the manuscript and identify any medical errors. I am greatly indebted to them for their expertise.

There were almost too many beta readers to name for this book. I have lost track of how many people have read early drafts—Michelle Power, Brad Kusy,

Dave Tudhope, Mike Newton, Pam Redmond, Mark Kusnir, Kim McCullough, Lisa Sweeney, Jackie Ellis, Bernice New, Dave Campsall, Vivian Campsall, Mike New, my entire bookclub from Victoria, and the list goes on. I know I have forgotten several people, and I truly am sorry. It has been seven years after all. All my beta readers were all incredibly supportive and offered fantastic feedback. They might be a bit surprised to see where the book has gone—I am pretty sure some of them will barely recognize it as the novel they read in 2008 or 2009.

Second to last in the editing lineup, this novel went to my fantastic editor David Gatewood, who as always made me laugh at my own idiosyncrasies, penchant for toque-wearing characters (must be the Canadian in me, eh?), and the ghost of Alan who had been cut from a scene but kept showing up. He also patiently explained commas before sentence-ending participial phrases, past perfect versus simple past when writing in present tense and any other number of esoteric, but important, grammar rules.

Then it was on to proofreader Warren Layberry, who did an amazing job, and flagged still more things for me to fix. He also made me laugh at some of my characters and writing habits. Editors and proofreaders are a hilarious lot it seems.

I have Andrew Brown of Design for Writers to thank again for the unbelievable cover. I can't say enough about his skills and talent.

The final stop was my formatters: Jason and Marina Anderson of Polgarus Studio, who did a rush job for me at the end, and Shelley Ackerman, who did a beautiful job formatting the print version.

I feel truly lucky to have been once again able to work with such a great team of professionals on this book.

Of course this book would not have happened without my ever-supportive husband and children. While sometimes their "sacrifices" involved clearing out of the house and skiing the powder so that I could be left alone to write, they all pitched in to make meals and offer words of support whenever they were needed (well, most of the time anyway). My children did note, however, that my characters tend to swear a lot.

And to everyone else who drifted in and out of my life over the past seven years, and said the right thing at the right time, and somehow helped me move this project forward, thank you.

ABOUT THE AUTHOR

Jennifer Ellis writes contemporary action-adventure fiction with a dystopic edge for both adults and children. She lives in a small ski town in Canada with her husband and two boys where she skis, does ballet, cooks, joins too many book clubs, and works as an environmental researcher. She blogs randomly but regularly at *www.jenniferellis.ca* and can be found on Twitter at *@jenniferlellis.* Her first novel, a middle-grade novel for adults (and children) entitled *A Pair of Docks*, is a rollicking adventure that explores the intersection between science and witchcraft. The sequel to *A Pair of Docks, A Quill Ladder,* will be released in December 2014.

www.ingramcontent.com/pod-product-compliance
Lightning Source LLC
Chambersburg PA
CBHW060347260626
47160CB00006B/2230